INEVITABLE

CARTER KIDS #5

CHLOE WALSH

The right of Chloe Walsh to be identified as the Author of the work has been asserted by her in accordance with the Copyright and Related Rights Act 2000. All rights reserved. No part of this publication may be reproduced, stored in a retrieval system, or transmitted, in any form or by any means – electronic, mechanical, including photocopying, recording, or by any information storage and retrieval system – without the prior written permission of the publisher, nor be otherwise circulated in any form or binding or cover than that in which it is published and without a similar condition being imposed on the subsequent purchaser.

This e-book is licensed for your personal enjoyment only. This e-book may not be re-sold or given away to other people. If you would like to share this book with another person, please purchase an additional copy for each reader. If you're reading this book and did not purchase it, or it was not purchased for your use only, then please return to your favorite retailer and purchase your own copy. Thank you for respecting the hard work of this author.

Published by Chloe Walsh
Copyright 2014 by Chloe Walsh
All Rights Reserved. ©

Inevitable,
Carter Kids #5,
First published, October 2017
All rights reserved. ©
Cover designed by Bee @ Bitter Sage Designs.
Edited by Aleesha Davis.
Proofread by Bianca Rushton.

DISCLAIMER

This book is a work of fiction. All names, characters, places and incidents either are products of the author's imagination or are used fictitiously. Any resemblance to events, locales, or persons, living or dead, is coincidental.

The author acknowledges all songs titles, song lyrics, film titles, film characters, trademarked statuses, brands, mentioned in this book are the property of, and belong to, their respective owners. The publication/ use of these trademarks is not authorized/ associated with, or sponsored by the trademark owners.

Chloe Walsh is in no way affiliated with any of the brands, songs, musicians or artists mentioned in this book.

All rights reserved ©

PREFACE

If two people are truly meant to be together, eventually they will find their way back to each other's arms.
It is a prerequisite of love.
It is inevitable.
Right?

– Hope Carter, The Carter Kids

RECAP

Hope

ebruary

I COULDN'T REMEMBER THE LAST TIME I WANTED MY DAD.

It must have been years, but sitting here, opposite the man who'd broken my heart repeatedly, I really wanted my dad. I needed his strong arms around me. Telling me that everything would be okay. Promising to make things right for me. But instead, all I had was the source of my pain.

I couldn't figure Jordan Porter out.

Why he'd come here or why he hadn't left already.

It didn't make sense.

He'd run all too quickly out of my life many years ago, and now he wouldn't go.

"Are we going to talk about anything important?" I asked when Jordan attempted to bring up the past for what had to be the tenth time. "Because our past is a hard limit for me, Jordan."

2 | INEVITABLE

"There's no shame in loving me, Hope," Jordan whispered and I balked.

Oh no he didn't...

"No shame in loving you?" I shook my head in disgust. "You married me and then you abandoned me!"

He ran a hand through his hair and sighed heavily. "I didn't do it on purpose."

"But you still did it. On purpose or not. You still broke my world. You self-destructed and you took me down with you," I hissed. "I think that's pretty damn shameful."

The mixed signals he was sending me weren't doing my heart any good. I was up in a heap trying to figure out what he wanted from me. He was gone for so many years that I'd learned how to cope. How to adjust to life without him, but he was back now. What the hell was I supposed to do with these feelings?

It wasn't as if I'd gotten over him.

We'd been so young. I'd fallen so hard for him. My feelings hadn't changed. I was broken inside because I seemed to be solely programmed to love Jordan Porter. But I knew what I needed to do. I needed to make him go away. For the sake of my sanity, I had to break free from the chains he had wrapped around my heart.

"You were always with me!" Jordan roared, chest heaving as he finally rid himself of that infuriating cool demeanor. Standing up, he stalked over to the living room window and looked out. "Just because I wasn't with you in the flesh, doesn't mean you stopped being the pivotal fucking element of my world."

"Well that's too damn bad," I screamed. Standing up, I kicked the coffee table, my temper out of control. "Because I signed your papers. I've suffered enough and I'm tired, Jordan." Looking him dead in the eye, I said, "So do me a kindness and walk away from me because I'm not willing to put myself through another round with you. I always lose and it's too hard."

"I am leaving, Hope," he replied, eyes locked on my face. "I don't have a choice."

"Why am I not surprised to hear you say those words?" I squeezed out, feeling like the air had been dragged clean out of my lungs. Blinking rapidly, I took several steps backwards. "Do you enjoy this?" I gestured to myself. "Do you enjoy hurting me?"

Overflowing with unrecognizable emotion, I stalked towards him, and unlike every other time, he didn't shy away from me. "Why'd you come back here, Jordan?" I demanded. Curling my fingers in the front of his shirt, I resisted the urge to thump him, letting out a harsh cry instead "I mean, why bother coming back at all if you're leaving again, huh?"

"I came back because I realized I'd left something behind," he told me, voice gruff and thick.

He stepped closer to me and I shivered.

Achingly slowly, he placed his hands on my waist and dropped his brow to rest on mine. "Something I've spent a very long time looking for."

"What?"

"You." His hands circled my wrists. "I've been searching for hope."

"No!" I shook my head, rejecting his cruel words and torturous promises. "You don't mean that."

"I do," he rasped, claiming the space I'd put between us. "I mean it so much I want to carve it on my body."

"You don't." Tears filled my eyes. "You can't." I looked around aimlessly and shrugged my shoulders. "You left me."

"And I spent every waking moment regretting that," he choked out. He reached out and cupped my face with his hands. Immediately, I clenched my eyes shut, desperate to block this out.

4 | INEVITABLE

"Look at me." When I refused, he shook me gently. "Hope, look at me."

Slowly, I opened my eyes and looked into his.

"I am so sorry," he whispered. "For lying to you and leaving you." He exhaled a shaky breath. "I swear to you, everything I've done has been for you." His hands moved to knot in my hair. "I know I don't deserve you, but that doesn't change the fact that I'm in love with you. I want you, Hope, and I'm too fucking weak to walk away again. So, I'm going to ask you for the impossible." He pressed his brow to mine. "Come away with me, Hope Carter."

"You can't just say that and expect me to be okay with it, Jordan," I sobbed brokenly. "You can't just barge your way back in my life and ask me to go with you! I've risked it all for you before and look where it got me."

"I know I've fucked up," he countered hoarsely. "I know I've hurt you and screwed everything up. But I need to be honest with you, Hope –" His voice broke off and it took him a moment to continue. "If I don't do it now, I'll never do it, and I can't fucking leave again with you believing that you're not the most important person in my life. Because you are. You always were and you always will be."

"Then why did you do all of this to me?" I sobbed. My hands reached up and cupped his face of their own accord. "Why did you break me?"

"I have a lot to explain," he whispered. "I know that."

"If I go with you," I said in a shaky voice – weighing up my options. "I want full disclosure."

Jordan cocked a brow and I stared hard back at him.

"You won't ever look at me the same," he replied.

I shook my head. "I don't care. I want to know."

"You will care," he muttered.

Taking a step back from me, Jordan unbuttoned the cuffs of his shirt and rolled up his sleeves.

"What the hell is that?" My voice was barely more than a

Recap | 5

soft cry as I stared at the insides of his wrists. I could hardly breathe. I wasn't sure why I was asking Jordan to explain something that I clearly already knew, only that I needed to hear it from his mouth.

"You know what that is," he choked out, green eyes locked on my face, imploring me not to pry.

Stepping closer, I took his left hand in mine and carefully rolled the sleeve up to his elbows. "These cuts?" My eyes were locked on the ugly crisscross welts on the inside of his wrists.

"Self-inflicted."

"Why?"

Jordan sighed. "Because sometimes the physical pain is easier to deal with than the emotional pain."

My fingers trailed over the scars on his wrists. I touched the lines of his marred flesh. The purple swell of his bruised and battered veins. The marks on his veins caused a tremor of unease to roll through me.

This was evidence of his lifelong pain.

"When did all of this start?" I asked, not trusting myself to say any more and scare him back into that shell he loved to hide in.

"Not long after I left The Hill," he replied. "I was...struggling with some stuff." Sighing, he ran a hand through his hair. "I wanted to forget. It started off with alcohol and a little weed." He laughed harshly. "But I obviously have a lot of Derek in me because it wasn't long until I was out of control."

"Out of control," I repeated numbly.

My world felt like it had been pulled out from under my feet.

"Heroin, Hope," Jordan explained, tone flat and cold. "You think I fucked you over by leaving, but I was toxic. I left to protect you from my bullshit."

"Bullshit?" I shook my head in confusion. "You're no druggie, Jordan."

6 | INEVITABLE

"Aren't I?" he countered. "Because I have a file as long as your arm saying otherwise."

"I can't believe this," I whispered, struggling to take it all in.

"She was my sponsor," Jordan whispered, finally breaking the horrible silence that had been suffocating us.

I looked up at him. "Annabelle?"

Jordan nodded. "I never slept with her."

Now I was the one to recoil. "You're lying." He had to be. She was his fiancée.

"I'm not lying to you," he countered, stepping closer. "The only woman I've ever been with is you."

"How?"

"How?" he shook his head in confusion "What do you mean how?"

"Sex, Jordan," I spat. "Are you honestly trying to make me believe that you haven't slept with that woman?"

"You gave me everything I ever needed," he growled, sounding oddly offended. "Why would I be with her for sex?"

"Because you're a man," I hissed, pressing my fingers to my temples. This was too much to take. "So why were you engaged to her?"

"Because she needed me."

"I needed you."

"I know, Hope. God, I know. But Annabelle.... I helped her out of a hole with an abusive ex by pretending to be her fiancé and she helped me out of a hole with...."

"Me," I deadpanned. "Go on. Finish your sentence."

"I needed you to move on," he choked out. "It was a horrible fucking lie, but one I thought you needed to hear."

"Why?" I demanded. "And why the hell would you put that crap in your body?"

"Because I wanted to forget and I didn't care if I killed myself in the process," he replied honestly. "In fact, I was sort of banking on it."

"That's what I don't understand," I admitted, feeling torn between my emotions.

One part of me wanted to throw my arms around this man and comfort him through his pain.

The other part of me wanted to slap him silly.

"You don't need to understand," he whispered. "Just know that I did you a favor by leaving."

"No," I hissed, shaking my head. "You don't get to call the shots and leave me hanging like this." I tightened my ponytail and struggled to reign in my emotions. "You ruined me. I had to live these past seven years not knowing what I'd done wrong. You broke me so bad. And no amount of success or money could fill the void you left inside of me. You took my heart away, Jordan. I can't go on not knowing why. It hurts too much."

"I was going down, Hope," he hissed. "I made a decision not to take you down with me."

"Liar."

"I'm not lying to you," he ground out through clenched teeth.

"You've been walking around pretending I'm a freaking stranger, Jordan!" Every time I looked at his stupid, beautiful face, another smidgen of my dignity slipped away, fueling my rage, and igniting my wrath. "Tell me why you left me that night. Tell me or I'll walk. I swear to god I will walk away and never come back!"

"Because I was raped, okay!" The words tore from his chest, bringing with them an onslaught of emotion. "I was fucking raped and I couldn't bear to look you in the eye afterwards!"

My hands shot to my mouth. "Jordan..."

"My stepfather raped me, Hope. Over and over. For days. He tied me to the bed and the bastard raped me with his body. He raped me with...Fuck, I can't even say it..." Pulling on his hair, Jordan backed away from me, chest heaving. He looked like he was struggling to breathe. "And when he was finished, he left me there." He dropped his head in shame. A sob tore from his

8 | INEVITABLE

throat when he said, "By the time Derek found me, I had almost bled out."

I couldn't hold back the scream that ripped from my throat.

This was a nightmare.

I was having a nightmare and I so desperately needed to wake up...

"Afterwards, I wanted to die." Jordan continued to talk, filling me in on a lifetime of painful memories. "I wanted to be fucking dead, Hope."

Meanwhile, I sank to the floor and wept.

"I left you because I loved you, not because I didn't!"

"I could have helped you..." I began to say but he cut me off.

"How, Hope?" Jordan demanded. "How could you have possibly helped me?"

"I..." I felt sick. I didn't know what to do or say. "I'm so sorry."

"That day I left you?" Jordan sank down on the floor beside me. "Derek took me to a facility that day." Wrapping his arms around his legs, he hung his head. "I stayed there for eight months."

I gasped, appalled. "He locked you up?"

"I locked myself up!" Jordan corrected me. "I didn't want to be near anyone. Derek was against it, but he did what had to be done." He pinched the bridge of his nose. "He signed the papers."

"Why didn't you tell me?" I cried.

"What?" he demanded, crying too. "What was I supposed to tell you? That I tried to fight back and I couldn't?" He grabbed his hair and pulled, clearly in pain even talking about this. "Do you have any idea how that feels? To be a grown man and unable to protect yourself?"

"It happens to men, too," I whispered, blinking back the tears.

"Yeah," he laughed humorlessly. "It does."

"Would you have left me, if it had been me who had been raped?"

Recap | 9

"It's not the same thing."

Shifting onto my knees, I crawled over to him and wrapped my arms around him. He stiffened under my touch, but he didn't push me away. "Would you have left me because of something I was a victim of?"

"No!" he hissed. "Of course not."

"Then you should have told me."

"I couldn't," he whispered.

"Why?"

His green eyes were glassy and full of self-loathing when he said, "because it wasn't a one-time thing."

"What do you mean it wasn't a one-time thing?" My blood ran cold. "Jordan." My voice was shaky. My body was trembling. "What do you mean?"

"It started about a month after mom married him."

"But you were only fourteen...Oh god." I heaved. I physically heaved, feeling like my insides were being dragged out of me.

"It stopped when I left," he whispered, trying to assure me. "I got bigger. Stronger. I could fight back..."

"Jordan," I wept.

"But sometimes I didn't..." He shuddered violently. "Sometimes... oh god, sometimes I just laid there and took it... " His voice broke off and it took him a few moments to continue. "I thought that when I came to you, that it was my fresh start. I thought I was free. Free to start my life with you." He laughed humorlessly again. "I was wrong."

"I hate this," I choked out. Reaching up, I gently cupped his cheek, and pretended not to notice when he slightly recoiled from me. Allowing my fingers to trail over his cheek bone and down to his stubbly jaw, I sighed. "I want to go back in time and change things for you."

He stiffened beneath my touch. "This is why I didn't want you to know." Clenching his eyes shut, he continued to speak.

"The way you're looking at me now. The tone of voice you're using."

"What tone?"

"Pity," he hissed. "Disgust." My hand fell on open space when Jordan suddenly jumped to his feet and stepped away from me. "I need to go."

I watched him run out of the room and instantly I was on my feet, running after him.

He wasn't leaving me.

Never again.

Rushing down the steps, I reached him just as he kicked off the pedal of his motorcycle.

"I'm not stable, Hope," he said in a warning tone, face down.

"I don't care," I replied as I swung my leg over the back of the motorcycle and got on.

"I can't guarantee you anything," he whispered, shivering. "I'm an addict with a record for fucking shit up."

"And I'm a Carter with a heart that belongs completely to you." Wrapping my arms around his waist, I pressed my cheek to his back and said, "Where you go, I go."

1

Jordan

*H*ope climbed onto the back of my bike just as recklessly as she had when she was sixteen – without thought for the consequences. She was doing what she did in most situations; rushing into it. I shouldn't have been surprised really. Hope Carter had never taken longer than a minute to make a decision, regardless of how life altering the consequences may be.

She was an *all or nothing* kind of person and I had always loved her for it.

Her latest impulsive decision scared the hell out of me though.

She was promising to be with me, dangling a future in front of me I wasn't entirely sure I could ever have.

She didn't get it.

None of it.

I wasn't the person she remembered.

I was the victim of a fucking crime and I was the one serving a life sentence.

It didn't go away.

My past was never truly in my past and I struggled every damn day to get out of bed.

I was nothing like the guy she'd fallen in love with all those years ago. I wasn't easy to love and I was even harder to live with. I had limits and issues and constrictions. Drugs had taken hold of me for years. While I had managed to gain some control back, I was now, and would always be, an addict.

Did she understand that?

Did she realize that I couldn't give her that perfect love she had been obsessed with having since childhood?

Sex was a fucked up area for me, and I was allergic to even contemplating the idea of having a family. The experiences and ordeals my life had thrown at me meant I never wanted to procreate.

Was that something Hope would want further down the line?

If so, we were going to have a problem.

I was thirty years old and I knew full well I didn't want to be a father.

Fatherhood wasn't something I had much experience with; I'd never had one growing up and the one I had been given fucked me up so badly, I still had moments daily when I wanted to set myself on fire and burn the skin from my bones.

"I'm not stable, Hope," I forced myself to say, giving her an out.

"I don't care." Her response was exactly what I predicted it to be. *You will,* I thought to myself, *when you learn it for yourself.*

"I can't guarantee you anything." She needed to get that. She needed to hear my words.

Every fiber of my being demanded I clamp my hand on top of hers and pull her closer, but I knew doing that would be the most selfish thing I could do; bringing her back into this, dragging her into yet another uncertain future. I loved her too

Chapter 1 | 13

much to put her through that twice. "I'm an addict with a record for fucking shit up."

"And I'm a Carter with a heart that belongs completely to you," was her response – again, not thinking this through. "Where you go, I go."

Pain, disbelief, and deep seeded gratitude flooded through me, threatening what was left of my ability to function.

How could she do this?

How could she kill me with words and bring me back to life with promises?

My heart was fucking breaking. It had been breaking from the moment I walked away from her. I was to blame. The wrong one. I could always admit my mistakes and leaving that girl was my biggest one.

Goddamn, this woman was going to bring me to my knees all over again. No words in the spoken language could ever express how important this moment was to me.

She knew my secrets – my deepest, darkest experiences and hidden pain.

And she was *still here*, still willing to risk it all on me.

She doesn't know everything, a voice deep inside my head hissed.

And she never would!

I had no idea how I would, or ever could, manage to keep up with her.

But I wanted to.

For the first time in a long time, I wanted to be selfish.

I wanted to claim my wife.

I wanted to keep her.

2

Hope

$\mathcal{N}$oah was fighting the most important fight of his career tonight, and I had just made the most important decision of my life.

I'd taken him back.

Never in my wildest dreams had I ever imagined myself to be one of those women who fall into their husband's arms as soon as they apologized, but that's exactly what I did.

My prodigal husband had finally returned from his eight-year – and some change – hiatus, and I had welcomed him with open arms.

Maybe I wasn't thinking clearly, and maybe Jordan was right in saying I was rushing into this, but what could I do?

Stand back and watch him walk out of my life again?

No.

No freaking way.

That wasn't a viable option for me. Not one I could live with anyway, and not after his revelation.

My husband was abused.

Chapter 2 | 15

He was *raped.*

The pain I knew he had to be carrying was unimaginable to me. I couldn't begin to empathize with how he must be feeling. I only knew that if I let him go now, after telling me his deepest, darkest secrets, he would never feel safe enough to trust me with anything again.

Throughout the course of his entire life, Jordan had been let down and abused by the people that were supposed to take care of him. He was raped when he was a child and he was raped when he was my husband.

By his stepfather.

By the man who was supposed to love him and take care of him.

It had happened right under my nose, over and *over* again.

And I had done *nothing.*

I had said *nothing.*

All of those times I had just known something wasn't quite right about him; all of those times when I'd seen the bruises on his body, I had done *nothing!*

The memories I had of the childhood version of him entered my mind and I was filled with a screwed-up concoction of guilt and happiness. Guilt for not being able to save him from him demons, and happiness for how he'd been the most important part of my life back then.

I couldn't remember the first time I met Jordan Porter.

In fact, I couldn't remember a day in my life when he wasn't around. I couldn't pinpoint the exact moment in time I knew I was in love with him, the same way I couldn't pinpoint a time when I knew I wasn't.

For me, it felt like my entire existence had always been entwined and interloped with him.

At first, it was an innocent kind of love between two children; young, kindred spirits thrust together because of circumstance, embarking on a slow burning love.

Over the years that followed, that love ignited into some-

16 | INEVITABLE

thing much more, much deeper. Like white, hot fire rinsed with desire and scorching teenage hormones.

I did always remember one specific thing though, one niggling complication that had played on my vulnerabilities since puberty; deep down inside, I had always had the distinct feeling that I loved him more than he loved me. I had always cared *more*, invested *more*, worked *harder* for us. I had always been the one in the driver's seat of our relationship and, to my deepest chagrin, it had sometimes felt as though Jordan was an unwilling passenger.

He had always been hard to make out, hard to crack, and hard to truly read. But I had grown up believing that true love existed. I felt it in our home every day of my childhood; my brothers and I had always been surrounded by love. I watched it unfold every day when my parents looked at each other. Because of this, being a believer of love and fate and happy ever afters came naturally to me, almost like a preset inside of my body. Which was why, when Jordan proposed we elope in my senior year of high school, I jumped at the chance.

We married in secret. I was eighteen years old and that day I gave him everything I was; my heart, my soul, my youth, my body. Everything I would ever be. I offered my entire existence to him without terms or stipulations. I was wholly his. Forever and always.

But then he left me, and everything I'd ever known to be true had been turned upside down. Which was why, at twenty-six years old, I found myself struggling deeply with my torrent emotions, drowning in a pool of uncertainty, and feeling like everything I had ever known and believed in to be true just... *wasn't.*

And now, I felt like my life hung in the balance of a few short questions.

Did I still love the man I vowed to share my life with when I was eighteen?

Without a shadow of a doubt.

Did I understand his behavior now I had full disclosure?

Undoubtedly.

Could I forgive him for abandoning me all those years ago?

...

Did I still see a future with him?

...

Those were much harder questions to answer.

Putting aside all of the pain and betrayal I had endured and was still feeling because of his abandonment, I knew that I had to go with him. I *had* to. I loved the man, and if I'd learned anything from my parents, it was you didn't run away from the person you loved when things got hard. You stuck it out and fought for them. You fought for them when they weren't fighting for you. That was true love. I knew he was capable of giving me that. I just had to stick it out and do the fighting for both of us.

Jordan didn't have the childhood I'd had. He wasn't coated in layers upon layers of unconditional love and support to help him grow into a confident and self-assured adult.

I had.

The way our parents had raised us had a lot to do with how successful all four of us had been as adults. Cash and Casey were still young, but I had no doubt they were receiving the same great childhood Cam, Colt, Logan, and I had been given. Our home had always been a safety net for us to fall back on – a safe haven. I had always known I was loved by both parents. They wanted every one of us, even Cam, and they were always in our corner.

I could do that for Jordan.

I could give him the unconditional love he'd been deprived of.

I didn't allow the niggling doubt inside of my heart to take ahold in this moment, nor did I listen to the voice inside my head when it screamed, *'you've been the only one fighting these past eight years'* or the even more depressing voice that whispered, *'I'm tired of fighting for this...'*

Instead, I did what I'd done every day of my life for the past twenty or so years; I closed my eyes and placed my blind faith in Jordan Porter.

3

Jordan

"Is this where you're planning on staying?" Hope asked when I pulled up outside a run-down looking semi on the south side of Denver and helped her off my bike. The area we were in was a far cry from the luxury she'd grown up around, and the way she was trying to hide her disdain was kind of adorable. "What happened to staying with Derek?"

"No, Hope, I'm not staying here. This is where I work."

She looked up at me with a surprised expression. "You work?"

"Yes, I have a job," I replied, unable to fight the smile spreading across my face. When I was around my wife, I found myself smiling more. "I have two of them actually."

"Huh." Hope made this clicking sound with her tongue as she looked up at my face like this was the first time she was ever seeing me.

"What do you do...here?" she asked, gesturing towards the halfway house with a dismissive wave of her hand.

"I volunteer as a drugs and alcohol abuse counselor."

20 | INEVITABLE

Stuffing my hands into the jacket, I looked up at the building that, for a long time, I'd called my home. "I usually work a couple of shifts here each week." Shrugging, I added, "My way of giving back to the community, so to speak."

Her blue eyes widened in surprise. "You're a counselor."

"Among other things." Hope and I had a lot to relearn about each other. My fault, I acknowledged. But this was another reason I feared she was jumping into this too quickly. She didn't even know what I did for a living. She never asked. We were virtually strangers to each other now and had a long road to go to get back to where we used to be.

"So, um... you've been here? All this time? In Colorado?" Her questions were laced with the resentment I knew she was desperately trying to hide. But I could see straight through her, just like I had always been able to.

"I have a house a few blocks from here," I replied, unsure of where this conversation was going.

Hope clicked her tongue again as she looked around at our surroundings before slowly turning to face me once more. "And you were staying with Derek because...?"

"I wanted to be closer to you." That was the truth. Boulder and Denver weren't too far away from each other, about an hour's drive, but I had wanted to be closer to her. "I wanted to see you."

"And when you said you were leaving," she spoke slowly and almost carefully, like she didn't want there to be any confusion. "You meant that you needed to leave because you had to go to work?"

"I had some vacation time owed to me." I shrugged helplessly before saying, "I'm due back today."

"Well, I feel stupid," she finally announced with a heavy-hearted sigh. "Making that big gesture of coming with you," shaking her head, she laughed humorlessly and stared down at her shoes, "when you were only leaving for work."

Chapter 3 | 21

"Hey." Reaching forward, I tipped her chin upwards. "Don't hide from me."

The moment her eyes landed on mine, I felt like I had been sucker punched in the chest. She took the breath clean out of my lungs. There were so many things I wanted to say to Hope Carter, so many things I wished I was capable of doing for her, but I settled on a smile instead. It was the best I could do right now.

And thankfully, it seemed to be enough because she returned my smile with a megawatt one of her own, revealing that dimple in her cheek, the one that had always made me feel lightheaded.

"Any regrets?" I asked. My voice sounded calm, when the truth was I was anything but. I couldn't stand the thought of her regretting this. Regretting coming with me. I knew she was better off without me. I knew there was a list as long as my arm of reasons we shouldn't be together anymore, but still... There was a part of me that needed her unconditional love and support. After all, she was the only one who'd ever given that to me.

"No regrets," she replied just as quickly and impulsively as always, and it made me smile.

"Then come on," I said, voice gruff, as I fell into line with her and gently nudged her shoulder with mine. "Let me introduce you to my world."

"What's the rush?" she shot back teasingly, returning my nudge as she walked beside me towards the building. "I've only been waiting a decade for this."

"Funny."

"You don't know half of it."

No, I didn't know half of it.

Of her.

But I planned on learning.

4

Hope

*W*ell, this was... awkward.

Driving off into the sunset on the back of my husband's motorcycle had seemed like the most romantic and endearingly beautiful gesture earlier. But now that I had time to think about what a huge plunge I had taken? Well, my mind was *reeling* and in complete and total overdrive.

You know that feeling you get when you make an impulsive purchase at the store, an expensive purchase you haven't quite thought through? A purchase that's going to affect your spending for the next six months? You know that horrible feeling of dread that settles in your stomach when you come down from the high and realize that 'hey, actually, I shouldn't have done that'?

Well, I was in the throes of said feeling.

And I felt horrible because of it.

What was I saying; I *was* horrible.

Who thought like that?

Bad people, that's who.

Chapter 4 | 23

I wasn't sure what I had been expecting to see when I walked through the doors of that halfway house in Denver earlier either, but I had felt humbled. The seriousness of the environment, and the sheer devastation of those men's situations, made the mortification inside I had been feeling fall onto the back burner. Sure, there were people in that building I would have crossed the street to avoid in normal day to day life, but it was an eye-opener for me.

Jordan was a counselor.

He *helped* people.

Those desperate and lonesome looking people I'd seen back in that house? Jordan took *care* of them, gave them *hope*, and the foundations of a drug-free future.

I thought that was pretty amazing and, when I hadn't been worrying myself into an early grave about the repercussions of my rash life choices, I had been in awe of Jordan the entire time.

I even ended up watching Noah's fight in the common area of the house with the residents. Unable to express the pain and heartbreak I had felt when I watched Teagan scramble into the ring and throw the fight on Noah's behalf had been too much for me and I had bawled like a freaking baby – along with at least two other big, butch men. I had tried calling her at least a dozen times since the fight ended, but she never picked up.

Those unanswered calls bothered me long after Jordan finished his shift, and when we finally arrived at his house after midnight, the fight was still on my mind.

We had come straight to his house after his shift and I was still trying to familiarize myself with my surroundings.

His house was tiny – only slightly bigger than my apartment back in Cork. The only difference that I could see was the fact that the two bedrooms and bathroom in Jordan's house were on the second floor. My apartment was all on the same level. Back in Ireland, I had a decent sized, open plan kitchen/living area. Jordan's kitchen and living area were split

24 | INEVITABLE

into two tiny rooms and separated by a narrow hallway; his living room at the front of the house, and the kitchen at the back. And where I had a balcony, Jordan had a tiny eight feet by eight concrete yard outback that was home to a clothes line and nothing else.

The kitchen was a small, lemon painted room, tiny in size, with just enough room for the two-chaired table we were sitting at.

The cupboards were an off-white color and the countertops were littered with copious amounts of paperwork and text-books, not to forget at least half a dozen dog-eared paperbacks strewn into the mix.

The clutter was chaotic and it kind of reminded me of what living with Teagan used to feel like –pre-Noah. She was a hot mess to live with and from the looks of this kitchen, so was Jordan.

"They're fine, Keychain," Jordan announced, breaking my thoughts, as he set a cup of coffee down in front of me before joining me at the small breakfast table in his kitchen. "Noah's probably pissed she threw the fight," he added before taking a sip from his mug.

"Did you see his face?" I heard myself snap, immediately jumping to Teagan's defense. "If I had been in Teagan's shoes, I would have thrown the fight three rounds ago."

Jordan's brows raised in surprise. "I didn't say I didn't agree with what she did, Hope. I just meant that it may have caused an issue between them."

Guilt churned inside of me. "Sorry," I mumbled, feeling like a dick for getting ratty with him. Jordan was obviously trying to soothe my anxiety and I was being a bitch.

"It's okay, Hope."

No, it wasn't.

Nothing about this was *okay*.

Something felt wrong.

I was antsy and agitated and it was taking every ounce of

Chapter 4 | 25

my self control to make myself stay in this chair and not pace the floor. I was feeling on edge about something. Not allowing myself to believe that my edginess had anything to do with the huge life altering decision I had just made, I focused on Noah and Teagan. It was a safer topic for my frazzled mind to concentrate on. I was worried sick about them and I couldn't explain that to Jordan. I couldn't delve into details because those were details I needed to take to the grave. Dangerous and illegal details. The only one who could even begin to comprehend what I was feeling I didn't *dare* think about.

Pulling my thoughts away from Noah and Teagan, I cast a glance around the tiny kitchen, trying to distract myself only to stiffen when my gaze locked on three or four baby bottles on the draining board next to the sink.

Baby bottles?

What the fuckety fuck!

With my body alive with suspicion, I began to search for more incriminating evidence. It didn't take me long. On the window sill, next to the back door, were a handful of unused diapers neatly stacked one on top of the other. Beside them was a container of baby wipes and what looked like a tattered stuffed rabbit.

"Do you have something you need to tell me, Jordan?" I heard myself ask, tone demanding and laced with unspoken accusation. His eyes landed on mine and I inclined my head towards the sink.

If Jordan had a child, I was done. Seriously. If a miniature version of my goddamn husband popped out from behind the woodworks, I was hightailing it out of here. I liked to think of myself as a tolerant woman, but him having a child was not something I could put up with. It would be too much. Knowing that he'd lied to me and *procreated* while I'd spent the majority of my adult life in a foreign country mourning him? Hell no.

"I don't own that bottle," he announced, roughly clearing his throat. "Or the baby it belongs to."

26 | INEVITABLE

Inhaling a deep breath, I bit out, "Then whose *is it*?" Pressing my fingers to my temples, I foresaw my head spinning clean off my shoulders if he didn't hurry his ass up and explain this to me.

"The bottle and every other piece of baby equipment in this house belongs to Ryder," Jordan was quick to respond. "And Ryder belongs to Annabelle."

"Annabelle," I repeated, deadpan. "As in your fake, former, whatever-the-hell-it-was fiancée Annabelle?"

"Yes." He cleared his throat again before adding, "She, ah... she and Ryder sort of live here."

"You're kidding?" I asked flatly. When he shook his head, my mouth fell open. "Jesus Christ, Jordan."

"As roommates, Hope," he was quick to add. "That's all it's ever been. Just roommates and friends."

"Are they *here* now?" I shrieked, wide-eyed and dumb-founded.

Jordan nodded. "They have their own room upstairs."

Okay breathe, Hope. Breathe. Don't lose your shit on him right this minute. You've just gotten back together. Give it a day at least...

"And Ryder's father?" I bit out, tightening my grip on my cup so tight I was surprised it hadn't shattered in my hand. I was struggling with this revelation. I really was. In fact, I was having a hard time staying in my seat. Some of Teagan must have rubbed off on me because all I wanted to do was *run*. "Who is he? *Where is he?*"

"He's a bad guy who's not in the picture anymore."

"Okay," I muttered, striving to remain composed and not reach across this table and scratch his stupid, beautiful face. "That's not going to work for me. I think you better tell me everything."

I surprised myself with how calm I managed to remain as I listened to Jordan explain how he first met Annabelle six years ago when he came to live at one of the sober living projects in

Chapter 4 | 27

the city. She was his counselor and sponsor back then and the only one who had absolute faith in his ability to become sober. They had bonded over their similar home lives – she, too, was from a broken home with no parental role in her life and, once he'd gotten clean and finished his social studies degree, had later helped him gain employment in the sector.

He told me about how even though they had drifted over the years as their careers took them in different paths, they had always remained close friends.

And then Jordan revealed to me how she had come to him for help two years ago when she had taken one punch too many from her violent ex.

She'd been four months pregnant with Ryder when she arrived on the doorstep of this very house on a cold night in December with nothing but a duffel bag and a broken nose to show for herself. She'd been here ever since. He'd been at the birth, held her hand through the labor, and had been the only consistent male in Ryder's life these past eleven months. He had even been honored with the title of Ryder's godfather, the same role my parents had given his father when I was born.

"Why?" I heard myself ask before blowing out a breath. I tried to form some semblance of an intelligent thought to explain how I was feeling in this moment, but the only thing I could say was, "*why*?"

"Why?" Jordan looked at me in confusion. "Why what?"

Why had he done all this for them?

Why were they still living here?

Why was he shacking up with another woman?

Why was he raising another man's child when he could have given me a chance and raised babies with me?

He didn't know her.

Not really.

He knows her more than you, a voice in my mind hissed, but I silenced that voice with a shake of my head.

"I'm trying to understand this," I whispered. And truly, I

28 | INEVITABLE

was, but it was hard to comprehend. "Does she know?" I heard myself ask then, locking eyes with him across the table. "About you. About what happened to you?" I swallowed deeply. "Does she know about that?"

"She was my sponsor, Hope," he replied, and I felt the floor fall out from underneath me. "She knows everything about me."

She knew.

About his life.

About everything.

He had confided in her while he had blocked me out.

"Hope," Jordan said gruffly before reaching across the table and covering my hand with his. "I know this is a lot to take in one night, but I promise there has never been anything but friendship between me and Annie. I love *you*."

Annie.

Ugh.

Christ.

We drank our coffee in silence after that, with me deep in thought and Jordan sensibly silent. Finally, when the last remnants of coffee were drained from both our cups, Jordan pushed his chair back and stood. "It's late." He paused and looked down at me before exhaling a shaky breath. "Should I call you a cab or..." his voice trailed off as he slowly reached for his phone, obviously waiting on me to make the decision about our future.

"Put your phone away," I muttered, exhaling a weary sigh.

I watched as relief flashed across Jordan's face. "You sure?"

No, I wasn't sure. I wasn't sure about anything anymore. A bitter taste had settled in my mouth, and I could only pray that it was a temporary thing. "I'm sure," I whispered as I pushed my own chair back and stood.

When we reached the top of the staircase, Jordan walked over to the last of three doors and pushed it open before gesturing me inside. I couldn't help but feel a pang of resent-

Chapter 4 | 29

ment towards the woman sleeping behind the other bedroom door as I walked past and into the bedroom my husband had been sleeping alone in this past almost decade.

As I looked around at my surroundings, the small double bed with a dark navy comforter strewn messily across it and matching closet and dresser, it was with a bolt of annoyance and my mind began to reel.

This was where he had been all those years. Every night I had cried myself to sleep over him, he'd been here. *Here!* In this house in freaking Colorado.

As much as I tried to fight it away, the knowledge of seven years of nothing continued to torment me, picking away at my trust and contentment like a horrible intrusive thought I couldn't defeat.

No calls.

No text messages or emails.

Seven long years of silence.

And then there was Annabelle, the fake fiancée, his current roommate, and her baby.

I didn't want this; I didn't want to hold a grudge.

I wanted to be happy with him.

More than that, I wanted *him* to be happy with me.

How was I supposed to handle this?

I wasn't known for my grace. I was one of six children, five of those being boys. Grace and tact weren't my strongpoints. Ugh, my father and brothers were going to freak out when they found out about this. My mother was going to rush out and buy a wedding hat – she didn't need one of course, but I knew she would be ecstatic at the thought of Jordan and I getting back together.

Maybe I was jumping ahead of the gun here.

We hadn't actually spoken about what we were to each other now.

I'd made an impulsive decision at the spur of the moment that decidedly and unintentionally changed the course of my life. I needed to have a ten second delay. It would be so much easier...

"It's okay to feel on edge, Hope," Jordan said, breaking me from my worried thoughts. I looked across at him guiltily and he smiled. "I let you down," he explained, tone soft and gentle. "And I've put a lot on you tonight. It's okay to feel wary of me. I'd be surprised if you didn't."

I felt my cheeks burn as I quickly denied what Jordan had so aptly figured out. "I'm not wary of you," I said, not really lying, but not completely telling the truth either. When it came to my husband, I was a wreck. My emotions and feelings were all over the place and I didn't know how I felt most of the time.

For the best part of my life, I had been so focused on *being with him* that I hadn't thought of how I might feel when we finally were together.

I had been hunting this man down since childhood and now that the day had finally come that we were together without any barriers or pretenses, it wasn't what I had expected it to be.

I didn't *feel* how I had thought I would.

Instead of elation, I was feeling oddly...numb.

That thing I had been chasing my whole life, the thing I had been so sure was Jordan and then my career and then Jordan again, still felt like it was *missing*.

I still felt...hollow.

Time, I decided.

I just had to give this some time.

I was twenty-six years old and hadn't been with him properly since I was eighteen. I needed to adjust and give it a little time. Everything would fall into place.

It had to.

I'd spent my life dreaming of having what my parents so effortlessly had with each other, with Jordan. He was my first love and, like my mom with my dad, I had every intention of him being my last.

Chapter 4 | 31

I just needed to focus.

I knew I wouldn't win any wife of the year awards, it simply wasn't in me, but dammit, I was going to be the best wife to Jordan that I possibly could.

I couldn't lose him again.

I refused to go through that twice.

But I wasn't sure how this was going to work. Did we fall straight back into man and wife? Boyfriend, girlfriend?

I didn't know and apparently, I didn't have to make a decision about it either. Jordan made it for the both of us when he said, "It's okay, Hope. I'll take the couch tonight."

I guess we were reverting to the friend's zone for now.

Was I being friend-zoned?

Why the hell was he moving to the couch?

Was it because he thought I wanted to sleep in here alone? Because I most certainly did not. Or was it because he didn't want me sleeping in here...with him? I didn't want to ask, because I wasn't sure I could handle the answer.

What he had endured at the hands of that bastard tore me up inside. I didn't want to make him feel uncomfortable by bringing up sex. We could work up to that. I'd managed for eight years without any, I could do it a little longer.

"No," I blurted out, quickly sinking down on his bed. "I want you to stay here. With me." He wasn't going into any damn spare room or whatever. Jordan and I were going to be happy together and I sure as hell wasn't going to ruin what I worked so hard to get by bringing up my horny female reproductive parts.

But what about children?

Would we have them?

And if we did, how many would he want?

How many did *I* want?

And what about his live-in surrogate family?

Would we all live here *together*?

Did he even want me living here with him?

With *them*?

Oh god, shut up, Hope. Shut your stupid, overactive imagination up right this minute before you ruin this!

"Are you okay?" Jordan asked me, his raspy voice drawing me back to the present, and I balked before swinging my gaze to meet his. My heart ached at the sight. He was so beautiful and I loved him so much. I truly did. I hated that there was a part of me that wasn't okay with this... a part that wasn't accepting. I'd always given myself fully to this man and having a part of my subconscious pull away from my decision troubled me deeply.

"Hope?" Jordan's soft voice flooded my mind and dragged me from my terror inducing thoughts.

Blinking rapidly, I looked up at him and smiled sheepishly. "Huh?"

"Stop overthinking this," he replied with a knowing smile etched across his handsome face. "We can take this one day at a time, okay?"

I nodded and returned his smile, all while I buried down the feeling of disappointment churning inside of me. "One day at a time?" I heard myself ask. "And what does that mean exactly?"

He cocked a dark brow. "I think the term speaks for itself, Keychain."

I shook my head. "What does it mean for you?" *For us?*

Awareness dawned in Jordan's eyes, as he caught onto my meaning, and he let out a heavy sigh. "I'm not the person you remember. I'm not that boy anymore, Hope."

I nodded in agreement.

Neither was I.

It was impossible to expect the boy who walked out on me almost a decade ago to return inside the man standing before me.

But that didn't stop me from admitting, "I miss that boy."

"That boy is dead," he replied. "So don't waste your time

Chapter 4 | 33

searching for someone who isn't inside me anymore," Jordan added, voice gruff and full of emotion. "Just..." Closing his eyes, he looked up to the ceiling and pinched the bridge of his nose. "Just accept me for the person I am now."

"I am," I croaked out.

Silence enveloped us then and I strived to find the words to break it.

"Maybe we should take this back to the start," Jordan finally said, breaking the uncomfortable silence. He walked around to the other side of the bed and emptied the contents of his pockets onto the nightstand before looking over at me and smiling. "I'm Jordan, I'm thirty-years-old, a meat-eating Virgo with a master's degree in sociology. I split my life into working two full time jobs, one of which is with a local charity that works with victims of sexual abuse and rape. The other is St. Luke's hospital where I work as an on-call crisis counselor in the psychiatric department. In my spare time, I volunteer at some of the shelters and halfway houses I used to reside in, and for some of those residents, I am their sponsor. Oh, and I'm also married," he added with a smirk. "And I've been in love with the same woman since I was four years old. I've been a shitty husband, but I plan on changing that." He unfastened the clasp of his watch and placed it on the nightstand alongside his wallet, keys, and phone. "I'm recovering from an alcohol and drug dependency that almost cost me my life. I've been sober for six years, three months, and twenty-two days." He sank down on the opposite side of the bed and smiled the brightest smile at me before saying, "Any questions?"

"Only a couple million," I mumbled, feeling completely stumped. "Okay." Shaking my hands out, I stood up and turned to face him. "I'm Hope Carter, a twenty-six-year-old Taurus with a penchant for story-telling and a vivid imagination." My cheeks flamed as I spoke. I felt suddenly very stupid and foolish, like I was reading the biography on the back of one of my novels. I was rehearsing four or five lines I knew by heart. And

34 | INEVITABLE

as I spoke the words, describing who I was, the feeling of being lost grew inside of me. "I'm the only girl out of a family of six kids." Was this really me? "I'm obsessed with reality television shows." Was this all my life entailed? "I've only ever had one boyfriend." Christ, I was boring. "And I married him."

"Talk about lucky," Jordan mused and I balked.

Why in God's name was he asking me about *him*? "What's there to say?"

Jordan's brows rose in confusion. "What?"

I stared back at him. "What?"

"It's a figure of speech, Hope," he explained slowly. "I meant that I was lucky."

"Right," I laughed nervously. "I knew that." *Totally didn't, but anyway...*

We stood at opposite sides of his bed, both staring at the other. His green eyes were locked on my face, taking in every frown, every blink of uncertainty I was feeling. He was so aware of me, so keenly observant that it both unnerved and delighted me. The way he looked at me, the way he gave me his complete and absolute attention excited something inside of me and I wanted nothing more in this moment than to drag him onto this bed and straddle him.

But I wouldn't.

Not yet, at least.

Unless he wanted me to.

Did he want me to?

Ugh, I *hated* this – I hated second guessing myself.

"Relax," he whispered gruffly as he opened the buttons on his shirt, revealing a lean, ripped stomach with tightly cut muscles and a sprinkling of dark hair trailing beneath his navel, disappearing beneath the waistband of his black slacks.

Immediately, my gaze landed on the jagged scars marring his otherwise perfect skin. "Jordan," I whispered, broken at the sight. It crippled me; knowing he'd done this to himself.

I took a step towards him.

Chapter 4 | 35

Immediately, he stepped back.

"I don't..." Words trailing off, I hung my hands limply at my sides. "I feel so bad."

"This is on me, Hope Carter, not you." His voice was full of heat and certainty as he spoke. "These marks are on my body because there was a time in my life when the physical pain was easier to deal with than the mental fucking torture." His green eyes were locked on mine as he spoke, "Again, not on you, Keychain." Inhaling deeply, he reclaimed the space he'd put between us. "Never on you."

"I feel like I failed you," I strangled out, barely able to breathe.

"Don't be sad for me," he whispered. "I'm the one that failed *you*."

When his shirt was gone, Jordan's hands moved to the buckle of his belt and I felt my body sag a little, my heart hammering hard in my chest, as he stripped. He never took his eyes off me as he slowly unbuckled his belt before undoing the zipper, revealing his tight, black boxer shorts.

He looked at me expectantly, his green eyes piercing through every wall and cover-up I had built to keep him out.

My hands shook with the effort as I yanked my shirt over my head and tossed it carelessly on the floor at my feet. I was trembling from head to toe, fear and anticipation residing inside of my heart, as I kicked off my sneakers and jeans before reaching behind my back and unclasping my bra, baring my breasts to him, my hardened nipples straining for his touch.

Clad only in a pair of plain, cotton white panties, I knelt on my side of the bed and paused, unsure of what to do next. In any of my novels, I wouldn't have to think twice about this because the hero would take complete control of the situation, but this wasn't one of my stories. This was real life, and this was Jordan. He continued to stare at me for the longest moment before finally releasing a ragged breath and mirroring my actions by kneeling on the bed.

36 | INEVITABLE

Plucking up the courage to do what I wanted, I closed my eyes, knelt forward, placed my hands on his shoulders and leaned closer. Prepared for rejection, surprise and lust flooded through my body when I felt his lips cover mine, warm, tender and oh so familiar. His mouth was on mine and it felt right. Like I was home.

This man was mine.

All of him.

Even the broken pieces.

Moving slowly, I pressed myself closer, and probed his bottom lip with my tongue. He opened for me, willingly accepting what I was offering. Excitement thrummed inside of me, joined by lust and desire, forming a desperate need to be underneath this man right now.

Tightening my hold on his shoulders, I gently probed his skin with my nails, telling him with my touch that I was thoroughly enjoying what he was doing to me and I wanted more. He seemed to get my meaning because he gave it to me. Harder kisses, more impatient, fast, heated, longing. I wanted him so desperately, I wouldn't have been surprised if I was oozing the smell.

Breathless, I gasped into his mouth and moaned loudly when his hand curled around my hip and pulled me closer. This was amazing. It was everything and more and I needed to have him inside of me. Growing more frantic with every kiss, I slid my fingers under the waistband of his boxers and tugged him closer, desperate to feel his skin on mine.

"You're so beautiful," he whispered as he cupped my face in both of his hands and exhaled shakily. "It hurts." Pausing, Jordan lowered his face to mine and kissed me softly before pulling back. "How much I love you?" He kissed me again, harder this time, before whispering, "It's physically painful for me," against my lips. "Loving you hurts, and leaving you hurts. It all hurts, Hope. Every bit of it."

My heart swelled so much I felt it crack clean open in my

Chapter 4 | 37

chest. Reaching up, I covered his hands with mine and squeezed. "I'm here." An outpour of love and unconditional devotion for this man poured from every part of my soul. I wanted to heal him. I wanted to love him so hard he never had to feel another ounce of pain for the rest of his life. "I'm right here, Jordy."

"I'm so hollow inside, Hope," he whispered, tightening his hold on my face. I welcomed the pressure. It meant he was really here with me. This wasn't a dream. He was back in my life, and I was back in his bed. "But I'm done disappointing you. And I'm done running away. I'm done *pushing* you away."

"It's okay," I breathed, my heart racing dangerously fast.

Leaning forward, he pressed his forehead to mine and said, "I know what I am, Hope – all kinds of fucked up and broken. I'm not even sure if I'm capable of giving you everything I've promised. But I'm here, and I'm yours, and I'm willing to try..."

I couldn't hear another word of it, his pain was threatening to overtake me, so I kissed him instead; reclaiming his mouth with mine.

I was starving for him; his attention, his love, his affection. Nothing could sate this desperate need I had inside to be filled up by this man.

Unable to bear the extreme heat burning through my body, I tugged at the waistband once more, clumsily trying to free him from the restraints of the fabric.

"Slow down," he whispered between kisses as I practically mounted him.

Nope.

Uh-uh.

No way in hell was I slowing down now.

Dragging his body down on mine, I clawed at his back like an attention starved, semi- deranged kitten, and rocked my hips frantically. I wasn't a stranger to orgasms, I'd had plenty over the years with the help of my trusted vibrator, but what I needed right now was something much more. What it was, I

38 | INEVITABLE

wasn't entirely sure, but I had no doubt I was searching for *something*.

Closeness.

Intimacy.

Love.

His body moved above mine as he kissed me into a drug-induced trance of ecstasy. Aroused and drowning in the feel of him, I slid my hands down his back, desperate to feel every inch of his skin. Slipping my hands beneath the fabric of his boxers, I moved my palms over his tight ass, unable to stop myself from squeezing his pert cheeks.

As soon as it had started, it was over and everything went to hell.

Ripping his mouth away from mine, Jordan jerked clean off the bed, backing away from me like I had just scalded him. "What?" I breathed, panting, as I leaned up on my elbows to look at him. "What's wrong?"

"Don't ever do that again," Jordan shot back, tone hoarse and shaken, as he glared at me with accusing eyes.

"Do what?" I gaped at him in sheer confusion. "What did I do?"

"Touch me there," he snapped, eyes wild and full of fury. "Never again, Hope." He ran a hand through his curls and rolled his shoulders. "*Never again.*"

"But I thought you wanted–"

"No!" he snarled. "I don't want... just no, Hope. Fucking no."

And that's when it sank in.

What I'd done.

What I had unintentionally provoked.

One innocent move had caused the walls of Jordan to fly up faster than the bullet from a gun.

"I'm so sorry," I blurted out, mortified, as I scrambled off the bed and rushed to his side.

Jordan dodged my embrace and stalked out of the room

Chapter 4 | 39

before closing the door quietly behind him, leaving me standing in his bedroom reeling.

Oh my god.

What did I do now?

Go after him and force him to talk to me?

Wait here and see if he came back?

I felt like a rapist. Like I had just forced my own husband into doing something he didn't want to. Disgust laced through me, followed by a heady amount of resentment. I didn't mean it. Didn't mean to upset him. I was trying to show him love.

"Fuck," I muttered as I padded over to where my shirt lay on the floor with my jeans and bra. With a heavy heart, I dressed quietly before flopping down in misery on the mattress.

I was so out of my element here.

I had no idea how to handle this man and the demons that came hand in hand with being with a man that had endured the suffering he had.

I debated leaving, wondering if that's what Jordan wanted me to do, if the reason he was staying away for so long was because he wanted me to go, but decided against it. I wasn't a coward. I would face this like I faced everything else in my life; head on.

Jordan was missing for so long that I ended up slipping under the covers and dozing off.

When the mattress finally dipped beside me, signaling Jordan's return, I was drowsy and barely awake. "Are you okay?" I whispered as I turned onto my side to face him, not daring to reach for him. I did not want a repeat performance of earlier. I already felt like shit and didn't think my ego could take another Jordan sized blow.

"Yeah," he whispered in reply, laying on his side facing me. "I'm sorry."

My heart squeezed tightly in my chest. "Me, too."

"I thought you'd be gone," he added, his voice barely more

40 | INEVITABLE

than a whisper as he looked into my eyes. "Wouldn't have blamed you."

Believe me, I thought about it... "Running is your forte," I replied, resting my face on my hands as I looked across the bed at him. "Besides, I think I love your mattress."

My words caused him to crack a small smile. "I love you."

I bit back a weary-hearted sigh and told him that I loved him, too, even if being here and not being able to touch him was breaking my heart a little.

I must have watched him for hours after that, long after he'd fallen asleep, memorizing the plains of his face and the shadows under his eyes. Jordan looked more like the man I used to know when he was sleeping. His features softened. He wasn't so on edge. He wasn't so...haunted.

I debated, several times throughout the course of the night, on reaching over and stroking his face, his hair, his beautiful, scarred body, but decided against it. I didn't want to sleep alone anymore and I knew that's exactly what would happen if he woke up and caught me trying to cop a feel.

It was after three o'clock in the morning when my eyelids finally began to flutter shut from exhaustion, and it was at this exact time my phone chose to vibrate obnoxiously on the nightstand beside my head. Snaking a hand out from beneath the covers, I swiped my cell up and looked at the screen.

One missed call from Teagan.

But it had barely rung out?

Redialing her number, I held my phone to my ear and waited. The call went straight to her voicemail.

Anxiety gnawed inside of me and I tried four more times to call her back before throwing the covers off myself and sitting up.

Something was wrong.

I couldn't put my finger on what exactly, but I just had this horrible feeling of dread in the pit of my stomach.

None of this was sitting well with me.

Chapter 4 | 41

Why hadn't she called me back?

Why was she not answering now?

What the fuck was going on?

Unable to just lay here with no answers, I slipped out of bed and quietly kicked on my sneakers. I took one more glance at my sleeping husband before slipping out of the room and creeping downstairs.

When I reached the kitchen, I called a 24hr cab company. I kept on my phone's speed dial and shrugged on my coat. I needed to make sure they were both okay. Call it strange, but I couldn't wait until morning. I needed to go home. I had this feeling in the pit of my stomach, a feeling that was screaming at me to *go back.*

"Where are you going?" I heard Jordan ask just as I was opening the front door.

Burying the shriek of surprise on the tip of my tongue, I swung around to face him. "I need to go check on Teagan."

"Right now?" He stood on the middle step of the stairs, still clad in his boxers and sporting a confused, sleepy expression. "Hope, it's like three in the morning."

"I know." My cheeks reddened in embarrassment. I knew it sounded dumb and I looked insane, but I couldn't exactly explain the reasons for my anxiety – at least not without incriminating Jordan. "I just have to, okay?"

He stared hard at me for the longest moment before finally nodding. "Let me get dressed and I'll drive you home."

"No need. I've called a cab." I checked the screen of my phone before saying, "It should be here any minute now."

"Well, just let me run up and change and I'll come with you–"

"No!" I interrupted bluntly, flinching when I saw the pain in his eyes at my rejection. "Noah doesn't like strangers in the house. Not since Einín," I began to ramble, and technically it wasn't a lie. He was incredibly cautious of who was around his wife now. "I'm just going to go on my own, okay?"

"Stranger," Jordan mused softly.

"I didn't mean that –" the sound of a car horn beeping both signaled my cab and interrupted my train of thought.

"It's fine," Jordan mumbled before turning on the staircase and heading back up the steps. "Goodnight, Hope."

"Yeah," I squeezed out. "Goodnight, Jordan."

5

Hope

When the cab finally pulled up outside Teagan and Noah's house, it was four in the morning and the place was lit up like the fourth of July. Teagan's shiny white range rover was parked in its usual spot, but there was no sign of Noah's Lexus. Immediately, a trickle of unease rolled through me.

"Thanks for the ride." Tossing a bundle of cash at the driver, I shoved the cab door open and practically threw myself out of the back seat. Dashing up the porch, I took two steps at a time, my lanky legs a great asset in times of emergency. I didn't need to knock; the front door was wide open.

The silence, when I stepped inside the foyer, was eerie and my hackles rose.

Something was wrong.

I could feel it right down to my bones.

Something bad had happened.

Maybe it was a good thing Jordan had come home when he

44 | INEVITABLE

had. My uncle Noah was involved in some dark and shady shit, and I was beginning to slip into this crazy world of underground violence. Maybe Jordan was my way out.

However, every thought, fear, and obstacle my day had thrown at me disintegrated into thin air the moment Noah burst through the front door of South Peak Road, shirtless and drenched in blood.

"Oh my god," I gasped. I threw my hand up to my mouth in horror and gaped at him. Were those *stab wounds* on his stomach and chest?

He didn't seem to see me or even notice I was there. He moved primitively, on instinct, as he grabbed a throw off the back of the couch and quickly disappeared outside and into the darkness.

Shocked and unsure of what to do, I just stood in the foyer, gaping out the wide open front door. A few minutes passed before he returned in through the doorway, this time with a small frame bundled up in the throw and cradled in his arms.

The moment I recognized Teagan as the bundle Noah was cradling, a scream tore from my throat, and this time he did notice me.

"It's okay," he continued to soothe as he plowed through the house with his wife in his arms. "I've got you, Thorn." Storming past me, he bit out, "Call Lucky."

"Lucky?" I balked, shaking my head in sheer freaking horror, all while I battled down the very inappropriate swell of excitement in my chest at the sound of *his* name. Swatting down that unwelcome sensation, I asked, "Shouldn't I be calling an ambulance? Or the cops?"

"No cops!"

"But, Noah, you're bleeding all over."

"Just do what I motherfucking say, Hope," he roared, "and call *Lucky*."

I moved to follow after them, but Noah warned me off with

Chapter 5 | 45

an almost animalistic growl. "Do not come up these stairs, Hope Carter," he snarled, "stay the fuck down here and *call Lucky*!" before climbing the staircase and disappearing out of sight.

"Omigod, omigod," I muttered to myself because no one in this stupid house had any interest in listening to me. "Okay. It's okay, Hope. Just breathe..." Rushing over to the front door, I quickly slammed it shut and locked it before sliding across the many deadbolts. The trail of blood that Noah had left in his wake caused my stomach to churn inside of me and I shook my head and blew out a harsh breath before rushing back into the kitchen to retrieve my cell. With trembling hands, I quickly scrolled through my contacts list until I found the contact *Hunter*.

Jesus, what the hell had happened tonight?

I knew something was wrong.

I freaking *knew* it!

I pressed call and held my cell to my ear while I quickly dashed around and locked every door and window I feared an intruder could use. My heart was racing so hard, I was sure anyone within a three-mile radius could hear it. I didn't dare delve into the reason why my body seemed to be thrumming with anticipation. There was nothing good about this situation.

Nothing at all.

When Hunter's phone rang out and went to voicemail, my fear spiraled to new heights and I quickly hung up before redialing. "Answer your phone, asshole," I muttered to myself as I frantically paced the room.

"Hello to you, too," I heard Hunter reply, clearly amused.

"Oh, *thank god*." I sagged in relief and quickly began to relay tonight's events to my uncle's best friend and former cellmate. "Hunter, I don't know what's happening, but Noah just walked in here and he's covered in blood, like completely drenched! And he told me to call you." My voice was rising with every word I spoke. "And Teagan? I don't even know if she's *okay*. He's got her wrapped up in a blanket...and he's taken her upstairs. Shit, Hunter, I tried to help, but they went upstairs and he told me not to follow them. God, I don't know what to do..."

"Hope, breathe," I heard him say, and weirdly enough, the tone in his voice soothed something deep inside me. "I'm on my way, sweetheart."

I sagged, visibly sagged, against the kitchen island. "I don't know what to do," I squeezed out.

"I'm coming," he replied. "I'm in my car now. I'm twenty minutes away. Lock all the doors."

"Okay." I nodded, trying to calm myself down. "And they're already locked." Hunter was coming. He wouldn't be long. He would fix all of this. I just knew he would. "Should I call an ambulance? Or the police? Hunter, there's a lot of blood –"

"No cops," Hunter was quick to interrupt, repeating the words my uncle had spoken to me just a few minutes earlier. He wasn't as aggressive as Noah, but I could hear the warning tone in his voice just the same. "Just hang in there, sweetheart. I'll be there soon."

"Don't hang up!" I practically shouted the words, my desperation evident in my tone. Pathetic as it was, hearing Hunter's voice on the other line made me feel safer. "Just...just stay on the line and talk to me."

He paused for a long moment before saying, "I'm not going anywhere."

"I'm scared," I blurted out, biting every nail on my free hand until I was left with nothing but stumps. "This has something to do with JD, hasn't it?"

Lucky didn't reply and his silence only caused the anxiety inside of me to skyrocket.

"Oh god." *Of course it does.* "What if he's coming here?" I prided myself on being a strong woman, but right now, I was a weeping, crumbling mess. JD Dennis was violent and unpredictable. There was no level of violence he wouldn't stoop to in

Chapter 5 | 47

his search of revenge. "Maybe you shouldn't come here, Hunter." I knew he was involved in the fire. I'd protected both him and Noah from the police by lying about their whereabouts that night. I'd told the detectives I had spent the evening watching movies with both men and when my uncle had gone to bed, I had taken his best friend into my bed. It was a lie, but it had fallen so easily from my mouth that morning that the police had believed me. And why wouldn't they? I had a perfect record. I was the ideal citizen. I was in so much shit here.

"No one is going to hurt you," I heard him say in such a confident, reassuring tone that I almost felt a little relief. I could hear horns honking and the sound of an engine revving in the background as I clung to the phone like it was going to somehow fix all of this. "Do something for me, Hope," he added, voice slightly muffled. "Go into the kitchen."

"I'm already in the kitchen."

"Okay," he coaxed. "Good. Now see the cupboard under the sink? Open it up."

I did as he instructed without question. "I'm here."

"Good girl," he said coaxingly. "At the very back, you'll see an opened box of laundry detergent. Can you see it, sweetheart? I think it's purple."

"I see it," I told him as I used my free hand to retrieve the detergent box. It was heavier than it should have been, and when I looked inside and saw the black shiny barrel of a gun, my heart stopped in my chest. "That's a gun, Hunter," I spluttered.

"Pick it up, Hope," he ordered. "It's fully loaded, no safety, so be careful."

I reached inside and froze. "I've never held a gun before," I whispered. I was anti-guns. My mother was shot when I was a child. Noah was shot last year. Guns and my family did not go well together. "Where did you get this?" I asked, gaping at the black, metal life taker in my hand. "Why isn't it stored in a secured gun safe?"

48 | INEVITABLE

"Do you really want me to answer that?" was his response.

Oh god.

No.

No, I really did *not* want him to answer.

"What now?" I asked instead, choosing not to incriminate myself further into this man's world.

"Wait for me," he replied. "I'm nearly there. And if any motherfucker tries to get inside that house before I get there, shoot 'em in the nuts."

Half laughing, half sobbing from the sheer craziness of the situation, I walked back into the foyer and sank down on the step of the stairs. "Why the nuts?" I heard myself ask as I stared down at the gun in my hand. "Why not the head or the chest?"

Lucky let out a low chuckle. "I was trying to spare you from taking a life, but have at it, sweetheart. You shoot 'em in any damn place you want."

The sound of tires screeching outside filled my ears and I stiffened. "Is that you?"

"Yeah, sweetheart, I'm here."

Four words.

Four magnificent fucking words.

I tossed my phone on the step and leapt to my feet. With the gun still clasped tightly in my left hand, I ran to the door and quickly unbolted every lock and deadbolt before throwing it open just as a car door slammed loudly.

From the porch light, a pair of muddy black boots entered my peripheral vision. My gaze followed those boots upwards to the dark, faded jeans and then the red plaid shirt, unbuttoned and revealing a white wife beater, finally landing on a stubbly jaw, slightly crooked nose from being broken more than once, and piercing blue eyes. His signatory man bun was on full display, holding his dirty blonde hair back from his almost inhumanly gorgeous face, as he walked with purpose towards me.

My heart skyrocketed in my chest at the sight of him and an

Chapter 5 | 49

unwelcome gasp tore from my throat. I didn't think twice about running out into the darkness, the relief of seeing him, driving me forward. He had barely made it to the bottom of the porch steps when I threw myself at him. "Thank god," I breathed, wrapping my arms around his neck in a death grip.

"Take it easy," Hunter replied in an oddly nervous tone. He didn't return my hug, choosing to keep his hands held up instead, and when I realized why, I quickly stepped back. I had unintentionally been pressing the nozzle of the gun against his back.

"Oh god," I gasped, holding out the evil piece of metal for him to take. "I'm so sorry."

"That's alright," he replied with a smirk as he took the gun from me. "At least it wasn't my nuts."

"That's not funny." Only Hunter could crack a joke in a situation as volatile and precariously dangerous as this.

"Then why are you laughing?" he shot back with a wink as I watched him fiddle around with the gun expertly before sliding it into the back of his jeans. The move sent a shiver down my spine to think how often this man had so obviously handled a gun. It disturbed me even deeper to realize how much I liked it.

"Nerves," I croaked out.

"Come on," he said then, breaking me from my less than stellar thoughts. "Let's go inside and clean our best friends' latest mess up."

When we were back inside the house with the front door locked, Hunter disappeared upstairs, but not before instructing me to boil some hot water. What the heck was I to these people; a tea maid? I did it anyway, much to my chagrin.

When twenty minutes had passed by and neither Hunter or Noah had come back downstairs, I contemplated going upstairs and demanding to be told everything, but the sound of a car pulling up outside quickly rid me of all thoughts. I kind of reminded myself of Chunk from *The Goonies* in this moment as

50 | INEVITABLE

I panted like a panicked dog and ran around like a headless chicken, attempting to call out for Hunter and Noah, but I couldn't get my words out loud enough for anyone to hear me.

A loud knock vibrated on the front door, followed by the sound of the doorbell ringing and I crept towards the front door like I was walking across a minefield. "Please, don't kill me," I whispered to myself as I peeked through the keyhole. "Dear God, don't let me die tonight."

Surprise, confusion, and a huge abundance of relief flooded my body when I looked through the keyhole and my locked eyes on Max Jones standing on the porch with a medical bag in his hand.

I quickly set to work on unlocking every deadbolt and chain before swinging the door inwards. I'd never been a huge fan of Teagan's doctor uncle, but right now, and considering the amount of blood splattered on the floors in this house, I was damn glad to see him.

"Where are they?" were Max's first words as he strode past me like a man on a mission.

"Upstairs," I offered, closing the door behind him before locking it once more. I turned to show him the way but he was already halfway up the staircase. "Go on up," I muttered under my breath.

Max had no sooner disappeared upstairs when Hunter rejoined me in the kitchen.

"Is someone going to tell me what's going on?" I asked, trailing after Hunter as he walked into the adjoining mudroom and retrieved a mop and bucket.

"You sure you're ready for it?" Hunter responded by asking as he walked over to the sink and filled the bucket with boiling water before adding bleach. When he was done, he turned around and placed the bucket on the floor and sank the mop inside. "There's a reason Noah told you to stay down here." He paused before adding, "You want full disclosure. I get it. But our

Chapter 5 | 51

world isn't exactly...kosher." He squeezed out the mop head before walking back into the foyer.

Swallowing deeply, I picked up the mop bucket and followed after him. "Whatever it is, I know I can handle it," I replied, and in that moment, I *meant* it.

"There's no going back once you know," Hunter warned me as he mopped up every blood and mud stain splattered across the floor tiles. "Last chance to run."

"I'm not running," I heard myself say. Walking over to where he was cleaning, I reached forward and placed my hand on the mop handle, stopping him in his tracks, and said, "Tell me."

Hunter looked at me for the longest moment, his blue eyes piercing me, before releasing the mop and shrugging. "Alright, HC." Gesturing towards the staircase, he added, "Don't say I didn't warn you."

The sounds of puffing and pained grunts came from just behind Noah and Teagan's bedroom door, causing me to stall. Bracing myself, I inhaled a deep calming breath and pushed the door inwards. The sight of my uncle's bare and clearly wounded stomach as he sat on the edge of their huge bed filled my vision and I balked. Max was using one hand to press what looked like a bloodstained towel against Noah's ribs while holding a suspicious looking metal contraption in the other. I guessed the towel had been white in its previous life, but I couldn't tell tonight, not with the sheer amount of blood smeared on it. The image caused my stomach to churn violently. Another half dozen or so neatly strapped bandages were littered across Noah's upper body, all of which were tinged red, and I heaved at the sight.

"Oh my god, Noah!" I managed to wheeze out, the sight of the bloodied towels and instruments splayed on top of their bed causing the bile in my stomach to rise up my throat.

"What the hell is she doing in here?" Noah demanded, looking behind me to glare at Hunter.

52 | INEVITABLE

"She carried a watermelon," Hunter shot back mockingly. "Why do you think, asshole?"

"Noah," I sobbed, gaping in absolute horror. I'd known he was wounded when he stormed into the house earlier tonight. I just hadn't really known how badly.

"I'm good, Hope," Noah managed to squeeze out seconds before a pained grunt tore through his lips. He seemed to be breathing through his nose, concentrating on not moving as Max appeared to be stitching him up.

"Are you guys sure I shouldn't call an ambulance for him?" Fear and concern rushed through my body. My gaze moved from his battered body to the blood smeared bedsheets. Staggering back from the blood, I pressed a trembling hand to my forehead and sagged. "Or for me?"

"You *would* be afraid," Noah grunted with a small shake of his head. "My own niece is afraid of blood. How the hell am I related to you?"

"I'm not afraid of blood," I ground out, averting my gaze from the horror scene in front of me. "I'm afraid of you *bleeding out* and dropping dead in front of me."

"Calm her down or take her out of the room," Max muttered in an irritated tone. "I'm trying to concentrate and she's a distraction."

Just then a warm hand landed on my shoulder, grounding me, and eliminating some of my trembling. I didn't have to look behind me to see who it was. I already knew his touch. For two whole months before Jordan returned, Hunter and I had been virtually inseparable. I'd know that comforting touch anywhere. I turned and walked straight into his arms. Screw the way we had left things when he left The Hill. And screw the fact that our friendship had been fractured by almost sleeping together. I needed a damn hug and the man had great arms.

"Hope?"

Teagan's voice came from somewhere behind me and I

Chapter 5 | 53

swung around, desperate for the reassurance that she was, in fact, alive and in one piece.

When my eyes landed on her willowy frame standing in the doorway of their ensuite bathroom, and her bruised and battered body, something that rarely happened to me occurred.

I cried.

"Teegs," I wept as I practically threw myself on the fragile blonde. Wrapping my arms around her frail body, I hugged her tighter than I knew was safe, but I couldn't help myself. From the moment Noah had shuffled her upstairs until now, I hadn't been sure she was even *breathing.*

"I'm okay," she whispered as she squeezed me back fiercely, comforting *me.* "I'm okay, Hope."

How, I wanted to scream!

How in God's name was she okay?

How was any of this *okay*?

"What's happening here, Teegs?" I asked, tone wobbly as I took in the sight of her bruised face. God, her face was so badly marked she didn't even look like *Teagan.*

Wordlessly, Teagan took my hand in hers and led me out of their room and across the hall to the family bathroom. And when she closed the bathroom door and finally opened her mouth, I knew the secrets she confided in me would haunt me until my dying day.

JD Dennis had found her and Noah.

After years of hunting and hiding, dodging and ducking, their long-lived feud had finally come to a boil. At the Ring of Fire, no less.

Blood had been shed, lives had been taken, and I was now one of the few people privy to the information that not only had Noah killed tonight, but so had *Teagan.*

When Teagan had explained everything that had happened to them tonight, my mind was blown. Seriously, how could so much drama and bad freaking luck follow her and Noah?

I couldn't wrap my mind around all of it.

54 | INEVITABLE

When she told me about how they had threatened to slit open her cesarean section scar, I felt faint. "I'm okay, Hope," she assured me for what had to be the fiftieth time since her revelation. She was sitting on the toilet lid. Meanwhile, I was kneeling beside her, clinging onto her hand like it was a lifeline. "I promise," she added, forcing a sad, teary-eyed smile. "Stop worrying."

"Stop worrying?" I had been worrying about this girl since she bombarded her way into my life senior year of high school. Teagan was like the sister I never had, and coming from a family of five brothers, that was saying a lot. I loved her. I trusted her. The thought of anything else happening to her, having seen her go through all she had this past year was almost too much to bear. I'd been right there by her side, watching helplessly as she grieved the death of her baby at the hands of JD fucking Dennis.

"Do you trust him?" I asked, inclining my head in the direction of the bathroom door to where her uncle was still treating Noah's wounds across the hall. Max had never been a fan of Noah. Having him here kind of worried me.

Teagan nodded slowly. "I do. He doesn't know everything. He says he doesn't need to..." She paused and swallowed deeply before adding, "That's probably for the best."

"And Hunter?" I croaked out. "What does he know?"

"Everything and more," she whispered, ducking her face, her blonde hair like a curtained halo framing her face. "Lucky is Noah's right-hand man. It's more than friendship between them, Hope. It's like they're brothers. You know, sometimes I think he knows more than I do."

"Maybe that's a good thing," I offered gently. "Maybe it's better if you *don't*?"

"Maybe," she replied quietly. She was quiet then for the longest moment, seemingly lost in her thoughts, before she finally whispered, "Hope I have something I need to show you." As silent as a ghost, Teagan stood up, tightened her white

Chapter 5 | 55

bathrobe around her waist, and walked over to the vanity unit surrounding a pair of chrome sinks. I watched as she reached into a drawer and retrieved a long rectangular stick before returning. She thrust the stick in my hands and sat back down, never saying a word.

Confusion filled me until I looked down and realized what I was looking at. "Oh my god!" Two pink lines formed the positive result of the pregnancy test I was holding. "Congratulations!"

"Yeah." Teagan smiled, but I could see the anxiety circling her eyes. "There's a dozen more in that drawer. Same result."

"How long have you known?" I asked, still staring down at the test in my hand.

"I was late," she whispered, "so I took a test a couple of days ago." She ran a hand through her hair and exhaled a shaky breath. "And every day since. All positive."

"What does Noah think?"

"I haven't told him yet."

"Why not?"

"Because he was busy with his fight and I didn't want to distract him," she choked out. "But mostly because if I lose this one, I don't think I can handle seeing that look on his face again. I don't think I can watch that disappointed look twice in one lifetime, Hope."

"*That* is not going to happen again," I vowed passionately.

"Won't it?" Teagan shot back, voice void of all emotion. "Then why am I bleeding?"

Oh god.

No. No. No. No.

"Much?" I squeezed out.

"A little," she choked out. "But enough to make me believe it's gone."

"Okay, Teagan, we have to tell Noah." Scrambling to my feet with the test still firmly clutched in one hand, I hurried to the bathroom door.

56 | INEVITABLE

"I can't go back out there," she blurted out. "I don't want the rest of them to know."

"Okay," I coaxed. "That's fine. I'll get Noah for you."

"I'm scared, Hope," she called out. "I'm just...I can't go through...*that* again."

"You *won't*."

"Do you promise?" she asked, and she looked so young and vulnerable in that moment that my heart cracked clean open. She wasn't a murderer. Not to me. She was just *Teagan*.

"Yeah, Teegs, I promise," I replied, making a promise to my friend, something I wasn't entirely sure I could keep.

When I slipped out of the bathroom, I bumped into an exhausted looking Max in the hallway.

"Oh, Max, thank god. I need to talk to you about –" I began to say, but he quickly silenced me with a weary shake of his head.

"Please don't say another word, Hope. I don't think I can handle another crisis tonight."

"But –"

"I mean it," Max interrupted, all but biting my head off. "There's a kitchen downstairs with two very capable men inside it – one of which is mobile. Go and hound them with your troubles. I've seen and done things tonight that question everything I believe in, not to mention jeopardizing my medical license. So please, if you don't mind, and for the sake of what's left of my sanity, I've had quite enough for one night." Max sighed heavily once more before wishing me farewell and disappearing down the staircase.

Well, he was as sociable as always...

Rushing down the staircase, I barreled through the foyer and into the kitchen. Noah and Hunter were both standing at the kitchen island.

"It needs to be now," Noah was saying as he leaned against the counter, shirtless and all bandaged up. "Tonight." Still clad in a pair of blood stained jeans, Noah held a tumbler of amber

Chapter 5 | 57

liquid in his hand as he spoke in a low voice, "Can't leave it up to G and his pricks to clean this up." He tipped the glass to his lips and tossed the whiskey down the back of his throat. "Not when she's involved. Don't have beef with the man, but I'm sure as fuck not putting her future in his hands." Slamming the glass back down on the counter, Noah let out a hiss before saying, "This can't fall back on her, man. I need a guaran-damn-tee she's in the clear."

"I'll handle it," Hunter, who was zipping up his black jacket, announced before pulling a black beanie cap over his head. "Stay here and take care of your woman. I've got this."

"I can't put this on you, Lucky –" Noah began to say, but I chose this moment to burst in, not caring that I was inter-rupting what I knew had to be a serious conversation.

"You need to go talk to Teagan," I announced. Both men swung around to face me, but I kept my focus on Noah. "Seri-ously," I added, pointing with my thumb to the kitchen door behind me. "Like, right now."

Noah took one look at my face before darting out of the room, calling out, "Thorn! You okay, baby?" moving faster than any man with his injuries should have been able to.

When Noah had disappeared from the room in search of his wife, Hunter turned his attention to me. "Hope," he acknowledged with a small smile before grabbing a set of car keys off the counter and slipping past me. "I'll be seeing you."

"Where are you going?" I demanded as I chased after him.

"I've got some business to attend to," he replied as he yanked open the front door and stepped outside into the night.

I knew exactly what *business* Hunter was talking about and it wasn't the 9-5 type. I wasn't a stupid woman. I knew that in order to survive an eleven-year prison sentence, a man would have to get his hands bloody. He was barely more than a child when he was locked away all those years ago – a crime of passion, they called it. Romanticizing the fact that he had taken the life of his lover's killer. It didn't take a genius to put two and

58 | INEVITABLE

two together and come up with the very real fact that Hunter Casarazzi left that prison with more blood on his hands than when he walked in there at eighteen. It should have made me want to run. And it did. Problem was, I wanted to run *to* him, not away from him. "Wait!" I called out, following him out into the darkness. "You're not seriously going on your own?"

Turning back to face me, Hunter tilted his head to one side and looked at me peculiarly. "Are you... *gasp!*Worried about me?" Grinning, he added, "There's no need, sweetheart. I've been cleaning up his shit for years now. It's part of my job description."

"But you *can't*," I reaffirmed, ignoring his bullshit sarcasm. "I'm serious. I won't let you."

"You won't *let* me," he mused, chewing the thought around all while trying to keep a straight face. "What are you proposing?"

He was going back to the Ring of Fire.

To face God knows what.

And he was going alone.

For some strange reason this *horrified* me.

I was going to regret this until my dying day. I knew I was. But still, I said, "I come with you."

"You're already in too deep, HC," Hunter replied as he unlocked Noah's black Lexus and swung open the driver's side door. His tone was serious, his eyes full of warning, as he said, "Turn back now, sweetheart."

Of course Hunter was right. A million-freaking percent right. I was in too deep and needed to turn back.

But what had happened tonight to my best friend in the world had changed something inside of me.

What had happened to my uncle had changed me.

I was done being a spectator on the sidelines, watching helplessly as the people I loved most in the world were tortured and crucified. I was done with doing *nothing*!

Something inside of the darkest part of my mind had

Chapter 5 | 59

switched on, and I was beginning to realize that, like my father and uncle, I was willing to stoop to *any* level to protect the ones I loved.

"You're right," I agreed, feet still moving towards the car he had just climbed into – towards the darkness I knew there was no escape from. Stopping outside the passenger door, I pulled the door open and said, "But I'm still coming with you."

6

Hope

I set fire to a car tonight.
Not just any car.
Noah's Lexus.

I also aided and abetted a convicted felon by driving his truck to the scene of a murder crime, and then for good measure, I waited for him in said truck while he met with some very unscrupulous looking men and dealt with the horrifically unappealing task of making half a dozen or so dead bodies disappear.

In a sick and twisted way, tonight's events were like a life lesson in science 101. I learned more about human anatomy tonight than I had in four years of high school biology. I had also learned a great deal about chemistry and the unusual methods and concoctions of acid and other substances required in order to make a human body disappear.

I could still smell the salt and smoke and acid. I could still taste the stench of death and deception. It was scorched inside of me, and I had a feeling that if I looked in the mirror tonight, I wouldn't recognize the woman staring back at me.

I spent eight years on the outskirts of this world, watching the drama unfold. This underworld, the one Noah and Teagan had unwittingly exposed me to, was something I now *craved*.

"Tired?" Hunter asked when we were parked outside the house several hours later. He killed the engine and exhaled a heavy sigh before turning to look at me.

Dawn was breaking, bringing with it a brand-new day, and even though I hadn't slept a wink and should have been exhausted, I was thrumming with a weird, almost addictive buzzing energy.

"Oddly enough, I'm wide awake." I turned sideways in my seat and stared at him. He looked worn out. Deep shadows had settled under his eyes and he seemed to have aged in a matter of hours. Like a heavy weight had settled on top of his already laden down shoulders. "But you look shattered."

Hunter cast a glance at me and smiled before pulling a packet of cigarettes out of his jeans pocket and lighting up. "Never gets easier." He inhaled a deep drag and seemed to hold it in his lungs for an abnormally long amount of time before finally exhaling the cloud of smoke through his nose. The move should have disgusted me, but it evoked the opposite reaction from my body. My heart hammered against my ribcage as I drank in the sight of him. It didn't make any sense – the way I felt when I was around him was the opposite of anything I had ever experienced.

The man sitting next to me had disgusting habits. He smoked excessively and drank without thought for his liver. He cussed like a sailor. He laughed at every inappropriate moment imaginably possible. He flirted with everything with a vagina and a pulse and he taunted the hell out of me. He was who he was and he made no apologies for it. The man was the polar opposite of everything I had ever known and I hated him for making me like that.

62 | INEVITABLE

"What you did tonight?" Hunter turned to face me. "Helping me? That was survival." His blue eyes scorched me as he spoke. "You get that, right?"

I nodded slowly.

I did.

I got it.

I didn't know what kind of a person that made me, but I didn't feel any guilt for my actions. Like Hunter, I had made a decision to protect two of the most important people in my life, and I could never regret that. "Do you?"

Hunter's brow furrowed as he looked at me with a peculiar expression before taking another pull from his smoke. He never answered me though; he just continued to stare – right into my freaking soul.

"What?" I asked, blushing from the heat of his stare.

"Nothing," he replied in an oddly amused tone, "nothing at all," before adding, "I'm gonna need your clothes."

My eyes widened. "What– like, right now?" My hand automatically moved to the hem of my sweater as I looked around at our surroundings. "*Here*?"

He grinned and flicked his cigarette butt out his window. "I was going to suggest you go inside to change, but here sounds like more fun."

"Funny," I shot back with a glare, not liking the way my heart had suddenly begun to race at the prospect of getting naked in a car with this man. After what I'd seen Hunter do tonight, the thought should have sickened me.

It didn't.

He was staring at me in such an intimate way that in this moment, I felt completely naked and exposed to him. It was like he was staring into the darkest part of my soul, and liking what he saw. Hunter Casarazzi unnerved me and he knew it. Memories of him restocking my candy stash when we both lived at South Peak Road flooded my mind and I smiled fondly at the countless late-night chats we'd shared...

Chapter 6 | 63

He didn't believe in ghosts. I did. He watched crappy sitcoms with me, even though I knew he hated it. He once said there was something lonely about me. He had these ice blue eyes that, when you looked deeply enough, showed you a glimpse of his soul.

Memories of him kissing me bombarded me. My lips tingled from the raw memory of his mouth on mine, his hands on my body, evoking more sensations and feelings from me than I had ever felt before.

It was at that very moment my phone began to ring in my pocket, breaking the moment, and clearing my thoughts of all prior notions.

Reaching into my jacket pocket, I retrieved my cell and, seeing Jordan's name flashing on the screen, I pressed accept without hesitation.

"Jordan," I greeted, tone hushed, as I adjusted myself so that I was once again facing forward in my seat. "Are you okay?" I cast a sneaky glance in Hunter's direction, but he wasn't looking at me anymore. His jaw was clenched, his attention focused straight ahead, as he sparked up another cigarette and took a drag.

"I wasn't sure if you'd be up yet or not when I called." His warm voice filled my ears, a stark contrast to what I'd done tonight. Suddenly, I felt cold to the bone. "Did I wake you?"

"Um, no," I muttered, chewing on what was left of my nails. "You didn't wake me." I cast another nervous glance to Hunter. This time he did look back at me. His blue eyes burned straight through me and the subtle shake of his head only reaffirmed what I had already known. I could never tell Jordan about what happened tonight. I could never tell a soul.

"So, is she okay?"

"Huh?"

"Teagan," Jordan affirmed. "Is she okay?"

"Oh yeah, she's fine!" I lied. "You were right. I was worrying about nothing."

64 | INEVITABLE

Jordan was quiet for the longest time before saying, "You didn't come back."

"That's because I've been writing," I heard myself say, never taking my eyes off Hunter, and the bare faced lie came out so naturally that it surprised the hell out of me. "Yeah, when I realized everything was okay, I just went up to my room and started on a new chapter in my latest WIP."

"You've been writing?" came his response, tone surprised, and if I was being honest, a little bit skeptical. "All night? Hope, it's like six-thirty in the morning."

I cringed in shame. "I, ah, must have lost track of time and wrote through the night." Hunter nodded in what seemed like approval before resuming his front window staring. "Did you want something?" I asked and immediately hated the way that had come out and sounded.

"I start a twelve-hour shift at eight," Jordan replied, tone puzzled. "Do you want me to come and pick you up first and grab some breakfast?"

"No!" I blurted out before quickly saving myself by saying, "I need to get this scene nailed down. It's really important to the story and if I stop now I'll lose my train of thought." I wasn't sure what scared me more; the lies that were coming out of my mouth, or how easy it was for me. "I'll call you later... when I get this chapter nailed down, 'kay?"

He was silent for the longest time before saying, "Hope? If you're having second thoughts it's okay–"

"I'm not, I swear," I interrupted, desperate to end this phone call – and the lies. "I just really need to work. I'll call you later okay?"

"Yeah, okay," he replied, voice quiet. "I love you."

"I love you," I whispered, mentally flinching at how uncomfortable this entire situation was. "Bye," I added before hanging up and dropping my phone down on my jean clad lap.

"Husband cracking the whip already?" Hunter taunted, sporting that cocky smirk that I pretended I hated but secretly loved. "Gotta give it to the guy; he moves fast." His blue eyes landed on mine, making me feel a million different unwelcome sensations. I shivered involuntarily under the heat of his stare. "What's he expecting? You at home waiting for him with his slippers and a hot meal?"

"Stop it," I snapped before blanching when I realized what he'd just said. I was pretty sure I'd said that exact same sarcastic thing to Jordan a long time ago. *Weird.* "I'm back with Jordan," I added, feeling the need to justify my actions but not knowing why. "We're giving it another shot."

"I gathered that," Hunter replied in an amused tone before swinging his truck door open and jumping out. "But here's a friendly forewarning," he added with a cocky smirk. "It won't last," he finished before closing the door and walking away.

"What– now just wait a damn minute!" Throwing my door open, I practically fell out of the truck and chased after him. "It will last!" I hissed, finally reaching him just as he turned his key in the front door. "It's for good this time."

"*This time,*" Hunter snorted. "Whatever you say, sweetheart."

"What's that supposed to mean?"

"It means that you are too much of a woman to ever be fully satisfied with a man like him." He turned his key in the door, unlocking it before pushing it open. "Oh, and don't forget, I need your clothes before you run home to lover boy."

"A man like him?" I spat, feeling both wounded and defensive by his offhand comment and even worse tone. "What the hell does that mean – hey, don't walk away from me," I hissed when he moved to walk away. Grabbing his arm, I yanked him backwards. "Finish what you started, Hunter."

"What do you want me to say, Hope?" Hunter chuckled, swinging around to face me with that cocky smirk still etched on his face.

"What did you mean by that 'too much woman' comment?" I demanded.

"I meant exactly what I said," Hunter shot back, eyes locked on mine, daring me to look away. "You might fool *him,* and everyone else in your life, with that 'I'm daddy's little perfect angel' bullshit façade you hide behind, but I see right through you, Hope Carter. I always have."

"You don't know me –" I began to say, but the words were swallowed by a loud gasp when Hunter caught my shoulders and shoved me against the house siding.

The rough way he handled me didn't hurt me – quite the opposite. And I felt a wave of desire roll through my body when he pinned my body to the house with his much larger one.

His voice was husky, his eyes darkened as he trailed up a hand up to cup my throat. "See?" he purred in a voice so insanely seductive I was instantly wet. "You *need* excitement in your life. And you *crave* danger." He made the slightest rolling movement with his hips and it was enough to make me audibly moan. "I can see it in your eyes. And you're never going to be satisfied with anything less," he whispered as he ducked his face so that his lips were within millimeters of my ear. "You're afraid of me, but not because of what *I* am. You're afraid of me because I make you see what *you* are. What you *want*..."

"That's not true," I whispered, desperately fighting my body's urge to give in.

"We both know it is," he chuckled softly, his breath fanning my ear. "I'm right, Hope. And one of these days, you're gonna have to come to terms with it."

With my heart hammering against my ribcage, I mustered up every ounce of self-control I had and pushed him away before saying, "Watch me prove you wrong."

That was too much, too close a call, too...everything. I needed to avoid that man.

I needed to go back to the life I'd worked so hard to have.

For the sake of my sanity and my marriage, I needed to give Lucky Casarazzi a wide berth.

7

Lucky

"You're making a mistake," I couldn't stop myself from taunting as Hope ducked under my arm and backed up several feet, putting space between us. "And for all the wrong reasons."

"*Wrong reasons?*" she seethed.

"Damn straight," I shot back, not giving two shits that she was furious with me. Let her. If it stopped her from making the biggest mistake of her life, then she could spend the rest of her life angry with me. "Guilt isn't exactly a lasting foundation to base a marriage on."

Hope's face paled. She visibly shook with fury as she spat the word, "Guilt?" like it was poison. "You know nothing about our relationship." Her blue eyes flashing with anger. "How dare you insinuate that!"

"Maybe I don't," I forced out casually, striving to keep my cool. "But I know what he's put you through."

"That wasn't his fault." Her voice warbled. She tucked her hair behind her ear; a nervous trait I'd come to learn. "If you

68 | INEVITABLE

knew the whole story, you wouldn't be blaming Jordan for any of this..."

"I don't give two shits about what he's been through." My response stunned her and her mouth fell slightly open. "He was a dick to you, repeatedly, which, in my books, makes him not even close to deserving you," I added salt to the wound by saying. She might be used to being spoon-fed bullshit by everyone else in her life, but she would get nothing but honesty from me.

"He was raped, you ignorant ass!" Hope practically screamed, glaring at me. "He was sexually abused by his stepfather – repeatedly. Is that his fault, too?"

"No," I shot back heatedly. "Is it yours?"

She opened her mouth, no doubt to toss some cutting insult my way, but I got there first.

"Just close your mouth, open your mind for two damn minutes, and listen to me." I moved closer, probably a really bad fucking idea on my part, but I couldn't help myself. When she didn't take a step back from me, I reached out and cupped the back of her neck. "Life isn't easy for any of us. Shit happens all the time. Bad shit. Shit that makes a person want to die. Makes a person want to run." Exhaling heavily, I lowered my face to hers, making sure she saw me, right into me. "What defines us is our reactions." My heart was racing as I spoke. "What makes us who we are is how we react when shit hits the fan."

"Hunter–" Hope began to say, but I interrupted her.

"Just hear me out," I said gruffly, still cupping her cheek in my hand, eyes locked on hers. When she nodded slightly, I continued. "I'm not saying I'm a better man for you." Hell, I was worse. Much fucking worse. "And hell, I'm not even saying this because I want to keep you for myself –" I paused for a moment before smirking. "Well, maybe I am. But I care about you." Did she get that? Hope Carter was the first woman I'd put myself out there for since Hayley, and she had the ability to crush me.

Chapter 7 | 69

I had a feeling she would, and still, I stood here and fought. "And I can't stand back and watch you make a horrible fucking mistake out of a misconceived notion of duty."

Closing her eyes, she leaned into my touch. "He needs me," she whispered.

"And what about you, Hope?" I asked, stroking her cheek with my thumb. "What do you need?"

She was quiet for the longest moment before finally opening her eyes and looking up at me. "Him." Her voice was cold this time, frigid even, as she yanked herself away from me and rushed towards the front door of the house.

"You running, HC?" I called out, stung from her rejection. "Thought you hated cardio?" I didn't think it – I fucking knew it. I knew a lot about this woman. Like the fact that she hated anything that even closely resembled exercise, and that specific brand of shampoo she had to use to tame that wild head of curls – the strawberry scented one in the pink bottle that cost forty fucking dollars. Or the way she always had to erase every notification on her phone the minute it came through, and how she bit her damn nails off when she was anxious. I knew all about her weird ghost obsession and her addiction to trashy TV shows. I knew how she took her coffee – black with two sugars – and that her favorite candy was caramel. Unlike the man she was going home to, I had taken the time to figure her out.

I wasn't stupid.

I knew there was a marriage on the line, but to me, it was bullshit. The girl was trying to save the unsalvageable. For fuck's sake, my shoulder was still damp from the tears she'd spilled over him.

Putting aside the fact that I was insanely attracted to her, it pissed me the hell off that his return had cost me my friend. Hope was the first woman in over a decade I'd felt something sincere for and she'd walked away from me.

Worse than walking away, she had *settled*.

70 | INEVITABLE

I hated that for her.

"If you can't respect the fact that I am married, then you need to stay away from me, Hunter," she warned before disappearing into the house.

Respect the fact that she was married?

What fucking bullshit.

I remained outside when Hope stormed into the house, brawling with my conscience and every other piss poor decision I'd ever made. The cold, piercing air of the early February morning hit me hard, stinging my eyes and numbing everything else inside of me.

Silently, I dragged my pack of smokes out of my jeans pocket and sparked up. I always enjoyed the first cigarette of the day best. Standing outside in the fresh air, without four walls and caged bars surrounding me.

Well, I hadn't been to bed last night, but sleep deprivation seemed to give me the same buzz and the strain on my chest as I drew each puff into my protesting lungs, that tingling dizzy feeling that engulfed me for just a moment, was fucking lovely to me.

Exhaling a cloud of smoke, I flicked some ash onto the freshly fallen snow and thought back to the last time I stood on these steps.

It was the night Teagan tried to drown herself.

The night of the fire.

Noah felt responsible for what went down that night when he shouldn't. Scoping out JD's lair had been my idea. Taking them out had also been my idea. It was all on me.

Did I feel remorse?

Not a fucking ounce.

But I didn't like thinking about it too much.

About how dark I had become.

About how easily I could take life and not feel for it. I guess the course my life had taken me on had sculpted me into what I was now.

Chapter 7 | 71

It was survival of the fittest in prison and in the eleven plus years I'd spent inside, I had transformed into a goddamn lion – I'd had no choice.

Her precious fucking Jordan wasn't the only one on the planet who'd been through hell and had come out the other side. Did I feel bad for the guy now that I knew what he'd been through? Of course I did. I was human. But he wasn't the only damn person on the planet who'd been thrown a shitty hand of cards.

Rape wasn't a word that shocked me. I had survived eleven years in the state penitentiary filled with blood-thirsty bastards who wouldn't think twice about tearing a guy a second asshole to get their load off. Stabbings, beatings, and rape were all too familiar to an inmate serving hard time – to an eighteen-year-old kid. The shit I'd seen, the sick bastards I'd met, fuck me, I was surprised I made it out of that place with my sanity intact.

Bad stuff happened all the damn time.

Look at Noah.

Christ, look at me.

I watched my girlfriend die. I took the life of the man who stole her from me. And in the years that had passed, I killed again – more men than I had fingers to count on. I'd done some bad shit in the twenty-nine years I'd been on this earth. Some real bad fucking shit. I had to live with that. Every day. Every night.

Noah was in the minority there. There were maybe three or four dudes genuinely innocent on our block. I wasn't one of them. No, I was guilty as hell. But the ones we cohabited alongside? Fuck me, those were some bad dudes...

Because of the fire, returning to The Hill hadn't been an option for me. The cops were still looking for the arsonist and my ass needed to stay the hell out of dodge until shit simmered down. I couldn't take the risk. So, I spent the past god knows how many weeks holed up in a shitty motel in the city, laying low and staying out of trouble.

72 | INEVITABLE

Until tonight.

Until *she* called me and I heard the fear in her voice. I was in my car and driving back to her quicker than my mind could comply with all the reasons not to.

I hadn't even known about the alibi she had given us until Noah told me tonight.

Hope told the cops I was with her the night of the fire. In fact, she had done more than just say I was with her that night. She had invented a very detailed story to the detective that questioned her, consisting of her sleeping – or not sleeping – in my bed that night. She risked a hell of a lot for me and Noah that night, and hell if it didn't make me want her *more* for it.

I knew I needed to take a step back. I scared her off earlier. She wasn't ready for me. But she was settling. She was doing it because she felt bad for the guy. Shit, *I* felt bad for him.

Not bad enough to step down, though.

I just had to be patient. Forcing her hand would be a mistake. She was stubborn and loyal.

That didn't mean I was giving up.

Not even close.

The way I saw it, we all had shit to deal with. I couldn't comprehend what he had suffered as a teenager, but then again, I was damned sure he couldn't put himself in my shoes, either. Goddamn, I was a fucking glutton for punishment, wasting my time on a woman who had no intention of leaving her husband.

The sound of the front door opening and quickly closing again behind me filled my ears, dragging me from the thoughts I had been absorbed in.

Moments later, a hand landed heavily on my shoulder. I didn't have to look sideways to know who the hand belonged to. Instead, I slipped the cigarette box out of my pocket again and offered it to him.

Noah took a smoke from the box before joining me in

leaning against the porch pillar. "You good, man?" he finally asked after lighting up and taking a deep drag.

Rolling the cigarette butt around between my fingers and thumb, I exhaled heavily and thought about how to answer that question. Finally, when no words came to me, I simply looked sideways at him and shrugged. "All good."

He nodded knowingly before taking another drag from his smoke. In this big motherfucking world, he was the closest thing I had to family. He knew me better than most. I knew he got my meaning. He didn't need to thank me. What I'd done tonight, he would do for me in a heartbeat. It was how we rolled.

"Teagan's pregnant," he finally announced. "About six weeks along."

My brows shot up and I turned and gave him my full attention. "For real?"

Noah nodded. "She had a small bleed. Took her to St. Luke's while you were... taking care of business. Got it confirmed there."

"Shit." I shook my head, at a loss. "How'd you explain her face?"

"Didn't have to." He took another drag of his smoke. "Nurse took one look at me and slipped Teagan a domestic violence shelter card." Grimacing, he added, "Don't know whether to feel relieved the nurse didn't ask any questions or disgusted she assumed I was beating on my wife."

"Damn."

"Yeah."

"Are you good with this?" I asked then. "The pregnancy?"

Noah exhaled a heavy sigh and nodded slowly. "Think so." He took one last drag from his cigarette before flicking it onto the snow. "You know, I've been fighting my entire life, man. Inside the ring. Out of it. Behind bars. My whole fucking life has revolved around fighting." He looked out onto the lawn as he spoke. "And I can honestly say that nothing has ever scared

74 | INEVITABLE

me like the thought of losing her does." He looked me dead in the eye then and I could see the fear there. "Can't watch her go through that again, Lucky."

"Jesus," I muttered before tossing my smoke and giving my friend my full attention. "Is that what you're worried about? That she's going to lose it again?"

Noah looked at me like that was the stupidest fucking thing I had ever said, and maybe it was, but I was still going to go there. The guy needed to hear it.

"That baby didn't die because of pregnancy problems, man," I told him. "Your daughter was murdered. Teagan can have more kids, man. This isn't going to happen to you guys again. What happened to Einín? It's not repeating. I can promise you that."

"And whose fault was that?" he shot back, dark eyes locked on mine. "Fucking mine, Lucky. Me, man. I'm responsible for my dead daughter and almost dead wife. I came *this* fucking close to losing her twice. And now what? She's putting her faith in me again? Giving me a second chance? I have enemies, man. What the fuck happens if another bastard jumps out of the woodwork and decides to take another crack at us?"

It was one of the hardest things I ever had to say to him, but if he was worrying about Teagan miscarrying or something, then he needed to hear this. "JD's dead. Your enemy is dead. Your *wife* put a bullet through the back of his skull. For you! She joined the horrible fucking club of killers for *you*. She took a life for you. So, suck it the hell up and get booted and suited. Cause you're gonna give her a football team of babies if that's what she wants. She deserves nothing less."

"It's fast, man," Noah muttered gruffly. "The baby..." he paused and hissed out a heavy breath before saying. "It's been less than three months."

"And?"

"And what if it's too much on her body?" he shot back

angrily. "She had a section, and I'm no doctor, Lucky, but don't those kinds of things need time to heal?"

I didn't know.

I had no fucking clue.

"All I know is that a baby's a blessing, Noah. And considering everything you two have been through this past year, I couldn't think of any two people who deserve a shot at happiness more."

8

Hope

I didn't go back to Jordan's house right away. I couldn't. Hunter had rattled me. I didn't like admitting that, even to myself, but it was true. I wasn't mentally prepared to deal with Jordan's questions either. I knew he would have them. How could he not? I ran out of his house in the middle of the night. It wasn't exactly normal behavior.

Instead, I packed up my stuff, borrowed Teagan's truck, and drove back to The Hill instead. I was going to have to face my parents sooner or later. Once my father got wind of Jordan and me getting back together, he was going to lose his shit. I'd rather he lost it on me than Jordan. I could handle my father. His bark was bigger than his bite – well, when it came to me at least.

I stood outside the red-bricked, two-story house on Thirteenth Street with a nervous disposition. Inhaling a calming breath, I forced my legs up the familiar porch steps I had played on as a child and let myself inside.

The usual hustle and bustle greeted me the moment I

Chapter 8 | 77

stepped foot inside my childhood home. It was still pretty early, Cash and Casey hadn't even left for school yet, so I knew Dad would still be here. He always helped Mom get the kids to school before leaving for work, and since she now worked with him, they shared a car to the hotel.

Bracing myself for battle, I walked into the kitchen and faced my family. "Guys, I really need to talk to you about something."

Mom, Dad, Cash, and Casey were all sitting around the table in the center of the room. To my absolute relief, Logan was the only one of the triplets here and I mentally sagged with gratitude. Logan was like our mother. He had patience and understanding and compassion and he was looking at me right now like he knew something was wrong. In typical Logan fashion, he didn't bombard me with countless questions. Instead, he simply raised his brow in question and waited for me to talk.

"Hope?" Mom's voice was laced with confusion and concern as she placed her coffee cup down and stared up at me. "What are you doing here this early, honey?"

Sharp as a razor, my father folded the newspaper he had been reading and turned to look at me. "What's wrong?" His eyes met mine and he gave me one of his no-bullshit gazes.

"I need to talk to you," I repeated, roughly clearing my throat. "It's important."

"Okay," Mom was the one to reply, fixing me with a concerned look. "Cash, Casey, go play in your room until I call you for school. Your father and I need to talk to your sister in private."

Casey stood up compliantly and moved for the door. Cash, on the other hand, decided to stay and push his luck. "No fair," he whined, folding his arms across his little chest. "Logan gets to stay."

"Cash," Dad warned. "Do what your mother told you."

Muttering his protests about how unfair his life was, Cash

reluctantly followed Casey out of the kitchen, but not before stopping in the doorway to poke his tongue out at me first.

When the twins were out of the room, I closed the kitchen door and walked over to the table, taking a seat beside my brother. Logan nudged me with his shoulder, an act of comfort, and I breathed a little easier. I loved him. If nobody else in the family understood or supported me, I knew Logan would. He was just that kind of guy.

"What's wrong?" Dad asked again. I looked across the table at him. He was bristling with tension and I was fairly certain the only reason he was still sitting down and *not* pacing the floor like he normally did when he was stressed was my mother's hand covering his.

"I'm...well, it's just that...I've decided..." Oh god, how was I supposed to word this? Did I ease them into this or just come right out with it?

"You're making it worse, Angel," Dad informed me, blue eyes locked on mine. "My imagination is going into overload here," he added. "And throwing around the worst possible scenarios. Are you sick?" he demanded. "Are you pregnant? What's wrong, Hope?"

"I'm getting back together with Jordan," I blurted out, then held my breath, waiting for the words to sink in around me.

When they did, Mom's face lit up in sheer euphoria. "Oh, Hope. I'm so happy for you both."

Logan leaned back in his chair and exhaled heavily. "Well shit..."

And Dad? My father threw his head back and laughed, "No, you're not." He laughed hysterically. "But good one, sweetheart."

"I'm not joking," I shot back angrily, glaring across the table at my father.

"You better be," Dad retorted, still laughing. "Because if you're not, I'm going to kill him and have you committed for mental evaluation."

"Kyle!" Mom growled, tone outraged. "That's enough. If

Chapter 8 | 79

Hope and Jordan want to give their relationship another chance, then we are going to support them."

"Support them?" My father turned and gaped at my mother. "Are you fucking crazy, Princess?" he demanded. "Over my dead body will I *ever* support my only daughter getting back in the ring with that asshole." Turning to look at me, Dad snapped, "What the hell are you thinking?" he hissed. "Getting back with a guy like him?"

"Don't judge me," I warned as anger roared to life inside me. I loved my dad but he could be such a judgmental *asshole*.

"Judge you?" Dad asked in a tone of pure outrage. "I'm seriously considering booking you in for a lobotomy because you've obviously lost your goddamn mind!"

"Kyle..." my mother began to protest, but dad wasn't listening. He was on a roll now.

"This is fucking ludicrous," he growled as he shoved his chair back and began to pace the kitchen floor. I wasn't surprised by his actions. I had been expecting the pacing. To be fair, my revelation deemed pacing entirely appropriate. "This is not good," Dad continued to mutter as he walked circles around us, pulling at his tie and raking his hand through his dark hair. "Fuck."

"Kyle, please calm down," Mom said, but it was more of an optimistic suggestion than an order. There was no calming dad down right now. He needed to work this out of his system. I had expected Dad to be annoyed, but the vein bulging in his forehead assured me that he had passed annoyed about forty fucks ago and was chugging full steam ahead into batshit crazy territory.

Logan, who had remained silent until now, looked at me and asked, "Are you sure about this?" My racing heart seemed to level out at his question and I smiled at my brother. He was so logical. So freaking calm and composed. I had no idea how this man had managed to share the same egg as Colton and Cameron at one point.

80 | INEVITABLE

I nodded to Logan before turning my attention back to my parents, specifically my father.

"I'm not here for your permission or blessing," I told them. "I'm here because you're my parents and I love and respect you enough to tell you firsthand what's happening in my life."

Wow. You know, sometimes I really surprised myself with how mature I could be. Of course, I also surprised myself with how quickly I could revert back to a bratty teenager and that's exactly what I did when my father said, "Good, because my blessing is something you and he will never get."

"Oh my god!" I threw my hands up in pure frustration. "You are such an asshole, Dad."

"I sure am, dear daughter," he shot back sarcastically, not batting an eyelid. "But I'd rather be the asshole that tries to protect you from getting your heart crushed again than the one that sits back and says nothing while *he* traipses all over your goddamn happiness again."

Mom shook her head in obvious dismay. "Kyle," she said in a weary tone and I had no doubt my mother was weary. Weary of putting up with his stupid ass for the last twenty-eight years. "You are handling this all wrong."

"Eight years, Lee," Dad snapped, turning his attention to my mother. "Eight long years was the price she paid last time. What's it going to be this time? A life-sentence?"

"Everyone deserves a second chance, Kyle," Mom snapped.

"Not him." Dad ran a hand through his hair in frustration. "He doesn't deserve shit from her, Lee."

"The same could have been said about you, Kyle Carter," Mom countered, leveling my father with a stern look. "I can't count on one hand the number of people who told me to walk away from you when we were young."

Dad flinched like my mother's words had physically wounded him.

Meanwhile, I folded my arms across my chest and smirked smugly.

Go Mom.

"You're right," Dad said after a long moment of silence. "And I deserved their disapproval back then. I was an asshole and I made a lot of mistakes with you." With his eyes locked on my mother, he added, "Difference is, I broke my goddamn back to make it right. I stayed, Lee, and I fought for you. I fucking tried. I didn't run. I didn't leave you when shit got tough. I stayed because you were *worth it*. Because I love you and you don't walk away from the person you love. You can't! Because when it's real? When it's honest to god, slit your wrists if you can't be with that person, true love, it's physically *impossible* to walk away."

"Kyle," Mom began to say, her voice much softer now.

"No. Just hear me out, Lee," Dad interrupted, holding out his hand. "I need her to hear this." He turned to me then and exhaled a heavy sigh. "Hope." He sounded almost defeated. "I know you think you love him, sweetheart."

"I do love him," I snarled, unwilling to remain quiet while my father belittled my feelings and spoke down to me like I was a child. "I *love* Jordan, Dad."

"Because you don't know any different!" Dad shot back, tone exasperated. "And neither does he."

"He does love me!"

"Then, where is he?" Dad demanded, waving a hand around in a form of gesturing. "Why isn't he sitting beside you right now?"

"Stop," I snapped, unwilling to listen to this. It was too hard. Too painful.

"Come on, Hope, and think about this for a minute," Dad urged. "He was your childhood best friend. I get that. Hell, even I'm capable of understanding that the bond between you two runs deep. But love? Honest to god love between a man and a woman?" Dad shook his head and threw his hands up helplessly. "I don't see it between you and him. I have *never* seen that between you and Jordan."

82 | INEVITABLE

"You're just saying this because you can't let go," I argued defensively. "You can't stand seeing me grow up, Dad. That's what your problem is."

"No," Dad countered in a heated tone. "My problem with you and Jordan Porter – what my problem has always been with you two– is that you have always confused friendship with love."

"He has a point," Logan interjected and I gaped at him like he had slapped me.

"Not you, too," I whispered, horrified.

"Finally," Dad shrieked in relief. "I have one sensible child."

"Why can't you just be happy for me?" I choked out, battling back the tears that were threatening to spill. I didn't want to cry. I fucking hated crying. It wasn't something I did without good reason. But right now, listening to all of this hurt, I felt like bursting into tears. "I do love him, Dad. I do." My voice cracked and a traitorous tear slid down my cheek. "Why can't you see that this is what I want and just accept it? Accept *Jordan?*"

"You are asking me to accept a man who went behind my back and married my child when she was still in *high school.*" Dad spat the words like it pained him to say it aloud – a horrible reminder of my secrecy and lies. "And maybe I could have," he added. "If he hadn't made a mockery of those vows."

"Dad..."

"You ran away from home when you were eighteen years old," Dad said in a pained voice. "Because of him. You lived with your pain and your secrets for almost a decade. Because of him. And you were *alone*. Because of him." Dad crunched his nose up, like the words he was speaking were causing him physical pain. "How can I accept that?" he asked then. "If you know how I can get past all that, then you better tell me now, sweetheart, because I have no fucking clue."

"If you knew his reasons for leaving me, you'd understand, Dad," I whispered, clenching my eyes shut. This wasn't easy for me. Being reminded of the pain and betrayal made my chest

Chapter 8 | 83

constrict so tightly I found it hard to breathe. "All of you would."

"Then tell me," Dad replied, taking a seat beside my mother once more.

"I can't," I squeezed out, dropping my gaze to my hands. "It's not my secret to tell."

"If there's something we should know, then you need to tell us, Hope," Mom added in a worried tone. "You can tell us anything, honey. You know that."

I did know that.

But this wasn't mine to tell.

It was Jordan's.

I already felt bad enough for blurting it out to Hunter earlier.

"He'll never forgive me if I do," I whispered, forcing myself to look at my parents. Two pairs of worried eyes gazed back at me. One set a piercing blue color, the other a shade of stormy gray.

"Whatever is said at this table, stays at this table," my father announced in a tone that sounded like a command.

"Agreed," said Logan.

Reaching across the table, Dad caught hold of my hand and squeezed reassuringly. "I promise," he whispered, looking straight at me. "I've got you, sweetheart."

I had a feeling I was going to regret this, but I couldn't hold it in. I needed my parents. I wasn't strong like Jordan. I couldn't block the world out and be happy alone. I needed their support and their acceptance.

Inhaling a deep, steadying breath, I tightened my grip on my father's hand and for the second time today, I blurted out the words I had promised I would never tell a soul, "He was raped, Daddy. Paul Smith raped him!"

9

Hope

I felt like the worst piece of shit on the planet when I returned to Jordan's house later that day. I had broken my promise to him. I had told the secret he had spent years trying to protect. And worse, I wasn't brave enough to admit it. I knew I would never tell him what I had done. I couldn't. I had just gotten him back. Revealing that I'd told my parents all about the horrific abuse he had suffered could make him run again. I couldn't bear that.

So, when I walked into the kitchen later that afternoon with two suitcases full of my possessions, and Jordan asked me about my day, I lied to his face.

I invented an elaborate tale about why Teagan had needed me last night, and then I rambled on and on about the book I should have been working on, but wasn't.

Jordan believed me. Every single word. And why wouldn't he? I had never lied to him before. Disgust filled every pore in my body, laced with the knowledge of what I had helped Hunter do this morning, until I was oozing with self-loathing.

Chapter 9 | 85

"So, how is this going to work?" I heard myself ask later that night as I stood in front of Jordan's already overflowing closet with my suitcases on the floor by my feet and a look of despair on my face. None of my stuff was going to fit in this house. It was too small. "I'm never going to fit in here."

"We can toss out most of what's in there," Jordan offered as he continued to empty the drawers of his dresser. "I don't wear any of it."

"No." I shook my head and closed the closet door. "We're not dumping your belongings, Jordan. I'll manage with the chest of drawers."

Jordan must have heard the uncertainty in my tone because he stopped what he was doing and gave me his full attention. "We'll make this work, Keychain." Tossing an armful of shirts on the bed, he walked over to where I was standing and opened the closet door. "You'll always fit in here." He then proceeded to wedge both of my cases into the bottom of the closet before shoving the protesting doors shut. "With me."

I wanted to ask him if Annabelle and her baby belonged here with him, too, but I held my tongue. She had been here when I got back, and hell if I wasn't feeling put out with her presence. I could hear her and the baby right now. They were in their bedroom next to ours. The walls were paper thin and I could hear her playing and cooing with Ryder. I didn't like acknowledging jealousy. It wasn't an emotion I was used to feeling, and one I liked even less, but right now I was bursting to the seams with the green-eyed monster.

"What's on your mind?" Jordan asked, breaking through my thoughts.

"I'm just trying to register everything," I admitted honestly. Walking over to the foot of his bed, I sank down and released a heavy sigh. "It's been a crazy twenty-four hours."

"Yeah," Jordan agreed. Sitting down beside me, he leaned forwards and rested his elbows on his thighs. "For me too."

86 | INEVITABLE

"Are you having regrets?" I dared to ask, not looking at his face when I added, "About me?"

"Not about you," he finally replied after the longest damn pause known to mankind. "But maybe about the speed everything seems to be moving at."

Now I did look at him. "The speed?"

"This is fast, Hope," he explained. "Really fast."

My heart sank clean into my butt. "Do you want me to leave?" I asked, unable to mask how appalled I felt at this moment. When he didn't answer immediately, I sprang to my feet in pure horror. This wasn't happening. This couldn't be fucking happening! "Oh my god," I shook my head and laughed humorlessly. "You do!" I was such an idiot. "You want me to leave."

"No. Of course, I don't – Hope, sit down."

I couldn't sit down, not when he sounded so uncertain. "Tell me what you want," I demanded then, unable to pretend I hadn't just heard that tone in his voice. The tone that told me he was still very confused. "I can't read your mind. If you're having doubts, then I deserve to know now."

"I'm not having doubts," he was quick to say – too quick. "This is what I want, Hope. To be a family with you. I just don't want to do anything to mess it up. I don't want us to rush into anything. The way I see it is we have our whole lives to rebuild this relationship." He shrugged helplessly, then patted the mattress. "Come here."

Helplessly, I returned to where I had been sitting, but this time I tucked my feet up on the bed and sat cross-legged. Call it crazy, but I needed to be comfortable for this conversation.

"I love you," he told me. "That has not and will not change."

"I love you, too," I replied, and that was the complete truth. I did love him. My love for him was the reason I was here, throwing myself into a foreign environment and ignoring the gut instincts that had protected me my whole life. "So, what happens now?"

Chapter 9 | 87

"Now?" Jordan turned and smiled at me, his green eyes piercing and full of love. "I guess we adjust to being in each other's lives again and live."

"It's not going to be easy, is it?" I asked with a rueful smile.

"No," he mused, playfully nudging my shoulder with his. "But nothing worth having comes easily."

"We can do this, right?"

Jordan took a moment to think about what I had said before nodding firmly. "We'll take our time. One day at a time. Step by step." He reached for my hand and squeezed reassuringly. "But yeah, Keychain. We will do this."

10

Jordan

"I love you. That hasn't changed. I still do. Just as much as always," I whispered as I sat side by side with my wife. Her slender hand was in mine. "I'm giving you everything I can."

My life with her meant everything to me. I didn't think she had a clue of just how important she was to me. I knew she was feeling unsure. She was frightened of our situation and uncertain of me. I could see it in her eyes. In the way she moved. In this moment, I thought she was the bravest person I'd ever met. She was putting her blind faith in me even though I was unable to give her guarantees for the future. If I was a normal man, I could comfort her in the ways she obviously needed me to, but I couldn't. I didn't seem to work right anymore. Everything inside of me was all fucked up and clouded.

"Right back atcha," she chuckled, squeezing my hand with hers. "Always."

I didn't say anything to that – there wasn't anything else to

Chapter 10 | 89

say in this moment. I had laid it all out there for her, and she had, too.

It was enough for now.

"Do you have a Wi-Fi password?" Hope asked after several minutes of unspoken silence. And just like that, the moment was gone.

Turning to look at me, she pulled out her phone and shook it gently. "I need to check some work emails. Smiling indulgently, I reeled off our internet password and watched as she keyed it into her iPhone. "Thanks."

"No problem." I stood up and stretched my arms above my head. "Are you hungry?"

"Starving," she muttered, attention glued to her phone. "I could eat a horse," she added, tapping furiously on the screen with a deep frown set on her beautiful face.

"I'll go downstairs and get dinner going," I told her, heading towards the door. "Come on down when you're ready."

"Sure, sure," Hope muttered, though I wasn't sure she had even heard me.

I smiled to myself as I slipped out of the room. She'd always had the attention span of a goldfish.

"Jordan?" she called out.

I halted mid step and swung around to face her. "Hmm?"

"Don't let me down," she whispered, blue eyes laced with uncertainty as she looked at me. "Okay?"

I forced myself to nod.

I was going to.

It was inevitable.

I only hoped that when I did she would find it in her heart to take me back.

To let me back in.

11

———

Hope

$\mathcal{I}$ found myself struggling to acclimatize to my new surroundings, which was ridiculous considering they weren't exactly new surroundings anymore. I had been with Jordan for more than a month now. It should be more than enough time to settle into a home.

Not for me, it seemed.

I still felt as out of place in Jordan's house as I had the very first day I stepped through the doorway. But then, our marriage hadn't exactly been smooth sailing this past month either.

The settling cracks I had felt in the beginning had turned into a full-blown ridge that mirrored the Grand Canyon. It seemed to be one thing after the next with me and Jordan. We still hadn't slept together, either. I had even taken to sleeping in my underwear in a bid to seduce my husband. Needless to say, it didn't work.

Not one time during our intimate kissing sessions had he lost control and had sex with me. I pretended like I understood, but it was a lie.

Chapter 11 | 91

The truth was, I didn't understand and couldn't accept the lack of contact. I knew Jordan was battling his demons, and I was incredibly proud of him for being so strong, but his demons were taking me down, too. I felt unloved and, if I was being really honest with myself, less of a woman. I didn't turn my husband on. Nothing I did or tried ever came close to tempting him into sleeping with me. *God knows I had tried on enough occasions.*

A better woman would have the compassion and maturity to handle a man like Jordan, but I wasn't a better woman. I was human, starved for affection, and desperately *lonely*.

Kissing and cuddling wasn't enough for me.

I wanted to be *wanted* by him.

Maybe that was selfish of me, but the more I tried to repress my feelings and desires, the more resentful I grew. His home was a drug and alcohol-free zone. I respected that. I was proud of him for overcoming the demons that had threatened to take him down. I just... didn't quite *fit* here.

I hated myself for the prominent thought I had first thing every morning. The one that told me, *"I didn't sign up for this life..."*

But as it happened, I wasn't just good at telling tales for a living, I was a mighty fine liar in real life, too, and a master at masking my feelings.

For example, whenever Jordan and Annabelle hung out together, I smiled and nodded like I didn't have a care in the world, or when they needed to work late and asked me to sit Ryder, I agreed and pretended it didn't rip my heart clean out of my chest or remind me of the family he had belonged to while I was alone.

Or when my dad asked questions about how I was doing, I would smile and reassure him with 'Great Dad, couldn't be better.' And when mom hinted about grandchildren, I had perfected the 'we'll see' or 'you never know' responses.

What a croc of shit.

92 | INEVITABLE

Mom had a better chance of getting pregnant than me, and Dad had a freaking vasectomy eight years ago.

Jordan wasn't the only person different now, either.

My mother was, too.

She was quiet and withdrawn these days. She had been this way ever since my revelation about Jordan. I hated it. I wished I had just spoken to Dad and left her out of it. I knew me telling her about Jordan had brought to the surface terrible memories from her own childhood. She had asked me on more than a dozen occasions if she could have my blessing to go and talk to Jordan about it. Every time, I shut it down with a firm no. He couldn't know that I betrayed him. And sure, my mother was battling with her guilt, but it paled in comparison to what would happen to my relationship if she talked to him. Jordan would talk when he was ready. Not before it.

Meanwhile, Dad never spoke about it again. True to his word, Dad kept it to himself and never brought it back up. He also never brought up the bazillion reasons he had about Jordan being a bad idea for me. He kept his opinions to himself now. It was strange. I wasn't used to my father being so... not opinionated.

I think the truth affected both of my parents deeply and in different ways. They were both drowning in different versions of guilt. Jordan was their best friend's son. He'd grown up alongside their own children. Knowing that something of this horrific magnitude had happened to one of us rocked their worlds.

I noticed Mom hugged us all a lot more. She was a hugger normally, but the news of Jordan's past had turned her into a helicopter mom, especially around Cash and Casey who were still short enough for her to hover over.

Derek and Dad were having problems, too. Their bromance was on the rocks. I guess Dad was struggling to come to terms with the fact that Derek had never told him. Derek was still under the impression that my father didn't know anything, while Dad was dealing with knowing and *not* telling. Overall, it was a horrible situation and I was the one that had put them in it.

Scared to death with the prospect of losing Jordan again, or worse, being the cause of him having a relapse, I slapped a smile on my face every morning and trudged on. Because it had to get easier, right? The first year of marriage was the hardest. We'd been married almost nine years, but I considered us to be in our first year. Eight years of separation didn't exactly constitute a happy marriage. No, we just had to get through the next few months. Everything would eventually work itself out. It had to, right?

"Do you want to go out tonight?" I asked. I was sitting up in bed watching him get ready for work. "Teagan and Noah invited us out for drinks."

"I can't tonight," Jordan replied, keeping his back to me as he buttoned up his shirt. "I have to –"

"Work?" I filled in wearily. "Yeah, I know." He always *had to work*. "But I really want you to get together with them, Jord. They're my best friends." Shrugging, I added, "You making an effort with them is important to me."

"I know," he muttered before swinging around to face me. He looked so beautiful it hurt. He was so handsome. His black curls were trimmed tight and the white shirt he had on emphasized his tanned skin. I wanted to crawl over the mattress and throw my arms around him, but I didn't. The guaranteed prospect of rejection kept me rooted to the bed.

"I'm training a couple of new guys at the Charity so the next few weeks at work are going to be crazy for me," he said in that soft raspy voice of his that I had always loved. "Once everything settles down, we can talk about going out with them." His green eyes burned into mine as he spoke. "Okay?"

I swallowed deeply and nodded. "Okay."

With that, Jordan walked over to my side of the bed and

pressed a kiss to my hair. "I love you, Keychain. See you tonight."

When the door closed behind him, I flopped back on the mattress and sighed heavily.

A million different emotions and thoughts coursed through me in this moment, but I clung to the one that gave me hope.

It can only get better...

12

Jordan

"What are you doing on the last weekend in May?" Hope asked when I walked into the kitchen after work on Thursday night. She was sitting at the table with her beloved laptop in front of her and one of those Happy Planner's laying open.

"The last weekend in May?" I dropped my keys and wallet on the counter and headed for the fridge. "As in two months from now?"

"It's nine weeks actually," she replied, tapping a pen against her planner. "So, are you working that weekend?"

"I don't know." Grabbing a carton of milk, I walked over to the sink and retrieved a clean glass from the draining board before pouring myself a glass. "I usually get my work schedule a week in advance."

"So, you could book that weekend off?" she asked, tone hopeful. "If you wanted to?"

"Sure, I guess." I nodded and took a gulp of milk. "Why?"

She typed furiously on her laptop for a few seconds before

96 | INEVITABLE

turning to grin at me. "Then book it off, because *we* are going to Aspen that weekend."

"We are?" My brows shot up in surprise. "Why?"

"I have just agreed to sign at the Indie's Book Bash in Aspen, and you, my gorgeous husband, are coming with me."

"You want me to come with you?" I frowned. "To a book signing?"

"Uh, *yeah!*"

Anxiety gnawed at my gut. "Why?"

Hope looked me dead in the eye and asked, "Why not?"

Because it's not my thing?

Because I struggle being in that sort of environment?

Because I can't fucking stand the thought of it?

"No reason," I lied. "I'm just surprised you want me to come. Don't you usually take Teagan to those things?"

"Those *things*?" Hope questioned, brow raised.

"Business trips," I corrected.

"That's better," she replied. "And you're right. I normally take Teagan as my assistant, but she's pregnant, and there's no way Noah's going to let her out of his sight."

"Why don't you take both of them?" I offered, pouring myself another glass of milk. "I'm sure they wouldn't mind."

"You want me to take Noah '*The Machine*' Messina to a *book signing*?" Hope shook her head and gaped at me like I had just told her the world was flat. "You do realize he was voted the third sexiest man in sports last year?"

"Yeah?" I shrugged. "He looks like those guys on the book covers – he'd fit right in."

"He would cause a riot, and Teagan would commit a felony!" Hope shot back. "Besides, I don't want to take them. I want to take you." She waggled her brows suggestively. "We could make a weekend of it – a belated honeymoon of sorts. I've heard amazing things about the hotel we're staying in. Apparently, it's crazy romantic, so I've booked us into this huge suite. And I've got some surprises in store for you..."

Chapter 12 | 97

"Hope, I really don't know about this –" I began to say, but one look at her fallen smile caused me to stop. "You really want me to go with you?" I asked instead, running an anxious hand through my hair.

She nodded eagerly. "I really do."

I released a heavy sigh before nodding. "Okay, I'll come."

"You promise?"

"Yeah," I forced myself to say. "I promise."

13

Lucky

I sat on the porch steps of my childhood home in the small town of Gunnison, Colorado and looked out onto the pretty, suburban neighborhood with neatly trimmed gardens and white picket fences I had grown up in.

I had shit to tie up here, shit I'd been putting off for months, but couldn't anymore. It hurt coming back here. It hurt to see the life I'd once lived. But here I was, sitting in the middle of my personal breakdown, with memories attacking the walls I had managed to build up over the years.

This neighborhood shaped me. I learned to ride a bike on this street. I had spent more summers than I could count camping in the backyard of my next-door neighbor. I had my first kiss in the house across the street. For the first eighteen years of my life, this small town had been my home, and everyone in it had been my family.

But time had a habit of changing things and it had been almost thirteen years since I stepped foot in this place. The people of my youth were gone now and new families had

Chapter 13 | 99

taken their place, raising their young families in suburban bliss.

Coming back here made me think about how differently my life had changed from what it once was.

I used to be good. Pure. A decent human being. I played football in high school and got drunk on the weekends with my friends. I had a loving mother, a great bunch of friends, a girl I adored, and a future with endless possibilities.

It was all gone now.

Shaking my head, I sparked up a smoke and inhaled deeply, welcoming the stinging sensation as my lungs protested. Good. Fucking burn. I didn't care.

Exhaling a cloud of smoke, I took another deep drag, and cast my gaze towards the house at the end of the street.

Her father was waiting for me inside that house.

The house that, once upon a time, I used to walk in at least twice a day, and the people who once called me son. Now there was no reason left to call me *son*.

That reason was six feet under.

My thoughts flicked to Hope and I came to the conclusion that women and my heart were a bad fucking idea.

Last time I fell in love, I went down for murder.

This time, I was positive *she* should go down for murder because the woman was *killing* me slowly. And I was fucking letting her do it.

I was pushing myself on her, the masochistic bastard I was, and enjoying the goddamn rejection.

The thing that got me through it was the knowledge that Hope Carter *wanted* me. I knew she did, and she could run around protesting the hell out of it and ignoring her feelings for me until the cows came home, but it wouldn't change a damn thing.

She brought me back to life. I'd been living a life of stone for more than a decade. Hope Carter walked into my world and splintered the concrete protecting my heart.

100 | INEVITABLE

Fuck, she blew the damn wall down by just being herself.

I was never going to be able to live a normal, mundane life like her husband did. I couldn't offer her that. I had a rap sheet and list of dangerous people I needed to watch my back from. I was thrown in prison when I was eighteen years old and I'd done a lot of shady shit in order to survive that place. I'd made deals with devils, and double crossed a lot of uncrossable people.

I wasn't good enough for her.

I got it.

Fuck, I got it loud and clear.

But neither was *he*.

I loved the ugliness inside her. She didn't have to be perfect when she was with me. She just had to be real. There was no pedestal in sight when she was with me. I didn't hold her to any damn vows or expectations. She was free to be whoever the hell she wanted to be when she was with me. I would take her in any of her forms. One of these days, she was going to wake up and not be able to lie to herself anymore. One of these days she was going to figure it all out. I knew I'd be standing there on that day with open arms...

I smoked three more cigarettes before I finally plucked up the courage to walk down the street towards the Clarke house. A part of me wanted to get in my truck and drive away from this town without looking back, but I'd never run from my responsibilities before and I wasn't about to start now.

"Lucky," Hayley's father greeted when I opened the garden gate. He'd been waiting on me. I'd seen the curtains in his front room twitching all damn day. "Good to see you, son."

I could drop on my hands and knees and beg the man before me for forgiveness but it wouldn't change anything, so I inclined my head and shook his hand instead. "Good to see you, too, sir."

"Well, come on in," Mr. Clarke said with an encouraging clap on the shoulder. "Margie's been waiting on you all afternoon. She baked your favorite cookies. Told her not to – that you might not be hungry, but you know the way she is."

I forced a smile and followed the elderly man into the house only to freeze when my eyes landed on the silver haired woman standing in the kitchen doorway. "Lucky Casarazzi," Mrs. Clarke gushed in a voice thick with emotion. "Oh, my boy!" She rushed towards me and threw her arms around my waist, making what was left of my heart shrivel up and fucking die.

"Mrs. Clarke," I managed to squeeze out as I gently hugged her back. "It's good to see you again." *I'm sorry I couldn't save her...*

"I was worried you weren't ever coming home," she mused, concern etched across her features. Reaching up, she cupped my face in her hands and smiled. "You look so much like Georgina. I still miss your momma, Lucky. She was my dearest friend and there's not a day goes by that I don't say a prayer for her."

"Yeah," I choked out as pain ricocheted through my body. "Me, too."

"It was such a terrible thing to happen," Mrs. Clarke added as she took my hand and led me into the kitchen. "Her passing while you were wrongfully locked up in that *cage*."

"I wasn't wrongfully locked up," I replied gently, taking a seat at the table. "I killed a man."

"You performed a civic duty by eliminating a horrible threat," she hissed, brown eyes welling up with unshed tears. "That *creature* raped and murdered our beautiful daughter." She reached for the teapot in the center of the table and shakily poured three cups of tea. "He deserved no mercy – the same as he showed Hayley. And you should have been given a medal for stopping him – not locked up in prison."

"Spoken like the true wife of a sheriff," I chuckled, though I felt anything but humorous. I had to face myself every damn day when I looked in the mirror and saw the reflection of a man who had taken a mother's son away from her. I wasn't the hero she portrayed me to be.

"It's done now," I added, reaching for my cup and taking a sip of tea. "I've served my time and I'm a free man."

"It still is not right," Mrs. Clarke continued to rant. Taking the seat beside me, she hovered over me and dropped two sugar cubes into my cup the moment I set it back down. "It's horrendous enough that Hayley lost her life over that vermin, but for you to lose eleven years of yours?" She banged her slender fist on the table and hissed, "There's no justice in the world."

"Leave the boy alone, Marge," Mr. Clarke grumbled, tone weary. "He didn't come over here to hash this all up." Taking his usual seat at the head of the table, he looked at me with pained gray eyes and forced a smile.

And in that moment, all I could feel was compassion for the old man. Chris Clarke had been a force to be reckoned with when we were kids. He was the town sheriff and a horse of a man. Now, he just looked old and weathered. Time and pain had obviously taken its toll on him – on both of them. Hayley's parents were a mere fraction of the vibrant people they used to be.

"Have you been to Hayley's grave yet?" Mrs. Clarke asked, causing her husband to sigh heavily. "I laid fresh flowers yesterday. Lilies. Hayley's favorites."

I shook my head and took another sip of tea. "No. Not yet." And I had no plans on going, either, but I left that out.

"You should go see her," Mrs. Clarke added. "I know she would love that."

"That's enough," Mr. Clarke said in a low, warning tone, but his wife didn't listen.

Instead, she continued to shred me apart with her words and hopeless hopefulness. "I like to sit under that big old oak and read to her when the weather's fine. Of course, I haven't been able to do much of that lately with the weather being so

Chapter 13 | 103

unpredictable, but I know she hears me. The sun always opens through the clouds when I read to her. It's a sign she likes to give me –"

"Dammit, Margery," Mr. Clarke roared, slamming his palm against the wooden table. "That's enough. Hayley's dead. Standing in front of a piece of black marble with her name on it doesn't mean shit. She's *not there.*"

"Excuse me, Lucky," Mrs. Clarke warbled as she jerked to her feet. "I have to go and check on something..." A small sob tore from her throat then as she hurried out of the room.

"I'm sorry about that, Lucky," Mr. Clarke said, clearing his throat. "She's still...struggling to cope. It got a lot worse after your momma passed on." He sighed again and rubbed his eyes with his thumbs. "I think Margery used to lean on Georgina for support. In many ways, your mother was the last connection she had to you. And you were her last connection to our daughter."

I didn't know what he wanted me to say. I loved his daughter and she died. I had spent more than a third of my life grieving that loss. I'd had thirteen years to come to terms with it, to grieve Hayley, and eleven of those I'd spent alone.

I cleared my throat a few times before daring to speak. "Living with grief isn't easy." It probably wasn't what Mr. Clarke wanted to hear, but it was all I had.

I loved his daughter and a part of me always would, but I was tired of being judged and stuffed in a box that was labeled *'damaged goods, don't touch.'*

I didn't want to end up like his wife.

I wanted to *live.*

I was built up to look like some goddamn martyr, avenging my dead woman. And yeah, that's exactly what I did. But my actions were selfish. I'd left her there, dying on the ground while I beat the life out of some loser I would never remember.

I was only eighteen years old back then, dammit, and his

daughter had been my first love. She was my first fucking everything and she was gone.

And as horrible and fucking horrific as it sounded, there was no guarantee we would have made it. It hurt to acknowledge that even to myself, but there it was.

She was a year older than me and had already left for the University of Colorado in Boulder when I was still in my senior year of high school. I'd never intended on following Hayley to Boulder. Football had been my entire life before I got the taste of her pussy and had been sidetracked. That didn't mean I never loved her. I had, deeply, and had planned on putting a ring on her finger back then. But my heart had been set on a football scholarship to the University of Alabama. And that's exactly where my life had been heading until that night...

"I heard the sale of your momma's house has gone through," Mr. Clarke stated gruffly.

"Yeah." Nodding slowly, I took another sip of my now cold tea. "I packed up the last of our stuff this morning." The family that had bought my mother's – my – house had needed a fast sale and were moving in next week. "I have some boxes of my mother's stuff packed up that Margie might like," I added, tone a little too hoarse for my liking. "I'll drop them off on the porch before I leave."

"You've put down roots in Boulder?"

Again, I nodded.

"With the fighter and his family?"

"Yeah." I smirked. "With the fighter and his family."

"Good." Mr. Clarke nodded. "Family isn't all about blood. It's what you make it." He paused before asking, "You got a girl waiting on you back there?"

I felt my body tense up. I had no fucking clue how to answer that question.

"It's okay to live again, son," he added gruffly. "Hayley would've wanted that for you... and so do I."

I exhaled a heavy sigh and whispered, "I'll always love her."

Chapter 13 | 105

"You're a good boy, Hunter Casarazzi," he finally replied. "Always were." Shoving back his chair, he stood up slowly and motioned for me to follow him towards the door.

Wordlessly, I got to my feet and walked behind him.

"Go and build yourself a damn fine life, son." Reaching for my hand with his, he shook it tightly. "Take chances, go after what your heart desires, and don't you dare waste another minute of your life... God knows enough time was taken away from you."

This was my closure, I realized.

The closing chapter on this part of my life, and Chris Clarke was giving me his blessing.

And until this moment, I hadn't realized just how badly I had needed it.

"I will," I choked out. "I promise."

He released my hand and took a step back. "Goodbye, son," he whispered before closing the front door, leaving me standing on the porch steps of the first girl I had ever loved.

When I walked back up the street towards my truck, I knew it was for the last time.

I wasn't going to be coming back here.

This town was my past.

And I was moving forward now.

To my future.

14

Hope

$\mathcal{I}$ once read somewhere that a person falls in love three times throughout the course of their lifetime.

Your first love: the love that is the hardest to get over, the one that takes root so deeply inside your soul it's damned near impossible to recover from.

Your second love: the healing love, the adventurous, crazy and blind, hard love.

And finally, the third love: the unexpected love. The love that ruins you. The endgame love.

I wasn't sure if I agreed with this theory or not, but I guess it was a valid one. But then I wondered if a person had the ability to feel this with the same person. Like, falling in love with a person in three different ways or loving three different versions of that person throughout three different stages of life.

That had to happen, too, right?

If not, then how did they explain those lifelong relationships between two people that met in high school or college?

Chapter 14 | 107

I knew my mother had only loved one man her entire life and she was in her forties.

And Teagan? Her heart had only ever belonged to Noah.

Maybe a person didn't feel all these forms of love in a lifetime at all.

Maybe you only fell in love once and it was one of the three.

And maybe Teagan and Mom had lucked out and skipped straight to the third love. Every character in every book I had ever written ended up with that third love.

Or maybe I just had too much time on my hands to overthink this?

My brothers always said I lived in my own little love-bubble and that I was born to be a writer. I wasn't sure if that was supposed to be a compliment or not, but I didn't care. I loved being inside my bubble. I adored my fictitious world of alpha males and epic love stories. There was only one thing more appealing than drowning myself in my latest one-click love story and that was writing one.

Somewhere in the back of my mind, I wondered if this was normal. I wondered if it was normal to feel more excitement from a story than from real life. If it was wrong, then there was something seriously broken inside of me, because working on my latest WIP these past few months had given me more satisfaction than anything in my real world had.

"Hope, would you mind dropping Ryder off at daycare this morning?" Annabelle called out from the doorway of the living room where she was adjusting one of her pearl earrings.

The grey pantsuit Annabelle was wearing was pressed to perfection and fitted her like a glove. It was a far cry from my baggy gray sweatpants with my fluffy socks pulled over them, not to mention the ratty black tee-shirt I had on with the words *World's Okayest Sister* – courtesy of Colton – emblazoned in neon pink letters across the front.

"I am running so incredibly late for this meeting," she continued to ramble as she kicked on a pair of killer black heels and adjusted her perfectly styled bun. "And if I don't leave now, I'm never going to make it on time."

I glared up from where I was sprawled on the floor with my laptop open and a bunch of detailed notes for my current WIP surrounding me, and bit back the urge to scream *'Fuck off and do it yourself!'*. But then my eyes landed on the tiny, dark haired child with a head full of lush curls pulling at his mother's leg and my resolve weakened. Ryder was so stinking cute.

"I wouldn't ask," she rambled. "But Jordan's not back from his night shift yet and, well, you're not doing anything important, are you?"

"No, I'm not doing anything important," I replied in a sickly-sweet tone, masking my absolute outrage at her blatant disregard for my career. "Just penning my latest book." Closing the lid on my laptop, I climbed to my feet and stretched. "You know, the books that paid for that Range Rover parked out front."

"Oh god, I'm so sorry," she was quick to say, cheeks staining pink. "I didn't mean to offend you. I just meant that you didn't actually need to go to work like the rest of us."

Irritation gnawed at the frayed tethers holding my temper in check. "Newsflash, honey, this is work."

"Of course, but you know what I mean; a real job."

Breathe, Hope, breathe...

"Yep," I bit out. "It's one of those, too."

"I thought your father bought you that car," she mused before slapping a hand over her mouth in embarrassment. "Oh god, I'm putting my foot in it, aren't I?"

Choosing to take the high road, I walked over to where she was standing and scooped her son up in my arms. "What time does he need to be at daycare?"

"Daycare opens at eight-thirty," she said with a smile before planting a lipstick smudging kiss on her son's forehead. "Thank you for doing this, Hope," she gushed in that soft, feminine tone of voice I envied. "You're the best."

Forcing myself to mask my emotions and distaste, I smiled

Chapter 14 | 109

at my husband's full-time roommate and part-time fake fiancée. "No problem."

She flashed a megawatt smile before turning on her heels and walking off like a model on the catwalk in Milan, with her blonde hair shining like a halo of light and purity.

Christ, I couldn't put into words how uncomfortable this woman made me.

"Oh, could you let Jordan know that I'll call him later?" she added as she yanked open the door and hurried out. "I may need him to pick Ryder up this evening."

With that, the front door swung shut with a bang and she was gone.

"Looks like it's me and you again, buddy," I cooed as I bounced with Ryder in my arms. He was adorable. I didn't start off with the intention of bonding with the enemy's baby, but that's what happened. I liked spending time with Ryder. I found myself caring about him. And when he called me "Opie", it always melted my heart. How freaking cute!

Ryder rewarded my cooing with a big, one-toothed gummy smile that blew my ovaries to hell. "Come on, handsome," I laughed as I carried him into the kitchen. "Let's go wash Mommy's icky lipstick off your face."

15

Hope

When Jordan rolled in from work thirty minutes later, Ryder and I were in the kitchen wolfing down a yummy breakfast that consisted of mashed bananas and baby rice. *Delicious...*

"Morning," my husband announced in a weary tone when he walked in and hung his coat on the hook on the back of the kitchen door.

"Good-morning!" I replied in a baby voice, attention focused on Ryder who was bouncing like a maniac in his highchair. "Ryder, can you say *good morning*?" I cooed, reaching over to tickle under his chubby chin. "Say *good morning, Jordan*."

"Da-da," Ryder babbled, face alight with pure adoration as he stared up at Jordan like he had brought the sunshine with him. "Da-da-da-da-dad."

"No, Ryder," Jordan was quick to correct in a gentle tone. Walking over to the table, he pressed a kiss to my cheek before crouching down in front of the highchair and smiling at Ryder. "Jordan," he said in a soft tone. "Can you say *Jordan*?"

Chapter 15 | **III**

"Dada," Ryder babbled, his hands splaying wildly with excitement. "Up. Dada up!"

With a rueful shake of his head, Jordan exhaled a heavy sigh and picked the baby out of his chair. "He'll get it when he's older," he said by way of explanation before pressing a kiss to Ryder's head.

"I bet," I replied before popping a piece of chopped banana in my mouth.

"Are you alright?" Jordan looked down at me when he asked that, searching my face for the anger he presumed I was feeling. But the truth was, I could never feel anger at this baby. In the four weeks I had been living here, Ryder had become my favorite roommate – my husband included. It wasn't Jordan's fault he came in second place to Ryder. I rarely saw him. I knew that sounded like a ridiculous statement considering we lived together now, but it was the truth. Jordan worked crazy long and sporadic hours that consisted of several twelve-hour night shifts during the week, not to mention the eight-hour days he put in at his other job. He was either going to bed when I was getting up or he was rushing for work. And on the rare occasion when Jordan wasn't working, he was playing daddy to Ryder. And I didn't want to even think about the lack of intimacy between us. It was too damn depressing.

Resentment roared to life inside of me and I felt a huge amount of shame. Little Ryder wasn't to blame for any of this. He was fatherless and utterly innocent. His mother, on the other hand, drove me batshit crazy. Until moving into this house, I hadn't realized I didn't do well with other females. I hadn't been aware of how much of a tomboy I was. Living with Teagan didn't count. I never considered her to be a girly girl. She was like the other part of me. We'd been together since high school. But Annabelle? I was struggling to make a connection with her. We had nothing in common and it was hard to find and level ground between us.

"I'm good," I shot back, forcing my dark thoughts from my

mind. My gaze flicked to the clock hanging above the kitchen door. "But I better get going if I'm to get this little guy to daycare on time."

Jordan's brows furrowed in confusion. "Where's Annabelle?"

"She had an early meeting," I reeled off her earlier bullshit excuses as I took a protesting Ryder from Jordan's arms and put his coat on. "She said she'll call you later." I placed a wriggling Ryder into his car seat and fastened the safety clips around him before retrieving my own coat from the back of the door and shrugging it on. "She might need you to pick him up this evening," I added before reaching for the handle of the car seat and hoisting it up.

"Do you want me to take him?" Jordan asked, following after me as I carried Ryder to the front door. "I know you're on a deadline."

Yeah, I mentally snapped. *I am on a deadline, but apparently, no one in this house gives two shits about my job.* "Nope, I'm good," I said instead. Walking out into the early morning rain, I opened the back door of my truck and battled with strapping in Ryder's car seat. "I'm probably going to stop by Teagan's for a catch up after I get this guy to daycare."

Leaning against the side of my truck, Jordan handed me the baby bag I'd stupidly forgotten to bring with me and smiled. "A catch up?" He shook his head and chuckled. "You girls live in each other's pockets. Don't you ever get bored of talking to each other?"

Closing Ryder's door, I turned and gave Jordan my full attention "Bored of talking to my best friend?" I asked, feigning shock. "What is this blasphemy you speak of?"

"Get out of here." Jordan rolled his eyes and pressed a kiss to my cheek. "Have fun with Teagan."

"I will." I grinned up at him and patted his chest before walking around to the driver's side of my truck and climbing in.

Chapter 15 | 113

Cranking the engine, I rolled down my window and called out, "See you tonight," before pulling out of the driveway.

When I was halfway down the street, I cranked the stereo, needing music to drown out my thoughts.

Pink's song *Just Give me a Reason* filled my ears and I momentarily debated on switching it off or changing the song, but decided against it, choosing to drown in the lyrics.

Every time I heard this song, something chipped away inside of me. I wanted to believe it was a piece of my pride, but I knew better.

My heart, still battered and barely patched back together, was still aching, and the words of that song brought me back to that night.

The night he walked away.

The night my world fell to pieces.

16

Jordan

There were so many things I wanted to say to my wife. So many promises I longed to make her that I knew I wasn't capable of keeping. But unspoken words were easier to live with than broken promises, so I kept my mouth shut as I watched Hope reverse out of the driveway.

My heart, my stupid, dysfunctional heart somersaulted around in my chest like it was the first time I'd ever seen her. It didn't make sense, but then, nothing ever did when it came to my feelings for my wife.

Once her truck was out of sight, that feeling of elation quickly turned to dread in my chest. And just like every morning since rekindling my marriage, every single one of my deepest, darkest fears and secrets roared to life inside of me.

What was she doing with me?

How long would she stay?

How could I keep her happy when I wasn't sure when *or if* I could get to a place in my life when I would feel ready to satisfy her in the ways she needed me to?

Chapter 16 | 115

I felt like I was drowning, and in all honesty, I didn't have the faintest clue of how long I was going to be able to keep her at arm's length before she snapped.

Most of my teenage years had been consumed with inappropriate thoughts and sexual urges all directed at Hope.

Hell, at thirty, they still were.

But it was different now.

My needs were different.

Sex, I could handle.

Intimacy, not so much.

And Hope was the kind of woman that needed both.

She deserved *both*.

I couldn't give that to her.

I kept love and sex in two separate compartments in my brain.

I guess somewhere in between being raped and fucking butchered by my mother's husband, I'd forfeited all notions of romance.

I was fourteen years old when it first happened.

September 2nd.

The first day of eighth grade.

The last day of my innocence.

The day I died inside.

I still remembered that day like it was yesterday.

I remembered every fucking detail...

Every smell.

Every sound.

Every move he made and every pathetic fucking sob and plea for help that tore from my mouth as he held me down and impaled me.

As he raped my body and pillaged my life.

No one saw it.

No one helped me.

No one stepped in and saved me.

No one cared enough to take a closer look and see just how fractured I was on the inside.

That's why over time, when I was asked if I was okay or if something was wrong, I kept my mouth shut and remained quiet.

Admitting you were raped wasn't easy for a guy.

Who would believe me?

How would they understand?

And what would happen to my mom if I told? The truth would kill her, and if it didn't, Paul certainly would.

Back then, I hated the world and blamed every person I had ever come into contact with for the soul-destroying life I had been dealt. For my life being over before it had even started.

And when I had finally crawled my way out of that world, when I had finally escaped, I'd been dragged back in. That's what hurt the most; my whole life I'd been on a road to destruction from childhood and just when I peaked, when I was free and got the one thing my heart had always desired, I had crashed and burned.

Hope told me not to go back there.

I didn't listen to her and it ruined my life.

I had spent eight months in a rehab facility to repair the broken pieces inside of me –trying and failing to fight my demons – and many years since clogging up the therapist's waiting rooms. I had been trying to come to terms with what had happened to me since getting sober, to find some semblance of peace inside of me, but it turned out that I was better at healing others than healing myself.

My job had become my coping mechanism. Helping people in similar situations as I had been soothed something deep inside of me. I had replaced drugs with work and I was thoroughly hooked. A slow work week for me was an eighty hour one. I was addicted to keeping busy. I had found my passion in

Chapter 16 | 117

helping others and I had clung to it like a lifeline, giving everything I had to my work.

I was in a better place now, but I still had days when I couldn't stand the man looking back at me in the mirror. I still had days when I wanted to peel the skin from my body and set it on fire. Days when I wanted to bleach my skin clean and disappear from this cruel fucking world.

Keeping myself closed off was how I stayed sane.

Avoiding physical intimacy was how I erased *his* touch.

I wanted to be with Hope sexually. Problem was, every time we came close to it, she caressed and cuddled and touched me in such a way that brought the painful images and memories to the forefront of my mind, rendering me paralyzed and eliminating any desire.

Certain ways she touched me triggered violent memories. Random smells and situations caused me physical pain. I was struggling being in close proximity of Hope which was fucking ridiculous, but the worst part was she seemed to have given up on me.

She never tried for more than a chaste kiss from me now. It was as if she had accepted that I was never going to be able to fulfill that need and it shredded me.

Loving me had caused Hope Carter pain and scars and tragedy, but she was still here. Problem was, she wasn't here with *me*.

Not really.

Sure, she slept beside me each night and lived in my house, but her mind, that beautiful mind of hers, was far away. I didn't like thinking about it and selfishly, I pretended it wasn't happening. I pretended I wasn't losing the only person I had ever loved.

I knew deep down that I deserved this.

How could I not?

Walking out on my wife eight years ago without a call or a

118 | INEVITABLE

text was a shitty thing to have done. Falling into the pits of darkness and drugs had been my punishment.

For breaking her.

For breaking us.

When Hope forgave me, I knew it was too good to be true.

And I was right.

I knew she still loved me, she wouldn't be here if she didn't, but it was different now.

That far off expression Hope wore when she thought no one was looking was enough for me to know that I didn't own her heart anymore.

A piece of it belonged somewhere else now.

Somewhere I couldn't reach.

She was the sweetest girl in the world and I let her down in the worst imaginable way. I walked away from my home. From my safety net. From my hope...

I noticed the familiar silver Ford Kuga drive up the street towards my house and had to force down the surge of resentment that tried to force its way out of me.

Derek.

My father pulled into the spot Hope had vacated and killed the engine. I watched as he got out of his car and walked towards me, laden down with a stack of containers in his hands, filled with desserts and treats no doubt. That was Derek's answer to everything. When he didn't know what to say or do to help a person, he cooked and fed them.

I hated my father.

Hatred was a strong emotion and maybe I didn't feel that strongly about him, but I certainly didn't love him like a son loved his father.

And in my defense, he'd never given me much to love.

Absent and uncaring.

That's how I remembered the man walking towards me.

Missing.

Not there.

Chapter 16 | 119

Fucking gone.

Like every time I ever seemed to lay eyes on the man, I was bombarded with memories from my past...

"She can never know."

"Jord—"

"I mean it, Dad. Hope can never know about this...about me. None of the Carter's can."

My father's face was a map of pain, contorting in agony as he watched me watching him from a hospital bed. Finally, after what felt like forever, he bowed his head and sighed. "I wish I could take this all away for you," he whispered. "All the pain... All the memories." Glancing up with tears in his eyes, Dad whispered, "I feel useless." Shuddering, he added, "I could have done more."

Grasping the bed clothes with more force than necessary, I nodded stiffly. "You can't change the past."

"Maybe not, but I can change the future," he shot back, adamant. "I mean it, Jordan, I don't want this life for you." Sighing, he added, "You've seen me. You watched first-hand what living with your demons can do to a man. I can't sit back and allow what happened to me happen to you."

"My situation is nothing like yours," I hissed...

"You hungry, Jord?" Derek asked, stirring me from my memories. "I brought plenty for all of you guys." Juggling the half a dozen or so containers in his arms, he added, "I packed some toddler friendly goodies for the baby. Is he here?"

"Morning," I acknowledged, good manners winning out, as I fell into step with my father and walked back into the house. "And no. Ryder's at daycare."

"Damn," Derek muttered, sounding genuinely disappointed as he followed me through to the kitchen. "I was hoping he would be here." Setting the containers down on the kitchen table, he shrugged off his coat and hung it on the back of the chair closest to him. "The kid's adorable."

"That's you all over, isn't it, Derek?" I tossed out as I walked

120 | INEVITABLE

over to the coffee machine and grabbed a mug. "You're a sucker for other people's kids." *Never your own.*

Derek sighed heavily before slumping down at the table. "Are we really going to go through this again, Jord?" he asked, tone weary, keeping his back to me. "I fucked up. I'm a piece of shit. I ruined your life. I'm the one in the wrong."

"Whatever, Derek." He was right about one thing; there was no point in rehashing this conversation. His excuses never changed and I never felt any better from it. "How's work?" I decided to change the subject by asking. Pouring two mugs of coffee, I walked back to the table and handed him one before taking the seat opposite him. "Did you finish setting up that new menu at the restaurant that you mentioned last week?" My father was a chef, and a brilliant one at that. I guess taking care of other people's kids and cooking were his best traits.

"Thanks," he replied, accepting the mug from me and taking a sip. "And yeah, I finished it on Tuesday." He placed the mug on the table in front of him and leaned back in his chair before asking, "So, how's everything going with you and Hope?" his green eyes were locked on mine, and if I didn't know better, I would say he looked genuinely interested in my life. But I did know better and the reason he was asking about my marriage wasn't his paternal instincts kicking into gear; it was his best friend's. Hope's father was my father's best friend. Kyle Carter was also a father in all forms. He wasn't a blow-in like the man in front of me who'd fallen into my life when I was four and had fallen back out of it when I was fourteen. No, my wife's father had stuck around to raise her and her brothers. He'd been there every day of her life, and with the exception of me fucking things up for her, she'd been incredibly sheltered and protected because of the man.

"Who wants to know?" I shot back, mirroring my father's actions by leaning back in my chair and studying him. "You or Kyle?"

Derek frowned deeply and I saw the hurt in his green eyes.

Chapter 16 | 121

It was there and obvious for me to see. Thing was, I didn't care. I didn't care if he was hurt by the truth. That was life. "Me, Jord," he finally replied. "*I* want to know."

"We're fine," I answered him. That was all Derek Porter was going to get from me. He didn't have the right to any information about my personal life. Sharing blood, genes, and a surname with this man didn't mean anything to me.

We drank the rest of our coffee with me in silence and him making small talk that I either nodded along with or completely ignored. When I was finished, I shoved my chair back and got up. "I need to sleep," I announced bluntly. "I'm back on night shifts this week."

"Okay. No problem." Nodding, Derek drained what was left in his mug before standing up and slipping his coat back on. "Don't burn yourself out, Jord," was the advice my father gave me before leaving.

Feeling at a complete loss, I shook my head and watched him leave.

I knew he'd be back.

Same time on Friday.

It didn't seem to matter how rude I was to the man.

He wouldn't *go away*.

Twice a week for the past eight years, I had been tormented with awkward visits from my father. He came when I was in rehab. He came when I was high. He came when I was sober. He came when I wasn't. Twice a week, every damn week, the man kept fucking coming back.

I just wished he had that determined streak inside of him back when I had needed it most.

When it had mattered.

Because it sure as hell didn't matter now.

17

Hope

"How's my favorite live-in nanny?" Teagan teased the second I walked into her kitchen in South Peak Road fresh from dropping Ryder to daycare. "You know, I've been thinking and maybe you should move back in here with us. I could use a woman like you around the place."

Sarcastic bitch.

I responded with a middle finger gesture. "Shut up and make me coffee."

"Okaaay." Closing the door of the refrigerator she'd been rummaging in, Teagan turned and gave me her full attention. The sight of her looking like a freaking supermodel in a pair of her husband's gray Calvin Klein's and a skin-tight tank top only made me feel shittier than I had already been feeling and my shoulders slumped. "Rough morning?"

"Rough life," I muttered under my breath, sinking down on one of the barstools at the marble island in the center of the room. "Coffee, Teegs. Please."

"Coming right up." I watched my best friend bound around

Chapter 17 | 123

her kitchen a heck of a lot happier and more together than she had been four weeks ago. She had that beautiful glow about her that came with entering the second trimester of pregnancy. Everything about Teagan was tight and toned. And that cute little baby bump she was sporting that she thought was so huge? I was fairly sure I looked more pregnant after a heavy meal. Her silky hair looked like a freaking horse's tail swishing around as she made my coffee. Even though she had her blonde mane pulled back in a ponytail, it still reached the curve of her lower back.

"Black. Two sugars," she announced, placing my favorite mug in front of me.

"Thanks," I whispered, wrapping both hands around the mug, grateful for the warmth stemming from the porcelain. It was cold as hell outside, and raining to boot. I felt wet and cold to the bone. Teagan sank down on the stool opposite mine and waited for me to speak.

Coffee didn't give a person the same Dutch courage as alcohol did, but it helped set the jets of my brain in motion.

When I drained the contents of my mug, I finally felt able to verbalize my feelings. "I'm so fucking angry," I bit out, blurting out everything I had buried down inside since I woke up this morning and had once again been faced with dealing with the absolute horror that was my life. "Worse than angry. I'm raging, Teegs. Like, certifiably furious."

Like every morning for the past god knows how long, Teagan didn't say a word as I complained. She simply sat and listened to me rant on and on about my life until I had it out of my system.

My life was a fucking train wreck.

No, scratch that, because my life wasn't interesting enough to be a train wreck. My life was a bus stop. Yeah, a boring, old, stinky bus stop in the middle of nowhere. I was trying. God knows I was trying to make my situation work, but I felt...suffocated.

124 | INEVITABLE

That was so wrong, right?

Feeling suffocated?

I shouldn't feel that way.

I shouldn't be feeling stifled and repressed.

I shouldn't be feeling *trapped*.

Because I wasn't.

This was a choice.

I had *chosen* this path.

So why, after twenty-six years of certainty, did I feel so damn lost?

"You need to get laid," Teagan announced when I had finally run out of things to complain about. "Badly."

"What – do you want to have sex with me?" I huffed loudly and folded my arms across my chest. "Because that's the only way I'm getting laid." *Had she been listening to me at all this morning?*

"Hope," Teagan snickered. "Don't be so dramatic."

"Who's being dramatic?" I shot back, voice rising. "I'm being deadly serious here, Teegs."

"Hey," she laughed, holding her hands up. "I'd help you out, but I'm married and don't possess a penis."

Ha! "Not serious about *you*," I growled, rolling my eyes. "God, this is so fucking depressing." Resting my elbows on the counter, I leaned forward and dropped my head in my hands. "I don't even remember what it feels like," I admitted glumly. "Sex? It's practically a foreign concept to me."

"It's *amazing*," Teagan offered with a dreamy sigh.

"Thanks for that," I grumbled.

"Maybe I should give you a crash course in the art of seducing your husband?" she mused.

"It wouldn't matter if the entire playboy mansion sat down and gave me a lesson," I wailed. "I still wouldn't be able to get my husband to sleep with me."

"Oh, quit being so pessimistic," she tossed back airily. "So,

Chapter 17 | 125

your husband won't have sex with you. Big deal. Have sex with yourself."

My head shot up and I gaped at her.

Teagan stared blankly back at me and I felt like throttling her.

"Do you have any idea how inexplicably tired a writer's hands are?" I bit out. "I have *carpal tunnel,* Teagan." Dear god, no one understood my struggles. "Forget it," I moaned. "You'd never understand. Not with your nimble fingers and horned up husband."

"Just keep plugging away," Teagan advised. "Eventually he's going to have to crack and have sex with you –"

"Morning ladies." Noah chose this exact moment to saunter into the kitchen, causing Teagan's words to trail off and her attention to hone in entirely on him. Noah walked right over to us and planted a kiss on Teagan's head. Not content with that limited amount of affection, Teagan spun around on her stool and dragged Noah's face down to hers, planting a loud kiss on his lips.

Meanwhile, I concentrated on ignoring how disgustingly cute they were together.

Smirking, Noah winked down at his wife before stepping away and walking over to the fridge. "So, what are you two talking about?" Retrieving one of those disgusting protein drinks Teagan prepped for him from the top shelf, Noah cracked the cap off and drank the entire bottle in one go.

"Ew," I muttered, staring at him in horror. "How can you stomach that crap?" Those drinks tasted freaking disgusting. Honestly, I had accidently consumed a sip once and puked my guts up. "It's gross, Noah, and you're gross for putting it in your body."

Noah cocked a brow in amusement. "Someone's bitchy this morning."

"Nah," Teagan mused. "Hope just needs to have sex."

"Teagan!" I snapped, mortified. "God."

126 | INEVITABLE

Noah coughed loudly. "Excuse me?"

"Hope," Teagan clarified happily. "She needs the D."

"The D," Noah deadpanned, looking mildly horrified.

"Dick," Teagan clarified. "As in the male reproductive organ used to penetrate the fe–"

"Yeah, I got it, Thorn," Noah interrupted with a barely restrained shudder. "Jesus."

"Noah, how long would you go without fucking me?" Teagan began to say and I blanched. *Dear god, she was off again.* "I'm being serious," she added, hopping down from her stool, she walked over to a very uncomfortable looking Noah and said, "How long?"

Noah looked incredibly uncomfortable and slightly confused when he looked at his wife and asked, "What – like how long would I go without fucking you in one day?"

Teagan threw her head back and laughed and I groaned loudly.

"You know what? In my humble opinion, I believe that in order to have a successful relationship, a man needs to bring three things to the table." Teagan grinned before saying, "His dick, his heart, and a good sense of humor."

"And patience," Noah offered. "A shit ton of patience."

"Funny little fucker, aren't you?" Teagan shot back before turning her attention back to me. "Maybe we should start on those seduction lessons after coffee."

"Holy shit," Noah spluttered, eyes widening as awareness dawned on him. "Are you and Jordan not..."

"Let me die," I whispered. It would be a hell of a lot easier to handle than this particular conversation.

"Nope," Teagan blabbed, continuing to ruin my life with this conversation. "Which is why I really feel that she needs to have the D right away."

"Oh my god. Shut up!" I hissed.

"Jesus Christ," Noah muttered. "You two are so fucking

Chapter 17 | **127**

weird." He shook his head in disgust before hightailing it out of the kitchen.

"Admit it," Teagan shot back. "Just admit that you are in dire need of some crazy, hot sex and I will drop it."

"Fine," I snapped, losing my patience with her. "I need to have sex."

"What was that?" She teased, cupping her ear. "I couldn't hear you."

"Oh, you didn't hear me? Well hear this, bitch." Jumping off my stool, I threw my hands in the air and shouted at the top of my lungs, "I, Hope Sarah Carter, need to have sex with a penis! I *really* need a big, fat, ginormous, juicy dick inside me right this second!"

Teagan was laughing so hard that it was encouraging the teenager inside of me.

Laughing along with her, I continued to make a total ass of myself in front of my best friend by breaking into a verse of Nicki Minaj's *Anaconda.*

"Ahhhh!" Teagan screamed through fits of laughter. "I can't. I can't..." Crossing her legs to stop herself from peeing, she gasped and spluttered. "You're killing me."

"See this?" I called out, grabbing my own sweatpants clad ass. "This needs the D." Hip thrusting, I hopped over to where Teagan was squirming and dropped into the twerk position. "This ass needs a dick!" I sang out through fits of laughter as I attempted to twerk.

"Yeah, it does," Teagan half screamed from laughter as she began to play the drums on my ass. "Woo, go girl!"

"I need a dick," I laughed, thoroughly enjoying this bit of innocent fun between two best friends. Weird or not, this was exactly what I needed right now. *Fun...* "Give me the dick!"

"I volunteer as tribute," a familiar male voice said from behind me and I screamed loudly before falling on my face. The instant my gaze landed on the huge, tattooed man standing in the kitchen doorway with a shit-eating grin on his face, mortification crept through me. "Oh, sweet baby Jesus..."

"I'll have sex with you," Hunter declared with a wink, causing Teagan to burst out laughing. His words caused my heart to jackknife in my chest. Ice blue eyes stared into mine. His lips curled up in a predatorily smile. "And you're welcome to inspect my dick beforehand to see if it ticks all your boxes." His words dripped from his lips like honey. His blond main was pulled back in his signatory man bun. He cracked a huge smile before saying, "But I've had no complaints."

"I bet you haven't," I muttered, climbing to my feet, but I doubted he heard me with Teagan laughing like a freaking hyena.

"Where the hell have you been?" Teagan exclaimed, still laughing, as she rushed over to where Hunter was standing and threw her arms around him, enveloping him in a massive hug. "You said you'd only be gone a few days."

Immediately, something spiked inside of me. Something green and very ugly. I quickly batted it away, not daring to delve deeper into the reasons behind my sudden burst of emotion. Nothing was simple when it came to this man so I just blocked him out.

I had been avoiding Hunter Casarazzi like the plague since the night at the Ring of Fire for two very valid reasons.

The first; being in his presence reminded me of what I was capable of.

And second; he *disturbed* me.

Sure, nine times out of ten, he was here when I came over to visit, but I tried my best to keep my distance from him. I had to because the man had no filter. He was wild and flirtatious and he seemed to revel in making me squirm.

I couldn't take his measure because the man was absolutely unpredictable. I never truly knew what he was going to say or do next. I didn't like unpredictable. It wasn't safe or comfortable.

Chapter 17 | 129

The thought of how close I had come to giving myself to him last Halloween flooded my mind and I reddened even further. Like a cruel twist of fate, my brain reacted like a broken record, playing the memory of that night over and over again...

Frozen to the spot, I gaped after Hunter, and contemplated my options. I could sit around and live the rest of my life the way I had lived the past several years– miserable and empty. Or I could take a risk on the stranger who walked into my life two months ago and made me feel again...

Jumping off the bed, I ran out of my room and down the staircase, with only one thought in my mind. Stop him from leaving. I didn't want to be on my own again.

When I reached the bottom of the stairs, I spotted Lucky moving towards the front door. Leaving, my mind told me, flashing the word in bright neon letters, and I barreled towards him, the fear of spending another day of my life alone almost too much to comprehend.

"Hey, Hunter!" I called out. "Lucky, wait." I managed to catch a hold of his cape just as the front door swung inwards.

"Don't go," I panted, looking up at him.

"I'm not playing games here," Lucky told me, and the vulnerability in his voice hit me like a crater. "Don't mess me around, Hope."

My hand found his of its own accord. "I'm not trying to," I told him, shivering at the feel of his warm touch. "I need..." The words that had been on the tip of my tongue shriveled and died the moment my eyes landed on the person in the doorway of my parent's house.

Jordan was back.

From the moment I stepped off that plane and climbed into Hunter's truck, I had been in trouble. I remembered expecting my father to be the one to come and pick me up. I also remembered the excitement and desire I felt when it was

130 | INEVITABLE

Hunter instead. I remembered the burning intensity I had to figure him out. Those secretive smiles and double meaning comments he tossed about airily. Sure, I had seen him back in Cork, and like every red-blooded woman, I had admired his beauty. But the day he opened the door of that truck for me was my turning point. Whether I wanted to admit it or not, I had unwillingly opened myself up to him.

Feeling something for Hunter made me resent him a little.

How dare he come into my perfectly organized world and pull the rug out from under my feet?

How dare he make me feel things for him.

How dare he make me question everything I had ever known?

I was aggravated and frustrated and not myself.

I was a ride or die kind of girl, and I was Jordan's ride or die girl.

Hunter had no business busting into my world and making everything a million times more complicated. He was not supposed to be in the equation.

$1 + 1$ = me and Jordan – *not* me, Jordan, *and* Hunter.

And why the hell did I always call him by his real name?

I didn't want to.

I didn't mean to.

Lucky was his nickname. Everyone and their mother called him that, but every time I opened my mouth, *Hunter* came out.

"I had some stuff I needed to tie up," Hunter replied, drawing back to the present as he set Teagan back down on her feet before fondly mussing her hair. "Took longer than I expected."

I itched to ask where he'd been. Teagan had mentioned Hunter was out of town last week, but I was sensible enough not to ask questions about him. It still didn't stop me from wanting to know.

"But you're back now?" she asked, rearranging her ponytail. "For good?"

Chapter 17 | 131

Disturbingly, I hung on every word of their conversation, desperate to hear his answer, but I never found out because Teagan bounded out of the room like an over-excited puppy, calling out, "Noah! Lucky's home."

Hunter shook his head in wry amusement. "She seems happier."

"She is," I confirmed, watching his every move as he strolled over to the coffee machine and grabbed the glass jug. "Happy, I mean."

"And you?" he asked, keeping his back to me as he poured himself a mug of coffee. When he turned around and asked, "Are you happy now, HC?" The intensity in his eyes almost melted me on the mortal spot.

"I'm happy," I confirmed, backing up against the island and as far from him as I could.

Hunter leaned against the counter, giving me his undivided attention as he took a sip of coffee.

Fuck, why did he have to look so damn good in those Timberland boots, faded denim jeans, that fucking plaid shirt and those ray bans settled on top of his head?

Tilting his head to one side, his eyes took a shamelessly long appraisal of my body and I felt the burn all the way to the tips of my toes. This man had a hold on me. I couldn't explain the how's or why's and *I didn't fucking like it*.

When he finally looked into my eyes and said, "Good," all the earlier intensity I'd seen in his eyes was gone, replaced now with...indifference?

Oh shit, I really didn't want him to look at me with indifference.

And I really didn't want to care if he did.

Dammit.

"So, where have you been?" I let myself down by asking.

Hunter took his sweet time answering me. He wasn't unearthed by my demands or questions. He didn't care that I was unsettled by him and it was wildly refreshing.

132 | INEVITABLE

"I had to go home for a while," he finally answered. "I had some old scores I needed to settle."

"Illegal scores?" I couldn't stop myself from asking.

"Don't worry, Bonnie," he shot back with a smirk. "Clyde hasn't done anything illegal without you since our last escapade."

My face reddened. "I didn't mean–"

"Relax," he said with an easy smile. "I'm just kidding with you. Or is that off limits now, too?"

We used to kid around a lot before everything went to hell in a handbasket between us. I missed spending time with him. I missed my friend, but I couldn't trust myself around him anymore.

The things he made me feel were not safe for me and I had to keep my distance. I was a married woman. I had commitments and I didn't need the distraction Hunter Casarazzi posed to me.

Teagan returned then with Noah in tow and I didn't have to say anymore. I knew this was my perfect opportunity to make my excuses and leave, and I knew that's exactly what I should do, but I found myself taking a seat in the kitchen.

Because as much as I hated to admit it, the only time I felt like I truly belonged was when I was hanging out in this house with my three best friends.

18

Lucky

Teagan couldn't cook a decent meal for shit. She was too health conscious, too focused on calories and levels of proteins and all that shit a professional athlete was required to eat during training. Even though Noah was in retirement, he still ate like he was conditioning for a fight. We weren't all fitness fanatics, and thankfully, Teagan had a BFF that more than made up for what she lacked in the cooking stakes.

I watched from my perch at the island as Hope busied herself with frying chicken in a skillet at the stove. Fuck, I missed her cooking since she moved out. Hell, I missed more than her cooking. I missed everything about the woman, especially that round, sexy ass of hers as she pottered around the house looking like a lost puppy.

She had a pair of baggy sweatpants on today and an oversized shirt. Her curls were pinned to the top of her head, held up with a pencil, and I'd never seen anything so fucking beautiful. I had no clue why she continued to hide that amazing body

134 | INEVITABLE

of hers beneath clothes that were about four sizes too big for her, but she did.

She couldn't hide that fine ass though, I thought to myself as I studied her curves shamelessly. Hope Carter was built like a dream. Honest to god. And I should know. I'd had the pleasure of having that beautiful body beneath me once. And even though it had ended sooner than I hoped, I'd had a hard time forgetting how she felt.

"Hey, Hunter? How many pieces of chicken do you want?" Hope called out with her back to me, her attention focused on the food she was cooking. She crouched down to look through the glass oven door at the tray of roasted potatoes she had peeled, giving me a wonderful glimpse of the black thong riding up.

"Whatever's going is fine with me," I replied distractedly, tilting my head sideways to thoroughly enjoy the view.

"There's plenty to go around," she called over her shoulder. "Breast or thigh? What's your preference?"

Goddamn.

I had been with more than my fair share of women over the years and I could safely say that not a single one of them had ever evoked in me the feelings Hope Carter did. For Christ's sake, she was a married woman. She had turned me down more than once. And now, she was standing in ugly ass sweats and asking me whether I preferred breast or thigh, and I was burning the hell up inside.

"I'll take whatever you give me," I told her, and I didn't just mean the chicken or her ass. I was certain this was the longest Hope had spent alone with me since going back to her husband. Teagan and Noah had left for a walk twenty minutes ago, and I had half expected Hope to tag along with them.

That's the way it was between us now.

I smiled and she ran, I chased and she hid, and it drove me batshit crazy.

Hope was careful around me now. Reserved. A shadow of

Chapter 18 | 135

her former self, and I found myself itching to break her free from the chains and restraints holding the real her inside.

I missed that girl and everything about her. The way she slurped on her first cup of coffee of the day, and the way she stored pencils in her hair. I missed that adorable expression she wore every time she had to put down her laptop when she was only half way through writing down a new idea. I missed seeing the excitement in her eyes when she thought up a plot twist, and the way she cried when one of her characters was in pain.

I missed my friend.

Noticing all her little quirks and habits probably made me a fucking stalker but I didn't care. I wanted to be around this woman.

I always had.

From the moment she crashed into Noah's hotel room last year, Hope Carter had taken me by surprise. The very first time I saw her in the doorway, something switched on inside of me. It wasn't because she was gorgeous and I wanted to fuck her brains out – I did, but that wasn't it – no, it was the look in those big blue eyes of hers when she looked up at me. In that moment, I could see how lost she was. I could see the turmoil inside her heart. It was like something inside of her called out to something inside of me, almost like a kindred spirit sort of connection. This beautiful, intelligent, independent and head-strong woman was so full of secrets and hidden pain. Hope had burst into my world and intrigued me to the point that I found myself opening up a part of myself to her that had been closed off to the rest of the world.

Losing Hayley the way I had was the worst thing that had ever happened to me.

Accepting that she wasn't coming back was the hardest thing I ever had to do.

But I did it.

Hard as it was, I fucking *did it.*

136 | INEVITABLE

The way I saw it, loving someone wasn't a sign of weakness or something to be ashamed of. Not in the least. Loving someone and telling that someone was one of the bravest things a human being could do. Putting yourself out there, knowing there's a ninety-nine percent chance it will all end in pain and tears and fucking misery, but risking it all anyway because of that one percent chance it might work out – that it might be the jackpot bet you've been trying to win your entire life?

That was fucking bravery.

Love was insanity. It was choosing to bare you soul and ugliness with another human being and being okay with what you saw in the mirror because that person loved the parts of you that were unlovable. The parts you were most ashamed of.

I believed in that.

It didn't make me a romantic person. I was far from it. I just believed that there had to be some sort of a recess from the bullshit life humans were thrown into, and that recess was the love of a human heart.

Some people might say that made me a traitor to her memory, but I'd never given much thought to what others thought of me. In fact, I didn't give a damn. I was who I was. I had loved and lost, cried and mourned, and I wasn't about to shy away from the chance to heal and love and breathe again.

And the woman standing in front of me?

She made me *breathe* again.

She made me *want to.*

Hope gave me something I didn't realize I had been missing and now that I'd had a taste of it, I wasn't giving it up.

I wasn't giving *her* up.

Fuck her husband and the whole damn world. If he loved her as much as *she* said he did, he wouldn't have left her. In my humble opinion, the man was fucking crazy. He had walked away from a woman like her and had been touched by fucking god himself that she had waited for him.

Chapter 18 | 137

If he had only stayed away a couple more months, hell, even another week, I had a feeling the outcome wouldn't have been so positive for him.

"Hunter," Hope warned, stirring me from my reverie. She spun around to face me and held up a shaky hand. "Please don't."

Jesus, the way she said my name, the way the word rolled off her tongue, did something to me. I hadn't been called Hunter since pre-k, not even by my folks, but I liked hearing the name come out of her mouth.

"Don't what, sweetheart?" I cocked a brow and waited for her to enlighten me. I wasn't about to open my mouth and give her an out. I was baiting the girl and I wanted her to bite.

She looked head on, blue eyes wide and cheeks flushed bright red, before whispering, "Don't flirt with me."

"I wasn't aware that I was flirting," I shot back with a smirk. *Of course* I was flirting with her. It was impossible not to. "You asked me a question and I answered you honestly." Now, that part *was* the truth.

My response seemed to throw Hope and her brows furrowed in confusion. "Oh," she finally mumbled, redder in the cheeks than earlier. "Okay."

"Why?" I teased. "Did you want me to flirt with you?"

"No," she spluttered, almost choking on her words. I cocked a brow in response and it earned me a death glare. "Absolutely not," she reiterated. "No flirting."

"You sure?" I asked, unable to wipe the smirk from my face. The woman was ridiculously hot when she was angry.

"One hundred percent. Now stop being so...infuriatingly frustrating!" Her chest was heaving as she glared up at me, clearly pissed off.

I laughed at her response.

She was such a little liar.

We didn't speak much after that, and ended up eating our meal in silence. The woman was still very nervous around me

138 | INEVITABLE

and I didn't want to push her too far. I was enjoying being in her company far too much to fuck it all up and send her running back to *him*. She had a backbone worthy of a soldier and an uncompromising loyalty. Unfortunately, that loyalty seemed to be directed at Jordan. I had plans on fixing that.

Later that evening when she was about to leave – to go back to him – the heaven's opened up and blessed me with a fucking miracle.

"Dammit," Hope hissed, stalking back through the front door. "I left the lights on in my truck. The battery's as dead as a doorknob now."

"I'll drive you home," I was only more than happy to offer.

"Oh." Hope's cheeks turned bright red. "No. That's okay. I don't want to trouble you. I'll just call a cab."

"You're not troubling me." Grabbing my keys off the counter, I walked towards her. "I offered. Come on."

"But it's over an hour's drive to get to Denver," she spluttered, trying to find a way out of getting in my truck with me.

"I'm not doing anything," I shot back, not giving her an out. "Now, let's go."

19

Hope

*A*s I sat in the passenger seat of Hunter's truck, I felt an abnormal swell of annoyance roar to life inside of me, which was stupid considering he wasn't even speaking.

In fact, he had been nothing but pleasant and courteous to me throughout the duration of the car ride, but I still felt irked.

His choice in music pissed me off. The fact that he looked at me twice pissed me off, but not as much as the fact that he had *only* looked at me twice.

Uncle Kracker's *Smile* blasted through the speakers of his truck then and I folded my arms across my chest and huffed out a sigh.

That song!

Back when we had both been living at Teagan and Noah's, we had all gotten drunk one night and decided to hit the town, only to end up taking part in a couple's karaoke competition at a local bar.

Hunter and I had come last with our pathetically drunk version of Uncle Kracker's Smile. Partially because we had laughed throughout the entire song, but mostly because his singing voice sucked.

Hunter didn't comment on that so I huffed louder.

I got nothing but a smug little smirk.

Bastard.

"Turn it off," I finally snapped when I'd had quite enough of the taunting music.

"No," he replied without hesitation.

I swung my gaze to his face and gaped at him. "Change the goddamn song, Hunter."

Instead of turning it off, he turned up the volume and hummed along to the music.

"Asshole," I muttered before resuming my staring out the passenger window. I needed to get out of this truck. I needed to put some space between me and this infuriating man.

"Sing, Carter," he ordered.

"Absolutely not."

"Do it."

"Not happening."

"Come on," he teased. "For old time's sake." Winking, he crooned loudly, laughing when I cringed.

"If I sing, will you stop?"

"Maybe?"

Reluctantly, I began to mutter the words. That only made Hunter croon louder.

Without my permission, a laugh fell from my lips and I slapped a hand over my mouth.

He grinned devilishly.

Giving in, I sang along to the song, fighting down a smile the entire time, until it became impossible. How could he do this to me? Make me feel like a child? Make me give in? he was goofy and playful and I loved him for it.

I sang along until my sides hurt from laughing.

"There she is," Hunter mused when the song was over.

Chapter 19 | 141

Turning down the volume, he exhaled a contented sigh and added, "I've missed this version of you."

"*This* version of me?"

"Yeah," he replied without remorse or hesitation. "You know, the real you."

I didn't say anything back to that.

In truth, I was kind of stumped.

He had this strange ability of cutting me down to the bone with his words...exposing me, making me feel almost naked around him.

20

Lucky

"Can I tell you a secret?" Hope asked in a small voice, when I pulled my truck up outside her place in Denver.

Killing the engine, I turned to face her, giving her my full attention. "You can tell me anything."

"I can still see their faces at night," she whispered, blue eyes wide as saucers, as she stared up at me. I watched her carefully as she spoke. "The men we got rid of –" Her voice broke off and she shuddered. "I can still smell their burning flesh." She looked straight into my eyes and whispered, "It keeps me awake at night."

Exhaling a heavy sigh, I rubbed my jaw and strived to find the words to tell her to ease her conscience. "You didn't do any of it," was all I came up with. "It was all on me."

"No." She shook her head and twisted sideways in her seat, giving me her full attention. "Don't try and soothe me with lies." Leaning towards me, she whispered, "You might have lit the flame, but I handed you the matches." Her hands trembled

Chapter 20 | 143

slightly as she tucked a curl behind her ear. "The worst part of it all is that I'm *not* sorry."

What could I say to that?

The truth?

"I'm not sorry, either," I admitted honestly.

"And if I had to go back in time, I would still do it over again," she confessed, biting down on her bottom lip. "I have *no* regrets."

"Neither do I."

"Does that make me a bad person?" she asked then, voice soft and unsure.

"If it does, then what the hell am I?" I shot back. "I've done worse than what you saw me do that night." *Much fucking worse.*

Hope took a long ass time to respond; so long, I actually thought she wasn't going to.

Finally, when she unfastened her seatbelt and had her hand on the door handle, she whispered, "I don't know what that makes you." She pushed open the door and stepped out. "But I like you, Hunter Casarazzi," she added, turning back to face me. "Regardless of how much blood is on your hands."

With that, she closed my truck door and disappeared into the house, leaving me alone with her words.

Well shit...

21

Hope

I was in trouble. Not the kind that required an ultrasound and a gynecologist. No. This was much worse. This was catastrophically worse.

Staring down at the screen of my phone, my heart leapt in my chest as I read then reread the message that just popped up on my screen.

> Hunter: Your breasts were fucking delicious last week, HC. I can still taste your thighs on my tongue.

RED-FACED AND PARANOID, I LOOKED AROUND THE CAFÉ AT LEAST another half dozen times before plucking up the nerve to reply.

Chapter 21 | 145

> Hope: Well, I hope you enjoyed my 'breasts' and 'thighs', asshole, because that's the last meal I will ever cook for you!

I PRESSED SEND AND CONTINUED TO STARE DOWN AT MY PHONE, watching the little dots bounce around the bottom of the screen, letting me know that Hunter was writing a response.

> Hunter: Fine. I'll cook for you next time. I'll let you sample my sausage. Le Cock De Lucky. In English that translates to Lucky's Cock. You'll need to work up an appetite though. I've been told it's bigger than most.

JESUS! I BLANCHED AT HIS CRUDE RESPONSE AND HURRIED TO TYPE out a reply.

> Hope: Okay, that's not funny. You need to stop or I can't text you anymore.

> Hunter: Why?

WHAT DID HE MEAN *WHY*?
He knew very well why!

146 | INEVITABLE

> Hope: Because I'm married and flirting with me is inappropriate. And especially considering what happened between us at Halloween!

Hunter: What happened between us at Halloween?

NOW HE WAS PLAYING WITH ME.
Purposefully pushing my buttons.

> Hope: Do you want me to spell it out?

Hunter: Please do. I love it when you go all bossy-writer on me and spell shit out. It's so fucking hot.

OH MY GOD.

> Hope: You're unbelievable.

Hunter: You have no idea what unbelievable means, HC. But you will...

> Hope: Oh really?

Chapter 21 | 147

Hunter: Really.

> Hope: Now you're boring me with all your talk!

Hunter: You left me that night. I had a whole night of action planned for you.

> Hope: Stop it.

Hunter: Admit it. You still want me.

> Hope: I mean it. Stop!

Hunter: You're thinking about it now, aren't you? What you ran out on that night. It's driving you insane.

NO. NO. NO. I NEEDED TO STOP THIS AND FAST.

> Hope: Goodbye Hunter.

Hunter: I'll be seeing you real soon, HC.

> Hope: Why do you keep doing that?

Hunter: ???

> Hope: Why do you keep calling me HC?

Hunter: I like it. It suits you. And we have the same initials. Talk about fate. ;)

> Hope: You're crazy.

Hunter: It's possible. But it excites you. By the way – have you thought anymore about my offer?

> Hope: Your offer?

148 | INEVITABLE

> Hunter: To have sex with you. It's still on the table.

> Hope: This... you and me? We are NEVER going to happen.

> Hunter: Never say never, HC.

"ARE YOU OKAY?"

The sound of Jordan's voice pierced through my thoughts and balked. "Yes!" I squeezed out before tossing my cell into my purse. "I'm... fine." I could hear my phone vibrating and it took everything in me to resist the urge to grab it and read the message.

"You sure?" Jordan asked as he sat across from me, his intelligent green eyes focused on what I was sure was my scarlet colored face.

Inhaling a deep, steadying breath, I pushed Hunter Casarazzi to the back of my mind, choosing to focus on my husband instead. "I'm sure."

Happy to let it go, Jordan placed a triple espresso on the table in front of me. "Enough coffee for the author?" he joked, relaxing back in his chair.

"I don't think I deserve to be called an author," I murmured as I took a sip. "I'm still blocked." I hadn't written more than a chapter in months. Not a single one. "This has never happened to me before," I added with a frown. Whatever I felt, I wrote it down. I channeled my pain into words and splashed that shit all over the paper like a boss bitch. Not lately though... No, lately, I seemed to be broken.

Leaning back in his seat, Jordan continued to observe me as he nursed his mug of black coffee with both hands. "What's the cause of this dry spell?"

I choked on my coffee, spluttered and heaved loudly.

Chapter 21 | 149

Dry spell didn't even come close to describing my sex life...

My phone vibrated again.

Dammit!

Jordan leaned forward in concern. "Hope, are you okay?"

"Yeah," I squeezed out, cheeks flaming red, as my phone vibrated for the third time. "I'm good."

I knew the cause of the dry spell.

I was agitated.

Fine, I was horny.

Okay, so I was horny and agitated and maybe even hangry.

I hadn't eaten breakfast this morning and I had been without sex for years.

"Hope." Leaning forward, Jordan covered my trembling hand with his and smiled. "If you need something from me, you only have to ask." His fingers trailer over the skin covering my pulse and I shuddered in pleasure. "I *want* to help you." Intelligent green eyes watched my every move. "We're a team now."

God, he was so beautiful.

So beautiful *and broken.*

I needed to remember that.

Shaking my head in disgust, I scolded myself for being an inconsiderate bitch. My husband was going through hell as he fought his demons. I was being selfish, thinking about my *needs.* "I'll get over it," I told him, slapping a bright smile on my face. "Don't worry."

Jordan gave me a look that told me he wasn't entirely convinced. "You're okay, though, aren't you, Hope?" he asked, voice deceptively soft. "You're happy?"

"I am," I assured him, wishing I could mean what I was saying. But something inside of me had changed.

My heart, in the eight years we had been apart, had molded into a different shape and didn't quite beat for him the same way it used to.

Acknowledging that fact, even to myself, almost broke me. I

didn't want to feel differently. I wanted to be all in like I had been my entire life.

I had always had a plan, *him*, and I didn't want to change it. I didn't want to contemplate a life where Jordan Porter wasn't the focal point.

It crippled me, the feeling I had inside, the one that assured me that while I still loved my husband deeply, it wasn't the same as before.

And worse, the undeniable, heart-wrenching feeling in my gut that assured me I would never feel that way again.

I had always prided myself on having my shit together, and knowing where I belonged in the world – and to who I belonged. I had made a choice, and for the last twenty plus years, I had stuck to it.

Now, I was second guessing everything I had thought was permanent and unchanging.

I had spent my life fighting so hard to be with Jordan that I never stopped to think about what I was doing.

Our relationship had always seemed so... inevitable that I never gave another thought to a life without him.

I never thought about if this was what I truly wanted?

If *he* was what was *good* for me.

I had been so damn stubborn and determined that I had never given a second glance to any other men.

Until now.

Dammit, everything had been so much easier when I was a kid.

Back then, I knew who I was.

Hope Carter.

I knew where and who I belonged to.

Myself

I knew what I wanted to be when I grew up.

A writer.

And I knew who I wanted to marry.

Chapter 21 | 151

Jordan Porter.

So why now, when I had finally gotten everything I wanted, was I having second thoughts?

Why was I entertaining the doubt and fear that had crept into my heart?

"I have to go if I'm going to make work on time," Jordan announced then, breaking through my thoughts, and his words caused the loneliness inside of me to surge. I watched him stand up and shrug on his jacket. "Traffic is always hell on earth this time of day," he added as he reached for his cup and chugged back the remaining coffee. "I'll be home at about nine tonight. We can work on fixing that writer's block of yours then, okay?"

"Okay," I replied, smiling. I didn't bother adding that he couldn't fix my block. I didn't want to sound unappreciative. Jordan was trying and I was willing to let him.

He leaned over the small, circular table and pressed a kiss to my cheek. "I love you, Keychain."

I closed my eyes and cherished the contact. "I love you too, Jordy."

When I opened my eyes again, he was gone, and I was alone.

Only when my phone vibrated in my purse did I remember the unread messages. My heart jackknifed in my chest and I held my breath as I grabbed my phone and swiped a trembling finger across the screen to unlock it.

Hunter: BTW: I walked in on Noah giving it to Teagan in the kitchen yesterday. Fucking ruined my appetite.

Hunter: Sick bastards. They better stop that shit once the baby comes.

152 | INEVITABLE

> Hunter: So, I'm guessing you're not texting me back because you're with your husband dearest.

> Hunter: You know where I am when you're done being second best.

Well, fuck.

22

Lucky

"The fuck you grinning at?" Noah grunted, pulling me from my thoughts, as he bench-pressed twice my body weight. "You're supposed to be spotting me, asshole, not playing with your goddamn phone."

"Simmer down, precious," I shot back with a wink before slipping my phone back into my jeans pocket and taking the bar from him. "Believe it or not, I happen to possess this amazing ability of being able to do two things at the same time." I set it back down in the hold and tossed him a towel.

Sitting up on the bench, Noah grabbed the towel mid-air and wiped the sweat from his brow. "You possess the asshole gene is what you fucking possess, Lucky," he said with a smirk, and just like that, I was transported back to a time when all we had to depend on was each other.

Neither one of us would have made it out of that cell block without the other.

That knowledge, dependence, and respect forged a deeper kind of friendship than most.

154 | INEVITABLE

He wasn't just my friend or my partner in crime.

Noah Messina was my brother.

And just like he had mine, I'd have his back until I took my last breath on this earth.

"So, who's the girl?" Noah asked a little breathlessly as he stood up and stretched himself out. "You've had your phone glued to your hand all morning."

"Hope," I chuckled and his words made me automatically check my phone for a response to my earlier messages.

Nothing.

Maybe I had laid it on a little heavy with her, but I didn't give a shit that she was married. I knew that made me sound like a selfish bastard, but I didn't care.

He didn't deserve her.

Any man who could walk away from the self-proclaimed love of his life like he had didn't deserve a second chance. Besides, I'd been dead inside for too fucking long to walk away from the one person who made me *feel* again.

And Hope?

She made me feel.

I wasn't blind and I wasn't in denial. I could see the whole childhood sweethearts turned lover's bullshit fairytale was important to her. I didn't fit into that life she had planned out. Thing was, I didn't care because I knew there was a piece of her sectioned off for me.

Just me.

I knew it and all I needed her to do was wake the hell up and realize it, too.

She was worth so much more than the life she'd attached herself to.

I wanted to take care of her. I wanted to snatch her away from the bullshit life she'd unwittingly tied herself to and show her everything she deserved.

I wanted to show her how to *live*.

"That is one bad mother-fucking idea," Noah stated in a no-

Chapter 22 | 155

nonsense tone. "Take my advice, man, and run far, far away from that situation. Nothing good will come out of messing around with a girl like her." His brown eyes seemed to bore through me as he spoke, and I could tell that Noah was willing me to take heed of his warning. "Trust me when I tell you she will *never* leave that guy. Not for you, or any other love-struck fool who tries."

"We're friends," I heard myself reply and Noah rolled his eyes.

"Yeah," he snorted. "And I'm a fucking virgin."

When I didn't say anything further, Noah shook his head and said, "Alright, man. Do what you gotta do. But when she rips your heart out of your goddamn chest – and she *will* – don't say I didn't warn you."

"Wow. Thanks for the great advice and vote of confidence," I shot back mockingly. "Asshole."

"You don't need any more confidence, Lucky," Noah laughed. "You're already full of shit." He inclined his head towards the entrance of the gym and said, "Come on. Let's go grab a bite. I'm fucking starving."

"Yeah," I agreed, following after him. "Me, too. I've been craving chicken all day."

23

Jordan

"You look lost in your thoughts again," I stated, looking across the restaurant table to where Hope was resting her cheek in her hand and staring off into nothing. I had been promising to take her out for dinner at a nice place in town since getting back together, but because of my hectic work schedule, I was only getting around to it now.

"Oh, I'm fine," Hope replied. Straightening in her seat, she dropped her hands on her lap and flashed me a smile. "Just daydreaming about my book."

That was a lie, but I didn't push it. I had no idea what happened to Hope at South Peak Road that night. I only knew that in the time that had passed since she slipped out of my house in the middle of the night to go see Teagan, she was... different. Distant. Further away than before.

I wasn't sure if it had something to do with me, but either way, I didn't dare broach the topic. I was afraid if I did, I'd hear something I couldn't handle.

She kept secrets from me now.

Chapter 23 | 157

That, I was certain of.

I could see it in her eyes.

Somewhere along the way in our eight years of misery and separation, I had lost the right to be in Hope's internal circle. Of course, she'd vehemently deny it if I asked. But it was obviously to me that my spot had been filled by Teagan and Noah.

The waiter arrived at our table with our main courses then and we both tucked in. "So, how's it coming along?" I asked between bites of my salmon. "The book?"

"Okay," she replied as she devoured her steak. "Not as fast as I would have hoped, though."

"Isn't that normal?" I swallowed a piece of fish and took a sip of water. "You can't rush creativity."

"No, I suppose not," she agreed with her mouth full, both hands armed with a fork and a steak knife as she attacked the piece of meat on her plate. "But try telling that to a horde of eager readers and a demanding editor." She swallowed another bite of her meal before reaching for her glass of wine. "I've been steadily releasing five books a year since I first published. It's now March and I haven't released since August last year. That's an eight-month gap." She looked disappointed in herself and I couldn't understand why.

Maybe I was clueless about the business of indie authors and self-publishing, but I thought eight months was totally acceptable. "That's nothing," I tried to assure her. "Most authors I read have gaps of one and two years or more between releases."

"Most authors you read are traditionally published and financially cushioned by a publishing company," she shot back, stabbing her meat with her fork once more. "Trust me, I've been in the indie publishing business long enough to know that an eight-month gap between producing a book is *not* a good thing." She grabbed the stem of her wine glass and gulped down a large mouthful before saying, "Time breeds doubt in readers, and for every month that passes in this

158 | INEVITABLE

industry that you don't produce a book, you risk losing your ranking."

I didn't get it. I honestly didn't. Hope was writing stories, not racing against time to find the cure for cancer. She made it sound so cut throat and dire.

"Why don't you just try and get yourself a deal with a publishing house and be done with all this added pressure of trying to do everything by yourself?" I heard myself ask. I saw the long days and countless sleepless nights Hope invested into her work. It was a solitary and isolating career.

Personally, I didn't understand why she felt the need to do it all on her own. She was talented. She didn't need to be wasting all of her spare time on marketing and formatting and all that crap. She was good enough to get a deal.

"Have your agent send out some feeler chapters and see who bites?" I Immediately wanted to take it back. The look of outrage in Hope's eyes assured me that I had said the wrong thing.

"For your information, my being self-published is a *choice*." She spat the words like poison. "I've had plenty of offers from multiple publishing houses all over the world." Dropping her fork and knife down on her plate, she picked up her napkin and wiped her mouth before tossing that down, too. "I've turned them all down because I *choose* this route."

Dammit, I had clearly offended her. I opened my mouth to apologize, but she obviously wasn't finished ranting.

"I really hate that," she growled. "Someone sees a self-published author and automatically assumes that their one goal in life is to be traditionally published. Like anything else is second best. Ugh." Huffing loudly, she drained the last drop of wine before slapping the glass down on the table none too gently. "Has it ever occurred to them that maybe said author doesn't *want* to take that path in their career? Has it ever crossed their narrow traditionally published minds that the financial opportunities and freedom of choice that come with

Chapter 23 | 159

self-publishing just might be in that author's best interests? No, of course not. Because when they see that an author is self-published they automatically assume it's because they can't get a traditional deal." She blew out a breath before adding, "What fucking bullshit."

I tried and failed to come up with something to say to ease the tension that had settled between us. We ate the rest of our meal in silence, opting out of having dessert before paying the bill and leaving. It wasn't until we were pulling her truck into the driveway of my house, that Hope finally broke the awkward silence.

"So, I may have overreacted a tad back there," she announced, casting a quick glance in my direction.

A tad? "You're passionate about what you do," I replied, trying to smooth everything out. "I didn't mean to insult you."

"You didn't." Killing the engine, she unfastened her seatbelt and turned in her seat to look at me. "Okay, maybe you did, but I know you didn't mean to." She exhaled a heavy sigh and placed her palms on the steering wheel. "I'm very defensive about what I do, Jordan." Her voice was low as she spoke. "For me, writing has always been my therapy. My safety net. The thing I threw myself into when my life spun out of control. And now I'm struggling... It makes me feel uncertain. And when I feel uncertain, I get anxious. And when I'm anxious, I get blocked. I hate being blocked."

"I bet." Dealing with uncertainty couldn't be easy for Hope. She was always so sure of herself. "Is there anything I can do to help?"

"No," she sighed sadly. "I'll have to figure this one out on my own."

I understood that.

I knew all about needing to do things by myself.

So instead of telling her lies and promising I could fix something we both knew I couldn't, I remained quiet and let her think it through on her terms.

24

Hope

I wanted someone to swoop in and save me from the impending deadline of doom circling above me. The story I was working on had been driving me crazy for months now. I was blank, couldn't seem to strain a single word from my fingers and it was making me go insane.

Of course, I knew the only one who could do that was me, but it still didn't stop me from wishing for a knight in shining armor with an extensive vocabulary and fabulous story-telling abilities to come and save the day – or my book to be exact.

Because of my defensiveness, our first dinner date had gone to hell. Jordan had taken time out from his crazy schedule to take me out, and I'd ended up having a mini-tantrum.

I felt guilty as sin over the whole thing. But another reason I felt so depressed over our argument was that it was a very sudden and cold wake up call for me. Jordan and I were two very different people now.

As much as I loved him, and I loved him deeply, we didn't quite *fit* anymore.

Chapter 24 | 161

He didn't understand my work and I had no clue about his. It hurt my heart to even contemplate the idea that we had drifted apart since childhood when I wanted nothing more than to be wrapped up in all he was.

We walked into the house side by side, but I could feel the stinging ridge spreading between us; a ridge that ricocheted further apart when we walked into the kitchen and were faced with Annabelle.

She was dressed in a basic, lemon tank top and flannel pajama bottoms. Her long blonde hair was swept on top of her head in a makeshift bun and her face was bare of makeup, and I swear she still looked like a freaking supermodel. My eyes took in her swan-like neck and painfully lean body in envy.

How was this fair?

How did women like Annabelle and Teagan go through pregnancy and childbirth and come out looking like rakes?

Meanwhile, the closest I'd ever been to having a baby was when Teagan sat on me at eight months pregnant, and yet I was the one that looked like I had produced half a dozen kids from my ever-widening, childbearing hips.

I hated these cursed curves I had inherited from my mother. Thick hips, even thicker ass, cinched waist and painfully big breasts.

The only luck I had was my father had given me height to carry my body shape. It still sucked though, being around all these skinny, perfectly proportioned women. They looked like Victoria Secret models while I looked like a fucking walking porn star. Not a good look for a career woman – which was why I usually dressed in hoodies and jeans or sweats. Loose clothing saved me from the countless ogling stares I received from gross men.

Thankfully, Jordan seemed to think the same as me. In fact, he didn't seem to take any notice of her appearance at all.

It was obvious from watching them these past few weeks that their relationship was purely platonic. Sure, Jordan and

Annabelle were close, but it was a best friend type of close. I wasn't sure why, but sometimes that bothered me even more. It made me think of Hunter and the friendship I used to share with him. It made me miss his friendship...

"How was dinner?" Annabelle chirped in that soft, feminine tone of hers as she removed a tray of freshly baked cookies from the oven before placing them on a cooling rack on the counter.

"Ryder down for the night?" Jordan asked as he walked over to where she was standing and snatched a piping hot cookie from the rack before juggling it from hand to hand, obviously waiting for it to cool down enough for him to eat.

Meanwhile, I walked over to the kitchen table and took a seat. I still felt uncomfortable around them. I knew Jordan was constantly trying to put me at ease, and Annabelle, when she wasn't annoying as hell, was actually pretty nice to me, but it was still hard for me.

"Yeah, he was shattered and went down at eight," she replied, snatching the cookie back from him and returning it to the rack. "There hasn't been a peep out of him since, poor little guy." She then smacked the flour off her hands before turning and giving me a megawatt smile. "Let me guess, he got the salmon at dinner?" Her question was directed at me and when I nodded, she threw her head back and laughed. "You're so predictable, Jord."

"I know what I like," he shot back with a rueful smile. "The way I see it, there's no point in me messing around with other dishes when I've already found my favorite."

For the next hour or so, I watched them go back and forth with each other. Everything about this situation was different to what I knew – to where I'd come from. I found myself unable to relate to the topics of conversations they spoke about or the banter they used. I felt completely left out. Worse, I felt like the third wheel in my own marriage. I envied the easygoing relationship she seemed to have with my husband. I craved to be

Chapter 24 | 163

able to banter back and forth with him like she did without any fear of upsetting him or making him close up.

HOURS LATER, WHEN WE WERE LYING IN BED, I FOUND MYSELF staring up at the ceiling with an unbridled amount of energy coursing through my veins. Hell, maybe my parents should have had me tested for ADHD when we were kids, too, and not just Cameron. But then again, I was normally a heavy sleeper. Nine times out of ten, I was out cold the minute my head hit the pillow. Not lately though. Not in months.

Every time I closed my eyes, I was haunted by the godawful image of Teagan's lifeless body that horrible afternoon last year. Of the broken look in Noah's eyes when he dropped to his knees in that hospital waiting room as the doctor told him the worst news a parent could hear. Even though months had passed, and they were both in a good place now, my heart still broke for them. And when my thoughts weren't taking up with those horrible memories, they were replaced with mental images of what I had done that night in the Ring of Fire.

Of what I had helped *conceal*.

I had always known there was a dark side to me. As a teenager, the threat of the Ring of Fire had spiked illicit and dangerous levels of excitement inside of me when it should have scared me silly. As an adult, I had been exposed to a dark and illegal underworld of crime and violence, not to mention dangerous and ruthless men who showed almost book-boyfriend levels of devotion to their women. The danger drew me like a moth to a flame, and even though I managed to hide it well, it was always there, this wildness just beneath the surface, itching to get out.

What I did with Hunter that night – what I had *wanted* to do – had somehow released that darkness in me. And now here I was, a mediocre writer, with a vanilla existence, craving a life-

164 | INEVITABLE

style that was so far out of the bubble it should have sent me running.

It didn't.

Without permission, my thoughts drifted to Hunter and those stupid text messages he had sent me last week. Those messages were the reason I had avoided going to South Peak Road all week. They were also the reason I found myself tossing and turning at night.

I never texted him back that day and I despised the part of me that wished I had.

I was well aware of the tattoos he bore on his body, the instinctive marks that represented a life of crime and prison-gang violence. I knew about the guns. The loss of life. The danger he represented to me. And it only seemed to make me want to be around him *more*.

God, I was so completely *fucked up*.

Forcing my mind blank, I turned onto my side and studied my husband's sleeping frame as he lay on his side with his back to me.

My heart ached at the sight of him laying here with me. My thoughts drifted to much safer thoughts now. Memories I welcomed with open arms.

The bike rides we had taken together as children. Fishing at the lake. Backyard camping adventures and the cushion filled forts in my parent's living room.

I remembered the child my husband used to be and smiled. Those cute reading glasses he was always pushing up on his nose. The beautiful drawings he used to create and how he'd always made me feel like I was the most important person in his world.

Life was so different for us back then.

We had both been so different back then.

I was much darker now. I was capable of dreadful, unspeakable things that should make me feel remorse, but *didn't*.

"Jordan?" I whispered into the darkness, desperate to hear

Chapter 24 | 165

his voice and have him comfort me. "Are you awake?" I knew he wasn't, but that didn't stop me from selfishly reaching out and trailing my fingers over the bare flesh of his shoulders.

The moment I touched him, I realized my mistake, but of course, it was too late to take it back. Jordan sprang up in the bed, jolting away from me.

Instantly, guilt swarmed me.

God, I was a shitty wife.

"Sorry," I whispered, biting down on my lip, when he finally focused his startled expression on me. "I didn't mean to..." I reached my hand out again to comfort him before thinking better of it and quickly snatching it back.

He caught a hold of my hand midair and gently tugged, settling it against his chest. The small amount of physical contact caused my heart to flutter wildly in my chest.

"What's wrong, Hope?" His voice was thick from sleep as he tightened his hold on my hand. "Why are you still awake?"

Because I'm a horrible person and I can't sleep with all the blood on my hands.

"I was just thinking," I whispered instead.

Jordan turned on his side to face me, still holding my hand to his chest. "Thinking about what?"

"About life," was all I was willing to say, all I dared to say. Jordan could never know the things I knew. No one could. No one but Hunter. I would have to take my secrets to the grave. "It's family night tomorrow at the house of Carter," I said in a lighter tone, steering the subject away from my criminal activity. "Will you come with me this time?" I could hear the hopeful, almost begging glint in my tone and I hated it. I didn't want to have to beg my husband to hang out with my friends. But we had been back together over a month now and Jordan had yet to face my friends or my family. Every time I asked him to join me, he always came up with excuses as to why he couldn't make it, and I wasn't holding out much hope for tonight's invitation.

166 | INEVITABLE

"I'm volunteering at the halfway house tomorrow night," he replied after several moments of paused silence, proving me right. "Mark had to take a raincheck. His wife's due date is sometime next week and he doesn't want to leave her home alone at night." Shrugging, he added, "I couldn't say no."

"Okay." I tried to hide my disappointment and failed bitterly. I wasn't a masked person. Usually, whatever I was feeling was etched on my face. And right now, I was feeling disappointed in my husband.

Mom and Dad had hosted family night at their place every Tuesday since I was a baby. We all showed up to eat, hang out, argue, and watch movies.

It was a Carter tradition and it hurt me deeply that Jordan kept avoiding it.

How were we ever going to progress in our marriage if he wouldn't even try and make an effort with my family?

Growing up, my dad had always made a huge deal out of the age old saying 'you made your bed, now lie in it.' Well, I had made my bed – my marital bed with Jordan. Now, all I had to do was lie in it.

"Are you mad?" he asked then, breaking me from my thoughts.

"Not mad," I whispered honestly.

Just lonely.

25

Hope

"Where are you going?" Annabelle asked as she stood on the porch, looking like a polished beauty queen, staring down at me.

"Where does it look like I'm going?" I snapped, pausing mid-stretch to turn and glare at her. "I'm going for a run." I thought it was pretty fucking obvious considering my attire and the fact that I was outside warming up.

"A run?" She threw her head back and laughed. "Should I get the camera?" she teased, eyes alight with mischief. "This has to be a monumental moment in your life, right? Jordan told me you hate exercising."

"Jordan has a big mouth," I muttered under my breath. "Skinny bitch."

Annabelle frowned. "What?"

I shrugged innocently. "What?"

"Well, have fun," she called out after a pause. "Call me if you get into trouble. I'll come pick you up."

"Will do," I shot back sweetly before turning my back on her

168 | INEVITABLE

and shoving my ear pods in my ears. I would rather die from sweat and dehydration than call that woman to *come get me.*

With the soundtrack from the movie *Suicide Squad* blasting through my earplugs, I embarked on my first ever agreed-to run.

However, the moment I was out of the driveway and halfway down the street, I realized this was a horrible idea. I was unfit and already out of breath, but I needed to move.

I couldn't stay in that house another second watching Annabelle and Jordan play house with Ryder. Best friends or not, it was fucking torture to watch and I needed a temporary escape.

"Call me if you get into trouble. I'll come pick you up."

Over my dead fucking body!

Shaking my wrists out, I ran as fast as my legs could carry me.

When the hell did my life become so complicated?

My cheeks burned, my lungs protested as the fire in my body heightened to unmeasurable levels. Gasping for air, I drained the contents of my water bottle only to whimper in dismay when it was gone and my throat still felt drier than the Sahara Desert.

Breathe, Hope, just breathe.

Concentrate on the road ahead of you.

No, fuck that, just concentrate on not face planting on the road and dying!

I continued to run until I was sure the house was out of sight, and then I made a beeline for the dumpster in a side alleyway. Collapsing against it, I closed my eyes and tried to drag precious, valuable air into my poor, tortured lungs.

Yeah, I was so *never* doing that again.

Why did people do this to themselves?

And for *fun?*

I could think of a million different hobbies and activities that felt better than the run of death!

Chapter 25 | **169**

Giving up on the idea of getting fit, I caught my breath and composed myself before heading back down the street in search of the nearest fast food restaurant.

———

I was sitting in the corner of my favorite fast food joint, digging into the best damn burger meal I'd ever tasted, when a familiar voice asked from behind me, "Hungry?", causing my heart to stop dead in my chest.

Momentarily stunned, and with half a dozen fries stuffed in my mouth, I debated my options. Stay and face him like a grownup or run like hell.

Knowing I would never run again for the rest of my days on earth, I swallowed down the huge hunk of fries in my mouth and turned in my seat to face him.

The moment my eyes landed on his face, a tsunami of butterflies attacked my insides. His blond hair was slicked back off his face, the light stubble on his jaw undeniably attractive, and those eyes?

Jesus.

"What are you doing here?" I asked, still a little breathless from my earlier escapades.

"I'm on pregnancy-craving duties," Hunter replied, waving a brown paper bag in front of himself. "Apparently, no other franchise makes chicken nuggets as crispy as *this one*." He nodded to the chair opposite me. "Mind if I sit?"

"Sure," I muttered, shoving my tray aside to make room for him.

"So," Hunter mused when he sat down. A wide smile broke out across his face as he looked me up and down. "Care to explain why you're dressed like you're trying out for the Olympic track team?"

"Funny," I growled. "I was out for a run."

"A *food* run?"

170 | INEVITABLE

"Oh, shut up," I shot back, tossing a fry at him. I took a sip from my coke, before saying, "I suck at exercise, but I excel at eating." Shrugging, I added, "Don't judge me."

"I never judge," he replied, his piercing blue eyes locked on mine.

I ate the rest of my meal in companionable silence, not bothered that Hunter was watching me stuff my face with food. He'd seen me do this on many occasions, so I wasn't about to start worrying about what he thought now.

Besides, I felt oddly comfortable around Hunter. His accepting, happy-go-lucky nature was one of his best personality traits and one of my favorite things about him. He had this knack for putting me at ease.

"Do you want to come home with me?" he asked then, startling me.

"Home?" I squeaked.

"Yeah," he confirmed, giving me one of those sexy as hell half-smiles. "Home."

"Um..." I shifted uneasily in my chair. "I probably shouldn't."

"Shut that part of your mind up and think for yourself, HC," he countered calmly, eyes locked on mine. "What do *you* want to do?"

"I want to go with you," I admitted, my words nothing more than a breathy admission.

It was either go with Hunter, or swallow my pride and call Annabelle to come pick me up.

There was no contest.

It was Hunter.

Every single time.

He stood up and reached for my hand. "Then, let's go."

And god forgive me, I placed my hand in his and went willingly.

26

————

Lucky

$\mathcal{I}$ had no idea what had happened to make Hope Carter *want* to exercise on her own accord, but I was guessing it was pretty fucking serious. She looked completely miserable when I saw her sitting in the corner of the restaurant earlier.

She was sitting in the passenger seat of my truck now, looking like a lost puppy, as I drove us back to The Hill. I was glad she had come with me without arguing because there was no way in hell I was leaving her alone back there. The vulnerability inside this woman was plain to see – if you were willing to take a closer look. She was sad, and confused and fucking lost in her own head. *I hated it.*

"Why are you called that?" she asked.

Those were the first five words she'd spoken in almost an hour and it threw me.

"Huh?"

"Lucky," she clarified, turning to look at me. "Where did it come from?"

172 | INEVITABLE

I smiled as I thought about it. "When I was in kindergarten, I ran out of the playground chasing a ball one of my friends had thrown for me. There was a big U-Haul coming down the street, driving right over me."

"Omigod!" Hope gasped. "Were you okay?

"Perfect," I replied, smiling at the memory. "Not a scratch."

She gaped at me. "*How*?"

"I guess even at the age of four, my survival skills were boss," I laughed to myself at the memory. "I dropped to the ground and laid flat on my back. The truck drove straight over me, missing me completely. When the kids in my class called the teacher, she christened me Lucky – after she chewed me out real fucking good in front of all my friends, of course." Shrugging, I added, "The name stuck."

"Well, that's a pretty fitting nickname for a child who escaped death," Hope mused, smiling now. "The only pet name I was ever given was Hopey-Bear." She scrunched her nose in obvious distaste. "According to Derek, I was a 'sumo baby' and reminded him of a teddy-bear."

"All babies are chubby," I consoled as I tried not to laugh at how adorable she looked. "It's a cute nickname for a baby."

"Oh yeah, it's so freaking cute," Hope scoffed. "Try being twenty-six and still having the majority of your family call you that." She shuddered and crossed her arms over her chest before adding, "I have enough issues without my family referring to me as a fucking teddy bear."

"Well, I think you're beautiful," I announced, deciding to add my two cents into the mix. "And the most un-teddy-bear-like looking female I have ever laid eyes on."

"Yeah, yeah." Hope rolled her eyes. "Even in my Olympic tryout clothing?"

"*Especially* in your Olympic tryout clothing."

Hope was quiet for the rest of the drive, but the brightness in her blue eyes, the slight rosy stain on her cheeks, and the way she perked up in her seat assured me that I'd said something right.

"You know you can talk to me, right?" I said when we pulled up outside Teagan and Noah's house. I killed the engine and turned to give Hope my full attention. "About anything." I studied her face, taking note of the loneliness in her blue eyes. She looked so damn sad. It fucking tore me up inside knowing that she was living like this... a half-fucking life. "I'm here for you." I knew my words sounded like a come-on, but I meant it in the most literal possible way. I *needed* Hope to know that she wasn't alone. "For whatever you need."

I waited for what felt like a fucking age for her to finally look me in the eyes, and when she did, my heart jackknifed in my chest. Christ, she was something.

"Hunter, I..." she began to say, but quickly closed her mouth. She shook her head then and reached for the bag of takeout I'd bought for Teagan. "We better go and feed the beast," she joked before unbuckling her seatbelt and slipping out of the truck.

I didn't move to follow her. Instead, I stayed in my truck and watched her disappear into the house. As I watched her walk away, all I could think was; *I need to bring this woman back to life.*

I could do it.

I could give her all the things he was incapable of giving.

27

Jordan

$\mathcal{I}$ had been expecting a visit from Hope's father every day since she had taken me back, so when I saw his Mercedes pull up at the bottom of my driveway at lunchtime on Thursday, I wasn't surprised. What did surprise me, though, was the brown-haired woman on my doorstep when I opened the front door.

"Hello, Jordan," Lee Carter said as she looked up at me with that warm, loving smile I remembered from my childhood. The moment my eyes landed on my wife's mother, a feeling of relief and comfort washed through me.

"Hello, Lee," I managed to acknowledge in return, though my throat felt suddenly tight.

"May I come inside?" she asked in a thick southern drawl she had never seemed to lose through the years. Wordlessly, I stepped aside and gestured for her to come inside.

She followed me through to the kitchen to where I had been making a sandwich. I had just finished work at the hospital and was heading shortly to meet one of my

Chapter 27 | 175

sponsors; Terry, a middle-aged man who had recently weaned off codeine. "I'm sorry about the mess," I muttered as I cleared a chair covered in Ryder's toys for her to sit on.

"That's all right," Lee replied gently. "I've raised six children," she added with a genuine smile. "Trust me when I tell you that I understand how scattered a child's items can get around a house."

"So, uh, you know about Ryder?" I asked when she didn't question who owned the baby stuff. Even though I had been living an hour away from Hope's family, I kept my distance over the years. I stayed away from them and, thankfully, they had returned the favor.

Lee had sent birthday and Christmas cards every year which had always made me feel uneasy. I didn't like knowing they had my address and I knew deep down that my father had something to do with them never coming here. It was the only thing I could remember ever being grateful to him for.

Somehow, I had been allowed to heal in peace and quiet without the Carter's meddling in my life. They weren't bad people, not in the least, but I could never bear to be around them.

Not after pushing Hope away.

"Derek filled me in on Annabelle and little Ryder." Lee paused for a long moment before adding, "And Hope filled me in on the rest."

Anger washed through me followed by a swell of panic.

Did Lee know?

Did Hope tell her?

"Okay." Feeling lightheaded, I walked around to the other side of the table and sank down. I needed to think about this. I needed to take a deep breath and figure out how I was going to handle this conversation. With my elbows resting on the table, I pressed my thumbs to my temples and asked, "Did she tell you everything?"

176 | INEVITABLE

Years of rehab, therapy, and counseling and I still struggled to talk about it.

The only one in this whole world I truly felt comfortable talking about my past to was Annabelle, and it had taken six years of me pushing her away and her pushing right back to gain my trust.

Annie was the only person on this planet who knew everything.

No one else.

Hope only knew the bare bones of my ordeal. She knew what I needed her to know so I could sleep at night and not feel like a liar.

She knew only what I thought she could handle.

What I *knew* she could handle.

I was protecting her this way.

It was better for her.

I would take the rest of it to my grave, and I knew Annie would, too.

She was my best friend.

My secrets were safe with her.

Lee nodded sadly and I watched in horror as a tear slid down her scarred cheek. "I came here to apologize to you." Her voice was full of emotion, her eyes glazed over with unshed tears. "I am so, so sorry, Jordan."

I sat, frozen in my seat, staring across the table at the woman that had been a second mother to me for most of my childhood.

Just like always, everything about Lee Carter screamed *safe* to me. Her voice, her smell, the way she moved, even her touch when she used to brush my hair back from my face and clean up my cuts when I fell over. It was all safe to me.

When I was little, she had always reminded me of Easter Sunday. That satisfied, lazy, and comforting feeling you got in the afternoon having eaten all your chocolate eggs and playing hunt? I got that when I was around her.

Chapter 27 | 177

I didn't need to ask her what she was apologizing to me for. I already knew.

"My own mother didn't realize," I finally said, body flushed as a screwed-up concoction of boiling heat and freezing coldness filled my body. "How could you?"

"I should have," she whispered, tone ridden with guilt and remorse. "I knew something wasn't...right." Her voice broke and she dropped her head in her hands. "Your eyes were always so full of sadness," she cried. "You always looked like you had the weight of the world on your shoulders." Sniffling, she added, "And now, I know you did."

"Does Kyle know?" I heard myself ask and the question shocked the hell out of me, but not as much as my next one, "Does he...understand? Why I left? Why I..." I couldn't finish. Why did it matter to me what he thought? *It shouldn't.*

"Yes," she sniffled. "He knows and he understands, sweetheart. He truly does."

I didn't respond to that.

He didn't understand.

None of them did.

"He doesn't know I'm here," Lee added, pulling a tissue from her sleeve. "No one does. We promised Hope we wouldn't say a word, but I couldn't keep that promise." She wiped her nose and tried to compose herself before saying, "I feel horrible for breaking my daughter's trust, and for letting her down, but it pales in comparison to how badly I've let you down, Jordan." Her voice wobbled and her tears spilled over. "Kyle and I should have protected you from that. From...*him*!"

"No," I corrected stiffly. "My father should have protected me from him." Straightening my spine, I looked her dead in the eye. "You and Kyle aren't my parents. Derek is... or at least he was supposed to be."

"Oh, sweetheart," Lee began to say. "Derek loves you so much–"

"Don't," I snapped, throwing my hand up to emphasize that

178 | INEVITABLE

I was not prepared to listen to this. "I won't hear it," I warned. "No excuses, Lee. Please." I was thrumming with barely constrained rage right now, and hearing Lee make excuses for Derek being a shitty father would push me over the edge. I was mad at Hope, too. For breaking my trust. For telling *my* story. *My life.*

I was proud of myself surviving what I had. I had battled addiction and abuse and toxic parents, and I was still standing on my own two feet.

Coming back here could have been my breaking point but I was still sober. Still working on myself and battling my demons. Sure, I spent most of every day in a state of anxiety and despair, but I was doing it. I was surviving. I wasn't expecting Lee Carter or anyone else to walk into my world and save me.

I was doing that for myself.

Sniffling, Lee nodded and said, "Please don't be angry with Hope."

Too late.

I was furious with my wife.

Her inability to keep secrets was the reason I was suffering through this...conversation.

"The only reason she told us was because she knew it was the only way her father would accept your relationship."

"And does he?" I bit out, staring right at her. "Does Kyle accept me now?"

Lee nodded quickly, but I didn't miss the way her voice faltered when she said, "Oh, yes."

She was a horrible liar.

Her husband would never accept me as good enough for his daughter, no matter how much shit I went through as a child or how badly I tried to prove him wrong. He never had and he never would. I didn't bother stating that aloud, though. There was no point. Not when we both knew it.

Chapter 27 | 179

"I called your mother last week," Lee added, shocking the hell out of me.

Every muscle in my body stiffened to the point of pain. "You did?" I hadn't been expecting her to say that.

"Yes," she replied, worrying on her bottom lip. "The line has been disconnected."

No surprises there, then, I thought to myself as a swell of protectiveness roared to life inside of my body. "I don't want you blaming my mother, Lee," I gritted out through clenched teeth. "It wasn't her fault."

I could tell from the expression on Lee's face that she didn't agree with me, but she didn't speak her thoughts on the matter. Instead she said, "I didn't do enough for you, Jordan, and that knowledge will haunt me until the day I die."

What did she want me to say?

There was nothing I could say to ease her conscience and besides, that wasn't my job. I didn't particularly feel like easing the conscience of any of the adults from my youth.

Even though Lee was my favorite, a darkness inside of me said *good*. A part of me wanted to know that they suffered.

Whether they knew or not, I had been tortured.

I had to live with the memories of what had happened to me.

I had to live with the scars and the pain.

The least they could do was the same.

Why should I give any of them an out?

Of course, I knew this wasn't the appropriate way to think and if any of my patients came to me with this, I would try and talk them down and make them see that their anger didn't constitute as a valid reason for making others suffer.

But I *wanted* them to suffer. Even if it was just with their consciences. Why should I be the only one who suffered nightmares and sleepless nights? I was tired of being alone in my misery.

28

Hope

*J*ordan was in a horrible mood when I got home from Teagan's place tonight. The minute I walked into the kitchen, he stopped what he was doing, stood up, and walked straight past me.

"Jordan?" I called after him as I watched his retreating frame. "Are you okay?"

No answer.

"Jordan?" I repeated. "What's the matter?"

"Back off, Hope!" he snarled before storming up the staircase, leaving me staring after him.

Back off?

I immediately turned to Annabelle, who was sitting at the table feeding Ryder and asked, "What did I do?"

"Don't worry," she assured me as she plopped a spoonful of baby food into her son's waiting mouth. "It's not just you. He's been like a bear with a sore thumb since I got home from work – barely said two words to me all evening."

Huh.

Chapter 28 | 181

Frowning, I slipped off my jacket and walked over to the table to join her. "Should I go after him?" I heard myself ask, then felt a flash of annoyance for having to ask another woman how to deal with my husband.

"You can, but there's really no point, Hope," Annabelle replied with a heavy sigh. "Jordan won't talk until he's ready." She shrugged helplessly before adding, "Trying to talk to him when he's like this will be as productive as banging your head on the wall. Best to leave him to work through whatever is bothering him. Once he does, he'll come around."

"Oh," I whispered, anxiety gnawing at my gut. "How long will that take?"

"Don't give up on him, Hope," was all she replied.

"I won't," I shot back.

Not ever.

29

Hope

$\mathcal{I}$ decided to bite the bullet and go and see Cameron today. I had been putting it off for a while now, but I was starting to miss the idiot. Neither Colton, Logan, or I had heard from him in weeks, and as much as I tried to deny it, I *was* worried about him. I knew he was still showing up at the hotel every day for work. Dad had said as much when I asked him, but he was avoiding us.

None of us had been particularly warm or welcoming towards his girlfriend the last time we met her – which also happened to be the first time we met her – and while my feelings towards the Grayson family were still the same, I'd had some time to calm down and put myself in my brother's shoes. Now that I was back with Jordan, I was beginning to see Cam's situation in a different light. My family didn't exactly approve of Jordan, either.

I knew Cam was serious about Tillie Grayson – he had to go against his entire family for her. And while Mom and Dad didn't know of her true heritage, we did.

Chapter 29 | 183

Taking me out of account – their singleton sister – Colton and Logan were his triplet brothers. They shared a deeper bond than any of us. Knowing they weren't talking to Cam, and that he was prepared to make that sacrifice to be with her, made Tillie important enough to my brother. And her significance in my brother's life meant that it was time I pulled my finger out of my butt and listened to him.

But when I pulled up outside Cam's house, I was hit with a sudden jolt of butterflies in my stomach. Cam's place was nice. He lived about a fifteen-minute drive from Mom and Dad's, based on the lower part of the mountains.

It wasn't as concealed or private as Teagan and Noah's place in South Peak Road, but he had the exclusivity of living in a gated community with electric gating and a big ass pool in the lower level of the building.

Aside from me, Cam was the first one to move out of home. Unlike Colt, who would live on our parent's couch if he was allowed, Cam needed his space. I guessed Low would have liked his space, too, but his illness meant he couldn't live alone when he was having a flair up so he and Colt shared a penthouse apartment down on ninth instead.

It didn't seem to matter where any of us lived.

We always ended up back in our parent's house at Thirteenth Street.

It was our home and always would be.

Thinking of my childhood home only caused the butterflies fluttering around in my stomach to grow.

What if Tillie was there and I *couldn't* be nice to the girl? Even though I knew I would have to in order to get anywhere with my brother, it went against *everything* inside of me to break bread with a Grayson.

But then I thought about a conversation I'd had with Noah last year...

"My mother caused a shit-ton of trouble for your family. She was singlehandedly responsible for bankrupting your dad and she helped

184 | INEVITABLE

David Henderson concoct a plan that resulted in your grandmother being raped and your mother set on fire." Pausing, Noah looked around at the siblings and said, "Tell me again that it's not the same thing." When no one responded, Noah sighed in defeat. "Look, all I'm saying is that girl you're all hating on? That girl is a person in her own right. That girl has a mind of her own. And that girl could have been me..."

How would we have felt if we had known about Noah's true heritage back then?

I liked to think that we wouldn't have been so judgmental and would have taken into account what an amazing human Noah Messina was, but I knew that was a lie.

Reluctantly, I had to acknowledge the very obvious fact that Tillie was a different person to Rachel. Whether I wanted to or not, I couldn't judge her by her aunt's actions. Even if her aunt was a crazy bitch that had murdered *my* aunt and shot my mother.

It was dry outside today and the sun was finally shining. The wet and dreary spring we'd been having had finally given way to the gloriousness that was early summer and I reveled in the prospect of not having to wrap up in a coat, hat, and scarf for at least five more months.

Climbing out of my truck, I walked up to the front entrance of the house and rang the doorbell, all the while battling down a huge churn of anxiety and, if I was being honest, trepidation.

It took a few minutes before anyone came to the door, but when it finally opened inwards, and my eyes landed on the rounded stomach attached to none other than Tillie Grayson, everything fell into place for me. It wasn't a big bump, but it was definitely a bump. The girl was rake thin and it didn't take a genius to figure out what was growing under her shirt.

My brother's ferocious protectiveness of the terrified looking woman in the doorway?

His sudden absence from family life?

Chapter 29 | 185

His ability to walk away from his siblings when given an ultimatum over her without a second glance?

"Holy shit." I shook my head as awareness dawned on me.

Cam arrived to stand at the door beside Tillie then. "Hope," he acknowledged as he placed a protective hand over her swollen belly. "Should I invite you in?" My brother's voice was heated and laced with unspoken warning. "Or ask you to leave?"

He was giving me a choice; accept this or walk away. But he was also letting me know that regardless of what choice I made, this was his woman and there was nothing he wasn't prepared to do to keep her safe. Including turning his back on the world for her.

Jesus Christ, he really was our father's son.

My gaze flicked from Tillie's bump to my brother's face and back again before finally landing on her face.

Shaking my head to clear my frazzled – holy shit, I'm going to be an auntie – thoughts, I pushed past every doubt and concern I had before nodding my head and choking out the words, "Invite me in." My gaze dropped to her baby bump once more and I felt a smile spread across my face. "Definitely invite me in."

30

Hope

$\mathcal{M}$y mind was still reeling when I let myself inside Jordan's house later that night.

Cameron was going to be a *father*.

My little brother was going to be a daddy.

And I was the first one in the family to know!

I still couldn't grasp my head around it. I sucked as a sister for not being there for him.

I didn't care about what happened in the past anymore. it was exactly that; in the past. The prospect of a niece or nephew overrode all our bullshit history. At sixteen weeks pregnant, Tillie was right around the same stage of pregnancy as Teagan and were both due in September. *Jesus Christ...*

Whether I liked her origins or not, Tillie Grayson was the mother of brother's unborn child. And Cam loved her deeply. That was enough for me. I doubted our brothers would feel the same way as I did, but that wasn't something I would lose sleep over. I'd given up a long time ago on trying to control my reckless and headstrong siblings.

Chapter 30 | 187

Jordan was sitting up in bed reading when I practically danced into our bedroom. I was grinning like an idiot, but I didn't care. The thought of becoming an aunt for the first time had me on cloud nine.

"You're home late," he acknowledged in a quiet tone, flicking a quick glance in my direction before turning his attention back to the paperback in his hands. Come to think of it, those three words were the first he'd spoken to me in days. Whatever had gotten into Jordan the other day, he was still working through it, and I was taking Annabelle's advice and waiting for him to come to me.

"I was visiting with Cam," I replied happily. "I had the best day." Flopping onto my side of the bed, I exhaled a contented sigh and turned my face to look at him. "I want a baby."

Okay, so I knew that sounded reckless and irresponsible and completely out of character for me, but I didn't care. I always knew that in order to procreate, my husband would have to have sex with me and I hadn't been having much luck in that department as of late, but I was an optimistic woman. Everyone was having babies around me and I wanted one too.

I watched, with my heart in my mouth, as Jordan set his book down on his nightstand and removed his reading glasses. "Where's all this coming from, Hope?" he finally asked, still holding his glasses in his hands.

"Cam and his girlfriend are having a baby," I replied excitedly. Rolling onto my stomach, I leaned up on my elbows and beamed at my husband. "Can you believe it, Jord? *Cameron* is going to be a father!"

Jordan's brows furrowed. "*What*?"

"I know, right?" I chuckled. "And I'm the only one who knows."

He continued to stare at me like I had seven heads. "This pregnancy is a secret?"

"I guess." I shrugged. "But she's due in September, so I really don't see how they're going to hide it."

188 | INEVITABLE

"So, you make a habit of breaking people's trust?"

I frowned at his question. "What?"

Jordan sighed heavily and shook his head. "Never mind." He rubbed his jaw before adding, "So, Cameron Carter is going to be a father. Well, hell."

"Yes," I squealed happily, choosing to ignore his previous remark. I was too damn happy tonight to be dragged down right now. "She's due in September." Rolling onto my back once again, I folded my arms behind my head and smiled up at the ceiling. "Same as Teagan's baby." I plastered on my sweetest smile and winked. "Lots of babies, Jord. Sounds pretty tempting, right?"

"We're not having a baby, Hope," Jordan stated flatly.

Anger fused with disappointment inside of me and I wanted to scream, *And what about what I want?* But I found an inner strength inside of me and said, "I didn't mean right this minute. But down the line. In the future. A baby would be nice."

My husband looked at me like I had two heads. "You want to be a mother?" His tone was incredulous, his expression skeptical.

Yes! "I might." I was moving into my late twenties and this was exactly the kind of thought that poked at a woman of my age. I swallowed deeply before adding, "In time."

Jordan stared hard at me for the longest moment before expelling a huge breath. "I don't want to be a father, Hope." I watched with a heavy heart as he pinched the bridge of his nose. "Not now, further down the line, or ever."

My mouth fell open and I gaped at him in horror. "Why not?"

"Why not?" he repeated, clearly frustrated. "Why would I ever want to be partially responsible for bringing a child into this fucked up world?"

"Because it would be a part of *us*," I urged, pulling myself up into a sitting position.

Chapter 30 | 189

"And have half of my genes?" Jordan spat. "No." He shook his head. "I'm sorry, but that's not something I want."

"But shouldn't we at least talk about this before making a final decision?" I argued, striving to keep my cool as I watched my baby dreams fly clean out the window. "This affects the both of us."

"What's to talk about?" he countered. "I'm not interested in bringing children into this world, Hope."

"But...but you're so good with Ryder," I tossed out, clutching at straws.

"Ryder is not my son," he was quick to point out.

"I want to have a family, Jordan," I whispered. "Not right away. But eventually... I want that for my life."

"I'm sorry." He shook his head and exhaled a heavy sigh. "But I won't breed anything that has the remote chance of becoming what I am. Or worse, my parents."

"So, that's it?" I demanded, not bothering to hide my annoyance now. "Your decision is final?"

"I'm sorry," was all he replied.

"You're sorry." My words were laced with sarcasm and hurt. "How long have you known you don't want children?"

"Always," Jordan said with a shrug. "Children have never been in my future. I've always made it clear that I don't want to be a father, Hope. I don't know why you're acting so surprised about this."

Surprised didn't come close to how fucking crushed I was feeling right now. "You said those things when we were kids," I shot back defensively, thinking back to the few times we had ever talked about kids. "No teenage boy wants to be a father." I threw my hands up in sheer exasperation. "I didn't actually think you were serious."

"Well, I was," he whispered. "I love you, Hope – more than life – but I'm not going to change my mind on this. I'm never going to want children." With that, he rolled onto his side then, giving me his back, and whispered, "Goodnight, Keychain."

I didn't respond.

I couldn't.

Not bothering to get undressed, I slipped under the covers and turned my back to my husband. My heart was breaking and I didn't trust the words that could come out of my mouth.

31

Jordan

$\mathcal{I}$ had been trying to forget about the conversation I had with Lee last week or at least put it to the back of my mind, but it was impossible to do.

Every time I looked at Hope, I was reminded of her betrayal. Trust didn't come easily for me. I had closed myself off many years ago for good reasons.

Knowing she had broken that trust I had put in her changed something inside of me. I felt myself retracting back into my shell and I was powerless to stop it. It was, after all, a survival instinct rooted deep inside me and had kept me alive all these years.

I had decided to put my talk with Lee to the back of my mind and not tell my wife that I knew about her betrayal, but then Hope had hit me with the baby card. And everything between us since that night had gone to hell.

I still felt like a piece of crap for shutting her down the way I had. For being so unwilling to talk to her about something she obviously wanted. But I drew a line on having a family. In fact, I'd drawn a line under that particular question many years ago.

I wasn't doing it.

I wasn't breeding any child that may bear a resemblance to either myself or my parents. I wouldn't wish this life on my worst enemy, and certainly not any kid of mine.

Things were strained between us now and I found myself avoiding being alone with her. We had barely spoken to each other all week. She was hurt and I was, too.

Like now, for example, Hope was in the living room with Teagan, and I couldn't put enough space between me and them. I loved Hope Carter more than I knew what to do with it, but I was struggling to cope with the changes having her back in my life brought me. I could hear her and Teagan laughing and joking in my living room and all I wanted to do was run. A normal man would go in there and converse with his wife's best friend, make an effort and try to blend into her world.

I just *couldn't* do it.

So instead, I drained the remnants from my coffee mug before placing it in the sink and leaving. Work was my one solace in life and I had every intention of throwing myself into it today.

32

Hope

"What's his problem?" Teagan asked when the front door slammed and Jordan's tall frame passed by the living room window as he walked towards his bike.

My shoulders slumped at the sight of him pulling out of the driveway. He hadn't even come to say goodbye before leaving. It felt like Jordan and I were living separate lives, not reconciling our marriage. "We had a disagreement last week," I stated, thinking back to that catastrophic night.

"I love you, Hope – more than life – but I'm not going to change my mind on this. I'm never going to want children..."

Everyone was having babies around me and I felt stuck.

It wasn't fair.

It wasn't that I wanted a child right this very minute, but I wanted to know that kids were a part of my future. According to Jordan, he was not budging on the matter and it hurt so badly I could hardly look at him lately.

You know that feeling when someone tells you that you

194 | INEVITABLE

can't have something, you become absolutely obsessed with it? That was how I felt right now. I had baby fever and it was made a bazillion times worse by the swarm of pregnant women in my life.

Teagan was pregnant with her second child, Cam and Tillie were on the cusp of parenthood, and an email from my old high-school friend, Ashlynn Brookes, last week had informed me that, not only were she and her husband expecting their third child, but her brother Layton's wife had recently given birth to a daughter.

Meanwhile, I was still trying to tempt my husband to share a bed with me.

I wanted a child of my own. I had never realized how badly I wanted to be a mother until the choice had been taken away from me.

"Hello?" Teagan called out, snapping her fingers in front of my face. "Earth to Hope."

"Sorry," I mumbled. Shaking my head to clear my depressing thoughts, I forced a smile and said, "I'm spacing out a lot lately."

Teagan looked around the small living room from her perch on the couch and grimaced, "Don't blame you, babe. I'd space out, too, if I had to live with Mr. Fun."

"Teagan," I warned.

"What?" she shot back, batting her big brown eyes innocently when we both knew she was anything but innocent. "I'm just saying, Jordan isn't exactly the life and soul of the party." She shrugged her shoulders and took another bite from the candy bar in her hand before adding, "He's more suited to a wake."

"Teagan!" I snapped, voice firmer now. "Don't talk about him like that."

"Don't take this the wrong way, but maybe you jumped into this without thinking it through first."

"Are you seriously lecturing me on impulsiveness, Teagan

Messina?" I demanded. She was one to talk about jumping into things.

Rolling her eyes, she waved a hand in the air and chimed, "Yeah, okay. Whatever." She polished off the last of her candy bar before pointing down at where I was sitting on the floor with my laptop open. "So, are you going to be finished soon?" Gleaming with devilishness, she added, "Because I came over here to play, not do homework.'

"Play?" I cocked a brow. "What are we, Teegs, nine?"

"Come on," she whined as she drummed her fingers against her bump. "I'm bored out of my mind here, Hope. Let's go do something fun."

"Where's Noah?" I asked. "Why don't you go and do something fun with him?"

"He's training." She grimaced at the word. "Which is completely pointless because I told him there's no way in hell I'm allowing him back in that cage again."

Noah had recently retired from the MFA because of an injury he received from a shooting last year, and though it was supposed to be a permanent thing, I had a feeling the world of mixed martial arts and street fighting hadn't seen the last of my uncle. He was only twenty-six years old. I didn't see him hanging up his gloves just yet. He had a score to settle with his nemesis, Anthony Cole.

Of course, I didn't dare breathe a word of my thoughts to Teagan. She suffered greatly every time her husband stepped into the cage. If she so much as got a sniff of Noah and the MFA, she would go batshit crazy.

"Well, I can't play until I get my quota of five thousand words done for the day," I told her, drawing myself back to the here and now.

"Are you close to 5k?" Teagan asked with a hopeful expression etched on her face.

I looked at the screen and bit back the urge to pick it up and throw it out the nearest window. "No," I wailed. "Not even close."

196 | INEVITABLE

I had a grand total of three hundred and thirty-eight words to show for seven hours of work. "I suck, Teegs," I moaned. "Like, so bad it's not even funny."

"You do not," she scoffed with a roll of her eyes. "You're just distracted. You've had a lot happen in a small space of time. Anyone in your shoes would be struggling to get their creative juices flowing."

"My creative juices are about as dry as the Sahara Desert right now," I shot back with a sigh.

"At least they match your vagina."

"How have I been friends so long with such a bitch?"

Teagan grinned. "Because you love me."

"Yeah, yeah." Turning my attention back to my laptop screen, I quickly read over what I had been working on before saying, "Maybe I should make her end up alone?" The story I was currently writing was of a taboo nature and was based on a beloved secondary female character, Harley Jacobson, from a continual series of books I had been writing. This was book nine in the 'Unexpected Series' and the first with Harley as the main heroine. In the story, Harley was torn between two brothers – Rhett and Peter.

"At least it would surprise my readers," I added lamely, knowing Teagan would never go for it. She was almost as invested in these characters as I was. She'd been by my side while I wrote the previous books. "This one doesn't have to be happy ever after."

"Are you for real?" Teagan demanded. "It's bold enough that you're touching the cheating trope, and now you're planning on *not* doing a HEA?" She pretended to shoot herself in the head with her finger before adding, "You're a brave woman, Hope Carter. Career suicidal, but brave."

"Not every story has to have a happy ending, Teagan," I snapped haughtily.

"You write romance," she countered unsympathetically. "Romance is *supposed* to have a HEA."

Chapter 32 | 197

I shrugged defensively. "No, it doesn't."

"Yes, it does," she urged. "The romance genre *always* has a happy ever after."

"Then the romance genre is a lying bitch," I shot back with a huff. "That's not real life."

"It's not supposed to be real life," she argued. "It's fiction. It's an escape for us readers. Why on earth would we invest months of our precious reading time into a series of books if they don't end up together?"

"Because it's *my* story."

"No, it's not," Teagan countered. "It's your readers' story– and mine!"

"Nope." I shook my head and pouted like a child. "It's mine."

"Hope, come on. Harley and Peter have to end up together in the end. He's loved her since childhood. You can't not have them as endgame!"

"Why?" I was being defensive. Why should Harley get her happy ever after when I didn't get one with my real-life version of Peter?

"Because!" Teagan flailed her arms widely. "Because, I said so, now do it. Give that girl her HEA, Hope Carter."

"I'm being totally honest here, you're making me feel a little finger-stabby here." Grinning, I added, "I think I'll kill them all off."

"Ugh," she squealed like I had physically slapped her. "Don't you dare!"

With my hands hovering over the keyboard of my laptop, I began to type furiously. "Uh-uh, they're all dying." I looked up at Teagan's horrified expression and bit back a laugh as I continued to type without mercy. "Still dying...uh...uh...and now they're dead. The end."

"Okay, now you're just being a brat."

"For that snide comment, you can forget an epilogue," I taunted. "Maybe I'll throw in a cliffhanger ending, too."

198 | INEVITABLE

"Ugh," Teagan groaned, flopping back on the couch. "You have too much power over my happiness."

That comment made me smile. I loved hearing how invested she was in my characters. It gave me hope that I wasn't doing such a terrible job.

"You know what? I'm just going to close this down," I announced after ten more minutes of blank staring. "The words are just not coming and I'm done forcing it," I added as I saved my file and closed the lid of my laptop.

"Praise Jesus," Teagan cheered sarcastically. "Actually – I think I know what will help you with your writer's block."

"Oh yeah?"

"Yeah," she confirmed with a grin. "Cookies."

I shook my head in resignation before getting to my feet. "You're a cow. It's completely unfair that you manage to stay as tiny as you are." I shot her a glare before adding, "You eat your weight in candy daily and still look like a supermodel, while I only have to look at the batter and it goes straight to my ass."

I opened the cupboard with the baking goods and took out what ingredients I needed before setting them on the counter-top. "I'll make a batch for you if you promise to slap me if you see me eating any."

"You're such a weirdo, Hope Carter," Teagan snorted as she followed me into the tiny kitchen and took a seat at the table. "I would *kill* to have curves like yours."

"*Sure you would*," I huffed out sarcastically.

Teagan stared across the narrow kitchen at me with a frown etched on her face. "You have really low self-esteem." Her voice was gentle and laced with concern. "I never noticed it before."

Now it was my turn to snort. "Well, if you had to grow up alongside the infamous *Carter triplets* and have Kyle Carter for a father, your self-esteem wouldn't exactly be off the charts, either." I measured some flour and sieved it into a baking bowl before adding, "You have no idea how many times I wished to be small and petite like my mother when I was growing up."

Chapter 32 | 199

When I was done with the flour, I cracked an egg into the bowl and grabbed some butter. "Alas, I inherited the giant gene – not exactly a feminine look now, is it?"

"Hope, you're like 5" 9'," Teagan shot back. "Come on, that hardly makes you a giant."

I didn't respond to that. Instead, I focused on preparing her cookies.

"You've got huge boobs and one hell of an ass," Teagan added enthusiastically. "And killer legs."

"Thanks, Teegs," I muttered, concentrating on the task at hand. "But you don't need to pump me up with compliments. I'm fine with me."

"I'm being serious here, Hope," she urged, brown eyes locked on mine. "You have no idea how incredibly wonderful you are, do you?"

"Oh, I'm simply amazing," I crooned, my tone once again dripping with sarcasm.

"You are," she countered seriously. "You're beautiful, smart, and independent." She shook her head and held her hands up, as if she was pointing out the most obvious thing in the world. "You have an honors degree from one of the best universities in Europe. And you've built this amazing career all by yourself – without anybody's help. You're financially secure because of said career. You own your own car, and home–"

"In Ireland," I replied, dismissively. "Which isn't much good to me here..."

"But you still *own* it," Teagan corrected. "Which is a hell of a lot more than most twenty-six year olds can say."

"I guess," I muttered, feeling embarrassed.

"It's true," Teagan urged. "You've accomplished so damn much all on your own merit, without a man standing behind you to break the fall. You're a fucking rock star, Hope Carter."

"Yeah," I whispered, not bothering to tell her that I'd give it all up in a heartbeat to have what she had with Noah.

"Is that it?" Teagan whispered after a long pause. "Is your

low self-esteem the reason why you've never pushed yourself out of your comfort box?"

My brows furrowed in confusion and I gave my friend my full attention. "I'm not following you."

"You've been my best friend since we were seventeen," she explained. "And never once in ten years have I seen you put yourself out there with any guy other than Jordan."

"Maybe that's because I've been with him since we met," I filled in, clearly only able to answer in sarcasm at this point.

"Or maybe it's because he's your *safety net*," she countered.

"What are you trying to say here, Teagan?"

"You jumped back in with him so fast," she explained, brows still set in a deep frown. "And I've been busting my balls for months trying to figure out why you took him back so quickly or how you even could... but it's all starting to make sense now." She looked up at me like it was the first time she had ever seen my face and said, "You lack confidence and have no faith in yourself. You don't see what the rest of the world sees. In fact, I'd bet good money that you have the self-esteem of a mouse."

"A mouse?"

"A mouse," she confirmed. "A nervous, unsure, scared little mouse that has already been trodden into the ground by that big asshole you call your husband."

"Okay!" I held my hands up, warning her off. "You need to change the subject."

"I'm right, aren't I?" she pressed. "You're with him because he doesn't push you. The things he can't give you are the very things you are terrified of experiencing!"

"Teagan, you need to stop –"

"You put all your eggs in Jordan Porter's basket because he's a safe bet," she continued to say, ignoring my plea. "Because he'll never push you for more. As long as you're with him, you'll never have to dig deep inside that head of yours. You'll never have to push your boundaries."

"Teagan!" I snapped. "Stop." Maybe I had thrown all my eggs

Chapter 32 | 201

in his basket because it was safer than facing reality. I never realized how poor my self-image was until I was forced to face it. Jordan had been with me since childhood and I never felt self-conscious around him. Other men, however, made me nervous. I felt inferior and ugly. It was hard growing up and listening to how handsome your father and brothers were. Deep down I had always felt like the ugly duckling of the family. "I'm not talking about this anymore," I warned her. "Seriously, Teegs. Don't push me on this."

"Fair enough," Teagan conceded. "But let me just say this one thing and I swear I'll drop it."

Sighing, I nodded for her to continue. There was no point in arguing with her anyway. She always won.

"Boundaries are there to be pushed, Hope," she urged. "Otherwise, what's the point in living?" Leaning forward, she rested her elbows on the table and stared meaningfully up at me. "The best part of being in love is pushing those terrifying limits and coming out the other side with a whole new perspective... or as a whole new person."

"Why are you telling me all of this?" I whispered.

"Because I want you to stop existing and start *living,* Hope," she shot back heatedly. "I see you and it makes me sad, because you don't get it. You don't see how unbelievably brilliant you truly are. I want you to realize what an amazingly talented and beautiful person you are, inside and out, and I want you to take your life by the balls! You only get one shot at this – one ride on the crazy train called life – and I want you to make it a ride you'll never forget."

33

Hope

I loved family nights at my parents' house. Every Tuesday night for as far back as I could remember, my parents, brothers, Uncle Derek, and I would all gather in my childhood home and gorge on takeout and junk food while fighting like alley cats over crappy board games before wrapping up the night by watching a movie none of us agreed on.

It was during one of these family nights in the third grade that I received my first set of stitches. Cam, who was a terrible loser, had lost terribly to me during a game of Monopoly and had thrown the ornamental boot at me in temper. It hit me full force above my top lip and I had ended up in the emergency room with a frantic looking Dad.

Twisted or not, I had fond memories of family night and it was one of the things I had missed most about home when I lived in Ireland.

Tonight's family night was no different to a hundred others. The only exception was the addition of a few extra family members in the form of Teagan, Noah, and Hunter and a noticeably absent Cameron. I tried to keep all thoughts of Cameron and Tillie from my mind when I was around my family. Cam still hadn't broached the whole impending fatherhood thing with the rest of them, and while I was dying to tell them, it wasn't my news to share. Besides, Mom and Dad were still clueless as to the origins of his girlfriend, and I sure as hell wasn't going to be the one to tell them. There was no way in hell I was taking that particular Grayson-laced bullet for my brother. Everyone would find out soon enough anyway.

It wasn't the first time Jordan had missed family night, either. In fact, since getting back together, he hadn't made a *single* family-night at my parent's house. He was either working or had some other excuse. It hurt me deeply, but I didn't dare dwell on it too much. If I did, I know I would drive myself crazy. Tonight he'd made the excuse of having to cover a shift for a work colleague of his. I invited him anyway, even though he was still freezing me out, and held onto the hope that one of these nights he would show up.

Aside from Jordan and Cam's absence, family night was unfolding the same way it did every week. Derek had complained about the nutritional value of Chinese takeout, stating that he could do so much better, all the while stuffing his face with a chicken satay. Full blown war had been declared in the kitchen between Teagan, Noah, Hunter, and Dad. Apparently, Teagan was as competitive at Monopoly as my father was and shit was going down. In the past thirty minutes alone, I'd heard my father declare that the banker – Hunter – was, and I quote, 'a corrupt bastard'.

And Colton, the genius, had just been disqualified from the board game 'Game of Life', that I had brought back from Ireland, for tossing two carloads of his 'stick-figure kids' over a bridge on the board.

"They're not fucking real," Colt argued defensively when Mom told him to get away from the coffee table in the living

204 | INEVITABLE

room. "Christ, everyone's taking this way too seriously. It's not like I threw my own real-life children away."

"You worry me sometimes, Colton," Mom muttered as she shooed him away. "They were your children."

"I don't have any fucking children!"

"Colton," Mom scolded. "Language."

"Mom, come on," Colt chuckled, unable to keep a straight face. "It's a game." He snickered before adding, "I couldn't afford four-fucking carloads of children, so I kept my favorites."

"You're a bad influence on your younger brothers," Mom replied, not giving an inch. She waved a hand in the direction of where my little brothers were sitting and shook her head in dismay. "Cash and Casey just watched you do that," she continued to say as she folded away the board and put all the pieces back in the box. "What do you think you're teaching them?"

Colton looked at our mother like she had three heads. "Am I in the goddamn twilight zone here?" he asked, scratching his dark hair in confusion. He looked over to where Logan and I were sitting and gaped. "Hope, help me out here, will you?"

I couldn't.

I was too busy laughing my ass off at the absolute ridiculousness that was my family.

"Yeah, thanks a fucking bunch, sis," Colt grumbled before stalking out of the room with Mom hot on his heels, lecturing about how all god's creatures should be honored and respected.

"They're plastic fucking stick men you shove into a plastic fucking car, Mom," I heard Colt say from the hallway. "I don't know what kind of respect you expect me to give them."

The outrage in my brother's voice caused me to double over from laughing.

"Some things never change," Logan said in an amused tone.

"Tell me about it." Curling my feet up on the couch, I rested my head on his shoulder and asked, "How are you feeling,

Low?" Aside from Cash and Casey, who were our parent's surprise babies, Logan was the baby of the family. The youngest of the triplets, he was a lot different to Cam and Colt, and in some ways, had always been my favorite. I knew that was a horrible thing to do, to have a favorite sibling, but there was something so incredibly fragile about Logan that seemed to give him that little bit more of my heart.

"I'm okay, Hope," he assured me. His tone was bright and gentle and hid the truth. He was in pain. He was always suffering. Logan had MS. He was only twenty-four and was one of the unfortunate people in the world who had suffered this disease since childhood on top of Juvenile Rheumatoid Arthritis and Raynaud's Disease. Stress made his MS worse and cold weather literally crippled him. But Logan was also one of these incredibly rare people that didn't accept an ounce of pity even when he was in physical agony and confined to a wheelchair. He kept his pain on the inside, never giving us a glimpse into how he was truly feeling. He was so strong, so heroically selfless, and whenever I was around him, I always felt in absolute awe. I knew I could never accept an illness like MS the way Logan did. My brother inspired me. Every day.

"So, where's Jordan?" Logan asked, drawing me from my thoughts.

"Couldn't make it tonight," I muttered. Pulling my cell out of my jeans pocket, I glanced at the screen. No missed calls or messages. "Again."

"It's probably hard as hell for him, Hope," Logan said knowingly. "Coming back here?" He inclined his head towards the doorway. "And with Derek." Sighing heavily, my brother added, "I wouldn't take in personally."

I was trying not to, I really was, but it wasn't easy. Not when it felt so fricking personal. "Being married is so much harder than I expected it to be, Low," I admitted before confiding in Logan everything I never would in my other brothers. Cash and Casey were only eight and while I loved

206 | INEVITABLE

Cam and Colt, they were wildly outspoken. If Cam knew how I was feeling, there was a very likely chance of him kicking Jordan's ass. Cam had a horrible temper that he barely managed to restrain most days. And Colton? Hell, Colt was as unpredictable as the weather. He would either crack jokes or lose his shit. It was hard to tell with him. He was a strange guy.

"I can't figure him out," I continued to confess. "He's like a closed book and I'm only catching a glance at the back cover. It's like I know the summary of his life, and I've read the blurb, but I'm locked out of the important details – the inner chapters are hidden from me. I want him to be happy so freaking badly, Low. I'm trying so hard."

The abuse Jordan had endured was common knowledge within our family now.

Behind my husband's back, I had sat my parents and Logan down and explained everything to them. I had no doubt Cameron and Colton had been filled in. I was sure of it. Their knowing was the only fallible reason I could think of as to why they had left me be and not showed up at Jordan's house.

My mother had always been Jordan's greatest champion and was on cloud nine when I announced our reconciliation. My father and brothers, not so much. I felt absolutely horrible for going behind Jordan's back, and had sworn them all to secrecy, but telling them was the only way I could make my father and brothers understand why I had chosen to give our marriage a second chance. They had to know that Jordan's reasons for leaving me were valid and that he hadn't intentionally broken my heart. If I hadn't told them, they would never have accepted us as a couple.

"Your husband was abused," Logan stated in a calm and steady tone. "He had a horrific childhood and even worse start at adulthood. It's perfectly normal for you to want to make him happy." He paused for a long moment before adding, "But it shouldn't be at the expense of your happiness, Hope."

Chapter 33 | 207

"Who says I'm not happy?" I countered, forcing a weak smile.

"I'm your brother, Hope Carter," Logan countered, leveling me with a steady, gray-eyed stare. "I've known you almost your whole life. I can tell when you're not happy."

"I'm not unhappy," I offered lamely. "I'm just...adjusting."

"To?"

"To where I fit in his world now."

"What do you mean?"

"I feel like I'm back seated when it comes to his job," I choked out. "I come second to his work and it drives me insane. I want him. Our marriage needs to be saved, but the minute someone else calls, he's gone saving the world while ours crumbles around us." I shook my head and bit down on my lip, repressing the urge to cry. "He's healing and he's drifting away from me." My voice was low and pained. "I'm not what he needs anymore. He's his own person now and I feel like I don't fit into this life he's created for himself."

"Adjusting to what?" Cash piped up from where he was sprawled out in front of the fireplace building Legos with Casey.

"Are you earwigging on my conversations, Cash Carter?" I asked, feigning outrage when I was secretly relieved to be saved from this conversation.

"Earwigging?" Cash looked at me in semi-horror. "What's that?"

"It means eavesdropping," Casey explained in his quiet tone of voice, never taking his eyes off the Angry Birds Lego castle he was building. "And yes. He was. He listens in on everyone's conversations."

"Shut up, Case," Cash growled as he folded his arms across his chest and pouted adorably. "You do it, too."

"Yeah, but I'm better at it than you," Casey tossed out, not batting an eyelid at Cash's anger. "I won't get caught."

"Okaaay," I chuckled, patting Logan on the knee before

208 | INEVITABLE

standing up. "You can deal with these two. I'm going to get a cup of coffee."

When I walked into the kitchen and locked eyes on the Teagan and Dad still battling it out at the kitchen table, I couldn't hide the smile that spread across my face.

Teagan was trying to talk her way out of paying for landing on one of my father's hotels and Dad, being a competitive jerk, had his hand held out, waiting for her money.

"You're ruthless," Teagan snarled as she begrudgingly coughed up the dough.

"Name of the game, Blondie," Dad shot back with a huge grin before dramatically fanning his face with her fake money. "Ah. Now what should I buy with this?"

Noah, who was sitting in the middle of them, looked on with a pained expression. "Don't torment her," he groaned. "Or we'll be here all fucking night."

"Oh, you can bet your ass we'll be here all night, Noah fucking Messina," Teagan growled, shaking the dice almost violently. "I'm not leaving this table until I bankrupt your brother."

"You can try," Dad scoffed, taunting her with his huge stack of pretend money. "You won't be the first."

"Should I call security?" I half-joked as I walked over to the coffee machine and set to work with making myself a cup of coffee.

"Nah," Derek, who was sitting at the table watching the game unfold, chucked. "Kyle would never hit a girl."

"True," I shot back. "But I wasn't talking about him."

"Hey – I'm not a violent person," Teagan called out.

Noah scoffed loudly, obviously calling bullshit on that statement, but one glare from his pregnant wife had him quickly sobering his features.

"Is there any more of that on offer?" Hunter's familiar voice came from behind me and I swung around to face him. The moment my eyes landed on his face, that horrible, perplexing

Chapter 33 | 209

torpedo of stomach fluttering that seemed to overtake me every time I laid eyes on Hunter occurred like clockwork. Realizing he was still looking at me with an expectant expression, I managed a, "Huh?"

"Coffee," Hunter explained with a smile. "Never mind," he added before stepping around me and pouring himself a mug.

"Sorry," I mumbled when I realized he had been asking for cup of coffee. "I'm not with it tonight."

"Nah, I'd say you're with it just fine, HC" he shot back with an easy smile.

I didn't know what to say to that so I just smiled in response. Everything felt murky now when it came to Hunter. Our conversations weren't as simple and carefree as they had been before and I found myself questioning and second guessing every word he said to me, hunting for hidden meanings I wasn't sure were even there.

"I'm stepping outside for a bit." Hunter tipped his finger against the cigarette balancing behind his ear and said, "Keep me company."

Hunter turned then and walked out of the kitchen, leaving me pondering if it was a question or a command. It didn't seem to matter either way though, because against my better judgment, I followed him outside to our front yard.

Wrapping my chunky knit cardigan around my middle, I leaned against the side of my truck and watched Hunter watch me as he lit a cigarette and pressed it to his lips. "So," he said in a tight voice before exhaling a big cloud of smoke. "What's new, HC?"

"Nothing much," I replied, wrapping my arms around myself to fight off the March coldness. "You know, you really need to kick this habit." I nodded meaningfully to the hand he was holding his cigarette in and sighed. "It's disgusting and it's going to kill you."

My warning didn't evoke the reaction I had wanted from Hunter, and when he threw his head back and blatantly

210 | INEVITABLE

laughed at me, irritation roared to life inside of me. "I'm being serious."

"I know you are," he agreed, still grinning like a lunatic, baring a set of pearly white teeth he didn't deserve to have. Not with the pack or so of cigarettes he smoked daily. "It's adorable."

"Stop it," I warned him. "It's not a joke." I was trying to be mad at him, but it was impossible when he continued to smile at me like that. Pushing off the truck, I walked straight over to him and playfully shoved his chest. I was smiling now. Full blown grinning back at him and it made me feel at a loss. "You're an asshole."

"True," he replied with a chuckle before taking another deep drag from his cigarette. "Speaking of assholes, how's your WIP coming along?"

"Awful," I admitted glumly, not surprised in the least that he had asked about my book. Writing was one of a long list of topics Hunter and I had discussed freely before everything had turned to shit between us. He had even helped me plot the outline for this one. Problem was, I'd lost all motivation for the story and the asshole hero we had conjured up together wasn't talking to me anymore. "I'm seriously considering pulling the damn book from the series, skipping over Harley's story and sending out an apology newsletter to my readers."

"Bad bout of middle-of-the-book jitters?" he asked with a sympathetic glint in his eyes.

Nodding, I exhaled a huge sigh. "I'm supposed to have it ready in time for the Aspen signing in June. I have the freaking thing listed in my preorders." I shuddered at the thought of showing up to the book signing without the book everyone wanted from me. "God, I suck."

"I can help you," he offered then. "Help you brainstorm. You know ideas always come to you after spending some time throwing around ideas."

Excitement followed by a huge surge of anxiety flittered

Chapter 33 | **211**

through me then. "I don't think that's a good idea, Hunter," I forced myself to look at him and say.

He met my gaze head on with a frown. "Why?"

"Because I'm *married*."

Again, he frowned. "You being married isn't a new thing here, Hope."

"No," I agreed gently. "But reconciling with my husband is new."

"I'm not a masochist, sweetheart. You made your choice. I might not like it, but I respect you enough to accept it." He paused and ran a hand through his messy blonde hair before adding, "But throw me a goddamn bone here, Hope. We spent every day for three months together and now..." his voice trailed off and I watched as a vein ticked in his neck. "Fuck it," he muttered with a humorless laugh. "You do what you gotta do."

"No," I argued. "Don't close off like that. Say what you want to say."

"Fine," he countered. "I'm saying I miss my friend."

"I miss my friend, too," I whispered, feeling a gut-wrenching pang of loneliness inside of me. A lonely, aching hole that he had once filled without even trying.

He stared hard at me for the longest moment before taking another drag from his cigarette. When he was done, he tossed the butt on the ground and exhaled a smoky breath. "Do you know what you are to me?"

"Hunter." I shook my head and held a shaky hand up to warn him off. "Please, don't..."

"You're not his wife or one of the famous Carter siblings from University Hill," he replied, not listening. "You're not a bestselling author or the only daughter of hotel tycoon Kyle fucking Carter. You're not Noah 'The Machine' Messina's niece, or a conquest." His blue eyes burned into mine when he said, "You're Hope. Just Hope. And you're my best friend."

His words curled around my heart like a warm blanket on

the coldest night in winter. I tried to muster up the courage to tell him that at one stage in time, he had been my best friend too, and I missed him desperately, but I *couldn't*.

So, I just stood there, in my parent's driveway, staring up at the man who I missed more than I dared acknowledge.

"Tell you what, you come find me when you're done lying to yourself " Hunter said, breaking the uncomfortable silence that had settled between us. "I'm only one call away." With that, he walked back into the house, leaving me standing in the darkness, staring after him.

34

Hope

𝒲hen I let myself into the house later that night, I was met with the sight of Jordan and Annabelle sitting on opposite sides of the couch. They were engrossed in a movie I hadn't seen before and looked so comfortable around each other that I wanted to cry.

She had her feet slung across his lap, and he was resting a cushion on top of them. He didn't shy away from *her* touch.

They looked so natural and at ease together. I debated just sneaking upstairs to bed, not wanting to interrupt the moment, but then I grew a pair of lady balls and flicked on the light.

"Hope," Jordan acknowledged fondly, craning his neck to look at me. "You've got to come watch this."

"It's brilliant," Annabelle chimed in, glancing up at me from her perch on the couch. "Leo won his first Oscar for his role in this movie."

"I don't want to watch the fucking movie," I hissed, not even trying to mask my anger. "I thought you had to work tonight?"

My words hit Jordan hard, and he had the decency to flinch,

214 | INEVITABLE

but he didn't lie. He simply said, "What do you want me to say, Hope?"

What did I want him to say?

"How about you start with saying sorry for lying to me!" Ripping my coat off, I tossed it on the back of the armchair closest to me before leveling my gaze on my husband. I surprised myself with how cold my tone was when I said, "This is what was so important that you couldn't stop by family night tonight?" I looked at Annabelle and then the television screen before returning my gaze to him. "A fucking movie was more important to you."

Sighing wearily, Jordan rubbed a hand down his face before getting to his feet. "They're not my family, Hope," he finally replied, standing and facing me now with only the couch between us.

"Well, they are *mine,* Jordan!" I screamed, not caring that Annabelle was in the room and watching me lose my shit. "*My family.* And you won't even try and make an effort with them."

"Why would I?" he shot back, tone equally angry. "With the exception of Lee, none of your family even likes me. Your brothers barely tolerate me, and Kyle? Your father can't stand the sight of me, Hope."

"Jay," Annabelle piped up in a warning tone. "Calm down. *Now.*"

"Stay out of this," I snapped at her before turning my attention back to my husband. "Maybe they would like you if you made an effort once in a while." I didn't bother denying the fact that my family wasn't fond of my husband. "But you won't even try."

"No, I won't," he agreed, voice rising. "Because I refuse to put myself in a situation that jeopardizes my sobriety."

"Jordan!" Annabelle hissed, standing up now. "You need to calm down. Right now."

Meanwhile, I flinched, feeling like he had physically slapped me with his words. "And you're saying my family does that?" Clearing the lump that was trying to form in my throat, I rasped, "My family jeopardize your sobriety?"

"There's no point in trying to explain any of this to you," he growled impatiently. "Unless you've been in my shoes, you'll never understand."

Now *that* really was a blow.

"I can't believe you just said that to me," I choked out.

Of all the things in the world he could say, he used the most hurtful one.

No, I had no clue how he felt or was feeling. But I was here. I was standing by him and I was desperately trying to make our marriage work.

The guilt in his eyes as he looked at me only maddened me. He had no right to throw that kind of a comment in my face. I was thankful I didn't know how he felt. I didn't want to be in a horrible, life-altering club he belonged to. And I wouldn't change places with him for the world, but dammit, I was his wife and I was putting one hundred and fifty percent into making this marriage work. I thought it was only fair that he did the same.

My family was important to me. I loved them to death. We might not be perfect, but they were my blood and I cherished them. I understood he didn't feel the same about his, but he could make an effort for me. Nothing seemed to be about me. I felt like a fucking servant to his feelings and I hated it. I was done feeling this way.

"It's not all about you, Jordan," I heard myself hiss, regretting the words as they poured out of my mouth, but unable to stop them. The dam that held all of my truths and feelings inside had well and truly burst open. "You're not the only person suffering here!" My body was shaking, my heart hammering against my ribcage. "And you're not the only one who gets to make the decisions in this relationship!"

"Me?" he shot back, clearly outraged. "I'm busting my ass to make you happy, Hope!"

216 | INEVITABLE

"By blocking me out?" I threw my head back and laughed harshly. "And making decisions about our future without consulting me? Oh yeah, because that makes me so fucking happy, Jordan!"

Jordan's face turned purple. "I'm here, aren't I?" he snarled, running a hand through his curls. "Dammit, Hope."

"It's not *enough*!" I screamed at the top of my lungs.

"Okay, Hope, I think you need to take a breather," Annabelle chimed in, tone worried. Walking over to where I was standing, she placed a hand on my shoulder and said, "Why don't you just go upstairs and take a minute to calm down. I'll talk to Jordan."

Insulted and beyond aggravated, I roughly shoved her arm off my shoulder and turned my anger on her.

"Why don't *you* go upstairs?" I bit out, glaring. "Or better yet, why don't you just go, period!" The hurt in her blue eyes was evident as she looked at me, but I was beyond caring at this stage. "You don't belong here," I added. "You're not even family, so just go away!"

"She *is* my family," Jordan snarled, sounding more furious than I had ever heard him. "Her and Ryder. And she is *always* welcome in my home. They were my family when everyone in *my* life turned their backs on me."

"I didn't!" I screamed right back at him. My eyes were burning with tears that threatened to spill over. I wouldn't dare allow it. Not now. I was too angry to cry. "I never once turned my back on you." Furious, I lost every ounce of my frazzled self-control and let every bit of my hurt and pain drip from my tongue like poison. "You walked away from me! You. Not me, Jordan. Never me. You turned your back on us. On all of the people who care about you. You made the decision that we weren't enough to help you through it and you walked away. I'm not blaming you for doing what you did. I get that was what you needed to happen in order to survive what you have, but don't you dare stand here and try and put the blame on me."

Chapter 34 | 217

The sound of Ryder's startled cries brought me back down to earth with a bang. Immediately, guilt filled my body, threatening to swallow me up whole.

Ashamed of myself for raising my voice and waking the baby, I mumbled a quick apology to Annabelle before I turned on my heels and rushed upstairs to our bedroom.

Closing the bedroom door behind me, I flung myself down on the bed and remained completely still, not moving a muscle as I desperately tried to figure out where everything had gone so horribly wrong. I felt like running home to my childhood room and burying myself under my comforter. Childhood was so much easier than this bullshit, bill-paying, tax robbing, descending path to mortality.

Everything was better when I was little. I had my parents to do the worrying for me. All I had to do was be a kid.

Now?

Now everything was screwed up and cloudy and I couldn't see a straight line through the mess I had managed to get myself sucked into.

35

Jordan

"*A*re you just going to stand here?" Annabelle demanded when she stalked back into the living room with a startled looking Ryder in her arms. "Or are you going to go up those stairs and make things right with your wife!"

Sighing wearily, I sank down on the couch and dropped my head in my hands. Everything was so messed up. I couldn't think straight. Anxiety and adrenalin were coursing through my veins and I was craving something fierce.

"Jordan," Annie snapped when I didn't answer her. "You can't leave it like this. You have to *talk* to her."

"I don't have anything left in me," I confessed. "I'm so fucking tired, Annie."

"You *chose* this," she replied, this time in a gentler tone. "You said you were ready for this."

"Yeah?" I hissed, running my hands through my hair in frustration. "Well maybe I was wrong."

"I know you don't mean that," she whispered, sinking down

Chapter 35 | 219

on the couch beside me. "That woman upstairs has been your whole focus these past six years. And now you have her back, you're *lying* to her? Avoiding her?" She shook her head. "I don't understand."

"I can't go there," I bit out. "I can't be around those people."

"They're *her* family, Jord," Annabelle stated calmly. "It's kind of a package deal when you marry into a tight knit family like the Carters'."

"I can't do it," I choked out. "I am so fucking close to losing my goddamn mind here, Annie. I am hanging onto my sobriety by the skin of my teeth when all I want to do is find the nearest bar and drink myself into oblivion."

"It won't help," she whispered. "And it won't change your past."

She was right.

Of course, she was fucking right.

It still didn't change the way I felt though.

"Tell you what," she said then. "The next time they invite you over there, I'll come, too."

"What, and be my bodyguard?" I shot back, smirking now.

"If that's what you need," she countered with a smile. "

"Thanks," I sighed. "But I can't ask you to hold my hand every time I'm put in an uncomfortable situation."

"You're my best friend," she replied, blue eyes heated and locked on my face. "There's nothing I wouldn't do for you, and if I have to stand and face Kyle Carter and every one of his duplicates for you, then I will.' She shifted Ryder into her other arm and reached her small fist towards me. "Teammates?"

"Always," I whispered, fist thumping her back.

36

Hope

I could hear hushed voices coming from downstairs so I grabbed a pillow and held it over my head. I didn't want to hear what they were saying to each other. I wanted no part of it.

Pulling out my phone, I debated calling Teagan, but then thought better of it. She already wasn't keen on Jordan. If I told her about this fight, she'd hold it against him forever. I couldn't talk to my family either because as mad as I was at Jordan, I still wanted to protect him. I didn't want anyone to think badly of him.

Without giving much thought to what I was doing – or considering the repercussions of my actions – I opened my messages and tapped out a quick text before pressing send.

Six words was all the message contained. But I knew deep down those six words would change everything. The truth was, there was only one person in the world I wanted to talk to right now.

Chapter 36 | 221

> Hope: I really need my friend tonight.

Seconds later, my phone pinged in my hand.

Hunter: Holy shit, that was fast. Didn't you just
leave here?

His response made me smile.

> Hope: Yep. Are you still at 13th street?

Hunter: Hell yeah. I've got a bet going with
Derek to see how long it takes Teegs to crack
up and smash the board over Kyle's head.

> Hope: Oh, yeah? And how's that going for you?

Hunter: Derek has ten bucks on it happening in
the next fifteen minutes, but I'm holding out a
little longer. I know our girl's got stamina when
she's winning. I'm betting on 30 minutes.

> Hope: Lol.

Hunter: What's wrong, HC?

What was wrong? My entire life...

> Hope: Why would anything be wrong?

Hunter: I'm giving you a "don't bullshit me"
look right now. Talk, Carter.

I sighed heavily. Why did he always seem to know when something was wrong with me? And why did I always want to tell him exactly what?

> Hope: I just need a friend tonight, that's all.

Hunter: Then feel free to use me for as long as
you like. Your whole life, if you want...

222 | INEVITABLE

My pulse raced erratically as I read then reread his words before responding.

> Hope: Hunter...

Hunter: I'll be good.

> Hope: Thank you.

I paused and then quickly tapped out another message.

> Hope: I'm lonely, Hunter.

Hunter: Want me to come and break you out of the tower of doom, Cinderella?

His response made me smile, and knowing he was on the other end of my phone settled the lonely feeling inside of me.

> Hope: Cinderella? Try Rapunzel, douchebag.

Hunter: Wanna hear something that's both depressing and wildly amusing?

> Hope: Always.

Hunter: I lost the bet.

Seconds later, a picture message came through. I clicked on the link and burst out laughing when the image of Teagan smashing the monopoly board over my father's head filled the screen.

> Hope: Omigod. Is he bleeding?

When he didn't respond straight away, my heart sank. It sank further as another minute passed by. But just when I was about to give up on him and toss my phone on my nightstand, it rang loudly.

Chapter 36 | **223**

Hunter's name appeared on the screen and I pushed accept and pressed it to my ear. "Hello?" I spluttered, desperately trying to calm my racing heart.

"Sorry about that," he chuckled. "The she-devil caught me laughing at her and rushed me with a chopstick."

"Oh my god." I laughed loudly at the thought of Teagan chasing Hunter around my parent's kitchen before covering my mouth to muffle the sound. "Did she get you?"

"Do you really need to ask that?" Hunter replied, and I could tell he was smiling from his tone. "She's like a miniature, ninja assassin – of course she fucking got me."

"Where?" I laughed.

"My ass," he confirmed. "Thankfully, just the left cheek. She promised to ram it up, and I quote, *the highest part of my hole*." He put on an Irish accent to say that last bit and had me in near convulsions.

"Oh my god," I laughed, biting down on my knuckles to control myself. "Her hormones are driving her crazy"

"Don't blame pregnancy on this," he countered, laughing. "That girl is batshit crazy on a good day."

That was true. Teagan Messina had a temper that rivaled an aggressive animal. She might look like a cute, little Maltese puppy, but she had the temperament of a rabid Pitbull.

I loved her for it.

"I've been thinking about what you said," I whispered, biting down on my bottom lip. "And you're right. I want my friend back."

"Which one?"

"You, dummy," I shot back, smiling. "I want us to have what we used to have," I added. "You know? Before..."

"I know what you mean," Hunter replied, tone serious now. "And I want that, too. I miss being with you."

"But it's different now," I interrupted, needing to put this out there before I lost my nerve. "And I need you to promise me something first."

224 | INEVITABLE

"List your demands, HC," he chuckled.

I clenched my eyes shut and blurted out the words, "Promise you won't fall in love with me," before cringing in embarrassment.

Hunter was silent for a long time before finally saying, "You seem very sure of yourself, HC."

"I'm serious," I whispered. "You can't ever fall in love with me, Hunter. It will ruin everything, and I don't want to lose you again." *I need you in my life.* "If we want to be friends, this has to be purely platonic."

"Duly noted, HC," he replied. "But you'll have to promise the same thing."

I frowned. "Come again?"

"You can't fall in love with me, either," he said with a teasing lilt to his tone. "I know it's going to be a damn near impossible task since I'm such an awesome fucking person with irresistible characteristic traits, but you've got to try your best to resist the urge."

"You're so dumb," I laughed. "Okay. I'll *try* if you will."

"So, *friend*," he mused. "Since we're friends again, do you want to talk about whatever it is that happened that has you all riled up?"

"You called me," I said.

"You needed me," he shot back calmly.

I was stumped.

I *did* need him.

To talk to, at least.

"Then talk," I heard myself say. "Please."

And he did.

He talked and talked until my eyelids fluttered closed and sleep caught up with me.

37

Hope

"Hey, this is Jordan Porter. I can't get to my phone right now. Leave your name and number and I'll get back to you when I can...*beep*."

"Hey, it's me," I whispered into the phone. "I was just wondering what time you were coming home tonight?" Tucking my feet beneath me, I leaned back against the couch and closed my eyes. "We're going to have to talk about this because– *beep* – I'm lonely," I whispered before ending the call and tossing my phone down beside me.

Two weeks had passed since our fight, and nothing had been resolved.

Jordan was still freezing me out, still keeping me at arm's length, and I still felt like I was slowly dying inside. I wasn't sure how much more I could take.

Every day that passed caused the hope inside of my heart that we could somehow persevere and get past this to flicker and fade.

226 | INEVITABLE

The doorbell sounded then, loud and obnoxious, cutting through my aching thoughts.

I didn't have to get up to know who was at our door.

Another freaking one of his sober prodigies no doubt.

This house seemed to have a revolving door for broken humans. Jordan was a substance abuse and a victims of sexual abuse counselor, and apparently a pretty damn good one. He *healed* people. He made them feel better. But he couldn't heal the rift that was growing in our marriage. He couldn't heal *himself.* See, he was good and pure and brilliant. I was a professional liar, paid to invent fiction, while my husband went out in the world and make it a better place. I felt both inferior and insecure around him now. His goodness shone bright and brought to light the ugliness inside of me.

Maybe I had been naïve in thinking Jordan and I were beginning to make progress before, but that naivety was certainly gone now.

The progress we had been making was fading fast, disappearing at a rapid rate every time one of my many calls went unanswered, and every night I went to bed alone.

I was trying to do what Annabelle said, and give him space to work whatever problem he was having out on his own, but it was hard when I felt more and more isolated.

I didn't belong in this house, I never really had, and now with this ridge between us, I felt even more alien here.

The doorbell rang again and I bit back the urge to scream, "*Fuck off*" at the top of my lungs. Knowing that whoever was on the other side of the door would know there was someone in here was exactly why my pajama clad ass remained on the couch with my mouth firmly shut.

The ringing doorbell was replaced with window banging and I groaned into my hands.

Jesus...

"You do realize I can see you in there," a familiar voice

Chapter 37 | 227

called out from the nearby window, causing me to balk and my heart to jackknife in my chest.

My gaze went straight to the bay window, and sure enough, there he was, standing in the driveway with a cigarette dangling from his lips.

"Hunter?" Springing to my feet, I walked over to the window and gaped out at him. "What are you doing here?"

"I've had an epiphany," he called back, eyes locked on me through the glass.

"An epiphany?" I shook my head in confusion. "About what?"

"About your book," he replied, smirking.

"My book?" I squeaked.

"Yeah, I know where you're falling flat," he shot back. "So, go and get your laptop, planner, and all those stickers and scented markers you need when you're writing and let's go."

"Go?" I gaped at him. "Go where?"

"Home," Hunter told me, blue eyes piercing through the glass between us as they bore into mine.

"Home," I repeated, whispering the word almost longingly. I cast a glance around the living room before turning my attention back to the man outside my window.

Peace settled inside of me then. A thick cloak of comfort washed over me as I stared back at him. There was no judgment in those blue eyes, no anger, resentment, or pain. All I could see when I looked into his eyes was... unconditional acceptance.

I *wanted* the friendship this man was offering to me.

I *wanted* to be that carefree version of myself when I was around him.

Texting him had changed something inside of me. It was like I had made a monumental decision about my future and I had decided that I wanted him *in* it.

"Okay," I whispered, nodding. "I'm coming."

38

Lucky

"When did you do all this?" Hope gasped as she knelt over the coffee table in South Peak Road and gazed down at the countless pages and sticky-notes cluttering the table.

"Last night," I replied, sinking down on the couch behind her.

"Hunter..." she whispered as she read each note filled page with a look of pure awe etched on her face. "This must have taken you days."

It had.

I'd spent every night for the entire fucking week sitting at the kitchen table scribbling down ideas and notions for her WIP.

"It's no big deal," I assured her. I wasn't getting any sleep anyways. Not when every time I closed my eyes, I thought of her all alone in that fucking house. She was worried about so damn much, and most of it I couldn't help her with. But the book? The book I could try and help. "It's probably all bullshit,"

Chapter 38 | 229

I added, thinking about the crazy fucking ideas I'd had for her characters and the overly dramatic plot twists I'd invented in my sleep-deprived state. "But I thought you could use some of the ideas."

"Use some of them?" Hope whistled. "You're a fucking genius." She spun around to face me then. "I'm so impressed."

The excitement in her voice made me laugh. "I wouldn't go that far, but thanks, HC."

"You have a wonderful flair for creative writing," she urged, shaking one of the sheets of paper with my scrawled hand-writing on it.

No, I have a flair for you. "Do you think you can work with any of it?" I said instead, knowing full well that if I laid my cards on the table now, she'd run. Hope had just decided to give us a shot at being friends. That was huge for her. I had to be patient and not fuck this up for myself, because in all honesty, if being her friend was all I could have, then I'd gladly take it.

"Yes!" she gushed excitedly as she dragged her laptop out of its protective sleeve and flipped it open on the table. "I actually *want* to write."

39

Hope

I had no idea how he did it, but Hunter's notes on my WIP had shattered the wall around my mind. My inspiration burst to life inside of me and I managed to knock out thirteen thousand words by dinner time.

I couldn't believe it.

I hadn't managed to write that many words in three whole months.

Feeling proud, I saved the document and quickly emailed myself a copy before heading into the kitchen for brain fuel.

The moment I walked into the kitchen and my eyes landed on Hunter, a roar of laughter tore from my throat. "Oh my god," I spluttered as I laughed and pointed at him. "You look ridiculous." The sight of him clad in the novelty apron Colton had bought Noah last Christmas, the one with the huge penis hanging off, caused me to double up.

"I can whip out my own dick if you want," he shot back, not caring that he looked like a complete tool. "This one doesn't do the poor guy any justice."

Chapter 39 | 231

"The poor guy?" I couldn't stop the snort that escaped me. "You're so weird."

"I'll take that," Hunter countered with a smile. "Now go and sit. I've made..." his voice trailed off as he looked down at the casserole dish in his hands and frowned. "Something."

"Something?"

"It was supposed to be chili con carne," he replied, still frowning at the dish. "It *looked* like chili con carne when I put it in the oven."

"And now?" I laughed.

"Now?" He shook his head and grimaced. "I can't tell."

"Oh god," I chuckled, taking a seat at the table. "Will it kill me?"

"I hope not," he shot back. He walked over to the table and placed the incinerated looking dish of slop on the table and handed me a fork. "Maybe I should taste it first to be sure." He stabbed his fork into the dish and scooped up a tiny piece.

"Together?" I offered, using my own fork to pick out a slightly less burnt piece.

"You sure?" he asked, looking uncertain.

"Yeah. Let's just do it on three," I replied. "One...Two... Three –"

We both shoved our forks into our mouths and stared at each other.

"I can't do it," Hunter forced out, heaving as he chewed viciously, obviously trying to force it down his throat.

"Ugh," I gagged when the sour taste hit my senses followed by the burning heat of spice and peppers enveloping my tongue. "Oh god..."

"Jesus fucking Christ." Shoving his chair back, Hunter rushed over to the sink and shoved his face under the faucet. "Don't swallow it," he called out, still heaving as he held his tongue directly beneath the running water. "Don't fucking do it to yourself."

232 | INEVITABLE

"Don't worry," I promised as I reached for the dish and spat the food back out. "I won't."

"Fuck," Hunter muttered when he finally turned off the faucet. He shuddered and glared at the dish containing the substance that had almost killed us both. "Please get it out of my sight," he groaned, rubbing his stomach. "I can't fucking look at it."

Laughing at his reaction, I stood up, grabbed the dish and walked over to the trash can before scraping the poison into it.

"Just toss the whole lot," he ordered grimly.

"What – the dish as well?"

"I'll replace it." He shuddered once more before adding, "I don't trust soap to remove the god-fucking-awfulness of *that*."

I threw my head back and laughed. "I gather cooking isn't one of your specialties then?"

"I can definitely do more productive things with my hands," Hunter agreed, giving me one of those half-smiles. "Like use them to order pizza?"

"Pizza sounds great." I smiled brightly at his suggestion. "See, I knew you were a genius!"

40

Jordan

*E*xhaustion had crept inside my bones, and by the time I got home from work tonight, all I wanted to do was face plant on the mattress and pass out, but the laptop and scores of sheets and papers scattered all over our bed made that impossible.

"Sorry about the mess," Hope announced when she noticed me standing in the doorway of our room. Her hair was on top of her head, held up in a messy bun with three pencils. "I'm burning through this chapter," she explained as she typed furiously. "Give me an hour and I'll move my stuff."

"Don't worry about it," I croaked out, rubbing a hand over my jaw. *I was so fucking tired.* "I'll take the couch tonight."

Hope stopped what she was doing and turned to look at me.

"You don't have to do that, Jordan," she said, sounding hurt. "This is your house. I'll move my stuff."

"No, it's fine." I waved a hand out dismissively. "I'll grab a blanket from the cupboard and crash downstairs."

I left the room then, before she had a chance to say anymore, because I was too hurt and too goddamn tired to fight with her.

My trust was gone.

And every time I looked at her now, all I could see was a stranger.

41

Hope

"Come on," Teagan ordered. "Drop your ass, Hope!"

"I'm trying, slave-driver," I choked out. We were outside on the front lawn attempting to do some light and gentle exercise. Teagan was in her element. She was a fitness fanatic – always had been. From the very first day I met her, she had been obsessed with running and other satanic rituals like Pilates and – shudder – the dreaded treadmill.

Meanwhile, I was regretting ever entering the house of pain this morning. I had hoped coming over here would be better than staying at home and getting the silent treatment from Jordan, but now I wasn't so sure because I swear to all things holy, I had never felt more stretched apart and broken in my life.

"Come on now," she called out cheerily. "Drop that Kim-K ass to the grass."

"Shut up, Teagan!" I huffed as sweat dripped off of very embarrassing places in my body. "I'm just not as flexible as you."

236 | INEVITABLE

"It's all in your head," she dismissed as she twisted her limbs around in such a way a contortionist would be proud. "We all have the same limbs and muscles in our bodies. Come on, spread your legs. Feel the burn and enjoy it."

"You're a freaking sadist," I whined when I finally collapsed into the most painful, fucked up version of the splits known to mankind. "I feel like I should warn Noah."

"No need," she shot back with a grin. "He likes my sadistic tendencies."

"Gross," I whispered as I prayed to the gods not to let me have broken my vagina.

"Look," she said. "Imagine a thick pair of hips between your legs. Stretch for the thrust!"

"Are you *serious*?"

"Absolutely, now ass to the grass –"

"If you say that to me one more time, I'm going to stick my foot up your ass," I growled.

My worst nightmare occurred less than a minute later when I heard the sound of a car engine and gravel crunching in the near distance, causing my pride to shrivel up and die inside.

I watched in semi horror as Noah climbed out of his Lexus followed by *Hunter* – Hunter who could hardly stand up. He was laughing so hard *at me*.

I hadn't seen him since our study session last week, and while we had messaged every day since, this was my first time seeing him in the flesh. It was also *not* the position I had hoped to be in when we came face to face again. I did, however, happen to catch a glimpse of his *company* when she left the house at the same time I was pulling up this morning.

Yeah, I wasn't sure why that was still pissing me off.

It was none of my business who he entertained at night.

We were friends now.

Just friends.

It shouldn't bother me that he was seeing other women.

Chapter 41 | 237

Other women?

What the hell was wrong with me?

Why was I thinking like this?

It shouldn't matter to me if he had a different woman for every night of the week. If he wanted to act like a whore, then who was I to judge him?

"The fuck you doing now, Thorn?" Noah called out, tone exasperated, as he yanked his glasses off his face and glared at his wife. He held his Ray Bans in one hand as he stared across the yard at us in obvious dismay. "Can't leave you alone for a goddamn minute."

"Oh, hey, Noah," Teagan called out as she unlocked her limbs from the precarious and inhuman position she'd been practicing. "We're just doing some pregnancy yoga." Bouncing to her feet, she stretched her arms above her head and smiled sheepishly. "It's perfectly safe."

"For what it's worth, *none* of this was my idea," I felt the need to call out. I would have gotten up, but I was fairly certain I was stuck in this position until someone took mercy on me and helped me up. It was pathetic, really, considering I wasn't the one with a watermelon growing in my stomach. Even though it was only April, we were already in the low seventies today, and Teagan was dressed for the weather in a pair of tight black capris and a workout bra. She looked good, too freaking good considering she was in the eighteenth week of her second pregnancy. Her bump was small and tight and with the exception of a C-section scar that ran across her lower belly, she looked incredible. For fuck's sake, she was pregnant and still wearing a size 2 – a UK 6.

Meanwhile, I was a size 10 – a UK size 14 – and had been since freshman year of high school. I had an hourglass shape that no amount of dieting or food constricting seemed to change. I had come to the depressing conclusion that my curves were never going away, which was why I was currently sporting a baggy t-shirt and sweats.

238 | INEVITABLE

I knew I wasn't fat, but I had those pesky rolls that liked to appear when I put my body in any position that wasn't vertical.

"Get in the damn house," Noah groaned, looking at his wife in horror. "Before you pop something."

"Pop something," Teagan snorted. "You're cute."

I watched from my distorted position on the lawn as Teagan skipped over to Noah with a huge grin on her face. Her long blonde hair was swept back in a braid that reached her lower back, making it swish from side to side as she moved. A feeling of warmth settled in my stomach as I watched them embrace.

Yeah, Noah and Teagan were pretty damn perfect for each other.

I'd known it from the moment they clashed against each other like titans back in high school.

Noah was the fighter, but Teagan wore the gloves in their relationship.

She was the boss, the queen bee, and he seemed quite content to go along with it.

I found it comical to watch them together; the big, bad fighter and his teeny, tiny conqueror of a wife.

"Wait, I can't get up!" I heard myself wail when Teagan bounded off towards the house with her distressed looking husband in tow.

"I can't decide if I'm in awe of what a good friend you are right now, or completely turned on by how fucking incredible you look in that position," Hunter chuckled as he walked over to me. Stopping just short of where I was spread, for want of a better word, he looked down at me and grinned. "The latter. Most definitely the latter."

"Shut up and save me," I whimpered as I reached for his hand.

"You know," Hunter mused, ignoring my extended hand. "If you were looking for a workout buddy, I could make this a helluva lot more enjoyable for you." Crouching down in front of me, he hooked his hand under my armpits and hoisted me to my feet, laughing when I groaned in pain as one of my thighs rejoined its counterpart.

"Funny," I shot back, still clinging to his shoulders as I tentatively stretched myself out. "I thought we talked about this? *No flirting!*"

"I'm just saying that there are easier ways to loosen up," Hunter teased. "More enjoyable ways."

"And you know all about those ways, right?"

Hunter frowned, obviously hearing the cattiness in my tone. "You got something you want to say to me, *friend*?"

His tone of voice riled me further and I couldn't stop myself from saying, "Yes. As a matter of fact, I do, *friend*." Folding my arms across my chest, I added, "There's a lot of things I could say about the blonde I watched walk out of this house this morning."

Hunter seemed to enjoy the bitchiness in my tone because he grinned and mirrored my actions. "Have at it."

"So, you don't deny it?" I snapped, flustered. "That she was here because of you?"

"No," he replied calmly, still grinning. "Why would I deny it?"

"*Why*?" I shook my head and gaped at him. Ugh! He was so fucking frustrating. "Because...because..."

"Because I want you?" he offered, winking.

"*Yes*," I blurted out.

"But you're married?" he added with a rueful smirk.

"Exactly," I bit back, hating that I had walked myself into this screwed up conversation.

"If you want me, I'm yours, sweetheart," he replied with another one of those killer smiles. "All you have to do is say the word, and I'll be *only* yours."

"Just like that, huh?" I sneered as I took a shaky step back from him.

Hunter nodded. "Just like that, HC," he clarified with a snap of fingers.

240 | INEVITABLE

I stared at his stupid, beautiful face for the longest moment before shaking my head and moving away. "And why would I want a man like you?" I snapped, hating the feel of my cheeks heating. "You're a slut," I added, spitting the words at him. "I prefer a man who isn't an STD-ridden convict." Having said that, I brushed the sods of earth and grass from clothes before turning around and walking away

"And an STD-ridden convict?" Hunter repeating, chuckling. "Ever hear of condoms, sweetheart? Oh no, that's right, you haven't because you're a virgin," he snorted. "A twenty-six-year-old, *married* virgin."

"I am *not* a virgin!" I snapped, swinging around to glare at him. "And even if I was, my sex life has nothing to do with *you*."

"You mean your non-existent sex life?" he countered, waggling his brows. "I heard you, remember," he continued to taunt, making a poor attempt at imitating my voice. "I need to be fucked. Dear god, somebody fuck me." He placed one hand against his forehead and used the other to mock fan himself. "Someone show me their cock!"

"You know," I growled, red-faced and mortified. "There are *so* many things I want to say to you right now, Hunter Casarazzi, but I won't. Because, unlike you, I am a grown up and am going to take the highroad instead."

"The highroad?" Hunter called out in that rage-inducing humorous tone he used regularly to drive me crazy as I stalked towards the house – *and away from him.* "Is that the same road that leads you back to your husband?"

I didn't answer him.

I couldn't trust my mouth at that moment.

Everything I was longing to scream was on the tip of the surface and if I spoke those words, there would be no coming back.

"Because that's one boring ass road, HC!" he taunted from close behind me. "You should try going off-road for once in

Chapter 41 | 241

your life. You never know, maybe you'll find that big cock you're looking for."

"Shut the hell up, Hunter." I opened the front door and hurried inside before slamming it in his face. I managed to catch his body in the door and I gleamed in delight when he grunted in pain. "And just remember," I added when he opened his mouth to say something sarcastic, no doubt. "I know where you hide your gun and now, because of your wonderful teaching skills, I also know how to erase evidence." Hunter's mouth fell open and I flicked it closed with my finger. "Which is why making me mad is really not in your best interests, Casarazzi."

"Then I *really* shouldn't tell you how turned on I am right now," he replied in a tone that oddly resembled awe. "Now, all I'm visualizing is you holding my gun."

I shook my head in resignation and punched his shoulder. "You're impossible."

"Wearing nothing but my holster," he added.

Giving up on scolding him, there was no point since it only seemed to encourage him, so I walked into the living room and plopped down on the couch.

My ass was still aching so much from the yoga that when Hunter sat down beside me, I didn't bother getting up and moving seats. I was too sore and he'd probably follow me anyway, so why bother?

I did, however, muster up the energy to remove the arm he'd casually flung over my shoulders before giving him a scathing glare. He responded to that by mashing his full lips together and making an obnoxiously loud kiss sound as he leaned his face towards mine.

My hand shot up and I face-palmed him. "Don't even think about it," I warned, trying and failing to bury the smile that was spreading across my face. I was never sure of what would come out of his mouth and it was exciting. He was exciting. Exhilarating. Charismatic and magnetizing...

242 | INEVITABLE

Hunter responded to my warning by snaking his tongue out and licking – *yes, licking* – my hand.

"Did you seriously just *lick* my hand?" I gasped as shock encompassed my features and I snatched my hand away from his face.

"Would you prefer I lick you elsewhere?" he shot back, unashamed or embarrassed. "Because I'm totally okay with that."

"You're a terrible friend," I gasped, slapping his chest.

"I'm the best possible version of terrible," he countered with a devilish wink.

My mouth fell open and I could do nothing but gape at him, while my heart raced wildly in my chest.

He was flirting with me and being completely shameless about it, too. He didn't care. Not one bit. I wasn't sure if it made me mad or turned me on. Either way it was working. He was getting a reaction out of me. That was his intention.

What was he trying to do to me?

I was rooted to Jordan like the roots of a great oak tree, but then there was Hunter, pulling me away from everything I had ever known. Secretly, and to my deepest chagrin, I wanted to be pulled. He was wild and unattainable and charismatic. Everything I never knew I wanted was inside this man. Something inside of him sang to the deepest part of my soul. It was a call I couldn't resist or deny.

"Don't lick me again. Okay?" was all I could come up with. *Lame.*

"Are you sure?" Hunter shot back teasingly. "You'd be amazed at how good I could make you feel by licking you." He waggled his brows. "Over and over again."

"Oh, please," I laughed, rolling my eyes at his comment. "What bullshit."

"You don't believe me?" he asked, clearly surprised.

"Answer me this," I shot back, grinning. "Do you believe in giant, fire-breathing dragons?"

Chapter 41 | 243

Hunter frowned. "Is that a trick question?"

"No." I smirked. "Now answer the question."

"Um, maybe?" He paused for a minute, clearly thinking about my question. "I believe they existed at one point."

"Me too!"

"Yeah?"

"Do you believe in mythical creatures like unicorns and mermaids?"

Hunter grinned. "I don't think anyone over the age of nine believes in mermaids, sweetheart."

"Exactly," I agreed with an enthusiastic nod. "It's *fiction*. It's made up stories to make people happy."

Hunter stared at me for a long moment with an adorably confused expression etched on his face. "I'm not following you," he finally admitted, looking puzzled.

"Multiple orgasms and men that can make you come with 'their tongue' until you're crying out and begging them to stop because you're absolutely positive your body cannot take the pleasure?" I cocked a brow in disbelief. "Bullshit fiction created by people like myself who write fairytales for the eighteen years and older category."

Now Hunter was the one to gape at me in disbelief. "Wait, you don't believe a woman can have multiple orgasms?"

"Oh, I do," I shot back, smiling sweetly. "I just believe that in order to have them, she would have to do the job herself."

"Well, your husband sounds like a barrel of laughs," Hunter finally announced. "You're just an asset to that man's pride.

"I'm realistic," I corrected. "And it's not just my husband. It's facts. That kind of thing doesn't exist."

"What *rock* have you been living under?"

"Oh what-fricking-ever, Hunter," I scoffed. "Like you're the master at making women have multiple orgasms!"

"I've had no complaints," he shot back with a proud smile.

I grimaced in disgust. "You're a slut, you know that, right?"

244 | INEVITABLE

"Practice makes perfect, HC." Smirking, he added, "It's all in the clit."

"*Excuse* me?" I spluttered.

"The clit?" Hunter smirked. "Maybe you should dust yours off once and a while and use it. You'd be amazed what a good fu–"

"Good, you're both together," Teagan announced just then as she sauntered into the living room armed with a stack of pamphlets and glossy catalogs. "We need to talk to you."

"What's up, Teegs?" I said in a bright tone, giving her my full attention, all the while thanking God for her unintentional intervention.

Hunter Casarazzi was entirely too brazen in his flirting with me, and I hated the part of me that secretly loved it. Even though it was only banter for him, he unintentionally gave me the attention I desperately craved. I was lonely and he filled the aching by making me want to smile and laugh even when my inner turmoil threatened to swallow me up.

Because the sad facts of my life were; my husband was still avoiding me. I still had to endure living with Annabelle – the same Annabelle I had been horrendously rude to a few weeks back and never apologized to. My career was going down the drain, one wordless day at a time, joining my love life in the toilet.

"Have you told them yet?" Noah asked, joining us in the living room.

"I was just about to," Teagan replied excitedly.

"Tell us what?" Hunter asked. "Wait –" He gasped and widened his eyes in mock surprise. "Are you *pregnant*?"

"Real funny, asshole," Teagan quipped before glaring at me. "Hope! Stop laughing – you're only encouraging him."

"I'm sorry," I choked out as I tried to smother my laughter with a cough. "Continue with your news."

"We're getting married," Teagan announced, clapping her hands with excitement.

Chapter 41 | 245

"Um." Hunter held his hand up, like we were sitting in class and he was asking the teacher a question. "I'm pretty sure you guys are already married."

Noah shook his head and bit back a smirk. "Thorn means we're renewing our vows. Before the baby comes in the fall."

"And we want you both to be in the wedding!" Teagan looked so happy as she bounced up and down on her feet like a toddler. "Hope, I want you to be my maid of honor, and Noah wants you for his best man, Luck!"

42

Lucky

*S*o, I was the best man and Hope was the bridesmaid? I grinned at her, knowing she was thinking this exact thing, too.

This was going to be very interesting.

"*Of course,* I'll be your maid of honor." Jumping up from the couch, Hope rushed over and threw her arms around Teagan. "I'm still pissed you ditched me the first time round. This will make amends."

"You know how sorry I am about that," Teagan countered, hugging Hope tightly. "But in my defense, I was so drunk that night I could have married *Elvis.*"

"That's fucking reassuring," Noah muttered with a shake of his head.

"So, when's this happening?" Hope asked excitedly as she did this fucked up jiggling dance. I wasn't complaining though. Her ass looked amazing when she jiggled around like that and I was thoroughly enjoying the floorshow.

Goddamn, how did Jordan Porter ever walk away from this

woman? She had a face that needed constant supervision, a body to die for, and the personality of a walking fucking dream.

"Early August," Teagan replied, beaming. "I'm so excited, Hope. It's like our second chance at things." She paused then and I watched as a flurry of emotion rushed over her. Her voice was thick with emotion when she spoke again. "After the year we've had, I want to stand in front of our family and friends and show the world we made it. That what happened to me and Noah didn't break us."

"Because we're permanent, Thorn," Noah piped up.

"Yeah," she agreed, flashing a smile at her husband. "Like a sharpie, right?"

"Like titanium," he corrected before walking over to where she was standing and pressing a kiss to her head. "What do you say, man?" he asked then, turning his attention to me. "Will you be my best man?"

Did he even need to ask?

"Always, man." Mirroring Hope's earlier actions, I rose from the couch and enveloped Noah in a hug. "Fucking always."

"Appreciate it," Noah muttered gruffly, clapping me on the back before taking a step back. "Don't know what I was going to do if you said no."

I smirked. "Fuck that, man. You have three nephews who would be more than happy to take my place."

"True." Noah nodded, agreeing. "But you're the one I want standing beside me on the day."

"Awh, Hope," Teagan gushed sarcastically. "Maybe these two should get married instead."

Hope threw her head back and laughed. "They certainly love each other enough."

"Who says we already haven't?" I shot back. "Maybe he was my bitch wife in prison."

Hope's mouth fell open in horror.

"Real funny, asshole," Noah grunted. "He's obviously fucking with you, Hope."

"*Noah* as your bitch wife," Teagan scoffed, unaffected by my comments. "More like the other way around, pretty boy."

"He'd have an easier life with me," I countered mockingly, totally fucking joking, but enjoying Hope's reactions too much to stop. "I'm lovely."

"*Of course, you are*," Teagan cooed, patting my shoulder. "Now, go and put the kettle on. We have color schemes to talk about!"

Noah paled. "Color schemes?"

Teagan nodded. "Not to mention flower arrangements, potential venues, and wedding attire –" She paused mid-sentence and turned her attention to Hope. "We have to get a red dress for you. You look smoking hot in red, babe."

"Good choice," Hope agreed, equally as absorbed in this wedding shit as Teagan was. "And you need roses in your bouquet."

"And a live band," Teagan shot back with a grin. "I want to do it outside. In the open."

"Like a gazebo or something?" Hope replied, eyes dancing with delight.

"Exactly. You are my freaking soul sister." Teagan clapped like a maniac. "We should organize a night out to celebrate."

"Omigod, yes!"

"Tonight?"

"Yes!"

"For drinks?"

"And dinner."

"And dancing!"

"Jesus," Noah muttered, taking in the sight of the two girls chattering at ninety miles an hour. "You'd swear they haven't seen each other in months."

I liked it; knowing Hope had a friend she could be herself around.

I liked to know she wasn't lonely.

Chapter 42 | 249

I had a feeling she spent a lot of her time feeling that way. It made my heart ache less when I saw her with Teagan.

"Lucky, can I have a word with you?" Noah asked then, distracting me from my staring. "Now?" he added before stalking out of the room. I took one final glance at the girls before following him outside.

"What are you doing, man?" he asked when I stepped onto the porch and had the door closed behind me.

"Right now?" I drawled. "I'm standing here talking to you, with plans to smoke a cigarette."

"Don't give me that shit," Noah grumbled, watching me like a hawk as I sparked up a smoke and took a deep drag.

"Then step back," I countered, exhaling a puff of smoke. "And you won't have to inhale it."

"You're either one hell of a cocky bastard and don't care what anyone thinks," Noah argued, not taking the bait. "Or you're genuinely blind to how fucking transparent you are when you're around her." I could hear the disapproval in his tone – it was oozing from him in buckets – and almost instantly, my hackles rose. "You couldn't want her more if you tried, Lucky, and it's plain for the world to see, man."

"We're friends," I bit out.

"Friends," Noah mocked. "But you want more?"

I nodded and took another drag. I wasn't a liar, and besides, I had nothing to hide. The whole damn world could know how I felt and I wouldn't give two shits, just as long as Hope knew.

Hope thought I was fucking around.

She'd assumed as much when she saw my sister leave Noah's house this morning.

Hayden had called me, stoned off her face, and I'd brought her back there to crash with the strict stipulation that she got her ass out of the house first thing the following morning. I hadn't known what to do with her last night if I was being honest.

250 | INEVITABLE

Blood or not, I didn't really know my sister. Hell, I'd only learned about her existence in the last year.

She was a product of one of my father's many affairs, and if I was being honest, I suspected half a dozen more Hayden's littered across the state.

At nineteen, Hayden was only a baby. But she'd managed to get herself up shit's creek with cocaine streaks streaming from her nose.

Drugs weren't my thing.

Never had been.

Sure, I'd smoked my fair share of weed in prison, but I'd never touched the harder stuff. I'd seen firsthand what shooting your veins up with that shit could do to a man. It wasn't fucking pretty and the state penitentiary was littered with the aftermath.

"You're a glutton for punishment," Noah stated, drawing me back to the present.

I raised a brow. "Coming from the man who married a hellcat?"

"I think married is the key word here," Noah shot back, unaffected by my sarcasm. "She's *married*."

"Married," I scoffed. "And what a fucking joke that marriage is."

I knew she wanted me.

I fucking knew it.

And in all honesty, if this was any other woman rejecting me on a daily basis, I would've walked away by now, but she wasn't any other woman.

She was *Hope.*

I was fully fucking aware that I didn't stand a chance against golden boy. Christ, they'd been practically betrothed from birth. And yeah, a part of me knew I should take Noah's advice and bow the hell out of this race, but I wasn't going to. There was something inside of me forcing me to *stay.* Forcing me to risk it all on the one woman I could *never* have.

Chapter 42 | 251

"You're playing with fire chasing that girl," Noah muttered, glaring at me. "And there's only one person that's going to get burned, man. *You*."

"Why don't you stay in your lane, man, and I'll stay in mine." I didn't particularly want to get into it with Noah over this, but I sure as hell wasn't about to stand down either. "It's got fuck all to do with you."

"Like hell it hasn't," Noah shot back heatedly. "She's my goddamn niece, Lucky!" He growled loudly and ran a hand through his black hair. "Seriously, man. You need to find a girl of your own."

"Why?" I demanded then, losing my temper. "Because he owns her? Because he's treated her so fucking well in the past?" I shook my head and sneered. "Bullshit, Noah. He put a ring on her finger and ran." I took a step forward and ran a through my hair in absolute fucking frustration. He didn't get it. None of them fucking got it. "If I had put a ring on her finger, you know what I'd have done?"

"This isn't about what you would have..."

"I would have *stayed*," I roared, interrupting him. "Regardless of the bullshit and the fucking horror. I would have fucking stayed."

"And Hayley?" he hissed. "If she was alive, you wouldn't even be thinking about –"

"Don't fucking go there," I warned, shaking my head.

Hayley.

Everything always came back to Hayley.

Was I not entitled to move on?

Was I supposed to sit around and fuck random women for the rest of my life and never again feel anything at all?

I didn't appreciate the fucked-up opinion that I wasn't entitled to fall in love again.

Because I *did* feel and I *was* falling.

Hell, I hadn't thought it possible, either, but it was happening to me and it was the realest feeling I had ever expe-

252 | INEVITABLE

rienced. More real and more consuming than anything I had experienced at eighteen.

"You have to go there," Noah growled. "You have to think about this, man. Hope is not a rebound. She's permanent. You take her away from him and she's going to be so consumed in her own guilt she's gonna be dark. Real fucking dark. This isn't black and white, bro. This is all fucked up and you've dug yourself into a hole so deep I don't think anyone can reach you."

"You know," I mused as I exhaled a cloud of smoke and flicked the ash from my cigarette. "I'm pretty fucking content in 'the hole' I've dug for myself, but thanks for your concern – it's unnecessary, though." I took another drag of my smoke before saying, "I'm good with the decisions I've made, Noah, and when it comes to her, I've got no fucking regrets."

"Say this bullshit notion you have swings in your favor," Noah countered, throwing his hands up in frustration. "She's nothing like us, Lucky. Think she can handle all the bullshit and horror that comes with being with one of us?"

I didn't answer that.

I couldn't.

Noah had me there and he knew it.

Hope was good and pure and the opposite of everything in my life.

"And say you fuck up and end up back inside," he added, pouring salt on the wound. "What happens to Hope then? I'll tell you what happens; she's left wide open as a fucking target for every asshole you've ever crossed paths with."

"I could say the same about you, brother," I shot back defensively, masking my sheer fucking horror at the thought. "What happens to Teagan and the baby if you're tossed back inside?"

My words caused Noah to balk. "Don't fucking say that, man." He visibly shuddered. "*Jesus!*"

"Then don't say it about me, either," I countered heatedly. "Because I have no intention of going back inside. But thanks

Chapter 42 | 253

for the vote of confidence," I added, tone laced with disgust. "It's good to know where your loyalties lie in all this. Asshole."

"My loyalty lies with you, you dumb shit," Noah snarled. "Always has and always will. But I can see trouble coming like a fucking hurricane, man. You keep chasing her and this will end in disaster. And the collateral damage is gonna be *you*. So yeah, maybe it seems like I don't have your back in this, but that's bullshit. I'm trying to warn you, Lucky. I'm trying to help you get out of this."

"I love her," was all I replied, and those three words seemed to throw Noah.

It was the first time I had verbalized how I'd been feeling aloud and it came as no surprise to me. I'd been falling for this woman for almost a year now. Saying it aloud, and to my best friend, only seemed to cement my feelings.

Noah stared at my face for the longest moment before exhaling a heavy breath. "I know." He shook his head in defeat and said, "But she's gonna take you down, man."

"Maybe I want her to," I shot back quietly. *Or maybe she already has.*

43

Hope

*W*hen I left Teagan's place, I headed straight back to Jordan's to shower and change my clothes. We'd made plans to meet at Darby's, a local restaurant/bar we all liked in downtown Boulder, at six-thirty.

The house was empty when I let myself inside, so I went up to the room I shared with my husband and began the task of getting ready for a night out on the tiles with my friends.

I knew I was cutting it tight when I climbed out of the shower at 4:25pm and threw on my favorite black skinny jeans and the lemon peplum top I bought last week. The fabric of my jeans was incredibly forgiving and flattered my curves.

Happy that the cut of my top seemed to downsize my breasts into a somewhat normal size while still flattering my shape, I toed on a pair of black pumps before doing something I rarely bothered doing; straightening my curls. It was crazy how long my brown hair was when it wasn't blown up in ringlets, and reached the middle of my back when I was done. I applied a full face of makeup, choosing to give my eyes a smoky

Chapter 43 | 255

effect tonight before adding the finishing touch of red lipstick to my always swollen lips.

By the time I was ready, it was 5:15pm and the cab I had booked earlier was waiting for me outside. Even though I knew it was pointless inviting him, I still tapped out a quick text to Jordan, letting him know where we were going and inviting him along before shoving my phone into my purse and rushing out to my cab.

44

Jordan

"We are going!" were the first words Annabelle said when she read the text message Hope had sent to my phone. "Go and get changed," she added, handing my phone back to me before returning to the task of changing Ryder's dirty diaper.

"I'm tired," I admitted, sinking down on the edge of her bed beside them. Leaning on my side, I tickled Ryder's chubby little face, distracting him so his mother could get the job of cleaning him done without protest.

"Da-dad," Ryder babbled, grinning up at me. "Da-da-da-da."

"Hey buddy," I cooed, smiling down at his beautiful face. I'd long given up on trying to teach him to call me Jordan. I figured it would come with time. "Good boy – stay still for Mommy to clean you up."

"Da-da-da-da," he squalled, blowing raspberries with excitement. "Up. Da-da...up!"

"Soon, buddy." I stroked his curls and smiled. "But you've gotta let Mommy clean that stinky butt first."

Chapter 44 | 257

"You're always tired," Annabelle reprimanded as she handed me the dirty diaper.

I took the diaper down to the trash for her before returning to argue my point. "I'm not comfortable going there."

"And I get it," she agreed, as she cleaned her son up and redressed him. "I do. But we're still going."

If this was any other person trying to force my hand, I'd probably lose my shit. But this was Annabelle. I knew her history, had seen first-hand the horror she had lived through, and it humbled me. The respect I had for this woman was unmeasurable. I also respected the hell out of her opinions and advice. I might not always agree, but that was a different story.

"We don't have a sitter," I pointed out, clutching at straws.

"I'll call Sally," Annabelle offered, cutting me a 'we're going, stop trying to stall' look.

"No." I shook my head. "No way. You know what happened last time we hired her. The minute we were out the door, she had her boyfriend over." I grimaced at the memory. "I don't want strangers around him."

"Fine," Annabelle countered with a determined look in her eyes. "Then we'll take him with us."

"To a bar?" I gaped at her. "He's thirteen months old. He's not going to a bar."

"It's a restaurant."

"It's too late for him to be out."

"We're *going*."

"But –"

"*We* are going," she cut me off by saying, finality in her tone.

"So, now that we've established our plans for the night." She stood up and blew out a breath before handing me the baby and saying, "Any ideas on what I should wear?"

I shook my head and laughed. "You're unbelievable."

"Hey, it's not often I get a night out," she shot back, grinning. "And who knows, I might meet the man of my dreams tonight."

She sighed dramatically before adding, "I hope he likes buying in bulk."

I cocked a brow. "Buying in bulk?"

"Yeah," she replied with a wink. "You know if he buys me, he gets two men free."

"He couldn't afford you," I shot back, laughing. "You're too fucking expensive."

"I'm just priceless," she tossed out airily before walking over to her closet door and yanking it open. "Now, the red dress or the black one?"

"Really?" I moaned, flopping back on the bed with Ryder. "Are we really going to go through this every single time we go out?"

"Yes," she shot back sweetly. "Consider this the downside of having a female best friend."

"Mommy's crazy, Ryder," I muttered under my breath.

"What?"

"The red one," I said with a sigh and waited for her to choose the opposite of what I said – like always.

"Really?" she frowned. "Don't you think the black one looks, I don't know, nicer on me?" She held the dress in front of herself and sighed. "You can see my baby belly in the red."

"See," I cooed, resuming my tickling attack on Ryder. "I told you Mommy's crazy. She thinks she has a baby belly."

"I do have a baby belly."

"No, you don't."

"Yes, I do."

"*No...* you really don't."

"Jord, don't lie to me..."

Christ. "Fine, wear the black dress."

"So, you agree? The red one does show my baby belly."

"What?" I gaped at her. "How did you just turn this entire conversation around on me?"

She stared at me for the longest moment before shaking her head and saying, "Screw it. I'll wear the red dress."

Chapter 44 | 259

Dear Jesus.

45

Hope

*T*eagan was that friend everyone had; you know, the one you had to say *'be nice'* to before bringing them around new people? She was as unpredictable as the weather and could be downright rude at regular intervals.

She also happened to possess a heart as brave as a lion's and a rare quality of loyalty that was second to none. I loved her to death and I knew she felt the same for me, which is why I genuinely feared for Annabelle right now.

Teagan on a normal day was scary enough.

Pregnant, hormonal Teagan was a force to be reckoned with.

"Okay, she needs to fuck right off," Teagan announced, voicing my inner thoughts, as we sat at the bar and watched Annabelle walk into the restaurant with *my* husband trailing after her, holding Ryder in his arms.

"Be nice," I muttered. "He never comes out." When he didn't answer my text message earlier, I had figured he was just flat

Chapter 45 | 261

out ignoring me. But now he was here? He had actually showed up? I was... *reeling.*

"And when he does he has to bring *her*?" Teagan shot back, narrowing her gaze at them. "Screw that, Hope."

Teagan was right of course, and voicing aloud exactly what I was thinking inside.

Jesus, why did Annabelle have to come?

This was supposed to be a celebratory dinner for Noah and Teagan.

She had no business being here.

She didn't know my friends.

Why would she congratulate Noah and Teagan on their second wedding?

She wasn't around for their first fucking wedding!

She knew nothing about them or the horrific struggles they had endured this past year.

"Please be nice, Teegs," I added nervously as they got closer. "The baby's with them."

"Luckily for her," she huffed before tossing back her orange juice. "What the hell is she thinking, bringing a baby to a bar at this time of night?"

"Well, it is technically a restaurant, too." I waved around the room at the many families enjoying a meal together. "And she's not the only one with children here."

"Fine," Teagan shot back, jutting out her chin. "The baby can stay. But *she* can leave!"

"Repress your violent urges," I begged, tone low. "And unleash them on Noah tonight."

Teagan's face broke out in a cat-like smile. "Oh, I intend to."

"Ew."

"Hello, Hope," Annabelle chimed, reaching us. She leaned into me and pressed a kiss to my cheek. "You look lovely tonight."

"Annabelle...hey," I acknowledged awkwardly as I slid off my bar stool and forced a smile to greet her. "This is Teagan." I

262 | INEVITABLE

turned to look at Teagan and gave her my best 'don't you dare let me down' glare. "Teagan, this is Annabelle Walker."

"Congratulations on your wonderful news," Annabelle said brightly as she stretched a hand towards Teagan. "I'm sorry for high-jacking your night. I hope you don't mind me and Ryder tagging along."

Meanwhile, I held my breath and waited to see whether or not I was going to have to wrestle a pregnant woman out of the bar.

Hunter had slipped outside for a smoke before we were seated at our table, and Noah had gone with him – to smoke behind his wife's back no doubt – but right now, I was hoping they would hurry the hell up and get back in here.

There was no way I was going to be able to manage Teagan on my own if she decided to stretch her claws.

"Not at all," Teagan finally said, voice a little tighter than normal. "So glad you guys could join us."

I sagged in relief.

Thank you, Jesus...

"It's a great bar," Annabelle added enthusiastically.

"They have live music here on Friday nights," I offered, feeling the need to make an effort. "So we picked the right night to come."

"Are they good?"

"The band?" Teagan nodded. "They're brilliant. They do the best covers."

"They do?" Annabelle chirped. "Well, maybe I'll find a nice guy to take me dancing then."

"Yeah," I replied flatly. "Maybe." I swung around then, giving Jordan my full attention. "I'm glad you could come," I whispered, feeling ridiculously nervous. "It means a lot to me."

"Yeah, I know," Jordan replied gruffly, eyes locked on mine. "You look nice tonight."

"Oh." I blushed at the compliment. "Thank you." I looked like a sack of potatoes in comparison to Annabelle who was

Chapter 45 | 263

rocking a tiny red dress with kitten heels, and Teagan who was dressed like a Grecian goddess in a white maxi-dress that emphasized her pregnancy boobs. "I should have made more of an effort," I muttered. "Worn a dress..."

"You're beautiful," he whispered, shifting Ryder into his other arm.

"Opie," Ryder babbled happily. "Opie."

"See?" Jordan chuckled. "You've already got an admirer."

"Opie, up," Ryder cried out as he wriggled like a little worm and reached his chubby little hands out to me.

"How's my favorite little guy?" Snatching him out of Jordan's arms, I smothered him in kisses to which he squealed in delight. "We're waiting on a table to come available," I found myself explaining as I waved a dismissive wave around the jam-packed bar. "They don't take reservations here."

The words were no sooner out of my mouth when a table became open in the far corner of the bar. Teagan, ever the graceful one, made a beeline for it, beating an elderly couple to the table. When they gave her a dirty look, she pointed to her blatantly noticeable baby bump and poked out her tongue.

"How am I friends with her?" I whispered in mortification as I watched Teagan defend the table from a couple of geriatrics.

"She hasn't changed one bit," Jordan chuckled, clearly amused at the sight of Teagan waving us over.

Stop waving, you brat!

And stop looking so freaking proud of yourself...

"No," I agreed with a shake of my head. "And she never will."

"Here; let me take this little guy off your hands," Annabelle said as she stepped in front of me and reached for Ryder. "Why don't you guys go and sit with your friend? I'll go find a highchair."

"I'll do that," Jordan was quick to offer.

"I can manage."

264 | INEVITABLE

"You're holding the baby," he countered. "You can't carry a highchair as well."

"Jordan? I've *got it*," Annabelle shot back, lifting Ryder into her arms. "Go and sit with your wife."

Call it strange, but I had the distinct feeling that she was telling Jordan what to do.

I wasn't sure if it made me warm towards her for trying to make him spend time with me, or hurt because he had to be told to do it.

Either way, I didn't wait around to listen, making a beeline for the table instead. "Oh god," I groaned, sinking down on a chair next to Teagan at the fancily decorated round table. For fuck's sake, the table was dressed better than I was. I stared down at the crisp white table cloth and groaned. "Kill me now."

"I can still kick her ass for you," she suggested, patting my forearm. "I'd do it, Hope. Just say the word."

"I know you would," I half laughed, half groaned, leaning my head on her shoulder. "That's why I love you so much."

Jordan, Annabelle, and Ryder arrived at the table then. He placed a wooden highchair down at the table before taking Ryder from her hands and gently slotted him inside. Then he did something I had been praying he would do; he sat down in the chair next to me.

I did a little internal happy dance that he was sitting with me, but then Annabelle took the seat on his left, and my dancing alter ego shriveled up and died.

They placed Ryder's highchair between them, ever the doting *parents*, while I forced myself not to cry.

I felt Teagan's hand squeeze mine under the table, and that small moment of contact was what kept me in my chair because the sight of my husband with his little surrogate family made me want to bolt.

"Oh my god," Annabelle gasped loudly, catching all our attention. Her focus was on the two men making their way towards our table. "Who is *that?*"

Chapter 45 | 265

I looked across the room to where Annabelle was pointed and locked eyes on Hunter and Lucky who were being surrounded by some overly zealous MFA fans. I took a moment to appreciate how amazing my uncle was. It wasn't easy, being tackled and swarmed every place he went, but he was incredibly graceful. He stood and took photographs with everyone that thrust a phone at him. I knew that if I were him, I would never be able to cope with the continuous intrusion into my life. But Noah just... got on with it. He didn't bitch or throw tantrums when his life was disrupted by them. He didn't complain about his lack of privacy or the fact that he was trying to have a night out with his wife and friends. The man was humbling.

On the other side of the lens was Hunter, taking the pictures while he too was fondled and grabbed by fans. That, I didn't like. They had no reason and no business to be touching on him like that.

"*That*," Teagan shot back in a deathly cold tone, dragging my attention back to the table. "Is *my* husband."

"I know who your husband is," Annabelle giggled. "Everyone knows who The Machine is." She bit down on her bottom lip and cast a glance towards the men before saying, "I was talking about him." She pointed discreetly towards Hunter and sighed dreamily. "Please tell me that tattooed piece of man candy is single?"

"Tattooed piece of man candy?" Jordan mused. With an easy smile, he asked her, "Should I even ask?"

She shot him a knowing smile. "I told you earlier."

Jordan looked over to where Hunter was standing and shook his head. "Maybe you should set the bar a little higher, Annie." Smirking, he added, "Perhaps focus on someone who *hasn't* spent half his life in an orange jumpsuit."

Immediately, my hackles rose. I opened my mouth to defend him, but Teagan got there first. "And what the hell is that supposed to mean?" she snapped, glaring across the table.

266 | INEVITABLE

"I'll have you know that Lucky is one of the best men I know – orange jumpsuit and all." She sniffed before adding, "Unlike other men around here."

Jordan swung around to face Teagan. "It was a joke," he replied flatly. "A private one."

"He didn't mean anything by that," Annabelle interjected. "My ex is in prison. That's why he said that about orange jumpsuits."

"Well, I'll be goddamned," Noah whistled, arriving in the nick of time. "Look who finally showed up." He clapped Jordan's shoulder before taking his seat beside his wife. "Good to see you, man."

Jordan's entire frame went rigid from the contact.

My heart broke at the sight.

Noah was being genuinely friendly, welcoming him like he would any of my brother's, but the surprise of his touch caused my husband psychological pain.

"Are you okay?" I whispered, reaching over to cover his hand.

"Noah," Jordan acknowledged, forcing a smile, as he yanked his hand away from my touch. "Good to see you, too."

Mortified by the rejection, I quickly dropped my hands on my lap and feigned impassiveness as I watched Jordan and Noah converse.

Out of the corner of my eye, I caught Annabelle glancing at me with a sympathetic expression.

The sympathy in her eyes was quickly replaced with lust when Hunter took the last remaining free seat at the table, which just so happened to be beside *her*. He settled into his seat and winked at me before acknowledging Jordan with a curt nod.

Finally, he turned to look at Annabelle and smiled. "Hey," he acknowledged, tone friendly.

"Hey," she replied, tone husky. Turning in her seat to give

him her full attention, she reached a hand to Hunter and said, "I'm Annabelle Walker."

"I figured," he replied with a smile as he took her hand and shook it. "It's nice to put a face to the name."

"I'm sorry," she purred, her hand lingering on his. "I don't know your name?"

"Lucky Casarazzi," he replied, slowly retracting his hand from hers.

"Lucky?" she mused, leaning closer to him. "Is that a nickname or something?"

"Something like that," he shot back with a smile.

"Well, Lucky," she purred. "Looks like we're the only two singletons at the table. Talk about coincidence, huh?"

"Yeah," Hunter replied. His eyes flicked to me for a brief moment and then Jordan before returning to her. "It's a strange world, alright."

Annabelle giggled at his response – actually fucking giggled like a fricking school girl – and I frowned.

What the fuck was she laughing at?

"I have to tell you, I love your tattoos," she added, eyes roaming shamelessly over his inked arms and neck. "Do you have more?" She leaned closer and whispered, "In *other* places?"

Ugh.

She had no freaking shame.

I never realized what a jealous breed of woman I was until I watched Annabelle look at Hunter like he was a piece of meat. Suddenly, after twenty-six years of docile living, my cat claws had come out in full force and I was ready to cut the bitch.

It wasn't enough for her to take Jordan away from me but now she wanted to take Hunter, too.

I couldn't stand it.

He smiled at her and I wanted to *scream*.

I knew he was only being his regular, friendly self, but I wanted to drag him away from her, lock him away somewhere safe, and save all his smiles for me.

268 | INEVITABLE

I felt a high heel stab my foot and I jerked in surprise.

"What?" I hissed, rubbing my injured foot with my other one.

"You're staring at them," Teagan whispered in my ear so only I could hear. "And you're being obvious about it."

Flushing bright red, I turned and gaped at her. "I am?"

"Yes." She nodded, voice still a whisper. "You look like you want to jump across the table and strangle her."

Fuck.

It was at this exact moment that Noah, who had been staring at Ryder on and off since we'd taken our seats, turned to Annabelle and said, "Cute kid."

"Annabelle beamed in delight. "Thank you."

"No problem," He continued to stare at him for another minute or so before turning to Jordan and asking, "He yours?"

That comment almost caused me to choke to death on the mouthful of wine I'd been in the process of swallowing.

"No," Jordan bit out. "He's not."

Unaffected by Jordan's sharp tone, Noah took another good look at the baby before turning his attention back to my husband. "You sure he's not yours? Kid looks a helluva lot like you."

"Quite sure," Jordan shot back coldly.

"Da-da!" Ryder squalled out, causing Noah to cock his brow, and Hunter to snicker.

The waiter came to take our order then, and I was pretty sure I'd never been so relieved to see a man with a notepad and pen as I was in this moment.

Awkward...

Thankfully, everyone at the table skipped a starter and only ordered mains. I was glad. This night couldn't end quick enough for me.

During our meal, I made no less than seven trips to the bar, each trip a little wobblier than the last. I didn't care about the disapproving looks Jordan gave me every time I returned with

Chapter 45 | 269

an overly generous glass of wine. I needed the Dutch courage to get through this damned dinner.

I ate my food in silence, feeling too frazzled to try and make forced conversation. I wasn't rude about it, though, and answered the rare question that was thrown my way. It was safer keeping my face down and my concentration on my steak.

46

Lucky

I walked straight into what had to be the most awkward fucking dinner party known to mankind with the woman I was in love with, her husband, his fake fiancé, a baby that looked a helluva lot like him, my former cellmate, and his pregnant wife. Someone needed to call Dr.Phil right about now because I had a feeling we were going to need him.

To be honest, when I came back in from having a smoke and saw them all sitting around a table, I'd taken a second look and checked for a camera, thinking this had to be a fucking joke.

And the blonde I'd been dumped beside was freaking me out with all the staring. I was beginning to think she might have an issue with her eyes because there was no way she was daring enough to watch me like she'd been doing without there being a medical reason for it.

I had no issue with single-mamas, and I could appreciate how sexy she was, but I wasn't interested.

Chapter 46 | 271

In anyone.

Unfortunately for me, my dick and my heart seemed to be connected by a cord and the only one I wanted to put it inside was the woman sitting across from me with the ring on her fourth finger.

Fuck my life.

Why the hell had I agreed to come? This was fucking bullshit. Standing and watching her make a total fool of herself. I wanted to stalk over there and steal her back from her husband who had come home just a minute too soon.

Hope looked miserable during dinner as she sat between Teagan and Jordan. He wasn't speaking to her.

In fact, he barely looked in her direction the entire fucking time. He couldn't make it any more obvious that he didn't want to be here, with us, and she looked mortified.

I wanted to reach across the table and hold her hand. Tell her that it wasn't her fault and she had nothing to be embarrassed about. I wanted to tell him to pull his finger out of his ass and fast.

He focused his attention on the blonde and the baby, and bristled whenever Hope touched his arm or rubbed against him.

I would gladly trade seats with him.

She kept trying to get his attention and he kept ignoring her.

It didn't matter to Hope that she had all of my attention without trying.

I was consumed by the woman. Every frown, smile, and lonely look. I couldn't keep my eyes off her.

I hung on every word she spoke, even when she talked about shit I had no clue about, I still listened, the sound of her voice like a blanket of warmth around me.

Fuck me, it took everything I had to stay in my seat and not lean across the table and smack some sense into him. I wanted

272 | INEVITABLE

to tell her to *stop begging*. He wasn't bothering so why should she?

Because she loves him, a voice inside my head hissed.

Unable to stick another second of watching her being ignored and under-appreciated, I leaned forward and patted her hand to gain her attention. "How's the book coming along?'

"It's amazing, Lucky," she replied, her voice a little slurred. I wasn't surprised by that. She'd spent more time drowning her sorrows at the bar during dinner than she had at the table. And like usual, he didn't fucking take notice. "I'm almost done."

I wasn't sure if it bothered me that she only called me Hunter when we were alone or with or friends, or if I liked that it was something personal between us.

Either way, I was back to being Lucky tonight.

"Knew you could do it, HC," I replied, feeling a huge swell of pride fill my body.

"Oh yeah?" She laughed and leaned forward and dropped her face in her hand. "I feel like I should give you like fifty percent of the... the..." She frowned and twirled her finger in the air, and in that moment, she reminded me of a blue-eyed version of Pocahontas with her brown curls straightened.

"Royalties?" I offered, smiling at how fucking cute she was when she was wasted.

"Yes!" She nodded and laughed. "That's the word."

"I don't want your money, HC,"I shot back, smiling.

"Oh yeah?" she snickered. "Then how else am I supposed to slay you for your help?"

I raised a brow. "*Slay* me?"

"Yeah." She nodded, eyes wide as saucers. "Pay you."

"So, are you married?" a voice interrupted us, causing Hope to drop her gaze to her plate.

"No." I turned to look at the blonde whose name I hadn't taken the time to memorize and forced down the irritation I was feeling. "I'm not."

"Really?"

Chapter 46 | 273

"Really," I deadpanned.

"Girlfriend?"

"No."

"How old are you?"

"Thirty."

"Wow," she replied, smiling. "I was convinced a man like you would have been snatched up and dragged up the altar years ago."

A loud snort escaped Hope, and I turned to grin at her. "Oh, that's funny, is it?"

"I'm sorry," Hope snickered as she swayed in her seat, waving her wine glass around recklessly. "I'm just laughing at the mental image of you being dragged up an altar." She took another mouthful of wine before turning her gaze on Blondie. "Lucky's not religious."

"Don't you think you've had enough?" I heard Jordan say, finally giving Hope some attention.

She looked up at him with a guilty expression. "I'm thirsty."

"You're drunk," he corrected, staring down at her. "You need to stop."

I watched him take the glass out of Hope's hand and hadn't realized I'd been moving until Noah's elbow dug roughly into my side. "Don't get involved, Lucky," he said in a low, warning tone. "If you love her as much as you say you do, then you'll sit your ass down and let her work this out for herself."

I glared at him for the longest fucking moment as I strived to find the composure I needed to walk the fuck away from this. Noah was right. Of course he was right. Didn't make it easy though.

"Oh look, the band is starting," Teagan offered then, sensing the tension at the table. She pointed to where a four piece were doing a sound check in the far corner of the room. "I love these guys."

I tried to concentrate on the band as they began their set, I really fucking did, but it was impossible to do with Hope sitting

274 | INEVITABLE

less than three feet from me, looking like she was about to burst into tears. Every instinct inside of me demanded I snatch her away from him – save her from this absolute bullshit. But what I wanted didn't matter in this. I couldn't fuck this up for her. I didn't want to jeopardize her future, whatever path she chose to take.

Because hurting this woman was the last thing I wanted.

Oh Christ, I needed to get out of here.

I needed to *stop* looking at her.

I needed a fucking drink.

47

Hope

*J*ordan took my drink from me and scolded me like I was a fucking child.

"I'm *fine*," I growled, reaching for my glass again as the music from the band blasted around us. "I am *fine*!"

Jordan stared hard at me before shaking his head and exhaling an exasperated sigh. "Whatever, Hope."

Embarrassed, I turned my face away and focused on Hunter instead. I watched in clouded confusion as Noah spoke into Hunter's ear, tone inaudible as the sound of guitars and drums and all that shit boomed.

A few minutes ticked by before Hunter got up from the table and stalked over to the bar.

I tried not to be obvious about watching him, but the alcohol flowing through my veins made it difficult for me to care. After all, he was the only one who seemed to even take note of me all night.

The confidence that oozed from that man was undeniably

276 | INEVITABLE

attractive. He had sex appeal in buckets and every woman in the room seemed to pay attention to him.

Women were openly gawking at him as he leaned against the bar with a bottle of beer hanging loosely in his hand and talked to the bartender. He looked so relaxed in his own skin, so content with who he was, it made my heart hurt.

My stomach churned as I watched a tall blonde sidle up to him and place a hand on his shoulder. I watched him turn to face her, giving her his full attention.

I watched her lean closer and my breath stalled in my chest.

Was he going to kiss her?

Dance with her?

Buy her a drink?

Take her home?

Oh god...

I wanted to barge over there and drag her away from him, tell her not to touch what wasn't hers, but how could I?

He wasn't mine, either.

I didn't *own* him.

Wrenching my gaze away, I turned my attention to Jordan, only to feel my heart plummet when I noticed he was, once again, in deep conversation with Annabelle.

I looked to Teagan for support, but her attention was on Noah, who was whispering something in her ear as he nuzzled her neck.

Drunk and depressed, I grabbed my wine glass and gulped down the entire thing, not caring when the bitter tasting alcohol caused my stomach to roll in protest. My heart was aching, so my stomach could damn well join in.

When Hunter returned to the table a few minutes later with his hands full with several shot glasses, I sagged in relief. He was *alone*.

"Celebratory shooters," he announced in his usual carefree

Chapter 47 | 277

tone as he slammed a bunch of glass tumblers filled with brown liquid down on the table. "Let's toast."

Annabelle, Noah, and I all reached for a shooter and held it up, but Jordan made no move to take one.

Earlier in the night, I had cared about the fact that we were all drinking around a recovering alcoholic, but now?

I was too fucking drunk to care.

"The fuck is this?" Noah asked, frowning at the contents of his glass.

"Thought you of all people would know a *slippery nipple* when you saw one," Hunter shot back. He picked up the lone shot glass that had orange content in it and passed it to Teagan. "Virgin for you," he told her with a wink before claiming a glass for himself. "To lifelong friendships, unreserved love, and the honor of standing by your side as your best man."

Noah and Hunter clinked their glasses together and said, "Cheers," before tossing their shots back. I clinked mine against Teagan's orange juice and then quickly gulped it down, gagging a little at the bitter taste.

The band began to play their own version of Walk the Moon's *Shut up and Dance* then, causing Teagan to squeal in delight.

Leaping to her feet, she pointed at Hunter. "Come on, Lucky-boy. Let's see what you got!" Giggling, she crooked her finger at him as she danced backwards away from our table and onto the floor.

Grinning, Hunter picked up another shot and tossed it back before slamming the glass down on the table. "It's on, Blondie." Shoving his chair back, Hunter sauntered towards Teagan, all the while making ridiculous hand – and hip – gestures.

They danced around the room so animatedly, laughing and reenacting every lyric of the song playing from the DJ booth.

They were absolutely hilarious.

It was honestly a sight to be seen.

278 | INEVITABLE

Teagan was a firecracker – always had been – but it looked like she had met her match in the crazy stakes with Hunter.

He was just so fun and wild and carefree. And he danced around the bar like he didn't have a care in the world. I knew he did, but he hid it so well.

He didn't care what anyone thought about him and I felt in awe of that confidence he exuded. He lived life on *his* terms and didn't shake or rattle when people came at him. He kind of reminded me of that guy in school everyone wanted to be around.

The girls wanted to be with him and the boys wanted to be him.

Curiosity burned inside of me; the urge to know this man on a level no other ever had known before burned inside of me.

His outlook on life was infectious.

All the horrible things he had seen and done, and Hunter Casarazzi was still standing with his middle finger cocked in the air saying *fuck you all*...

"Does that bother you?" I heard Jordan ask Noah and immediately my hackles rose in defense.

Noah shook his head and laughed. "It probably should, but nah." He seemed to be enjoying watching Teagan dance around the place with Hunter. It was like watching two best friends in a dance off. "They're like brother and sister."

"Jord?" Annabelle called out, immediately capturing my husband's attention. "I'm going to take off." She pointed to where Ryder was beginning to fuss and stood up. "It's too loud for him in here."

"I'll come with you," was Jordan's automatic response as he rose from his chair and grabbed Ryder's changing bag off the floor.

"Don't leave now," I heard myself say and it sounded awfully like begging. Reaching up, I placed a hand on his forearm and said, "This is the first time we've been together like this in forever. Can't you just stay out and enjoy yourself?"

Chapter 47 | 279

"I have responsibilities, Hope," he whispered.

"They are *not* your responsibility," I hissed, the alcohol in my belly giving me the courage to finally speak my mind.

"Hope –"

"I'm serious," I urged, not caring if Annabelle could hear me or not. "You don't have to spend all of your time working and hanging out with her, you know."

"She's my friend."

"I'm your wife."

"I'm well aware."

"Then *act* like it."

"I *can't* be here, Hope." Jordan pinched the bridge of his nose and exhaled a shaky breath. "Being in an environment like this? Around alcohol?" He shrugged helplessly. "It's too hard for me. I need to go home. I can't afford to make any slip ups."

"Okay," I whispered, feeling a huge swell of guilt. Reaching under the table, I grabbed my purse and moved to stand. "I'll come, too."

"No. You stay and enjoy yourself."

"I want to enjoy myself with *you*."

"It's not something I'm able to do right now, okay." He leaned down and brushed his lips against mine. "I love you," he whispered. "But I'm not staying here."

Then he turned his back and walked away from me.

Sinking back down on my chair, I watched them leave, forcing myself to hold it together when everything inside of me was falling apart. Blinking away the tears that were filling my eyes, I looked around the bar in defeat. I felt utterly helpless. My life was railroading out of control and I felt powerless to stop it.

It was only when I felt a strong arm come around my shoulders that a hiccup of pain tore from my lips. "What am I going to do with you, huh?" Noah grumbled as he tucked me into his side.

Turning to face my uncle, I buried my face in his enormous

chest and cried. We were the only two left at the table and I was glad. At least he was the only one that was witnessing my personal breakdown. "He doesn't love me anymore, Noah," I choked out, drowning his clean, white shirt in my mascara stained tears. "And it hurts so fucking much."

"I don't think that's it, Hope," Noah soothed as he stroked my arm with his hand. "I think he really does love you, but he's too messed in the head to show it."

"You saw that just there," I objected, sniffling. "I *begged* him to stay and he just walked away – with *her*!"

"Doesn't mean he doesn't care."

"It feels like he doesn't."

"Look," Noah said, exhaling a sigh. "I've been through something similar to what you're going through now."

"With Teegs?" I whispered.

"Yeah." He nodded. " Seven years is a long ass time to be apart. Time changes things, Hope, and people grow apart."

"Including you guys?"

"Of course," he agreed. "We were different people when we found our way back to each other. It was hard as hell trying to find some middle ground to stand on together." He shook his head, clearly thinking back to an earlier time in his life. "We were so goddamn resentful of each other back then, both blaming each other for shit that didn't even matter anymore. Both of us too terrified to trust the other."

"But you guys found it." It wasn't a question, more like a statement of fact. "You found your way back to each other."

"I love her," he replied simply. "I'd die for the woman. There is nothing I wouldn't do for her – to keep her. Hell, if I couldn't find middle ground, I'd make it myself and drag her there with me."

"But that's the *difference*, Noah," I whispered, lifting my head from his chest. "That crazy passion you guys have? That 'I want to rip your clothes off and lose myself in you' feeling you get whenever you're around each other? That ride or die love?

Chapter 47 | 281

Jordan and I don't have that." Exhaling a ragged breath, I forced myself to admit, "We've never had it."

"What are you saying here, Hope?" he asked, frowning down at me. "You want out?" He stared right into my eyes and said, "Because that's okay, too. There's no crime in admitting defeat."

"I don't know what I'm saying anymore," I squeezed out, staring back at him. "I'm just a mess, I guess."

Noah frowned at me for what felt like an age; his dark eyes locked on my face, clearly taking my measure. "Yeah, you are," he finally said, cracking a small smile. "You look like a raccoon."

My hands automatically moved to my face. "Oh shit," I half laughed, half sobbed. "My make up?"

"Is now on your cheeks," he filled in, smirking. "Go and clean yourself up and put a smile on your face. Before Little-Irish comes back, sees you've been crying, and hunts down your husband."

"God, *she* would," I chuckled. I stood up and headed for the restroom, only to halt mid-step. "Noah?" I called, turning to face him. My uncle was a man of few words, but he'd given me plenty to think about tonight.

"Yeah?"

"Thanks for the talk."

Noah flashed me a sympathetic smile and said, "I'm always here, Hope."

48

Hope

*W*hen I finally managed to compose my drunk ass, and clean the mascara stains off my cheeks, I slipped out of the restroom.

My head was still slightly spinning when I returned to the bar, and I was starting to really regret the damned wine. I thought about how I would feel in the morning and I groaned in pained anticipation.

Wine hangovers were the fucking worst.

I walked back to our table, but frowned when my eyes landed on half a dozen unfamiliar faces. Confused, I searched the room for my friends, and spotted Noah and Teagan on the dancefloor.

The sight of them sickeningly in love as they danced together almost caused the wine in my stomach to make a reappearance.

Thankfully, I won the battle and managed to keep it inside.

Depressed and not wanting to interrupt the lovebirds, I slid

Chapter 48 | 283

my cell out of my purse and called a cab before heading for the exit.

I needed water and lots of it. And a burger. And maybe some fries.

Yeah, grease was a really good idea right now!

I was contemplating the likelihood of the cab driver making a pit stop at the drive-thru for me when I walked outside and my drunken gaze landed on Hunter.

He wasn't alone.

The blonde I'd seen him talking to at the bar earlier was standing under the awning with him. They were both smoking. She was talking animatedly, while he listened and laughed at whatever she was saying.

Rage burned inside of me at the sight. I had no idea why or where the horrible feeling had come from, but suddenly I wanted to walk right up to them both and throw a fit.

She was flirting shamelessly with him and I was jealous.

No, scratch that, I was beyond jealous.

I didn't want any woman looking at him, touching him, attempting to take him home.

The thought of her putting her hands on him made me feel physically sick.

Without thinking about the repercussions of my drunken actions, I stalked right over to where they were standing.

Hunter's glazed over eyes landed on mine and he smiled warmly. "I thought you left," he said, sounding genuinely happy to see me.

Reaching up, I grabbed the cigarette dangling from his lips and tossed it away. "Are you going to fuck her?"

"Excuse me?" I heard the skinny blonde hiss from behind me, but I didn't give a shit. Keeping my back to her, I glared up at Hunter.

"Well?" I demanded, chest heaving. "Are you?"

Hunter's brows rose in surprise, but he didn't make any reply.

284 | INEVITABLE

Instead, he just stared down at me, jaw slightly clenched.

"Answer me, dammit!" I hissed, pushing his chest. "Are you?"

"You're making a scene, HC," Hunter replied, voice soft, eyes dark and dangerous. "Go home."

"I can't," I managed to bite out while my body shook all over. I was making a scene. I could feel several pairs of eyes on us, but I didn't care. Not one bit. "Do *you* want to fuck *her*?"

When he didn't answer me, I lost it.

"Hunter, you better tell me now, dammit."

"What do you want me to say, Hope?" he demanded then, tone irritated. "How the fuck do you want me to answer that question?"

"I want you to say no," I screamed – yes, screamed – as I pushed him hard again. "Dammit, Hunter!"

"What does it matter?" His voice was resigned, his face weary. "We're not together, Hope."

It shouldn't.

God, it shouldn't matter.

"It matters," I countered shakily. "It matters to *me*."

"You need to stop," he warned, blue eyes narrowed on mine. "Now."

"Don't go home with her," I blurted out, stepping closer to him. Shaking his head, Hunter attempted to move away from me, but I didn't let him. "Don't do it," I begged, reclaiming the space he'd tried to put between us. "Don't."

"Relax, honey, we were only talking," the woman behind me sneered. "You really need to get a grip."

"And you really need to fuck off," I snarled, swinging around to face her. "He's not for you, *honey*!"

Hunter threw his head back and made a strangled noise, almost like a laugh, but it was pained. "Jesus fucking Christ, Hope."

"He's mine," I snapped, losing every ounce of my-self-control. Like the unhinged woman I was, I fisted his shirt in my

Chapter 48 | 285

hand. "Mine," I growled, glowering at the blonde. "You got that?"

The blonde glowered at me before turning her attention to Hunter. "You know, you really ought to buy a muzzle for your girlfriend," she spat before stubbing out her cigarette and stalking off. "Possessive bitch."

As soon as she was gone and the threat was eliminated, the reality of what I'd just done crashed down on me.

Oh god, what was happening to me.

I was losing my freaking mind.

Reeling, I turned back to face Hunter.

Every ounce of blood drained from my face when I looked up at Hunter's murderous expression. His jaw was clenched tight as he glared down at me, blue eyes dark and locked on mine.

"I'm sorry," I choked out. "I don't know what came over me."

"You can't do that to me, Hope," he bit out as a vein ticked in his neck. His voice was calm, but he looked like he was close to exploding. "Fuck," he growled. Shaking his head, he exhaled a harsh breath. "Fuck!"

"Please don't be mad at me," I begged, words slurring a little, as I took a tentative step towards him. "Don't hate me."

"I'm not mad at you." He exhaled a ragged breath and looked up to the sky. I could see his chest heaving as he took several sharp breaths. Finally, he swung his gaze back to me, he hissed, "Tell me what you want from me, Hope?"

"Nothing," I whispered.

"*Nothing*," he repeated, tone laced with disbelief.

"No, not nothing! I want...you can't...I just..." I shook my head and tried to make sense of my crazed thoughts. "I didn't want you to leave with her," I choked out.

"Why not?" he demanded.

"I don't know."

"Why not, Hope?"

"I told you, I don't know!"

286 | INEVITABLE

"Bullshit," he snarled. "Why the fuck not?"

"Just because."

"Because what?" he demanded, voice torn. "Because you don't want me to be happy? Because you want me to be alone and fucking miserable? Huh? Which is it, Hope?"

"Because the thought of you with another woman makes me want to die!" I screamed.

"Are you fucking with me right now?" he hissed, face reddening. Jerking closer, he cupped the back of my neck and dragged my face to his. "Are you fucking with me, Hope?"

"No," I choked out, forehead pressed to his. "The thought of you with another woman makes me crazy."

"Then how the fuck do you think *I feel*?" he snarled. Releasing my face, he shook his head, eyes still locked on mine. "There's only one woman I want," he roared, losing all control now. "*One*! And she's got a goddamn wedding ring on her finger."

"Hunter," I sobbed. "Don't –"

"I'm *yours,*" he snarled, chest heaving. He drew me closer, so close I could practically taste his breath on my tongue. "But you don't fucking want *me*."

"Because I *can't* have you," I cried. "You know that."

"But you do want me," he said calmly, his blue eyes heated and locked on mine, gaging my reaction.

"I don't," I choked out before exhaling shakily. "At least I shouldn't."

"So, because you can't have me, you don't want anyone else to have me?" he shot back, glaring, and drunk as I was, I didn't miss the pain in his eyes or the way his voice cracked. "Is that it?"

"No. Yes. God, maybe!"

"Then what do you want me to do, Hope?" he choked out, shrugging helplessly. "What do you want from me?"

"Hunter..."

The sound of a car horn honking blasted loudly, distracting

me. Twisting sideways, I saw the black cab pulled up at the sidewalk. "Hope Carter?" the cab guy called out from the wound down window.

"Yeah, that's me," I called out and held my palm up to him indicating I'd be there for five minutes.

The cab driver gave me a dirty look and tapped on his wrist.

"Go on, HC," Hunter said in a weary tone. He took one last final look at me before shaking his head and turning back towards the bar. "Go on home to your husband," he called over his shoulder.

He walked away from me, and I wanted to scream *stop*. I wanted to beg him not to go, but I didn't have the right.

He wasn't mine and I didn't belong to him.

I was a married woman with a husband and a life waiting for me.

I needed to allow him to nip this in the bud.

I needed to allow him to be happy, and I needed to be happy for him that he was able to do it.

I just *couldn't*...

"Wait," I called after him. "Don't go back in there."

"Why? You gonna keep me company, HC?" he shot back, swinging around to face me once again. "You gonna take some time out from playing happy little wife to fuck me?"

When I didn't respond, he stormed towards me. "You wanna come home with me, HC?" he demanded. Taking my arm, he walked me over to the awaiting cab. "Is that really what you want?" he hissed. Swinging open the door, he shoved me into the backseat then leaned into my face. "Because I've got no problem getting in this cab and giving him directions to my place."

Hunter stared hard at me before shaking his head and saying, "Didn't think so." He tossed the cab driver a bundle of cash and said, "Make sure she gets inside before you leave."

With that, he banged his fist on the hood of the cab and walked away.

49

Lucky

I woke at the crack ass of dawn to the obnoxious fucking sound of my cell ringtone as it pierced through my ears, vibrating loudly from somewhere on my bedroom floor.

Stretching out lazily, I snaked a hand under my pillow and pulled it over my face, sighing in relief when it finally stopped ringing, only to groan loudly when it started back up a few seconds later.

Goddammit!

Fisting the comforter away from my body, I swung my legs over the edge of the bed and reached for my jeans. Not bothering to check who was calling, I swiped my finger across the screen of my phone and pressed it to my ear. "This better be fucking good," I growled, rubbing my eyes, as the watery sun poured through my window, aggravating my already pounding head. "Really fucking good."

"It's me," Hope's familiar voice filled my ear.

Christ.

Chapter 49 | 289

"You okay?" I asked, voice gruff and thick from sleep, as I rubbed a hand over my jaw. She was the last person I had expected to hear from this morning. I had half expected her to run for the hills after our screwed-up confrontation last night. My gaze flicked to the alarm clock on my nightstand and I frowned. "It's eight-thirty, Hope."

"I know," she croaked, voice low and hoarse. "I'm at the front door." There was a long pause, and then she said, "I really need to see you."

My feet were moving before my brain had a chance to catch up. Like a glutton for punishment, I headed straight downstairs to let her in.

When I opened the front door, and saw her standing on the doorstep, holding both her hands up in the universal peace sign, I couldn't stop the smile that spread across my face. "Did you just fall out of bed?" I asked, gesturing towards her makeup smeared face and bedhead hair.

"I couldn't sleep," she admitted, not bothering trying to deny it.

"No?"

"I'm an asshole," she blurted out as she shifted from foot to foot. "But a really sorry one."

"You were a tad assholely last night," I confirmed, smirking.

"I was," she sighed, biting down on her bottom lip. "But I'm hoping that my previous demure and lovable character up until last night's brief meltdown counts for more, and you still want to be friends with me."

I frowned, trying to make sense of the long ass question she'd just thrown at me.

"Do you think you can forgive me?" she added, smiling sheepishly. "For being a bitch and cock-blocking you?"

"There's nothing to forgive."

"Do you mean that?"

I nodded.

Anger coursed inside of me. She didn't cock-block me last

night. She fucking *expressed* herself. She was *honest* with herself for the first time in months. Guess she was back to being in denial again.

"Yeah, HC. I do."

She kept coming back to me.

That was the crux of it.

The woman, no matter how much she claimed she didn't want me and tried to push me away, kept coming back to me.

She was a grade A mind fuck and I was getting caught up in the fucked-up hype that came with wanting a woman like her.

She would never know how hard last night was for me. Her standing in front of me all possessive and crazy was so fucking confusing. Screw confusing; she'd all but ripped my damn heart out. The way she looked at me last night? The begging in her voice? It took *everything* inside of me to put her in that cab and send her away when all I wanted to do was *keep her*.

"Do you think..." She paused for a moment before adding, "We could pretend last night never happened?"

"Which part?"

"The part where I stepped over the line."

I forced down a burst of frustration and nodded. "No problem."

"Great." She exhaled a huge sigh and smiled. "So, um..." Her gaze trailed up my body before landing on my face. Her cheeks were pink when she said, "Do you want to put some pants on and take a walk with me?"

Christ, this woman was fucking destroying me and I kept putting myself out there for her to ruin.

If she'd had met me first, I wouldn't be in this situation.

Her husband was an asshole and he didn't deserve her.

I could give her better.

I could give her *more*.

"Sure," I said, eyes locked on hers, breaking my own damn heart. "I'll take a walk with you, sweetheart."

50

***

Hope

$\mathcal{S}$ide by side, we walked for hours. It was incredibly warm outside; a sheen of dew lay on the grass beneath us as we trudged through the wooded area surrounding Teagan and Noah's impressive fifteen-acre property. Hunter didn't try to flirt or throw an arm over my shoulder as we walked and I was grateful. I already felt like I was being emotionally unfaithful to my husband. I didn't want to add physical contact to the weight on my shoulders.

I messed up last night.

Monumentally.

All night, I had tossed and turned, thinking about how I had come *this* close to being with him. His words still haunted me, the painful truth a harsh reality check.

"...Then how the fuck do you think I feel? There's only one woman I want. "One! And she's got a goddamn wedding ring on her finger..."

I shouldn't be here.

Not after last night.

But coming here was the only thing that made sense to my frazzled brain and *being* with him was the only thing that *felt* right to me.

Hunter Casarazzi stormed into my world and turned it upside down. He hit me like a wrecking ball that I never saw coming.

He seemed to make everything better. He brought this aura with him. Carefree, chilled. Relaxed. It was hard to explain. But he did.

He was just so easy to be around.

Like a breath of fresh air.

It was overwhelming and overpowering all in one. I was terrified of him. Not because he was a criminal. Not because the hands I craved had taken human life away, more than once, but because of the way he made me *feel*.

Right or wrong, I needed to be around him.

He was, after all, the best part of my day.

When we were together, it was as if we were running on a different wave frequency to everyone else around us. I became so caught up and consumed in him that I didn't have time to overanalyze and freak myself out like I usually did.

In a weird way, Hunter felt like home.

51

Hope

For the third time in a matter of weeks, I found myself sitting in Cameron's kitchen with a mug of hot chocolate in my hands as I poured my heart out.

I had no idea why I was coming to him with my troubles. Cameron was the last person on earth I usually shared my problems with.

But something inside him had changed, and he had confided in me about the baby.

It made me want to do the same.

Something about him now made me feel safe. I knew that sounded strange. He was still the same Cam, and yet, he wasn't.

I had five brothers, but Cameron was the one who reminded me most of our father. Stubborn and prideful, impulsive and strong – just like Dad.

It was weird, but Tillie had changed my brother. She had reached into that closed off heart of his and flicked on a switch. His resemblance to our father only seemed to be growing.

294 | INEVITABLE

Stepping out on a ledge with Tillie was such a typical Dad thing to do.

Going against everyone and everything he knew because he loved her? It was a crazy move and reminded me of something our father would do for Mom.

I felt more on the same wavelength as Cam now, which was a first. I had never been able to relate to Cam before. He was the sibling I was least close to.

Colton was the lovable, playful brother who always picked you up when you were down.

Logan was the deep and meaningful one who gave the best advice.

But Cam?

Cam was always the explosive one. The one you never quite knew how to be around.

Until now.

"Everything's so fucked up, Cam," I muttered as I took a sip from my mug and moaned in delight when the chocolatey goodness hit my taste buds. Cameron made a kickass hot chocolate. As kids, whenever he pissed Mom off, he would make her a hot-chocolate. At the age of twenty-five, and after countless times pissing Mom off, my brother had perfected his signatory drink.

"I'll say," Cam agreed with a snort.

"Not helping."

"Sorry."

"So?" I demanded expectantly. "Come on and tell me how to fix the car crash that is my life."

"Well," Cam mused, taking a sip from his mug. "You and Lucky are on good terms again, aren't you?"

"Yeah," I agreed with a relieved sigh. "Thankfully." When I relayed the antics at the bar to Cam, I had omitted the part about my deranged moment of madness when I had unilaterally cock-blocked Hunter. "We're fine again." Sagging in my

Chapter 51 | 295

chair, I continued, "But Jordan and me?" I shook my head. "Not so much."

"He's still giving you the cold shoulder?"

I scoffed. "I'd be lucky to get his shoulder."

Cam frowned sympathetically. "That bad, huh?"

"Imagine the worst," I shot back. "Then multiply it by ten."

"Ouch," he muttered. "You've fucked yourself over good this time, Hopey-Bear."

"Please don't call me that again," I shot back with a groan. "Otherwise, I'll have to reconsider the promotion I've given you."

His brows rose in surprise. "Promotion?"

I nodded and took another sip of my hot-chocolate. "You've recently become my favorite brother. So, don't screw it up with stupid pet names from our childhood."

"Duly noted," he snickered. "And thanks for the promotion."

"No problem – thanks for the niece or nephew." I blew into my mug and watched as steam rose from the rim. "So, where's Tillie this morning?"

Cam exhaled a heavy sigh and rubbed his jaw. "She had to go visit her parents in Redford."

I cocked a brow. "You didn't go with her?"

He shifted uncomfortably in his seat before saying, "I'm not exactly welcome around her family."

"And why not?" Defensiveness sprang to life inside of me. "You're not the one with the crazy fucking aunt!"

"Hope," Cam said in a warning tone, blue eyes locked on mine. "Don't go there."

"Fine," I placated with a huff. "I won't say another word on the matter."

"Thank you." He ran a hand through his hair before admitting, "But let's just say, I'm not the only one with a disapproving family. This is hard on Tillie, too. Her family aren't exactly stoked that she's dating a Carter." Shrugging, he added, "Whatever. I'm just trying to do whatever I can to make this as easy on her as I can."

I stared at my brother for a long time before saying, "You're a good man, Cameron Carter."

Cam gave me a look that said *are you feeling okay*' before smirking.

"I mean it," I added sincerely. "I'm proud of the man you've become... of how you're taking care of your responsibilities."

"I'm in love with her, Hope," he shot back gruffly. "More than I know what to do with it. Never thought I'd say that about a woman, but it's true." He smiled, revealing the deep dimple in his left cheek. "She makes me question myself and rethink everything I've ever done before. I am so goddamn sunk, it's not even funny."

I laughed then; hearing my little brother use our father's analogy of being sunk was surreal. "You're certainly changing."

"That's the thing," he replied, nodding eagerly. "She makes me want to do better – *be better*. I can't explain it properly – you know I'm shit with words – but when I'm with her, I need more, I need to get deeper. I'm always wanting *more*. And when I'm not with her?" He shook his head and laughed humorlessly. "It's like I can't fucking breathe until she walks back through that door and I see her again."

"Wow," I mused, resting my chin on my hand. "You really are sunk."

"What about you?"

"What about me?"

"It's the same for you, right?" Cameron grimaced before saying, "With Jordan."

"It used to be," I admitted honestly.

But things were different now.

I had spent eight years apart from Jordan, and in that time, I had learned to cope on my own. I was still licking my wounds, trying to recover from an eight-year-long open gash across the center of my heart.

Chapter 51 | 297

That wound he left was still open and I had a feeling it would never quite fully close up.

Reasons and excuses for our separation aside, I had been left broken in the aftermath of his abuse.

I had been the collateral damage.

And I was the one suffering for a bad man's crimes.

And even though it pained me deeply to admit it; somewhere in between Jordan walking away from our marriage eight years ago and then changing his mind, he had lost a piece of me.

Somewhere along the way, Hunter had squeezed his way into my heart and I hated myself for allowing it to happen, for being too weak to stop myself from caring, but it had happened.

I loved my husband, but I wanted to spend my time with another man.

How screwed up was that?

Every time I heard my phone vibrate or saw the screen light up, I was immediately attacked by an onslaught of butterflies in my stomach. My heart fluttered. My palms turned slick from sweat. I was completely enraptured with Hunter. It wasn't good or safe or sensible but it was exactly how I felt. And I craved the danger. I longed for the text messages and chance encounters. I longed for *him*.

He was like a vibrant color that had burst into my black and white world. He made me think about life in ways I never had before. He made me second guess myself.

He made me feel *free*.

It killed me inside, knowing that I had managed to remain completely faithful my whole life to Jordan, and knowing that I had only ever given my heart, my affection, and my body to him just for it to not be enough anymore.

It was *soul-destroying*.

I didn't know what to do to fix the problems in our relation-

298 | INEVITABLE

ship. I couldn't use my body because he didn't want it. I wasn't at the top of his list and it freaking gutted me.

All my life, I'd put him number one. And now I was expected to fall into the contented little house-wife role?

It wasn't me.

I was bored and I needed excitement.

I needed something else.

Something *more*.

"Hope, you know that you can always change your mind," Cam stated, pulling me from my thoughts. "This life you've signed up for?" he added as he stared at me intently. "It doesn't have to be permanent. Not if it's making you as unhappy as you look right now."

"What are you trying to say, Cam?"

"I'm saying that a decision you made when you were eighteen doesn't have to affect the rest of your life."

"I'm not giving up on him," I snapped, horrified that he was even insinuating I do that. "I'm here. I have been here for him, and I will continue to be here. I will never divorce him, Cameron. Over my dead body." I glared at my brother and hissed, "I would never be that selfish and it hurts me to know that *you* think I would!"

Cam shook his head and exhaled heavily. "Accepting the fact that you've grown apart and aren't the same people as back then doesn't make you a failure, Hope. And it doesn't mean you don't love him or have given up on him, either." Reaching across the table, Cam took my hand in his and squeezed. "This is your life, Hope. Your future isn't something you can base on someone else's feelings. Trust me when I tell you, there are times in life when you *have* to be selfish."

52

Jordan

*H*ope was sitting up in bed with her laptop open when I walked into our room after work.

The minute she noticed me, I watched her body visibly tense up, but she didn't say a word.

Instead, she continued to tap away on her computer.

"Hey," I offered, feeling like I had to say something to break the tension between us.

"Hey," was her one word response.

"How was your day?"

"Fine. Yours?"

Two words.

"Long," I admitted, kicking off my shoes and yanking my shirt over my head.

I was bone weary from a long ass day at work, and fighting with her was the last thing I wanted to do.

Thankfully, she seemed to feel the same because she whispered, "You look exhausted, Jord."

I was.

300 | INEVITABLE

So fucking tired.

Pulling back the covers, I pretty much face-planted on the mattress, groaning in relief when the pressure of standing left my body.

"Are we going to talk about this?" she asked, tone gentle. I heard the click of her laptop closing moments before her hand landed on the middle of my back. "We can't keep living like this, Jordan."

"Like what?"

"Strangers."

"I warned you that being with me wasn't going to be easy," I whispered, stiffening beneath her touch. "I'm giving you all I can."

"I know," she agreed, and resigned.

"I did the meet your friends thing," I added, grimacing at the thought of that horrible fucking night.

"And I appreciate it," she stated. "But I need more."

Exhaling heavily into my pillow, I closed my eyes and willed myself to be a better man – the man she needed me to be.

I knew what I looked like.

A heartless bastard.

I was fully aware that I was handling this badly, keeping her at arm's length, but it was all I knew. Every day was a struggle for me. Just living and breathing took so much out of me.

She wanted my words.

I couldn't give them to her.

I didn't trust her anymore, and even if I did, masking my pain and concealing the lifetime of abuse I had endured was all I'd ever known.

I'd made so many mistakes in my life.

Some, I had learned from.

Some, I knew there was no coming back from.

I didn't want Hope's understanding back then, and I didn't want it now.

Chapter 52 | 301

I didn't want her help or pity either.

I didn't want her exposed to any of that shit and I didn't want her to look at me differently.

I couldn't live up to her expectations.

I *couldn't*.

I was dirty. Sullied. A fucking mess. And she was pure and perfect and better than everyone else.

It fucking tortured me to know that I was hurting her.

I was doing that.

Me.

How the hell was I supposed to explain all of that to her?

How the fuck was I supposed to explain the fact that a piece of me resented her, too? For having a family that loved her. For being protected and loved and fucking cherished.

For years, I was cast to the outside. Looking back on a life I had left behind. A life I had been forced to leave behind. I had to watch my friends, my family, live their lives without me. It hurt. It fucking pained me. But I'd made the decision to step back years ago. I couldn't take it back. No matter how bad I wanted to.

I couldn't deal with it then.

I still couldn't.

"Goodnight, Keychain," was all I whispered.

I heard her heavy sigh and a part of me wanted to die inside.

"Goodnight, Jordan."

53

Hope

The horrible awkwardness that had settled between me and Jordan finally came to a boil the following Saturday. For the first time in months, Jordan wasn't working and we were home together. Annabelle had taken Ryder to visit her sister in Boulder, leaving us with an empty house.

I wanted to use the precious time to talk about things and clear the air between us.

Obviously, I was the only one.

He had been avoiding being alone with me since the night we talked about having children. I had tried to fix things between us on countless occasions since, but whenever I tried, he brushed me off by saying he was either too tired to talk or running late for work.

We were sitting on opposite sides of the couch.

Jordan was staring at the television screen while I was staring at his side profile.

I was totally confused by his behavior as of late. It felt like we had taken three steps forward in our relationship only to take ten more back.

I was running out of patience with this cold, standoffish version of my husband and I finally said as much. "What's wrong?"

"Hmm?" he replied, not looking at me.

"I asked you what's wrong," I repeated calmly, even though it was a hard thing to do. I hated being ignored. It was a hard limit for me. I had spent close to eight years being ignored by this man. I wasn't prepared to do it again, not when we sat less than two feet apart from each other. "You've barely said more than two words to me in over a month," I added, trying to remain cool and composed. We were both adults and I wanted this to be a civilized conversation. "Is it because I said I wanted a baby?"

"Is what because you said you want a baby?" he replied, jaw clenching, still watching the television.

Anger flared to life inside of me. "This silent treatment, Jordan." That had to be it. I knew it. Men freaked out about babies.

"No," he responded. "We talked about the baby thing. That's done with."

"Is it because of the bar?"

He frowned. "The bar?"

"Yeah," I snapped, flushing. "Because I got drunk?"

"You're a grown woman, Hope," he replied tightly. "You can do whatever you want to do."

"Then why are you being like this?" I demanded hotly.

"Like what?" he asked flatly.

"So *cold* towards me," I hissed, chewing on the inside of my mouth to stop myself from screaming.

"I'm not being like anything towards you," he shot back tersely. "You wanted to spend time together and I'm here. You wanted to eat dinner together, and I cooked us a meal. You

304 | INEVITABLE

wanted to watch a movie, and I'm watching it. I don't know what else you want from me, Hope. I'm doing what you asked."

"I want to talk," I said with a sigh of exasperation.

"And I don't want to," he deadpanned, shutting me down with the lack of emotion in his voice. Dammit, he was behaving like a fucking robot.

"Please talk to me, Jordan," I whispered. "Because I'm starting to feel like I don't even know you anymore." And the truth was, I didn't. He wasn't the boy I'd grown up loving. He certainly wasn't the man I'd pledged to halve my life with. That guy was gone.

"We used to be best friends," I choked out. "We used to tell each other everything." I shook my head, at a complete loss. "Don't you remember?"

"I remember," he bit out as his jaw ticked.

"You took me to my first dance. You were my first kiss. You were the first person I did everything with. And now?" I forced down the sob threatening to rack through me. "Now, it's fading."

"Hope, don't –"

"Why not?" I demanded. "It's the truth, isn't it? You don't talk to me anymore. You don't show me you love me. You don't even seem to *care*!"

"Of course, I care."

"Then prove it," I shot back, chest heaving. "And *talk* to me."

I watched as his body grew rigid and his jaw worked over. Finally, he said, "Okay. What do you want to talk about, Hope?"

"I don't know," I shot back. "How about our marriage? Or how you're feeling? How you feel about Derek now? Or maybe your mother?"

The mom question was one I had been dying to ask him for months now, but hadn't managed to scrape up the courage. I knew absolutely nothing about Karen or what had happened to her since leaving The Hill.

Back when we were kids, I resented her so much that I hadn't cared enough to ask. In my ten-year-old mind, she was

Chapter 53 | 305

the woman who had stolen my best friend away from me and could go to hell. As the years passed by, I thought about her on and off, but the resentment I felt was still very much alive, so I had never delved deeper. I had only cared about Jordan's well-being. Never his mother's.

Jordan stiffened on the couch but didn't respond. Instead, he continued to stare at the television screen, blatantly ignoring me.

This irked me.

"I asked you a question," I snapped in a tone a little hotter than I usually used with him. I didn't want to come off like a bitch, but I wasn't invisible either. I was his wife, and I deserved an answer.

"I know," he replied tightly. I watched as his jaw worked and his Adam's apple bobbed in his throat. "I'm not ready to talk about her, Hope. Talk about something else. *Please*."

I wanted to scream *well I am!* But it was his choice.

I couldn't force him to talk to me.

It was his decision on how far he wanted to let me in.

"I want to help you, Jordan," I announced before releasing a weary sigh.

I was weary.

Weary of fighting and losing ground.

Weary of standing on the sidelines, looking in. I wanted full disclosure.

I wanted to be the woman he confided in.

Not Annabelle.

"You are helping me." He turned to face me then and his eyes were like green emeralds burning bright. "Being here with me?" he croaked in an almost helpless tone. "Staying? Giving me a second chance? That all *helps* me."

But it's not helping me, I wanted to shout, *it's not enough for me.*

I held my tongue.

Arguing with him about this wouldn't give me the answers I

306 | INEVITABLE

needed. It would just add to the long list of growing problems we were facing.

So, I smiled at him instead before turning back to look at the television.

I had no clue of what was happening in the movie we were supposed to be watching and I cared even less.

I managed to keep my mouth shut for a good ten minutes before losing the battle with myself.

Reaching for the remote control, I snatched it up and switched off the television before turning to face my husband.

"I can't do this, Jordan," I told him as I knelt on the couch beside his stiffened frame and reached for his hand. "I can't keep walking on eggshells around you wondering if the next question I ask is the one that pushes you away." I shrugged helplessly, willing him to understand my point of view. "What am I doing here, Jordan?"

"What do you mean?"

"This isn't right," I bit out. "None of this feels *right* to me."

"Don't say that."

"It's the truth." I shook my head and exhaled a weary sigh. "I feel like I'm bending over backwards to make this work and you're just...slotting me into your world when I've moved mountains to make you happy."

No response.

"I'm your *wife*." I emphasized the word, praying that title still meant something to him. "I deserve to have my questions answered." I held one of his hands in both of mine and squeezed. "For better or worse, remember?"

Jordan remained completely motionless. He didn't respond or turn his face to look at me. He just continued to stare at the now blank television screen. He didn't squeeze my hand back. It was like dead weight in my hand.

The only clue I had that told me he was listening to my words was his increased breathing and the slight flair of his nostrils as he clenched then unclenched his jaw.

Chapter 53 | 307

"I told you," he finally bit out, still staring straight ahead. "I don't want to talk about her."

"Well, I do!" I all but screamed, and the shrill sound surprised me. "I want to talk about her," I added in a gentler tone. "I want to know, Jordan. Every damn thing. I want to know about your mother. I want to know about your thoughts, and how you feel? I want to know it all." My voice was rising again, but I couldn't help it. I had finally plucked up the courage to confront him on the life he kept hidden from me and I didn't dare stop now. "And Paul," I choked out. "I want to know how much time in prison he got." I was shaking now and so was Jordan. Maybe I had crossed the line bringing up his evil bastard stepfather, but I needed to know, dammit! "I want to know that rat bastard paid for what he did to you. I need to."

"Why?" Jordan roared, finally losing his cool. Leaping from the couch, he put as much space from me as the small room allowed before looking at me with the angriest expression I'd ever seen him wear. "So you can go running back to Thirteenth Street and report every fucking detail of my life to your parents?"

Every ounce of blood drained from my face. My mind was reeling. "How did you..." I began to say, but my words faltered when I saw the look of betrayal in my husband's eyes.

"How did I find out you told your parents about *my business*?" he offered in a harsh tone. "Because of your mother."

"My mother?" I gasped.

Jordan nodded. "She showed up here back in March like Mother fucking Teresa, begging for forgiveness." He ran a hand roughly through his hair before hissing, "I trusted you, Hope!"

"I know," I choked out, mortified. "I'm so sorry."

"That wasn't your story to tell," he continued to say, furious. "It was *mine*, and if I wanted the whole fucking world to know about what happened to me, I would have said. It wasn't your fucking call!" He ran his hand through his hair once more, but this time he yanked hard on the ends. "Who else did you tell?"

308 | INEVITABLE

He turned and glared at me then. "Noah and Teagan? Do they know, too?" he demanded. "And that felon they live with – how about him?"

"Who?" I gaped. "Lucky?"

Jordan nodded. "What about him? Does he know my business, too?"

I opened my mouth to say no, but quickly snapped it shut, knowing full well that Jordan could see through my lies. "I'm sorry."

Fury blazed in his green eyes. "God fucking dammit, Hope!"

"I'm sorry, okay?" I squeezed out, feeling winded. "I was trying to help you."

"Help me?" He laughed harshly. "Well, thanks for trying. I feel a lot better now."

"Jordan," I spluttered, feeling physically wounded by his verbal outburst. "I love you. I'm trying to help –"

"It's got nothing to do with you!" he roared, visibly shaking. "So, stop, Hope. Stop trying to help! My past doesn't affect you so stop asking goddamn questions. It's my damn business, Hope. Not yours. Mine!"

"How can you even *think* that?" I demanded, his words causing me to lose control. "*Of course* it affects me, too." Was he fucking serious. "I'm your wife, Jordan!"

"And I've told you everything I'm willing to tell you, Hope," he countered shakily and I could tell he was holding onto his temper by the skin of his teeth. "So, do us both a favor and stop fucking pushing for more."

"No!" I screamed, not backing down one bit. I couldn't believe this was happening. How had this escalated so quickly? "You stop! Stop being so selfish and fucking stubborn," I hissed. "And talk to me, dammit."

"Selfish?" he repeated, paling. "SELFISH?"I watched in a mixture of shock and horror as Jordan moved towards the television and yanked it clean off the wall mount before tossing it against the wall opposite me. When that didn't completely satisfy his need for violence, he kicked over the coffee table, but not before knocking all the photo frames off the mantelpiece. "Jesus fucking Christ!" he roared in a voice he had never used with me before. His tone was frightening, but my anger overrode all the fear inside of me

"You have some fucking nerve calling me that when everything I've ever done was to keep you safe–" His voice broke off and he rubbed his jaw, obviously trying to calm himself down.

It wasn't working though.

Jordan was still thrumming with fury. It was emanating from him in waves, and red flags were flying up around me.

But I didn't move.

Instead, I stood my ground and faced him.

Jordan wouldn't hurt me.

As furious as he was, I knew he would never put a hand on me.

"You're going to regret doing that when you calm down," I bit out, blinking away the tears that threatened to spill.

"Then I'll add it to the long list of mistakes I've already made," he sneered. "Including coming back here!"

"What's that supposed to mean?" I countered shakily.

"Nothing," he spat. "Forget it. You've probably never regretted anything in your life."

"I have regrets," I shouted out shakily. "I regret keeping your secrets when we were children. I regret being the one person with the knowledge and power to save you and not using that knowledge. I regret not saving you from becoming the heartless monster in front of me."

I flinched at the cruel words that came out of my mouth and tried a different approach.

"Look," I said in as calm a tone as I could muster given the circumstances. "We're both acting like teenagers." Raising my hands up in the peace motion, I added, "Let's both just cool down here and talk about this like mature adults."

"You're still not getting it, are you?" Jordan snarled, pinching

310 | INEVITABLE

the bridge of his nose like he was in pain. "I don't want to talk about it with you, and I'm not going to talk about it with you. Not now or ever! Do you need me to write it down for you, hot shot author, so you finally understand? Or are you actually going to listen to me for once in your fucking life?"

Yeah, I was so *not* staying here to get chewed up and talked down to like I was a piece of shit.

Snatching my purse off the coffee table, I jumped off the couch and rushed straight for the front door.

"Shit, Hope, I'm sorry – wait," Jordan called after me, but I didn't respond and I didn't stop walking.

Apologies in the heat of the moment meant nothing to me. They were automatic words thrown about to settle both pride and conscience. I had too much respect for myself to fall back into his arms right away after he spoke to me like that.

I needed a time out and, from the looks of the trashed televisions set back there, so did Jordan.

54

Jordan

"I fucked up," I whispered, clutching my phone in my hand like it was the only thing keeping me rooted to the ground. I stared in horror at the trashed living room and the carnage I'd caused after Hope left and hung my head in shame. "I fucked up so bad."

"Where are you?" Annabelle's familiar voice filled my ears and I sagged against the couch. "At the house." I clenched my eyes shut, forcing every bad image and memory that was threatening to overwhelm me away from the fore point of my mine. "She's gone."

She ran.

She fucking ran out on me and didn't look back.

Even when I called her name, even when I begged her to stay, she just kept running.

A part of me wanted to let her go. If she couldn't handle me now, what was the fucking point? This was mild. I could be worse. I could be so much worse.

I never wanted to be responsible for making Hope look at

312 | INEVITABLE

me like that again. I could see the devastation in her eyes earlier. It ruined me. Disgust and self-loathing filled every inch of my body. I wanted to drop to my knees and beg her for forgiveness. I knew she would forgive me. Problem was, I would never deserve it and couldn't promise her that an incident like today wouldn't happen again. My mood swings were unpredictable. I couldn't understand them myself. And right now, I was plummeting fast into the pits of despair.

"You warned me this would happen and I didn't fucking listen," I choked out, forcing myself to breathe through the pain that was threatening to overtake me. "I'm done, Annie. I need to get out of this place. I'm so fucking tired of this."

"It's going to be okay, Jay," Annie soothed. "Just stay where you are. I'm on my way."

"How?" I whispered brokenly. How was anything going to be okay? "They all *know*." Anger fused inside of me. "She fucking told them about *him*!"

Nothing was going to be okay again.

That was the only thing I was sure of.

55

Hope

I was used to feeling heartbroken.

It was a feeling I had become familiar with many years ago.

A feeling that had followed me throughout my adult life.

I had lived with the feeling for so long that I thought I might actually miss it if I were to wake up some morning and not have that gaping, unifiable feeling in my stomach – in my heart.

What I was feeling now, though?

This was worse.

I was hurt.

Badly.

The knife Jordan had stabbed me through the chest with was causing me problems. It was making it hard to breathe.

I felt like a fool; giving him everything I had only to receive coldness in return.

Why should I allow him into every corner of my heart when he obviously wasn't offering me the same in return?

314 | INEVITABLE

His earlier words continued to swirl around in my mind over and over again. He was trying to hurt me with those comments.

I got that it was a defense mechanism. I understood.

But that didn't mean it hurt any less.

He called me a hot-shot author and he'd said it in such a way that it was supposed to be an insult.

Call me crazy, but that hurt worse than everything else. My being an author was something I was proud of. I had accomplished that career without help from my father or him. It was all mine and I hated that he had sullied that for me.

I knew where I was going.

Home.

Realistically, I knew this wasn't a huge deal.

Teagan and Noah fought like that all the time. I couldn't count the number of plates that had been smashed off the kitchen walls by one or the other of them during their fights.

But I wasn't Teagan.

I was *Hope.*

And I didn't roll like that.

I wasn't a violent person and I didn't want to be in a relationship that produced toxic behavior. He smashed the freaking television set. He threw it at the wall right by me. It had been *this* freaking close to my face.

That wasn't *normal.*

Maybe it wouldn't bother other women, but it certainly bothered me.

I wasn't into that. Not in the slightest.

Call me old fashioned, but I preferred to use words to deal with my problems.

I knew he was upset and he had every right to be, but if I had stayed, then it would have given the reaction that I condoned that type of physical violence.

I didn't and would have no part in it.

Chapter 55 | 315

When I arrived at my parent's house, I had every intention of giving my mother a piece of my mind.

Why did she have to do that?

Why?

I wasn't stupid, far from it, and had quickly come to the conclusion that the reason Jordan had been freezing me out was because he didn't trust me anymore.

I had broken that tiny piece of faith he had put in me. I felt horrible over it, but not enough to stay in a house where television sets were thrown against the walls and ugly words were used in anger.

I parked my truck in its usual spot and stomped up the porch steps towards the house. When I let myself inside, I headed straight for the kitchen.

When I rounded the doorway, the last person I had expected to greet me was Hunter Casarazzi.

But there he was, with his ass perched on my mother's kitchen table, shirtless and entertaining my little brothers.

Whatever he was saying must have been funny because Cash and Casey were laughing uncontrollably.

"What are you doing here?" I asked, gaping at the sight before me. "Where are my parents?"

Hunter swung his gaze around to face me and smiled an honest to god, carnal looking smile. "Morning, HC," he purred before shoving a mouthful of dry cereal into his mouth.

I rolled my eyes at the sight.

The man had an obsession with dry cereal. He always ate it straight from the box without a bowl or milk and spoon.

Come to think of it, Hunter did everything differently. I could never predict his next move or what would come out of his mouth next.

"Hungry?" he asked, shaking the box of Cheerios towards me.

I shook my head and placed my hands on my hips. "Care to

316 | INEVITABLE

explain why you're sitting on my mother's kitchen table half naked?"

He raised a brow and smirked. "Would you prefer I be fully naked?"

"Don't start," I warned, not in the mood for his bullshit flirting right now. I was too damn mad. At Jordan. At my mother. At *myself!* "Just tell me, what are you doing here?"

"I'm babysitting," Hunter replied in a casual tone.

"*You're* babysitting?" My brows furrowed and I gaped at him. "You?"

Hunter raised a brow. "And what's wrong with me?"

"You just don't look like the babysitting type of guy," I muttered, blushing deeply.

"There's a lot you don't know about me, HC," Hunter shot back with a flirty wink. "I happen to be a great babysitter. Isn't that right, boys?"

"Yeah," my little brothers hooted in unison. "We love Lucky."

"Cute," I bit out, feeling a little taken aback by all of this. "So, *my father* trusted *you* to babysit *them*?"

"Why wouldn't he?" Hunter countered evenly. "I take care of my responsibilities, sweetheart. Your father knows as much."

Dammit, that was true.

Hunter did take care of his responsibilities and my father seemed to respect him – had from the moment he walked into our lives with Noah.

Dad had always treated Hunter like a *man*.

Like he wasn't the same age as his children.

Maybe it was because of the way he had stepped in and taken care of his brother when they were in prison.

Or maybe not.

I didn't get it, but then again, I never truly understood what my father was thinking.

Mom was like an open book. She wore her heart on her sleeve and was as beautiful on the inside as she was on the outside, but Dad?

Chapter 55 | 317

Dad was a deep one.

He was hard to make out.

Or maybe my father respected Hunter because he had something very dark in common with him.

They could butter it up and throw technicalities around the place, use money to bury the truth, but it was a well-known family secret that my father had killed Jimmy Bennett twenty-five years ago. And he had done so in a blind fit of rage to avenge my mother.

It was also pretty well known around here that there was no level my father would stoop to or no mountain he wouldn't climb to keep her safe.

My mother was walking and breathing because of my father's actions all those years ago, and he had survived the unsurvivable – a knife to the throat – not only because he was a stubborn bastard, but because he was incapable of leaving her behind.

The love they shared for each other?

It was an insane, delirious, once in a lifetime kind of love and the reason I wrote romance.

Hell, I didn't have a whole lot of experience in the love department, but my parents?

They *humbled* me.

The sound of my little brothers laughing and joking with Hunter brought me back to reality and I balked. "Where's Mom and Dad?"

"Mom and Dad had to go out of town for the weekend," Casey informed me with a small smile.

"And they left Lucky in charge," Cash snickered, clearly delighted with our parents' choice of babysitter.

For the whole weekend? "And they left *Lucky* in charge?" I repeated, dumbfounded. "Why didn't they ask me?"

"Because he's badass and way more fun than you?" Cash offered sarcastically, rendering a frown from me and a high-five from Hunter. "And he lets us eat cereal for dinner."

318 | INEVITABLE

"How would you like to get grounded all weekend, Cash Carter?" I shot back, glaring at the cheeky little fucker. "Because that's where this conversation is leading."

"Oh, please," he countered with a wave of his little hand. "You have no power over me. Dad left the reins to Lucky." Smirking, he added, "And Lucky loves me. He would never ground me, right, Luck?"

"I wouldn't be so sure about that," Casey, ever the wise one, interjected.

"Oh?" Cash turned his glare on his twin brother. "And why is that?"

"Because he loves Hope the most," Casey replied, and his words caused my heart to jackknife in my chest. I looked at Hunter for some sort of divine intervention, but all he did was wink back at me. He was laughing at my brothers and thoroughly enjoying the conversation unfolding between them. "It's so obvious," Casey continued, scooping up a spoonful of cereal. "Right, Luck?" he asked, looking up at him with his big blue eyes.

I watched as Hunter tried to smother his laughter before saying, "I love all of you guys."

"See," Cash scoffed. "He loves *all* of us, Case."

"Whatever," Casey muttered with a shake of his head. "I still say he loves her most."

"That's gross, Case," Cash grumbled. "Lucky doesn't love *girls*. He's cool."

"They smooched," Casey shot back. "I saw them."

"We did not smooch!" I blurted out, red-faced and mortified.

"Smooched," Hunter snorted.

"You're not helping," I hissed.

"Smooched," he repeated, like it was the funniest thing he'd ever heard.

"You did too smooch," Casey countered calmly. "I saw you."

"When?" I gaped in horror at my baby brother. "When did you ever see me and Lucky *smooch*?"

Chapter 55 | 319

"At Mom and Dad's Halloween party last year," Casey replied innocently. He turned his attention to Cash and said, "He was in her bedroom, and you know what Colton said?"

Cash paled and nodded grimly. "Girls invite you to their room when they want to smooch." He looked at Hunter with an expression of disgust. "You kissed my sister? That's fucking gross, dude."

"Watch your language, Cash Carter," I hissed, flustered, as I desperately tried to plot my way out of this one.

"I've got this," Hunter interjected, saving me. "Boys, did Colton ever explain to you that boys and girls can be friends without – dear god, I can't believe I'm saying this – smooching?"

Both Cash and Casey looked at Hunter like he was talking a foreign language. "No," they said in unison, shaking their identical little heads.

"Of course, he didn't," Hunter muttered as he ran a hand through his hair. "Do you have a best friend at school?" he asked then. "A friend you like spending time with? Someone who makes you happy and you want to be around all the time?"

Both boys nodded.

"Well, your sister is *my* best friend," Hunter explained, and again, my heart jackknifed in my chest. "And I was in her room that night because we like to hang out together." He looked over at me and smiled. "She makes me happy."

Casey nodded, seemingly mollified by Hunter's explanation, but Cash continued to gape in horror. "But she's so *boring*," he stated. "And a *girl*!"

"Boys and girls can be friends, too, Cash," I heard myself say, jumping on the friendship bandwagon. It was so much easier to explain away. "Girls can make great friends, too, you know."

"Ugh," Cash muttered with a shake of his head. "Rather you than me."

"Come and say that to me in about eight years, kid," Hunter said with a grin before hopping down from the table.

320 | INEVITABLE

He walked over to where I was standing and inclined his head towards the door.

Wordlessly, I followed him outside.

"Your father called me late last night," Hunter announced in a low and oddly serious tone when I joined him on the porch. "Your grandfather's sick and his attorney applied for a probation hearing based on compassionate terms."

"Compassionate terms?" I gaped. "David Henderson doesn't have a compassionate bone in his body."

"For what it's worth, I agree with you," Hunter replied. "But apparently, the man's dying with cancer and the court approved his application for early probation." Shrugging, he added, "Your Mom and Dad have gone up there to fight it. Derek went with them."

Pulling a packet of cigarettes out of his pocket, Hunter lit up a cigarette and took a drag before saying, "They didn't want to worry you or your brothers with this, so they called me to come and stay with the boys." He exhaled a puff of smoke and said, "Your uncle's flying in from England to support your father's objection to the appeal."

I gaped. "Uncle Mike is coming home for this?"

He nodded.

"What about Noah?" I asked. "He's David's son, too."

Illegitimate, but still.

"Noah doesn't know anything about it," Hunter said. "Your father wants him protected from this just as much as you guys."

"Oh god, this is bad, Hunter," I muttered, pressing my fingers to my temples as I tried to comprehend what I had just learned. "My grandfather is a very bad man."

I didn't remember the last time I'd seen my biological grandfather, Dad had kept him away from us when we were little, but I knew all about the day he and Noah's mother, Kelsie Mayfield, kidnapped me from my crib and held me ransom.

Even thinking about it caused me to shiver violently.

My father had given up everything that day to keep me safe

Chapter 55 | 321

and protect my mother. He had signed over the hotels and his money... everything!

The boys might not remember the struggles and poverty of our youth, but I did.

I remembered it all.

How hard Dad worked, juggling a dozen jobs a day just to keep a roof over our heads, and it had been all David Henderson's fault.

I remembered the midnight hushed conversations between my parents, and the countless nights my father sat at our kitchen table and worried himself to death about the overflowing pile of bills he couldn't keep up with.

As a child, I remembered looking at my dad and thinking he was the one who hung the moon. This big, strong, invincible giant of a man who could keep me safe from everything.

It was only in the dark of the night, when I crept out of bed to listen at my parents' bedroom door, that I would realize my father was human. The sound of him crying in my mother's arms had stuck with me for many years. Or when my brother got sick, and we didn't have the money for his wheelchair.

That was all on David fucking Henderson.

My dad worked so hard to win back everything that had been stolen from him.

I was just shy of thirteen years old when my grandfather was finally sent to prison for the crimes he had committed against my family. I had always assumed he would die in there.

Evidently not.

Shaking my head, I staggered a little, feeling completely overwhelmed. "If that man is released, he's going to come looking for us." Anxiety churned inside of me as reality hit me like a wrecking ball. "He's going to try and seek revenge against my father."

"Let him try," Hunter shot back. "He won't get far."

"You don't understand," I urged, trembling now. "You think

322 | INEVITABLE

JD Dennis was bad? My grandfather is twice as smart and ten times more ruthless."

"Hope –"

"I'm serious," I choked out. "If they let him out..." I flinched, unable to cope with the fear growing inside of me. "He's a cancer on our family, and he won't stop until he destroys everything my father has!"

Everything bad that had ever happened to my parents had been at the hands or the orders of that man.

My mother had been shot because of him.

My father, stabbed.

My aunt Camryn was in the ground because of him.

Because he'd twisted and manipulated Rachel Grayson into a weapon of mass freaking destruction...

I either hadn't realized Hunter had moved, or I had been too consumed in my thoughts to notice, but when his arms came around my body, I felt myself sag against him.

The strength of his arms comforted me.

Having him close, and knowing just how capable he was of keeping me safe, settled the anxiety in my heart.

He was bare chested, with a cigarette poking out of his mouth, and all I wanted to do was cling to his strength and have him never let me go.

"Nothing's going to happen to you," he whispered. "The boys aren't the only ones your father asked me to keep an eye on."

"What are you saying? He asked you to babysit me, too?"

"He asked me to keep you safe," he corrected, tone soothing, as he held me tight. "And I told him I would. With my life."

I believed him.

Every word.

It was more than just believing him; I *trusted* him.

With everything I had.

I didn't need to ask him to promise, because it wouldn't matter.

Chapter 55 | 323

He had made it very clear that I was important to him, and in this crazy and unpredictable world, it was comforting to know I was in the arms of a man who was strong and brave and equally as wild as the shit that was thrown at us.

It was when I was wrapped up in his arms that I realized why my father entrusted his youngest sons into Hunter's care.

He was a soldier.

An unlikely one, but a soldier nevertheless.

"I need to call my parents," I announced, breaking away from the hug I had been enjoying far too much for my own good. "I need to find out what's happening."

"Okay," he replied calmly. "Do you want to come back inside to do it?"

Yes! "No, you've got everything under control here." Shaking my head, I took a safe step away from him and forced a smile. "I'm going to go. If you need help with the boys, you know my number." Having said that, I swung around and hurried down the porch steps towards my truck.

I needed to get away from here.

Away from Thirteenth Street.

"HC?" Hunter called out when I reached my truck.

Reluctantly, I swung around to face him. "Yeah?"

He was frowning at me, like I was a puzzle he couldn't quite work out. "It's going to be okay, you know?"

"Yeah, I know," I agreed, forcing a smile. "No judge in their right mind would let that man into the world again." I didn't believe it, though. He was smart and cunning and manipulative enough to sway even the most righteous of men.

"True," Hunter agreed, brows still furrowed. "But I wasn't talking about him." He flicked his cigarette away and rested his hands on his hips, his beautiful face still etched with concern. "I've got your back. In everything."

"Thanks," I whispered, swallowing down the huge lump that was forming in my throat. "I appreciate it."

56

Jordan

"I don't know how you can trust me to be around him," I muttered, several hours later, as I bounced Ryder on my knee. "I'm a train wreck waiting to happen."

That was the understatement of the century.

Our trashed living room was a prime example of how erratic I could be.

If it weren't for Annabelle returning when she had, the chances of the rest of the house remaining unscathed were low.

"What you *are*," Annabelle countered heatedly. "Is a good man." She leaned across the table and covered my hand with hers. "I see you, Jordan Porter," she added, blue eyes locked on my face. "I see the compassionate, decent, wonderful person you bury deep down inside." She released my hand and leaned back in her chair. "And so does he." She inclined her head to where Ryder was grinning up at me. The sight of him, so innocent and perfect, caused the ice around my heart to melt.

I loved that baby from the minute he came into the world and the doctor's placed him in my arms. I'd made a vow to him that day; a vow to protect him from all of the horrible shit in life that I hadn't been protected from. I made a vow to his mother, too. A vow to always be there for them both.

Honestly, I wouldn't be sitting in this kitchen tonight if it hadn't been for Annabelle Walker; my therapist turned best friend. She'd been saving my life from the day she walked into it. And even today, when I had fucked up beyond repair, she waded in and helped me make sense of things. She made me see things clearly. I wasn't able to do that on my own sometimes. I got lost in my head a lot. She was always the one to draw me back out, and guide me back to reality.

"Do you know what you're going to say to her?" Annabelle asked.

I shook my head, at a loss. "Figured I'll start with sorry and go from there."

"Sorry is as good a place as any to start," she replied with a smile. "And flowers. They're good, too."

"I'm so damn mad at her," I admitted, locking eyes with her. "I trusted her and she went running with my secrets." I shook my head and released a shaky breath. "Makes it impossible for me –"

"To trust her again?"

"Yeah." I exhaled heavily. "Impossible to trust her again and I'm thankful I didn't trust her enough to tell her ..." I broke off, unable to put into words what Annabelle already knew.

"Jay," she sighed. "Hope's young and green. She didn't mean to hurt you. She probably didn't even realize how badly you would take it. You've said it yourself, she's led a sheltered life. But she loves you. She's here and she's trying, and she really does love you."

"I didn't want her family knowing," I bit out. "I don't want to see *that look* in their eyes every goddamn time I see them." That's what would happen now. I was sure of it. That's what *always* happened.

"I guess you have a choice to make," Annabelle said after a

long pause. "Try and move past this with your wife, or go back ten steps and continue to live your life in the shadows."

"You know I want to be with her," I choked out. "More than anything."

"Then *be* with her, Jord," Annie shot back, tone thick with emotion. "Just be with *her*!"

"Just like that, huh?" I whispered, then shook my head. "You know it's not that easy for me."

"I do know it's not easy for you," she agreed. "But guess what? Hope knows that, too. And she's still willing to *fight* for you. So, the question is, are you willing, Jordan? Are you willing to fight for *her*?"

57

Hope

*W*hen I let myself inside Jordan's house later that evening, I was surprised to find the place in pristine condition. Seriously, there wasn't a book out of place.

Confused, I trailed into the living room, searching for evidence of our earlier argument, and couldn't find any.

With the exception of the missing television and the dent in the wall from where he'd thrown it, it looked as if nothing had happened.

Feeling depressed and anxious, I padded upstairs to our room and slipped inside. Whipping off my clothes, I pulled on one of Jordan's t-shirts before sinking down on the bed and grabbing my phone to dial my father's number.

It rang three times before his familiar voice came down the line in the form of a clipped one-word answer, "Carter."

"Dad," I whispered, gnawing on my bottom lip. "It's me."

"Hope." His voice noticeably softened then. "Are you okay, sweetheart?"

328 | INEVITABLE

"Yeah." I kicked my shoes off my feet and sat cross-legged on the middle of the bed. "But I'm not sure you are."

Dad was quiet for a few moments before exhaling a frustrated breath. "Fucking Lucky," he grumbled. "What did he tell you?"

"Everything," I admitted hoarsely.

"Of course, he did," Dad muttered. "Sunk, son of a bitch."

"Is it true, Dad?" I asked, hating the way my voice wobbled. "Is David getting out?"

"Not while I've got air in my lungs," Dad shot back angrily. "You've got nothing to worry about, Angel. I've got the court tied up in so much red tape it's gonna take them weeks to sort through."

"And when they do?" I breathed. "Sort through the red tape. What happens if he gets out?"

Dad was silent then and his silence only encouraged the anxiety rising inside of me.

"Dad?"

"I'm doing everything I can to stop that from happening," he replied, his tone a weary sigh. "I'm trying real fucking hard to fix this, Hope. For your mother... and for all of you."

"This isn't your fault, Dad," I shot back heatedly. "You didn't choose him to be your sperm-donor."

Because that's all David Henderson was to my father.

A sperm donor.

My Dad had grown up in foster care. He was tossed into the system at the age of three when his mother committed suicide. He was an orphan.

We were the only family he had ever known, and he protected us like our lives depended on it. And sometimes, they did...

"He can't hurt her anymore, Dad," I heard myself say, desperate to comfort him. I knew what was going through his head. It was the same thing that always went through his mind.

My mother.

Chapter 57 | 329

"Lucky said he's dying of cancer. He'll be dead soon."

"Not soon enough," Dad bit out.

"No," I agreed sadly, knowing it was a horrible thing to wish on anyone, but wishing it all the same. "Not soon enough."

"All this pain because of Frank Henderson's inheritance," I half-laughed, half-sobbed, wondering if my great-grandfather had realized the trouble that would befall on my father when he left him everything in his will all those years ago.

"Do me a favor, Hope," Dad said then, drawing my thoughts back to the present.

"Anything," I promised.

"Don't let on to your mother or brothers that you know any of this..." he paused and I heard him exhale heavily down the line before saying, "She's not sleeping again, and when she does, she wakes up screaming. I don't need the boys losing their heads and running into this all guns blazing. Your mother has enough on her mind without worrying about them, too."

Oh god.

"The nightmares are back?"

"With a vengeance."

My heart sank, and all my earlier irritation towards my mother evaporated into thin air.

"She's struggling," Dad added, voice torn and laced with pain. "She's been blaming herself for what happened to Jordan. It's been eating her up, and now this?" He exhaled another heavy sigh. "I need to keep her –"

"Safe," I filled in, already knowing what he was about to say.

"Yeah," Dad agreed. "And life isn't exactly working in my favor right now."

"I won't say a word, Dad. I promise."

"You're okay, though, right?" he asked then. "You're dealing with... everything?"

"You don't need to worry about me, Dad," I assured him. "You just focus on handling your corner of the map and I'll handle mine."

330 | INEVITABLE

"You're my daughter," he shot back, tone lighter now. "I'm always gonna worry about you."

The bedroom door creaked inwards then, startling me and causing me to lose my train of thought.

When I saw Jordan standing in the doorway, with a bunch of roses in his hand, my heart skipped a beat.

"Dad, I'm going to have to go," I mumbled into the phone. "I'll call you tomorrow. Love you."

I didn't wait to hear my father's response before ending the call and dropping my phone on the bed.

"Flowers?" I croaked out, my entire focus latched on my husband. "For me?"

"Yeah," he said gruffly, still standing in the doorway. "They go with the apology I owe you."

"Well, they're lovely," I mumbled, tucking a stray curl behind my ear.

We continued to stare at each other, both frozen, until Jordan finally broke the tension.

"Christ, Keychain," he groaned as he closed the bedroom door behind him and walked straight for me. "I am so fucking sorry for how I reacted earlier."

Even though there was a part of me that wanted to make him stew in his guilt for how he treated me today, I still found myself scrambling off the bed and moving towards him.

"It's okay," I whispered, meeting him halfway in the room. "I'm sorry, too," I whispered, throwing my arms around his neck. "I screwed up telling them, but I never meant to hurt you."

"I know," he soothed, tightening his arms around me, flowers forgotten on our bedroom floor. "I get it now."

"I love you so much," I breathed. "I would *never* set out with the intention of breaking your trust or hurting you."

"I'm screwing this up, Hope," he choked out, burying his face in my neck. "Every day, we drift further away from each other and I have no idea what to do or how to fix it."

Chapter 57 | 331

I could feel his body trembling and I ached to heal him. To make every bad thing that had ever happened to him disappear.

"I'm fucking terrified you'll wake up some morning and realize I'm a bad fucking idea."

"Are you serious?" My heart broke at his confession. "I'm not leaving you, Jordan." My voice was hoarse and thick with emotion and I meant every word. "I swear to god, I'm not going anywhere!"

"I am so fucked up in the head, Hope," Jordan replied, voice torn. "And I know I'm not treating you right... the way you deserve to be treated. Christ, I *know* it! I just *don't* know how to fix it."

"Just love me," I whispered, eyes filling up with tears. "Just love me and be my husband and stop doubting us." My voice cracked then and I had to take a moment to compose myself before I could continue. "Because every time you doubt me, *I* doubt me!" I exhaled a ragged breath. "I love you. I do. And I know you love me back. Sex isn't something you want with me, and that's okay because I get it. I do. But we can get past that part and still build a life together."

"You think I don't want sex with you?" he asked, interrupting me.

"It's okay. I understand, Jordan." My cheeks burned bright with shame. "I'm not trying to force you –"

"All I've ever wanted my entire life, was to be with you," he interrupted, green eyes locked on mine. "In every single way."

I shook my head in confusion. "But I thought you couldn't –"

"I *want* to be with you, Hope," he growled, green eyes piercing through me. "But I need to be in control. Of where you touch me, and how it happens, and what position I take you in. I need the assurance that *I* am the one with the power. That I can stop when *I* want. That you're not going to – " His voice broke off and he exhaled a ragged breath before continuing, "It

332 | INEVITABLE

has to be on my terms, all of it, and I can't expect you to be okay with being a fuckbuddy doormat for me."

"You can have me!" I blurted, nodding my head eagerly. "I'll be your fuckbuddy doormat. I'm just so relieved to know that you actually *want* me," I continued to blabber, ignoring his frowns and protests.

"Hope, you don't understand what I'm saying here." Jordan frowned at me as he said, "If you did, you wouldn't be agreeing so quickly."

"I do," I urged, feeling unhinged with how excited the thought made me. "I seriously do and I'd be happy to do it... More than happy, actually. Fucking delighted is more accurate."

"Hope..." he shook his head and exhaled another ragged breath. "I can't be... I can't handle *gentle*."

Rough sex?

Hell fucking yes!

"Where do I sign up?" I breathed, forcing myself not to break out and do the happy dance in pure joy.

"Are you sure?" he whispered. "I'm not the boy you remember, Hope. I'm different now...rougher."

Fuck me.

Without a word, I took a shaky step back from him and reached for the hem of my shirt and yanked it over my head in one swift movement.

"I'm all yours," I whispered, standing before him completely bare. "If you want me."

"Oh, you better believe I want you," he groaned. "Badly." I watched as he pulled his shirt over his head and closed the space between our bodies. "Are you sure you want this?" he asked, tone gruff and thick as he pressed his body to mine.

"I want this," I blurted out, panting. His erection strained against me, making me feel weak with want. "I'm ready –"

Jordan's lips landed on mine harshly, painfully, and I loved it. I relished in the feel of him punishing my mouth with his.

Chapter 57 | 333

I wanted to erase the demons of his past, but not nearly as much as I wanted to take him inside me again.

Gasping for breath, I wrapped my arms around his neck as he lifted me into his arms and walked us over to the switch on the wall. He flicked off the lights, leaving us in complete darkness, before moving towards what I presumed was the bed.

Seconds later, my back hit the mattress followed by his body landing heavily on top of me.

"Oh god," I moaned, opening my thighs for him to slide between them. He was rough and urgent and I loved every second of it, so much so that I cried out in pleasure.

The feel of this man doing the things my body had longed for. I pushed everything else out of my mind, concentrating entirely on this moment.

On us.

Everything about this moment felt surreal.

Having him crushed against me, straining against me, his hands on my body and his mouth on mine.

It was everything I had ever wished for.

"You sure?" he whispered. Pinning my hands above my head, he trailed kisses down my neck, stopping to suckle on my collar bone. "I'm not like before."

"I am beyond sure," I cried out, writhing beneath him with my legs spread open. We were trying again. I wanted fresh and I wanted him. In any shape or form.

He pulled away from me then, breaking our kiss, and the sudden lack of contact made me cry out in frustration.

"Please don't stop, Jordan," I heard myself beg as I shivered violently on the mattress. I didn't care if I sounded desperate. I *was* fucking desperate, and I would say and do whatever it took to keep this man between my legs. "Don't do this to me again."

"I'm not stopping," he promised in the darkness.

Oh, *thank god...*

It was only then that I heard the sound of clothes ruffling

and realized he was undressing. "Come back," I moaned, bucking my hips desperately. "I *need* you."

His weight landed heavily on me again and I gasped in delight from the contact only to lose the ability to breathe when he claimed my lips in what I could only describe as a soul-searing kiss.

I didn't care that I was weighed down so heavily that I couldn't move, and I didn't care that my hands were pinned and I was unable to touch him.

I didn't care about any of that, because he was about to give me exactly what I had wanted for so long.

"On your knees," he ordered, tone gruff and impatient.

"Wh–what?"

Not waiting for me to respond, he lifted off me, grabbed my hips, and flipped me onto my stomach.

Seconds later, I was being dragged back onto my knees.

Oh my god.

Oh my god.

Oh my fucking good god!

I wasn't sure about this position. I was quite literally face down and ass up on the bed.

It felt sort of degrading.

But I didn't have long to ponder it when I felt the pressure of the head of Jordan's cock at my entrance and his voice in my ear.

"Open your legs," he growled, using one of his hands to press my upper body into the mattress, while he knotted the other in my hair. "Now, Hope."

Unsure of how I felt about this, but eager to please him, I did as he asked.

My entire body was trembling with a mixture of fear, lust, and anticipation as I spread my legs as far apart as I could.

And then he was inside me, slamming into my too tight entrance, impaling me with such aggressive forcefulness that I cried out in shock and pain.

Chapter 57 | 335

"Fuck," I whimpered, breathing through the pain that was coursing through my womb.

I'd lost my virginity many years ago to this man, but tonight, it felt like I was losing it all over again.

"Oh god," I bit out as the burn inside of me felt like I was splintering in half. "Slow down."

He didn't slow down.

Instead, he continued to fuck me like a dog, forcing my body into submission.

I wasn't sure what I had been expecting when he said he needed rough, and I knew I shouldn't be surprised, but this wasn't it.

I didn't like this.

There was no intimacy or love in this.

This wasn't husband and wife.

This was a man and his whore.

This was dirty.

Closing my eyes, I forced my trembling body to remain in position and not collapse in a heap like I felt like doing.

My body protested venomously to the intrusion, and I tried to make myself enjoy it. I honestly did, but all I wanted to do was cry.

When the first sob finally tore from my throat, I felt him still inside me. It was the first of many tears I cried that night, because when Jordan pulled out of me and whispered, "I'm sorry, Hope. This is all I know," I came to the ugly, unwanted realization that this was it for us.

"I'm sorry," he choked out once more before shoving on his jeans and leaving me alone in the darkness.

This was it, I thought to myself.

This was all I would get from here on out.

This was all he could offer me – the only form of affection I would ever receive.

And I wanted no part of it.

58

Jordan

I didn't think it was possible for my heart to break into any more pieces.

I was wrong.

The sound of Hope crying, and the knowledge that I was the one responsible, caused whatever was left of my black heart to shatter.

I sank to the floor outside our bedroom door, dropped my head in my hands, and listened to her breaking down a few short feet away.

I wanted to go back in that room and comfort her, but I couldn't. Not when I was the reason she was crying.

Again...

Disgust filled every inch of my body as I listened to her hushed sobs. I didn't think I could ever look her in the eye again.

I wanted to erase myself from her life, and save her from the horror that was me and everything that I touched.

Chapter 58 | 337

I should have known better than to take her like that.

I should have fucking known!

Seconds rolled into minutes and I remained exactly where I was, too ashamed and fucking shredded to move a muscle.

Tears filled my eyes and I let them fall, not bothering to wipe them away as awareness smacked me straight in the face.

Hope needed to be free. I loved her enough to spare her this pain.

This fucking torture.

She was the only thing that was right in my whole lifetime and she deserved better than *this*. She was the best person I knew and I loved her enough to keep my ugliness away from her light.

And I was ugly now.

I was fucking rotten inside.

I had to give her up.

There wasn't any other way around it.

I was filthy. Dirty. Fucking infected with *his* scum. Dying from the inside out.

More than an hour had passed by when the bedroom door opened inwards and Hope appeared in the doorway, dressed in her pajamas with her eyes puffy and cheeks tearstained.

My entire body stiffened when she lowered herself to the floor beside me. "I'm sorry, Hope," I squeezed out. "For tonight... for everything."

"Me, too," she whispered, resting her head on my shoulder.

"How are you still here?" I choked out, unable to comprehend how she could stand to be around me right now.

She was devoted to me, her actions just now proved it, but I wasn't sure if it was for the right reasons.

For the reasons that would last over time, over the course of a lifetime...

"Because I love you," Hope replied, shifting closer to me. "Always."

338 | INEVITABLE

Yes, she still loved me, except it wasn't me she was loving. It was the guy I *used to be.*

Before.

59

Hope

"Do you still feel sad?"

He nodded.

"Can I fix it for you?"

He shook his head.

My heart sank.

"I want to help you."

"Nobody can help me, Hope," he whispered. "I'm beyond repair."

Up until now, I thought I could.

Until tonight, I thought he was wrong.

I had thought I would be the one to save his life.

I had devoted twenty-six years of my life to saving the unsavable.

The truth was, I had been wrong, and I wasted a lifetime on proving him right.

And now here I was, right back in the middle of his world, fracturing my pieced together existence, the center point of his breakdown.

340 | INEVITABLE

Drowning with him.

"You deserve more than me," Jordan whispered brokenly. "I can't give you a normal marriage." He exhaled a broken sob and tears flowed freely down his cheeks. "I'm here, but I can't... that part of me isn't there anymore."

He was giving me an out.

I should take it.

After what happened tonight, I *needed* to take it.

But I wouldn't.

I *couldn't*.

I refused to be another name on the long list of people that had given up on him and let him down.

He deserved so much better.

"I'm not going anywhere," I vowed. "I'm here, I love you, and I'm not leaving you."

"Do you..." His words broke off and he hung his head. "Tonight... did I?" Shaking his head, he forced himself to look at me. "Force you?"

I shook my head. "No," I sobbed, joining him in our united misery. "Don't you dare think that wasn't consensual," I choked out, sniffling when my sobs threatened to overtake me. "You warned me it would be different."

"And now you know," Jordan whispered brokenly, tone laced with self-loathing.

"And now I know," I agreed, nodding numbly.

Neither of us spoke a word after that.

We just sat side by side on the floor in his tiny hallway in heartbroken silence.

The events of tonight had signified a monumental fracture in our marriage, and we both knew it.

60

Hope

Jordan never touched me after that night.

And I never asked him to.

We never spoke about that night again, either; both of us were either too embarrassed or too ashamed to put it into words.

At night, we lay side by side in bed, our entwined hands the only parts of our bodies touching, and during the day, we passed each other like ships on separate journeys.

I wanted to speak to someone about how conflicted I was feeling, about how distraught I was inside, but there wasn't anyone to tell.

My family wouldn't understand, and Noah and Teagan were finally happy for what felt like the first time in forever. I didn't want to bring them down with my bullshit drama, so I kept it inside, and told nobody about how absolutely broken I felt inside.

I didn't feel like facing them anyway, and had avoided contact with them all week, choosing to stay at home and work on my book. I didn't have the energy to pretend I was happy anymore, which, evidently, worked wonders for my work.

It became very clear to me that conflict and misery were an author's best friend. I had finally accepted that my life was shit, and it was doing amazing things for my writing. I managed to finish on Tuesday.

It was with my editor now, who had emailed me every night since, raving about how this was my best work yet. I seriously doubted it, but took comfort in the knowledge that my work life was stabilizing.

I would have the book in time for the signing in Aspen next month.

Aspen.

My heart plummeted at the thought.

It seemed like a lifetime ago that I had been organizing the romantic hotel suite, with champagne and rose petals and all that bullshit I had thought, in my naïve state of mind, would heal the rift in our marriage.

Yeah freaking right.

"Are you hungry?" Jordan asked, stirring me from my reverie.

I looked up from where I had been daydreaming and saw him standing in the kitchen doorway with a brown takeout bag in his hand. "I got Chinese."

My heart broke at the sight of him.

He was so beautiful.

So beautifully broken.

It hurt to know that there was nothing I could do to make it better, but I accepted it now.

I couldn't fix him.

I couldn't heal the broken pieces inside of him.

Acknowledging that caused another piece of my heart to chip away.

Forcing the dark thoughts from my mind, I smiled brightly and said, "Starving."

61

Jordan

"I'm going to try harder, Keychain," I said, breaking the silence that had settled between us, as I watched her from across the table.

I'd brought home her favorite Chinese food tonight, hoping that I could somehow make up for the life I'd dragged her into. Make up for being *me*.

Hope looked up at me with those big, blue eyes of hers and my heart squeezed tightly in my chest.

"I'm fine, Jordy," she replied with a small smile that didn't meet her eyes. "Don't worry about me."

She ducked her face again, concentrating on the plate of food in front of her, and it made me want to groan in frustration.

Hope was still here.

Still trying.

Still fighting for me.

For what was left of us.

Except she wasn't *with me* anymore.

Not completely.

Yeah, she was sitting in the chair opposite mine. She was with me in the flesh, but her mind was somewhere else entirely.

And it was all on me.

That wild, carefree girl I'd spent my life adoring?

She was gone.

I'd broken her spirit.

My life had sucked the happiness out of hers.

And now, she was living with everything I had tried to protect her from.

I watched as he ran her fingers through her wild curls and bit back a pained sigh.

She was magnificent.

So damn beautiful.

But her mind was the most beautiful part of her.

It was like a dark abyss of secrets.

I knew she was keeping things from me now.

I also knew I deserved it.

I wondered if I would ever be granted entry into that inner circle she seemed to reside with.

Deep down inside, I knew there was a part of Hope Carter unattainable to me now. A piece of her heart closed off and retired. It belonged somewhere else.

I just hoped that the biggest part still belonged to me.

62

Lucky

"Morning, Luck," Teagan chirped when I walked into her kitchen on Thursday morning.

It was the first time I'd seen her in over a week and her stomach seemed to have doubled in size. I'd been staying at Thirteenth Street, looking after Cash and Casey while Kyle and Lee were away.

They'd gotten back this morning and I headed straight over here.

"Do you want a fried egg?" Teagan offered as she stood in front of the stove with a spatula in her hand. "I'm craving grease this morning."

"Nah, I'm good," I shook my head, passing on the offer of breakfast as I sank down on one the stools at the breakfast bar.

I was too fucking worried to eat.

"What's wrong with Hope?" I came right out and asked.

I hadn't heard from her since last weekend when she showed up at her parents' house looking really fucking upset.

346 | INEVITABLE

I'd sent her a dozen messages since, and had tried calling her twice.

They all went unanswered.

Something was wrong, and I was anxious, which was an entirely new feeling for me.

I didn't get anxious about anything. I'd never had reason to. *Until now...*

I didn't feel and I didn't get involved.

I lived by those two rules and I was still breathing.

I fucked women, loose women, and I did it without an ounce of guilt.

I didn't make love.

Not to anyone.

That part of my soul was gone, it had been buried with her.

Until Hope Carter crashed into my world twelve months ago and knocked me on my ass.

The fucked-up thing was, I didn't even see her coming.

And hell if she hadn't taken me down like a hurricane.

"She's ignoring you, too?" Teagan spun around to face me and let out a huge sigh. "Oh, thank god. I thought it was just me."

I frowned. "She hasn't been coming over here?" She usually came here every day.

"Not since last week," she replied, brows furrowed. "I thought I'd done something to piss her off, so I was giving her space to cool down and remember what a wonderful person I am. But now? Now, I'm worried."

"Yeah," I muttered, rubbing a hand over my jaw. *Me, too.*

"I'll call her after breakfast," she said. "See what's going on." Her face darkened then. "If that dickhead has upset her, I'm going to kill him."

"Jordan?"

"Who else?" Teagan scowled. "He's made it his life's mission to crush that girl. There's no doubt in my mind he's the problem here.... ugh, you know what? Screw the eggs. I've lost

Chapter 62 | 347

my appetite," she groaned, dropping the spatula down on the counter before turning off the gas at the stove. "I'll do it now. I won't be able to eat until I know she's okay."

Teagan disappeared down the hallway for a few minutes before returning with a frown etched across her face.

"Well?" I demanded, feeling anxious as hell.

"She's fine," she mumbled, still frowning. "She's at the hotel – went to see her dad."

"Then why are you looking like that?"

"Because..." Teagan's voice trailed off. She stared down at the phone in her hands and blinked a few times before looking up at me. "I've got this bad feeling, Luck. In the pit of my stomach." She chewed on her lip. "She sounded like she'd been *crying.*"

I was off the stool and moving towards the door.

"Where are you going?" she called after me.

"To see her."

"Want me to come with you?"

"No," I shot back, heading for the door. "I've got this."

Whatever was happening with Hope, I was going to fix it.

Yeah, I was the fucking fix-it guy now.

63

Hope

*W*hen my father called this morning, asking me to meet him at the hotel later that afternoon, I just knew he wanted to talk about my grandfather.

They were just back from their trip and the seriousness in Dad's voice assured me that it had not gone his way. I was fully convinced he was going to sit me down and give me the bad news that the judge had decided to release David.

When I walked into my father's office later that afternoon and saw him sitting on the throne of the Henderson empire, looking every inch the ruthless businessman, I began to wonder.

"Take a seat, Hope," Dad said, all businesslike, when he spotted me hovering in the doorway.

"Okaaay," I replied, feeling extremely jittery as I claimed the chair opposite him.

For some reason, whenever I sat in this office, I didn't feel like the confident, self-assured, grown woman I was supposed

Chapter 63 | 349

to be. No, with my father looking at me the way he was, I was reverted to a bashful and secret-ridden teenager.

What was this about?

Was I about to receive bad news?

Was I in trouble?

"Is David out?" I finally blurted out, unable to stand the unknown.

"No," Dad replied, frowning at what had to be my terrified looking expression. "I managed to get his hearing adorned for two weeks."

I pressed a hand to my chest and sagged in my chair. "Oh, thank god," I whispered, as relief filled my heart. "I thought you called me here to give me the bad news."

"But I think we need to brace ourselves for the possibility that he might be," he said then, blowing my world to smithereens. "I've been talking to my attorney – several of them actually - and it's not looking good, sweetheart."

"What?" I breathed, wide-eyed and horrified. "But you said –"

"I know what I said, Hope," Dad bit out, blues eyes filled with pain. "But he's the perfect fucking prisoner. Perfect rap sheet. Perfect behavior. Smart enough to display remorsefulness to the right people. And he's already served thirteen years of his sentence." Swallowing roughly, he added, "Compassionate release or not, he was getting out next year anyway."

"But he's *dying*," I snarled. "Can't they just let him die in there?"

"Hope–"

"You can't let this happen, Dad," I choked out. "You have to stop this."

"It's not definite, Hope," Dad replied, tone worn and pained. "And I'll fight it every step of the way, sweetheart. But we're going to have to accept the fact that in a few short weeks, he could be a free man."

350 | INEVITABLE

"They can't let him out, Dad," I choked out. "He's going to come straight for us."

"I won't let that happen," he vowed. "I promise, he's not going to get anywhere near you guys."

"How can you promise that?" I squeezed out.

"Because I'm your father," he growled, running a hand through his hair. "And I would take the damn world down before I allowed a hair on your head to be harmed." He exhaled heavily and added, "Any of you! I'll keep you safe."

His phone rang then, distracting him from our screwed-up conversation, and he pulled his cell out of his pocket.

"Carter," Dad said in a clipped tone.

I watched his face as he listened to whatever was being said on the other line. "I'm tied up here, Kenny," he snapped, tone impatient. "What's the fucking urgency?" He frowned then and cast a glance towards me. "He's here?" Dad sighed heavily and ran another hand through his hair. "No, no, you can send him up in five." He smirked then. "Yeah, I didn't think he would."

"What was that about?" I asked when he had ended the call. "Pushy guest demanding to speak to the owner?"

"Something like that," Dad shot back with a wry smile.

"What are you *smirking* at?"

"Irony, sweetheart," Dad replied.

"Irony?" I frowned in confusion. "The irony of what?"

"Of history repeating itself," he finally answered.

I frowned in confusion. "History?"

"History," Dad confirmed. "Which brings me to the second thing I wanted to talk to you about." Shrugging, he added, "You know, without the rest of the family adding their two cents."

"There's more?" I asked, gaping. "Please tell me it's not more bad news, Dad?"

"Not bad, per say." Dad ran a hand through his hair and sighed. "How's... life?"

I gaped. "Life?"

Chapter 63 | 351

He nodded. "Yeah, life."

I shrugged uncomfortably. "It was going fine until you told me that my deranged, psychopathic grandfather could be released from prison."

"Crazy grandfather bullshit aside," Dad countered, frowning a little at his own words. "How's...everything?"

"Fine, I guess." I stared at how uncomfortable he looked right now and asked, "Are you okay, Dad? Is there something you want to talk to me about?"

"On the contrary, I was hoping there was something you might want to talk to me about," he replied.

"Me?" I frowned. "I'm fine, Dad. Nothing to report."

"Why do I find that so hard to believe?"

"I am *fine*," I repeated.

"How's everything going with Jordan..." His voice trailed off and he reached up and loosened his tie before saying, "Is he treating you right?"

"We're fine," I forced the lie from my lips and smiled brightly to boot.

"Yeah?" he shot back, looking unconvinced.

"Yeah," I confirmed.

My father continued to study my face with sharp blue eyes, a color spookily similar to my own.

Shoving back his chair, Dad stood up and walked around his desk. Leaning against the front of it, he comically ran his hand through his mussed up brown hair and blew out a breath. I had a feeling that whatever he was about to say was painful for him both to admit and verbalize so I gave him my full attention. "Look. I know what I've been like with you. I've treated you differently from your brothers. Held you on a pedestal. Tried to wrap you up in cotton wool." Sighing he added, "Obviously, I did the wrong thing..."

"Dad–"

"Hear me out." He sighed again before saying, "You ran away

from home at eighteen. You married him in secret and lived with that pain for almost a decade. You were... alone." He scrunched his nose up, like the words he was speaking were causing him physical pain. "Because you couldn't talk to me. Because I made it impossible for you to be a...a...

"Woman?" I offered, fighting back a smile at the huge change in conversation.

"Yes." Dad nodded. "Because I struggled to accept that you were becoming a woman." He shook his head and exhaled a sigh. "I'm sorry, Hope. I am. And I blame myself for where you are now."

"Dad–"

"I want you to know that you can talk to me," he interrupted. "Without being judged. I promise you, sweetheart, that the only thing you will get from me is my support and love. Because I love you so goddamn much!"

"What's this about, Dad?" I whispered, feeling my cheeks burn. "What are you expecting me to say here?"

"I don't know," he shot back. "Maybe the truth about how you're really feeling?"

I sat back and gaped. "What?"

"Do you think I can't see when one of my children is unhappy?" he asked, eyes locked on mine. "Hell, I can see it in your eyes right now. The pain inside of you. The secrets you're hiding."

"I don't have any secrets and I am not unhappy, Dad," I shot back, feeling unnerved at his perception. "I'm *fine*."

Dad cocked a brow at me. "Don't piss down my back and tell me it's raining, Hope Carter, and don't you dare say you're *fine* again." He was on the move again, pacing the floor. "I hate that fucking word, especially when it comes out of a woman's mouth."

"What's wrong with being fine?"

Dad snorted. "I've been with your mother for almost thirty years, Hope. You think I don't know how misleading the word *fine* is?" He smirked before saying, "Not my first rodeo, sweetheart."

"It's hard, okay?" I admitted, voice torn and thick with emotion. "Being back together after all those years apart?" I swallowed the lump in my throat before continuing, "It's taking some time for both of us to... adjust."

"Adjust?" Dad repeated, frowning. "I know I'm getting old here, but what the fuck does that mean? Is that code for something?"

"No," I grumbled. "It means what it means."

"Adjust," Dad repeated once more, still looking puzzled. "To what?"

"Ugh, Dad," I groaned. "Please don't make me spell it out for you."

His eyes widened as awareness dawned on him. "Adjust," he choked out, paling. "As in... romantically?"

"Do we really have to talk about this?" I wailed, mortified.

"Fuck no," Dad wheezed, sounding thoroughly disgusted. He stood up then and walked over to his office door. "Just go back to lying to me and telling me you're fine..." Pausing at the door, he turned around and said, "Just, answer me one question."

"Okaaay?"

"Do you love him?"

What kind of question was that?

"Of course, I love him," I shot back with an eye roll. "He's my husband."

"That's good," Dad replied without hesitation. "But I was talking about the second coming of Charlie fucking Hunnam. You know, your uncle's cellmate who hasn't stopped looking at you longingly since you came home?"

"Dad!" I hissed before taking a moment to mentally high fiving him for his accurate descriptive techniques. Meanwhile, my heart rate skyrocketed. "You can't be serious?"

"You must think I've been living under a rock," Dad shot

354 | INEVITABLE

back. "And hell, most of the time, when it comes to you, I prefer living under a rock, but when I can see it, how he looks at you? How you look at him? That's pretty fucking serious." He exhaled heavily before saying, "So tell me straight, sweetheart. Are you in love with the man?"

"He's my friend," I spat, as I desperately tried to calm my racing pulse. "That's all. Jesus, Dad!"

"Huh," Dad mused before placing his hand on the door-knob. "Well your *friend* is here to see you."

With that, my father yanked open his office door and my eyes landed on Hunter standing in the doorway.

The minute I saw him, I sprang to my feet, a knee jerk reaction.

He looked from me to my father and nodded in acknowledgement.

"Kyle."

"Lucky," Dad replied, gesturing him inside.

His brows were furrowed. Concern was etched on his face.

"What's wrong with you?" he asked, tone low and gruff, turning his attention back to me. "Teagan said you sounded upset on the phone."

Hunter didn't seem to give a damn that my father was standing at the door, watching our interaction.

He walked straight over to me and enveloped me in a hug. "Are you okay?"

Stunned, I could do nothing but stand there as he wrapped me up in his arms.

"I'm fine," I squeezed out, patting his back. "Honestly, I'm fine."

"She's all yours, Luck," Dad called over his shoulder. "Maybe you can get her to open up."

With that, Dad walked out of his office, leaving us alone.

"I think my father likes you." I frowned at the thought. "Scratch that; he definitely likes you."

Chapter 63 | 355

"Of course he does." Hunter looked down at me and grinned. "Everyone likes me."

"Wow, Hunter," I chuckled, taking a step back, and breaking our hug. "Cocky much?"

"There's nothing wrong with being self-assured, HC," he shot back with a wink. "You should try it sometime – god knows you have plenty to brag about."

"Really?" I countered as I walked around to my father's chair and sank into it. "How about my failing marriage? Should I brag about that?"

Hunter didn't say anything to that right away.

Instead, he took the seat opposite me and just stared across the table at me.

"Please forget I just said that," I mumbled, mortified at my gut reaction to blab like a baby to this man. "I was being over dramatic."

"No can do," he countered, icy blue eyes locked on mine. "What happened?"

"Nothing," I said, flushing.

"Bullshit," he countered, cocking a brow in challenge. "Bull-fucking-shit, HC."

"Well, how about I don't feel like talking about it?" I snapped a little hotly.

"Better," he replied, not missing a beat.

"And I especially don't want to talk about it with *you*." Okay, that sounded bitchy, but I couldn't help it. I also couldn't stop myself from adding, "You are the last person on earth I want to talk about my marriage with!"

Anger boiled inside of me, caused by Jordan, but directed entirely at Hunter.

I knew I was being a complete bitch right now, and taking my frustrations out on the wrong man, but he was the one that was *here*.

"You know, I didn't answer your calls for a reason, *Lucky*!" I sneered, hating myself more with every word I spoke. "You'd think you'd take the hint that I don't want to talk to you, but no. You had to come over here and torment me!" Exhaling a ragged breath, I hissed, "I don't want to be around you right now. And another thing; I don't even know why you'd think I'd *want* to talk to someone like you."

64

Lucky

*L*osing myself to this woman was a bad fucking idea.

I wasn't the kind of man they expected her to end up with. I wasn't clean collared and professional. I had baggage in my heart and skeletons in my closet.

Yeah, I knew she deserved to be with a good man; one who led a wholesome, clean life. She would never have that with me. I had too many enemies. But no one would ever come close to loving her like I did. She would be safer with me than anyone else. And I sure as hell could love her better than *him*.

The moment I saw her, I knew she was going to be trouble.

I should have heeded Noah's warning.

I should have stayed away.

I didn't.

And now, I was fucking hooked.

She was expecting me to leave.

She was fully prepared to watch me walk away from her.

That man she called her husband had fucked her up so badly, she didn't believe she deserved to be loved.

358 | INEVITABLE

Eight years of abandonment had fucked her up so badly, she was settling, living in a life she thought she deserved.

She deserved better.

More.

And I planned to give that to her.

I knew I must be fucked in the head, because instead of being angry at her cruel jabs and low blows, I was fucking thrilled to see her finally come to life.

She was erupting like a volcano, right here in her father's office, and I couldn't be happier about it.

It was about damn time.

65

Hope

*H*unter leaned forward, resting his elbows on the desk, and stared at me.

I sat back in my chair and just stared right back at him.

Why wasn't he leaving?

Why wouldn't he go?

"Someone like me?" he finally said, smirking.

"A criminal," I accused.

"I sure am," he shot back with a grin. "I've killed before and, chances are, I'll do it again."

Gah! He was so frustrating. He pissed me off so much I wasn't sure I could look at him again without losing the battle with good and scratching his eyes out.

Immediately, I slapped a censor sticker on that thought and scolded myself. I didn't think like this. I wasn't that kind of girl. That kind of wild and crazy was all Teagan. I was the mature, composed friend.

What was he doing to me?

What was he making me become?

360 | INEVITABLE

"Don't you see how wrong that is?" I hissed.

The smile that spread across his face only fed the fury inside of me and I couldn't stop myself from hissing, "You burnt down a house with an innocent woman inside."

Hunter nodded, not even trying to deny it. "I sure did, sweetheart, and you gave me an alibi."

He shifted in his seat again, but made no move to get up and leave.

Quite the contrary; he looked like he was getting comfortable.

That aggravated me to levels I'd never known before.

"And another thing," I snapped. "My father didn't want me to know about David, but *you* told me!" I spat the words like I was listing a crime he'd committed.

I had no idea where this sudden aggression had come from, but I couldn't seem to reign it back in. I was being reckless with my words, desperate to provoke a reaction from him.

Again, I had no clue why. But he was and, right now, he was the target for my pain.

He stayed.

He always freaking stayed.

Regardless of how indecisive and irrational I was being.

He didn't leave me.

He didn't walk away.

He *stayed*.

I hated that!

"You knew it would upset me to know and you still went ahead and laid it out there. Why'd you do that?" I demanded. "Jordan would never do that. He would *never* tell me something he knew would upset me."

I was baiting him by bringing up Jordan.

Why, I had no clue.

But I was definitely baiting him.

"Of course, he wouldn't," Hunter shot back, jaw clenching.

Chapter 65 | 361

"Because he prefers to leave you in the dark and lie." He sniffed before adding, "Real fucking stellar guy, he is!"

"He's a *good* person," I snarled. "And all he's ever done is try to protect me, which is more than can be said for you, *friend*!"

"So, because I give you full disclosure I don't have your back?" he asked. "I'm a piece of shit for that?" He ran a hand through his hair, clearly frustrated. "I'm not going to lie to you to protect your feelings, because it's bullshit! You're not a child, HC. You're a grown ass woman and deserve to be treated like one," he hissed gruffly, not giving me a chance to respond. "When you are with me, you are my fucking *equal*. There has never been any bullshit gender politics between us. You've never been one of those flailing women who want to be treated like a wallflower and shielded from the world because you possess a pussy, so don't start pretending to be one now."

When I didn't respond, he threw his head back and laughed humorlessly.

"I don't know, Hope. I really fucking don't." With that, he stood up and turned towards the door.

"Finally," I choked out, ignoring the pain in my chest as I watched him walk away from me. "You're taking the hint and leaving."

My words caused Hunter to halt mid-step. "You want someone to spar with, HC? Someone to take your pain out on?"

Swinging around, he walked right back to the desk and leaned over it.

"Fine. Give me your worst, sweetheart. Let it all out. Blame everything that fucking asshole's done to you on me. Because unlike your fantastic fucking husband, I *won't* walk away from you when you need me. I'm a horrible, selfish bastard like that."

"Just get out!" My heart was racing so hard in my chest right now, I feared it might burst. He was towering over me, closing in on my personal space, making me feel tiny in comparison to his huge frame, and I didn't like it. "Leave!"

"Not a chance," he shot back tauntingly.

362 | INEVITABLE

"Hunter, go away!"

"No."

Fury coursed through my veins, igniting much deeper and complex feelings that he was bringing to life inside of me.

Without giving a second thought to the repercussions of my actions, I swung my hand back and whacked his cheek. "Go away, dammit!"

"You call that a slap?" Hunter laughed, not even flinching. Lowering his face to mine, he taunted, "Come on, daddy's girl, you can do better than that!"

Losing all common sense, I stood up, reached across the desk and grabbed a fistful of his hair. Sinking my nails into his scalp, I dragged his face roughly to mine.

"You're an asshole," I hissed.

And then I kissed him.

The moment my lips crushed against his, I knew I was making a terrible mistake, but every ounce of common sense I possessed evaporated into thin air, replaced with a jolt of scorching heat in my core.

And when he kissed me back, and I felt his tongue touch mine, a ripple of pure, unadulterated pleasure shot through my body, causing me to moan into his mouth.

One of his hands was knotted in my hair, the other on the curve of my neck as he kissed me back with violent passion.

With his lips still on mine, and his tongue in my mouth, Hunter reached over the desk and dragged me towards him.

I went willingly; scrambling over the mountain of paperwork and other important documents on my father's desk in my rush to get to him.

To get to where my body so desperately wanted to be.

The flame I hadn't realized I had been holding for him had ignited like a fireball in my chest.

His hands came around my middle, tugging me closer. Unable to stop myself or talk myself down from the ledge I was inching towards, I knelt on the edge of the desk, shuddering at

Chapter 65 | 363

the wonderful feeling of having his hard, muscular chest pressed against mine.

It was only when a loud sound came from somewhere nearby that I realized what the hell I had done.

"Mr. Carter," Mrs. Brimble, my father's elderly secretary, called out from the other side of his thankfully *closed* office door. "Marcus is here for the quarterly report. Shall I send him up?"

"Fuck," I gasped, wrenching my mouth away from Hunter's.

"Don't answer her," Hunter groaned, moving to kiss me again.

Balking, I jerked my head to one side, avoiding his lips. "I can't..." I shook my head in horror. "I'm so sorry for doing that."

Hunter stared at me like I'd lost my mind. "What?"

"I..." My voice trailed off and I looked at his swollen, thoroughly kissed lips before whimpering in shame. "I shouldn't have kissed you."

Hunter glared at me. "Are you serious right now?"

I nodded in disgust.

"Mr. Carter?" Mrs. Brimble called out again with another impressive knock for an old lady. "He's waiting in the lobby. Shall I send him up?"

"Dad's not here right now, Mrs. Brimble," I croaked out, eyes locked on Hunter. "He went out for uh...for, um, lunch."

Every inch of my body trembled as I unattached myself from Hunter and scrambled off the desk.

"Hope, wait," Hunter growled. "Talk to me about this."

I couldn't.

Not right now at least.

"I'm sorry," I whispered.

Shoving past him, I ran to the door and threw it open.

"You should call him on his cell," I muttered to my father's secretary before darting past her.

66

——————

Hope

*J*ordan and Derek were in the kitchen when I barreled into the house a little over an over later, with my nerves frazzled and my brain a puddle of mush between my ears.

What the hell had I just done?

I kissed him.

I kissed Hunter!

"Where's the fire?" Derek joked when he saw my ruffled appearance and panting chest.

In my panties, a voice in my head cackled cruelly.

"Oh, hey, Uncle Derek," I choked out, still feeling breathless. My gaze landed on Jordan and I cringed before composing myself enough to say, "Hey Jord."

"Hope?" Jordan said with a frown, as he turned to face me. "Are you okay?"

No! No! No! "Yep," I squeaked out. "Perfect. Fantastic."

His brow creased in concern. "You sure?"

"Yeah!" I started to shake my head but ended up nodding

Chapter 66 | 365

frantically like a deranged idiot. "I'm just..." Shaking my head, I backed out of the kitchen. "I'll be right back!"

Turning on my heels, I ran full speed up the narrow staircase, not stopping until I was inside the tiny family bathroom with the door locked firmly behind me.

Sinking to the floor, I leaned my head against the doorframe and exhaled a shaky breath.

My phone began to vibrate in my pocket and I balked, horrified.

Digging into my jeans pocket, I retrieved the wretched device and whimpered loudly when Hunter's name flashed across the screen.

I stabbed the reject button and clenched my eyes shut.

I couldn't talk to him.

I couldn't fucking breathe.

Inhaling short, puffy breaths, I tried to get a handle on myself, but it wasn't coming easily.

Did a kiss constitute as cheating?

Because if it did, then I had just committed adultery.

"Fuck," I groaned, banging my head against the bathroom door. "Fuck!"

This wasn't me.

I wasn't the type of woman who kissed other men.

Maybe I had more of my aunt Cam in me than I had my mother.

I needed to focus on what was in front of me.

When my phone vibrated again, I slid my finger across the screen and put it to my ear. "I have no idea why I just did that!" My chest was heaving, my words coming fast and clumsy in my rush to fix the monumental fuck up I had just created. "Please..." Cringing, I clenched my eyes and exhaled a pained breath. "Can we pretend that never happened... *please*?"

I held my breath as the seconds ticked by, and waited for his response.

"Forget what, HC?" Hunter finally asked, tone light.

His response was so fucking perfect I felt like crying.

Exhaling heavily, I allowed my shoulders to sag and whispered, "Thank you."

67

Lucky

*G*oddamn. This woman. She broke me.

Fuck, worse than breaking me, she fucking *fixed* me.

I didn't ask for this shit.

I didn't ask to *feel* again.

I was perfectly content with the way my life was rolling out before her.

And now?

Now I couldn't fucking breathe, and it had nothing to do with the twenty pack of Marlboro I'd just consumed.

This woman wasn't mine, she would never be mine, and still it didn't stop me. I was willing to give it all to her, if she only wanted me to.

Fuck, I'd never been so twisted up in knots in my whole damn life.

If this was what it was all about, this love shit, then I was ready to throw my hand in and lay it all on the line for Hope

Carter. See, she was still a Carter. That had to mean something. She never took his name. She wasn't fully his. I still had hope...

Fuck me if I knew how I'd wrangled myself into a situation like this, but nevertheless, here I was. A fucking wreck willing to risk it all - my heart, my brain, my goddamn sanity - to be with a woman who bore the stamp of another man.

"Please..." Hope whispered down the line. "Can we pretend that never happened... *please*?"

Jesus Christ.

I couldn't forget it.

If I lived another hundred years, I wouldn't be able to erase the memory from my mind, or how unbelievably fucking right it felt when she put her mouth on mine.

For the millionth time in the past year, I wanted to burst in and drag her away, but I couldn't.

This was her choice.

I couldn't make this decision for her.

I couldn't force her to *choose* me.

If he'd just stayed away, then she would be with me now.

I knew what she wanted.

I knew what she liked.

I knew exactly what she needed and I was more than willing to give it to her.

I knew she wanted me.

Problem was, she didn't realize it yet.

But she was starting to. I saw it in her eyes when she broke our kiss. There was a brief look of wonder just before her face caved into a tortured expression. There was a part of me that wanted to kick my own ass for making her feel so conflicted. But another part of me was glad she was finally waking up.

She cared about me, and her awareness of those feelings was waking her up from a lifetime of lying dormant.

"Forget what, HC?" I forced myself to ask, giving her exactly what she wanted.

"Do you think I screwed up our friendship beyond repair?"

Chapter 67 | 369

Her voice came down the line and I bit back the urge to roar. "Hunter?"

Closing my eyes, I dropped my head against the door I was leaning against. "You didn't ruin anything," I whispered, playing along with her denial at the expense of my heart.

"You're sure?"

"Yeah," I choked out. "I'm sure."

68

Hope

*W*hen I woke up on Friday morning, it was with the sole focus of putting the spark back in my marriage.

The disconnect between us had to stop.

One of us had to do something to try and bridge the gap, so I decided that someone would be me. Which was why, by seven o'clock this evening, the house smelled like a florist had thrown up in the living room.

Okay, so maybe I had gone a tad overboard with the rose petals everywhere, but dammit, I was determined to make tonight a success.

I had even texted Annabelle this morning and asked if she could make herself scarce for the night.

Surprisingly, she had texted me back almost immediately with three huge thumbs up, followed by a message letting me know that she and Ryder would stay with her sister, and then a third and final text to wish me good luck.

I cooked his favorite dish – lasagna – and I shaved every

Chapter 68 | 371

inch of my body before dressing in the sexy, red baby-doll I'd bought at the store this morning.

I'd made a decision that I would try harder for him. I would make an effort. Yeah, I was still slightly traumatized from our last sexual encounter, but I wasn't a quitter. I figured I'd learn to enjoy it, and if that's all he could offer me, then I would take it.

When I had everything in order, I sat at the kitchen table and waited for him to come home from work.

And waited.

And waited.

When Jordan finally walked through the door at a quarter after ten, he looked exhausted. He walked into the kitchen only to halt mid-step when he noticed me sitting in what was as good as underwear at the table. His eyes widened momentarily as his gaze raked over me before noticing the trail of rose petals he'd trudged over.

"Hey," I said, cheeks reddening as I got to my feet. "I've been waiting for you."

"Hope?" Jordan frowned as he glanced around the room again before settling his attention on me. "What are you doing?" He looked around again, this time doing a full three-sixty, as if he couldn't quite figure out what was going on.

"I'm attempting to seduce you." Shrugging sheepishly, I gestured to my attire. "I thought it was kind of obvious."

"Right now?"

I frowned at his words. "What's wrong with right now?"

He looked at me, expression pained. "I have to go back to the hospital –"

"No," I blurted out, interrupting him. "No, no, no, you don't!"

"I really do," he groaned, looking pained as he stared at me. "I just came back to grab my notes."

"Cancel," I urged, prowling towards him. "Call in sick." When I reached his side, I pressed my body to his. "Stay here with me."

372 | INEVITABLE

"I can't," he choked out. "There's a patient that was just admitted. High risk."

"So?" I hissed. "There are other staff at the hospital, Jordan. They can manage without you."

"I told my boss I'd come in and work with him," he choked out. "He's a previous patient of mine. Relapsing. I'm sorry, Hope."

"Sorry?" I balked, taking a step back from him. "You're sorry!"

"I didn't know you'd be..." his words trailed off and he gestured to my near-naked body. "Waiting for me."

"I can't believe this." Jerking away from him, I placed my hands on my hips and glared. "Have you any idea how much work I put into planning this evening for us?"

"I'm sorry, okay?" He turned and grabbed a stack of paperwork off the counter. "Look, I really have to go." He paused and looked at me with a pained expression. "Can we talk about this when I get home?"

"Are you serious right now?" I gaped at him. "No, we most certainly cannot talk about this when you get home!"

"I'm sorry, Keychain, but this is my job. I *have* to go."

"No. I don't give a shit if this is your job or not," I snarled unsympathetically, following after him as he walked towards the front door. "Don't you dare walk away from this, Jordan!" I hissed as I watched him open the front door. "I mean it," I called out in warning. "Walk out that door and there's no guarantee I'll be here when you get back."

"I love you."

And then he was gone.

Again.

Leaving me alone.

Again.

"Asshole!" Furious, I stormed into our bedroom and grabbed my overnight bag from under the bed. With trembling hands and a growing temper, I began to pack my

Chapter 68 | 373

pajamas and a spare change of clothes, needing to get the hell away from this place. Not bothering to change, I slipped an oversized hoodie on before shrugging into a pair of baggy sweatpants.

I wasn't going to sit in this house and wait for him to come back.

I'd spent eight long years waiting for him to *come back*.

No more.

No freaking more.

I had to get out of here.

For the sake of my own sanity.

I couldn't put up with living like this.

Giving my whole, my freaking all, to him and getting a slither of him in return.

Why couldn't he stay?

Why couldn't he put me first for once?

Because he didn't want to, and because everything that ever happened in our relationship happened on his terms.

It was all about what he wanted, what he felt okay with, what he decided was right, and I was done with it.

It made me a horrible woman and a weak one, but I couldn't handle this life.

I wasn't selfless enough to live like this.

I couldn't fight his demons, not when they were crippling me, too.

I was losing myself in this and I didn't like it.

If he wasn't prepared to put our marriage first, then why should I?

When I had my overnight bag stowed away in my truck and was halfway down the street, I dialed Teagan's number.

She answered on the third ring. "Hey!"

"I need a favor."

"Okay..."

"Jordan and I had a huge fight." I looked in the mirror before pressing on my blinker and turning onto the street. "And

374 | INEVITABLE

I need a place to stay for the night. I can't go home and listen to my parent's bullshit, and they'll know if I check into the hotel."

"Yeah, sure. Come over."

I sighed in relief. "You're sure?"

"Of course–" She paused and I heard some ruffling and whispered murmurs in the background. "We're not at home, but you still have your key, right?"

I took a quick peek at my keychain and nodded. "Yeah, I do."

"Hope?"

"Yeah?"

"Want me to kick his ass?"

I bit back a smile. "God, I love you."

WHEN I REACHED THE HOUSE, I KILLED THE ENGINE AND JUST SAT for a moment, thinking everything over.

I felt so lost.

I felt like a freaking teenager again and I despised it.

I was beginning to resent myself for being so naively stupid for believing in love and happy ever after. Because if this was mine? If this was all I got, I wanted a freaking refund.

Anger and shame crept through me, causing me so many conflicting feelings that I lost it and smacked the shit out of my steering wheel.

Maybe I needed to go downstairs to Noah's basement and work out my frustrations on one of his punching bags?

I was so freaking frustrated and angry and bitter and a million other ugly, negative feelings.

Bummed out, I let myself into the house and trudged straight into the kitchen, dropping my bag on the marble tiles before making a beeline towards the refrigerator.

I needed something to drink.

No, I *wanted* something to drink and I wanted to be able to drink it without having the guilt of consuming it around my recovering addict husband.

Grabbing a chilled bottle of Savion Blanc, I retrieved a wine glass from the cupboard and plodded into the living room, preparing to spend the night in misery and mourning my failing marriage.

Doomed, was the word I finally determined best suited our marriage.

Jordan and I were fucking doomed from the get-go.

Love wasn't enough in our case and I didn't think it ever would be.

I didn't bother switching on the television.

I wouldn't be able to concentrate on anything anyway.

Not tonight.

I waited for what felt like forever for him to call me or send a text.

He didn't.

With every glass of wine I consumed, my cell became the enemy.

I was burning mad.

Hurt and rejection washed through my veins, blending with the alcohol and making for a disastrous concoction.

Finally, the silence was broken by the sound of the front door slamming.

Too drunk to get up, I remained where I was seated and decided to crane my neck around to see who was there.

When my eyes landed on Hunter, and the gorgeous blonde draped in his arms, the pain I had felt earlier laughed at me.

It was as if my heart was saying, *Ha fool, you think that's pain, you haven't seen anything yet.*

Scorching, blinding, paralyzing spasms of pain shot through my alcohol ridden body.

His eyes landed on my face and surprise filled his features before awareness dawned on him.

376 | INEVITABLE

But he didn't push her away or try to explain himself like I had half expected him to do.

No, instead he gently coaxed her up the staircase – to his bedroom no doubt

Jesus.

Oh, dear god.

Clutching my chest, I was almost surprised when my hand came away without any remnants of blood; it certainly felt like I had just been sliced through the heart.

Tears poured down my cheeks, but I remained silent, motionless, grief stricken on the couch.

My soul felt like it was being dragged clean out of my body.

I was surprised I was still breathing.

I felt like I should have been dead by now because this pain should have killed me.

One shrill, harsh sob tore from my throat and, angry with myself for letting it out, I threw my glass at the fireplace.

The sound of the glass shattering didn't help me or ease my pain, so I curled up in the smallest ball I could and rocked.

I heard his pained growl moments before I felt his hands on my body.

"Go away," I sobbed, barely able to breathe through the pain as Hunter hoisted me into his arms.

"No," was all he replied as he carried me up the staircase towards my old room.

When we reached my bedroom, he kicked the door inwards and walked us over to my bed before sitting me down and crouching on his hunches in front of me.

"Get out," I cried.

He didn't.

"I said go!"

He ignored my screams and he didn't leave.

Instead, he reached up and wiped my mascara stained cheeks with his thumb. "No."

Chapter 68 | 377

"I hate you so much," I sobbed as I leaned my cheek into his touch.

"I know," he whispered as he continued to clean me up.

"Why are you even here? Go back to your whore!" I hissed, shoving him roughly away with one hand, only to bunch his shirt in my other hand and pull him closer. I was beyond confused. In fact, I was sure I was going crazy. "Fuck!"

"I'm sure my sister wouldn't appreciate being called a whore," Hunter replied in a coaxing tone of voice. "Though, I've only known her for a year, so I can't really vouch for her on that."

"Your *sister*?"

Hunter nodded and wiped my cheek with his thumb. "That hot mess you saw me cart off to bed was Hayden." He paused to capture another traitorous tear from my cheek before saying, "I got a call about an hour ago from a friend telling me to come pick her up." Sighing, he added, "Guess she fell off the wagon again."

"I didn't know you had a sister," I hiccupped, feeling like a fool for my demented reaction. "How old is she?"

"Nineteen, though she acts like she's nine."

"Damn."

"What?"

"I remember what that age felt like." I cringed in sympathy. "Tough age for a girl."

"Seems to me like twenty-six isn't exactly smooth sailing either?" He gave me a knowing look. "Am I right?"

The grip I had on his shirt tightened as a pained sob tore from my lips. "God, I'm such a mess," I whispered, dropping my head in shame. "I think I'm going crazy."

"Oh, I don't know," Hunter replied with another overly-dramatic sigh. "Maybe just a tad." With his thumb, he tipped my chin upwards, forcing me to look at him. "But I like your crazy." With that, he tapped the tip of my nose with his finger and smiled sadly. "So, what happened?"

378 | INEVITABLE

I blinked in confusion. "Huh?"

"You're here," he filled in, "you're alone, and you're sad. What happened?"

"It's a very long, very drawn out story," I whispered, hiccupping as I tried to steady myself. Feeling both mentally and physically exhausted from tonight's events, I kicked off my sneakers and curled up in a ball on the bed. "But the ending goes something along the lines of 'he broke my heart again and now I get to live unhappily ever after' – again."

I watched Hunter watch me for the longest moment before he finally shook his head and rose to his feet. "Goodnight, HC."

"Don't go," I whispered when he turned for the door. "Please." Swallowing deeply, I added, "Can you just stay and hold me until I fall asleep?" Shivering, I added, "I just really need somebody to hold me tonight."

I watched as a tirade of emotions flickered across his face before landing on what looked like subdued resignation.

"Move over," he whispered and I did.

The mattress dipped when he sprawled out beside me.

Turning on my side, I snuggled my back against him and shivered when I felt his arm come around me. "You always make things better."

His breath fanned my neck when he whispered, "Goodnight, HC."

That night I slept like a baby.

69

Lucky

I woke to find her sleeping beside me.

For the longest time, I just stared at her, memorizing the way her face looked when dawn was breaking.

I knew I should wake her up, but I didn't have the strength to.

I wanted to keep her.

Selfish as it sounded, I was glad she'd fallen asleep last night.

I got to have her for a little while longer.

For a stolen moment in time, I got to pretend that she was only mine.

Of course, when she woke up and realized she'd accidentally spent the night in my arms, everything would go to shit and I would spend the next five days trying to reassure her of bullshit I didn't believe and wanted even less.

But I loved her.

And loving her made me bend all of my morals.

It changed something inside of me, softened something.

Made me willing to do whatever it took to keep her happy, even if that made me miserable.

70

Hope

Some days, the lonely, empty feeling inside my heart was harder to bear than others.

Today was one of those days.

When I woke up this morning, there were storm clouds outside my window and a pain in my heart. It felt like the ridge between me and Jordan was spreading at a rapid rate.

I figured this was how all women feel whose husbands had endured what mine had.

In a perfect world, I would be waking up this morning to my husband's smiling face.

Instead, I was waking up to the color of a cloud ridden sky and an empty bed.

A glutton for punishment, I curled up in a ball and took stock of my life.; it was something I did every year on this day.

Career wise, I had peaked at the tender age of twenty-two. Now I was riding the wave of success, having knocked out book after book for the last five years.

My publishing success left me feeling anything but fulfilled

382 | INEVITABLE

though. Most days, I still felt empty inside, and knowing that my marriage wasn't working the way I had hoped made me want to curl up and die.

Sitting up in bed, I read and then reread the note I had found on my nightstand when I woke up.

Raincheck on dinner tonight.
Got called into work the double shift at the hospital.
I'll see you in the morning.
J. x

I STRIVED TO FIND THE PART OF MY BRAIN THAT WAS PROUD OF MY husband for being such a compassionate and amazing man that gave every waking hour of his time to people in need, but all I came back with was the word *typical*.

This was so fucking typical.

Scrunching up the handwritten note, I tossed it across the room and dropped back onto my pillow, feeling depressed and wishing I was anywhere but here.

What the hell was I doing with my life?

Where was this going?

Jordan wasn't showing me that he wanted to make this work, and I was losing the will to keep going. I was growing weary of carrying the both of us, and a piece of my heart begged me to call it a day before it got any worse.

Every day since returning from my brief escape to Teagan's, I questioned my decision on coming back here.

I wondered if I was making a mistake.

But what could I do?

How could I give up now?

Chapter 70 | 383

I could hear Annabelle and Ryder downstairs, but I didn't dare go down and join them.

It was still early and, knowing my luck, I would be left with the baby while she rushed off for whatever meeting she had today.

Annabelle was beginning to rely on me for childcare like she did Jordan.

And while I honestly loved Ryder, I didn't want to become his built-in babysitter any more than I already was.

Feeling cranky and drowning in disappointment, I reached for my phone on the nightstand.

Unlocking the screen, I went straight into my messages and began to type.

> Hope: Teagan, I think I've made a huge mistake.

I STARED AT THE WORDS I HAD TYPED AND PRAYED FOR DIVINE intervention, but all I got in response was a huge swell of guilt.

How could I do that to Jordan?

How could I even *think* those words, let alone type them out with the intention of sending them to *Teagan*? She was already burning mad at Jordan over our last fight. If she had further confirmation of how unhappy I truly was, she'd reign hell down on him.

Thoroughly disgusted with myself, I erased the message and tossed my phone on the bed before wrapping my arms around my knees.

I was a horrible human being.

Releasing a heavy sigh, I clenched my eyes shut and tried in vain to calm my racing mind.

It didn't work, though.

384 | INEVITABLE

The silence around me only seemed to make matters a million times worse, and when I heard the sound of the doorbell ring around an hour later, I was still drowning in my rampant thoughts.

I paused mid-meltdown and decided that the walls and flooring in this house must have been pathetically thin because I could hear Annabelle clearly as she greeted the person at the door. "Hello, *you*!"

"Oh, hey... is Hope here?"

Oh my god.

Oh.

My.

Fucking.

God.

The minute I heard the familiar male voice, I leapt clean out of my bed in wide-eyed horror.

"Omigod. What the hell is he doing here?" I yelped as I dove towards the chest of drawers across the room, only to stub my toe on the foot of the bed, and almost killing myself in the process.

"Shit," I squealed, hopping to my destination on one foot. Throwing open the top drawer, I grabbed the first pair of pajama pants that came my way and roughly yanked them on. I grabbed a tank top and quickly pulled it on before hobbling out of the room.

Weeks had passed since my meltdown at South Peak Road, and while we had fallen back into platonic-friends territory and had hung out on several occasions since, things were different now. Everything had intensified and I found myself more aware of him; how he moved, the different smiles he wore, his laugh, the color of his eyes, and how they changed slightly with his moods.

When I reached the top of the stairs I was greeted by the sound of Annabelle's girlish laugh coming from the kitchen. "I

Chapter 70 | 385

can't believe how good you are with him, Lucky! He really loves your facial hair."

"Yeah well, I love kids."

"I can tell... do you have any kids of your own?"

"Um, no."

"But you want kids?"

"Uh, sure. When the time comes."

"That's really good to know."

Ugh.

That skank was laying it on thick.

With my bitch-mode in full force and my stubbed toe forgotten, I stomped down the stairs, fully prepared to shut this shit down.

It was bad enough that I had to suffer sharing my husband with the woman, I was *not* sharing my Lucky, too!

Okay, so I knew that made zero sense and Hunter wasn't my anything, but dammit, she couldn't have him.

No freaking way.

Like a woman on a mission, I marched towards the kitchen and slung the door open, feeling frazzled and, if I was being honest, a little territorial and deranged.

However, the moment my eyes landed on Hunter standing in the middle of our tiny kitchen bouncing Ryder up and down in his arms, my annoyance evaporated and my ovaries exploded.

No joke.

The sight of this bad-ass man, covered in tatts and, let's be real, oozing sex appeal, holding a freaking baby ,caused a very strong biological reaction inside of me.

My heart went wild at the sight of him.

I couldn't make it stop.

It was hammering in my chest like I had run a marathon.

Excitement at him being here and the anticipation of what he wanted caused my body to tremble.

I wasn't expecting this – *him*.

386 | INEVITABLE

I didn't know I could feel this way by simply having a man's eyes on me.

One look at Annabelle's face told me she was having the same problem.

Immediately, my hackles rose.

"What are you doing here?" my tone was curt, bordering on rude.

Hunter turned and looked at me. "Hey, friend." He winked and gave me one of those megawatt smiles. "Nice jammies."

I looked down at my pajamas in confusion for the briefest moment before turning beetroot red.

"I'm just a writer in my mid-twenties who spends her days in cat printed pajamas and eating my weight in Oreos."

"For the record, you look damn good for a woman who eats her weight in Oreos..."

SHAKING MY HEAD TO CLEAR MY THOUGHTS, MY GAZE LANDED ON the rectangular shaped envelope in his hand.

The sight of the envelope and the thought of what it could potentially be, caused my heart to hammer wildly against my ribcage.

"What's that?" I asked, not daring to get my hopes up.

He didn't remember.

He couldn't have.

"What – this?" Hunter asked, still grinning, as he held the envelope out to me. "Is for you."

Blushing furiously, I stepped forward and took the envelope from his hand before quickly tearing it open.

An abnormal swell of emotion rushed through my body as I stared down at the card in my hands, only to end up laughing when I read the message printed inside.

I hope your birthday is as great as your ass.

"Yeah, I thought you'd enjoy that greeting," Hunter chuckled. "Took me fucking hours to find it."

"How did you remember it was today?" I managed to squeeze out, though my throat was so dry it felt like sandpaper. I was pretty sure I had only mentioned my birthday once to Hunter and that was sometime last year.

"Uh, maybe because you told me?" he shot back sarcastically. I watched him snatch a huge bouquet of flowers off the kitchen counter and thrust them towards me. "Happy birthday, HC."

"Wait – it's your birthday?" Annabelle squeaked in surprise as she took Ryder from Hunter and placed him on her hip. "Jordan never said."

Because Jordan never remembered, I thought to myself.

"It doesn't matter," I replied, taking the flowers from him. "It's not a big birthday or anything. I'm only twenty-seven today." My face burned with heat as I walked over to the sink and placed the bouquet on the draining board. "Do we have a vase?"

"Under the sink." She frowned for a moment before adding, "Well, happy birthday, Hope."

"Thanks," I replied, retrieving the vase to place my flowers in. When I was done, I swung around to face Hunter. "You know, I can't believe you remembered." I smiled and, for the first time in what felt like forever, it was genuine.

He smiled widely back at me and I bit back a sigh. Someone really needed to frame that man's smile and hang it somewhere. It was fucking beautiful.

"You better go upstairs and get your ass dressed," he said

388 | INEVITABLE

then. "If I don't deliver you to your parent's house by three, your father will have my balls."

"Oh god," I groaned, covering my face with my hands. "What do they have planned this year?"

"I'm not entirely sure. But I overheard something about pink balloons and party hats."

"Fuck."

My response made Hunter laugh and Annabelle say, "Go on upstairs and get ready for your party, Hope. I'll keep Lucky company."

Yeah, I bet she would.

I wanted to stay right here in the kitchen and *not* leave her alone with Hunter, or better still, take him upstairs with me.

Knowing I couldn't do either, I nodded dejectedly and headed upstairs to get showered and dressed.

"Oh, I almost forgot," I heard Hunter say when I was halfway up the staircase. "Today's a big day for you, too, right?"

"Me?" Annabelle asked, tone laced with confusion.

"Yeah.," he replied "Today was supposed to be your fake wedding day, right?"

I could only imagine the expression on Annabelle's face in that moment. The gasp that tore from her throat was enough to know she was taken aback.

"Anyways, happy fake wedding day," he added in a carefree tone of voice.

I couldn't hold in the snicker that escaped me as I hurried up the rest of the steps.

That man was the best friend *ever!*

When I came back downstairs twenty minutes later, it was with a head full of wet and tangled hair.

Call me crazy, but I didn't want to waste a copious amount of precious time trying to wrangle my curls into submission –

Chapter 70 | 389

not at the expense of leaving Hunter alone with the blonde goddess that was my roommate.

To my immense relief, when I walked back into the kitchen, Hunter was alone at the table.

"Your roommate told me to let you know that she had to leave for the baby's doctor's appointment and to have a great birthday." He frowned before adding, "I think I hurt her feelings with the whole fake wedding comment."

I thought about it for a moment before shrugging. "Nah." I wasn't about to feel sorry for Annabelle over anything. "Serves her right for going along with that lie."

Hunter didn't say anything to that.

His focus was entirely on me.

"Christ," he muttered gruffly as he got to his feet, eyes still locked on me. "Are you trying to cause a riot, HC?" he purred, giving my body a slow appraisal. "You look gorgeous."

My face flamed with embarrassment as I forced out a nervous chuckle. I looked down at the red wrap dress I had on and grimaced.

My boobs were spilling out of the low-cut fabric, but I felt comfortable in this dress. It had an awesome way of hiding my less than perfect assets while emphasizing my better ones.

"Well," I mused, "if my parents insist on taking a family photo, like they do every freaking year, then at least I'll look halfway decent in this."

71

Lucky

"If my parents insist on taking a family photo, like they do every freaking year, then at least I'll look halfway decent in this."

"Are you fucking with me?" I asked, scratching the back of my head in utter confusion.

The woman was batshit crazy. She was standing in front of me, trying to talk down her looks, when I'd never in my thirty-one years on this earth seen anything like her.

Seriously, was she messing with me right now?

"Fucking with you?" Hope squeaked out with a confused expression.

"Jesus," I muttered with a shake of my head.

How did she not see what I saw?

How did she not know she was the most beautiful fucking woman I had ever had to misfortune to lay eyes on?

I loved the color red on her.

When she was wearing red, she looked like a blazing fire, resembling exactly what she represented to my heart.

Chapter 71 | 391

Because the woman set me on fire.

"You are the most beautiful woman I've seen in real life," I told her. Hope was gorgeous and she deserved to know it. No, scratch that; she deserved to *feel* it. "No exceptions."

My comment only caused her cheeks to grow even redder than before.

I didn't get it.

If I was a woman and looked like Hope, I'd be naked and in front of a mirror all-day long.

"Anyways," she squeezed out, clearly uncomfortable. "We should get going."

I thought about pushing the subject, but decided against it.

Hope wasn't the kind of woman who took compliments well.

I didn't like that, either, but it was something that would take time to change.

And time was something I had plenty of.

72

Hope

To my utter chagrin, when we got to my parent's house, I realized Hunter had been right about the party hats and cake.

My entire family was there, Noah, Teagan, and Derek included, and I was showered with hugs, kisses and all the attention that came with having a birthday.

It was disgustingly embarrassing and I loved every minute of it.

It was a nice feeling. To be surrounded by my family and friends. Even Cam showed up for cake – minus his pregnant girlfriend, of course.

I decided to leave shortly after eight, but not before Dad and Derek had told their annual tale of how they delivered me on the side of the road in what Derek liked to refer to as my father's *Maternity Merc*.

Watching my father playacting around with Derek was amusing to say the least.

Chapter 72 | 393

Those two were like two sides of the same coin – completely inseparable.

It didn't seem to matter what life threw at them; they *stuck together.*

Unrelated through blood, yet brothers of choice – of life.

An unbroken bond of forged brotherhood that seemed to be relentlessly resistant.

Watching them together made me think of Jordan.

And thinking of Jordan made me sad...

"Do you have plans for the rest of the evening?" Mom asked, trailing after me into the hallway.

"No," I admitted honestly as I shrugged on my jacket. I didn't have any plans and I didn't see any point in lying about it. My life was dull. Mom knew this. "I'll probably just order some takeout and read a book or something."

"Oh." Mom seemed nervous as she fingered one of her curls. "No plans with Jordan?"

I bit back the urge to cry at the mention of his name. "No," I said instead. "He's, uh, working a double shift at the hospital." Shrugging, I added, "He won't be home until the morning."

Mom frowned in concern. "He's working a double shift again?"

As always, I mentally cried. "Um, yeah. He works a lot."

"You two are okay though, right?" she asked, looking up at me with big, glassy, gray eyes. "You're doing okay?"

I knew what she was asking, and I knew the answer she needed to hear in order to sleep tonight. "Yeah, Mom," I lied, forcing a smile. "We're doing just fine." She wouldn't sleep if she thought I was having problems, and she barely slept as it stood. She didn't need to take on my demons. She had enough of her own. "We'll celebrate my birthday tomorrow," I added brightly. Another lie, but it seemed to appease her.

"That's good," she replied, smiling. "I love you both so much." Pressing a small hand to her chest, she added, "I just want you to be happy."

394 | INEVITABLE

"I know, Mom," I managed to squeeze out, smiling so hard I thought my face might crack. "And we are happy."

She was quiet then, looking up at me like a lost puppy.

"Mom," I whispered. "Are *you* okay?"

"Oh, I'm fine, honey," she soothed. "Just fine."

The fear in her gray eyes assured me she was anything but fine.

"What's wrong?" I came straight out and asked.

"Nothing," she assured me brightly – too brightly.

"I'm not stupid," I told her. "I can see something's bothering you." I was about to ask if it was my grandfather, but remembered I wasn't supposed to know. "I'm here for you," I said instead. "Always."

"I know that," Mom whispered, pulling me into a tight hug. "Lord, I love you so much, Hope Sarah Carter."

"I love you, too, Mom," I whispered, squeezing her back.

"Are you leaving?" a familiar voice called out, breaking the moment I was having with my mother.

"Yeah," I replied, turning my attention to Hunter who had joined us in the hallway. "I called a cab about thirty minutes ago."

"Cancel it," he ordered, stepping aside for my mother who was rushing back to the kitchen – no doubt to break up the growing argument between Colt and Cam I could hear happening. "I'll take you back."

"You don't have to do that," I mumbled. "It's a long drive."

I noticed how he never said home. It was always there, or back. He never once referred to Jordan's house as being *my* home.

"No," Hunter argued, reaching around me for his jacket. "I drove you here. I'll drive you back."

I thought about arguing with him, but decided against it when I realized I *wanted* him to drive me home.

"Are you sure?"

"I'm always sure," he shot back with a smile.

Chapter 72 | 395

My eyes trailed after him as he walked to the front door and slung it open.

"Besides," he added with an easy smile. "There's something I want to show you on the way."

"What?"

"I bought an apartment down on tenth and I want you to see it."

My mouth fell open in surprise. "You *bought* an apartment?" Racing after his retreating figure, I followed him outside. "But you live with Noah and Teagan."

"No..." he drawled as he opened the passenger door of his truck and gestured me in. "I *stay* with Noah and Teagan– when they need me." I climbed inside and Hunter closed the door behind me before walking around to the driver's side. "I *live* at my own place," he added, once seated in the driver's seat. "Buckle up."

"Hunter."

"Hope."

"You *live* with Noah and Teagan," I argued as I fastened my seatbelt, not taking my eyes off his face. "You've been living there for months!" What the hell was he talking about?

"I'm thirty-one, Hope," Hunter mused as he cranked the engine and pulled away from the sideway. "What makes you think I don't have my own place?"

"Because you *don't*!" I shot back, flustered.

He threw his head back and laughed at my response. "You're so fucking cute."

"Okay, okay," I conceded, throwing my hands up in resignation. "Show me your *house*."

"It's an apartment," he corrected with a wink. "And I will. But first, we need to go shopping."

"Shopping?" I gaped at him. "For what?"

"We're going to buy a cake," he simply replied.

"A cake?" Christ, he was so weird. "Can I ask why?"

396 | INEVITABLE

"Cakes are for celebrations," Hunter said, like he couldn't understand why I had asked him the question.

"Yeah, okay. And we need a cake because?" Frowning, I folded my arms across my chest and added, "if you say we need cake because it's my birthday, then we don't. I'm stuffed from the chocolate one Derek made earlier."

"No, we don't need cake for your birthday. It's for something else."

"What?"

"It's a surprise," he teased.

"You're going to tell me, right?" I asked.

"I might." He shot back with a grin. "If you help me find a cake."

"Fine," I replied, trying to smother the goofy smile that was spreading across my face. "I'll help you find a cake."

BY THE TIME WE GOT TO THE CONVENIENCE STORE, IT WAS LATE IN the evening and all the fresh cakes were sold out, so we ended up buying the ingredients to make one at his place instead.

"You sure you know how to make a cake?" Hunter asked as we rode in the elevator of his building to the fourteenth floor.

The elevator doors jerked open and I followed him down the pristine hallway to 29B.

"Of course," I shot back dryly. "I was taught by the best."

"Who – your mom?" he asked as he twiddled his key in the door and pushed it open.

"Try Derek," I snorted, stepping inside, only to freeze on the spot as my eyes took in my surroundings. "Holy shit."

I was kind of stumped.

I was thoroughly stumped, actually.

"This place is..." Breaking into a stride, I hurried into the enormous open plan kitchen/living room and spun around in awe. "*Amazing.*"

Chapter 72 | 397

The floor to ceiling window on the opposite side of the room caught my attention and I rushed over to it. "Wow," I gushed, staring out onto the night lights of Boulder. "I think I can see my father's hotel from here."

"You can," Hunter agreed. "It's a decent view."

"Decent?" I shook my head. It was more than decent. It was epic.

Nosily, and without permission, I wandered through his apartment, opening every door and cupboard as I went.

This was a great apartment. Two bedrooms, and a balcony. A massive, fully fitted kitchen. Super cute walk in closet in the master bedroom and a bathtub to die for in the master ensuite.

God, Hunter was so *neat*.

There wasn't a sock out of place. I'd heard about this from Teagan. She said that Noah was exactly the same.

Apparently, it had something to do with being caged for a half a decade.

Well, Hunter had been caged for twice that amount.

Thinking about that made my heart hurt.

Being here, in his apartment, alone with him, was about the last thing in the world I should have been doing, but like everything I did lately, I chose wrong.

I made a bad decision.

Selfishly, I went with the darkness inside of me – the part of me that craved his company more than my own sanity.

73

Hope

I wasn't even a drinker, I hardly ever touched a drop, but twice in the last month, I'd found myself consuming my annual quota.

And Hunter?

He didn't judge me or make comments about my poor decision skills.

Quite the opposite; he seemed to enjoy watching me let my hair down.

I guess that's why I felt so comfortable around him.

He touched something deep inside of me, something or some part of me that no one else could reach. A part of me that I was beginning to learn was reserved entirely for him.

He had this way of making me laugh. Of making me feel like everything was going to be okay, when it so clearly wasn't.

When we were together, I felt more like me and less like me all rolled into one.

My feelings were a contradiction and I was beginning to feel deeply conflicted.

Chapter 73 | 399

I was drunk, too drunk to be alone with this man, but that didn't stop me from accepting another drink from him. And it didn't stop me from enjoying the way he made me feel.

Hunter's eyes were glassy, his smile loose and carefree, as he enthralled me in conversation. My body language mirrored his as we both blocked out the rest of the world and concentrated entirely on each other.

"So, I have to ask," I announced an hour or so later, when I had consumed half a dozen beers and had our poorly proportioned cake placed in the oven. "How are you affording this place?"

Hunter looked up from where he had been washing the utensils we had used during the baking process in the sink. "What are you insinuating, HC?" His tone was light and full of humor, but I still felt heat flood my face.

"I was just wondering how a guy like you could afford –" I slapped my hand over my mouth, mortified. "I didn't mean it like that."

"A guy like me," he mused humorously. He shook off a suds-covered plate and placed it on the draining board before turning to face me. "God, you know how to compliment a man."

"I am so *sorry.*"

"Nah, it's cool." He walked over to the fridge and grabbed two bottles of beer.

Uncapping both, he handed me what I thought must be my seventh bottle of the evening before taking a deep swig from his own.

"I'm not poor, Hope," he finally said. "Don't know where you got the idea that I was."

"The orange jumpsuit might have had something to do with it," I offered and immediately regretted it. "Fuck."

Hunter threw his head back and laughed freely. "Yeah. Maybe."

"I'm sorry. I really shouldn't drink," I replied. "Seriously. I'm a lightweight." I raised my bottle and said, "A few of these and

400 | INEVITABLE

I'm already *way* past tipsy," I muttered, feeling like such a tool. How blunt could I get? I swallowed a huge mouthful of beer before adding, "I shouldn't have pried."

"Feel free to pry on me," he shot back with a wink. "You're the only one who has permission." He took another swig before adding, "Come on, HC. Ask your questions. I know you have them." Grinning, he added, "I'm an open book."

"Okay." Taking another slug from my beer bottle, I mustered up the courage to ask, "Where'd you get the cash to afford a place like this?"

Hunter leaned against the counter and met my gaze head on. "I inherited it."

"The apartment or the money?"

"The money."

I drank the contents of my beer bottle before asking, "Legally?"

Hunter smiled fondly. "Yes, Hope. It's totally legit and above board."

"So, did the money come from a relative?"

He nodded. "It did."

"Who?" We had never spoken about his family before now.

It wasn't something Hunter had ever brought into conversation before tonight, and in all honesty, it hadn't occurred to me. Not with all the Teagan and Noah drama that had been going on.

Hunter walked back to the refrigerator and grabbed another two beers.

"My parents," he confirmed before handing me one. "Contrary to popular belief, this *broke-ass felon* isn't so broke."

"What's that supposed to mean?"

"It means you're not the only kid with a rich ass daddy – whose entire life's work was willed to his first-born son."

"For real?"

He nodded. "Obviously, it's not a chain of hotels or anything so glamorous, but I'll be financially okay for a few years. And

Chapter 73 | 401

Mom left me the house back home in Gunnison, which I recently sold. My time in that town is over. Bought this place instead so at least I'd have a place to hang my head when I need it."

"Both of your parents are dead?"

He nodded.

Oh fuck.

Fuckety fuck, fuck, fuck...

His parents were dead and I was a nosey bitch.

"I'm so sorry," I whispered, mortified.

"It's okay, Hope," he replied, tone soothing. "They died a long time ago, sweetheart."

How was it that *he* was the one comforting *me*?

"How did they, you know..." I let my voice trail off, not wanting to finish the sentence for fear it would upset him.

"My mom passed away about seven and a half years ago, after a very long and very soul-destroying battle with ovarian cancer. And my father? He passed when I was eleven – not that it made much of a difference to my life. " Hunter took a swig of beer before saying, "He wasn't around much when I was growing up. Guess you could call him a check in the mail daddy – he split when I was four and left my mother to raise me alone. I did manage to catch that particular funeral though." Shrugging, he added, "I was still inside when my mother died." He took another swig from his bottle before saying, "She was buried a month before anyone told me."

"Jesus," I strangled out, unable to form a coherent sentence.

What was I supposed to say to that?

"I do have one living family member. My sister, Hayden – you remember?"

I nodded in embarrassment. "I remember."

"She happens to be an even bigger pothead than your husband," Hunter added brightly. "Guess my father was as much of a fuckboy as he was a shitty father." He paused for a moment before adding, "To be honest, I'm expecting plenty more half-sibling to fall out of the woodworks." Frowning, he added, "He was a whore."

I had no idea what to say to him and I was fairly certain my facial expression said as much. "I..." Shaking my head, I struggled to find the right words. "Hunter, I..."

When the words didn't come, I set my bottle down on the counter, walked over to where he was standing, and wrapped my arms around his waist. I poured all of my sorrow for all he had endured into the hug.

I thought I was doing a pretty good job at comforting him, until he hit me with the killer blow.

"I'm thirty-one-years-old today, Hope."

My entire body stiffened and I swung my gaze up to gape at him.

"It's your birthday, too?"

He nodded. "What are the odds, right?"

"Right." I swallowed the huge swell of emotion rising inside of me. "Is that what the cake's for?"

He nodded again, but this time a smile broke through, dazzling me.

"Hunter, why didn't you *say* anything earlier? We could have celebrated together."

"Because I don't care about my birthday." Hunter smiled down at me and tucked a wandering curl behind my ear. "I just wanted to spend yours with you."

"Why?"

"Because you're my best friend."

"I'm a terrible best friend," I muttered as I furiously tried to calm my racing pulse. I continued to hug him and he continued to stare down at me.

He was just so tall and strong and primal...

I knew I needed to step away, but my body refused to listen to my brain.

I knew there were a million reasons why I shouldn't be close to this man. And every time I wasn't with him, every

Chapter 73 | 403

single reason why he was a bad idea for me built up in my head until I had a bulletproof case against him with a list as long as my arm of all the reasons why Hunter and I shouldn't be friends. But those reasons always seemed to evaporate into thin air when he was close by.

It seemed like the only time I could stop overthinking and just *breathe* was when I was alone with him.

He wasn't judging me and I wasn't pretending around him.

I was *me* when I was with him and, surprisingly, being *me* seemed to be enough for him.

"I didn't even get you a card," I added lamely.

"But you baked me a cake," he offered cheerfully.

"I would have bought you a gift had I known."

"I don't want a gift," he countered. "I want the cake."

He wants the cake.

He wants your fucking cake.

Oh Jesus...

Why wouldn't my body just calm the hell down?

I was a married woman, dammit!

Jordan, I mentally repeated over and over. *You're married, Hope. You're back with your husband now. Hunter... Lucky... He means nothing to you. Nothing!*

The timer rang, startling me and breaking the tension building between us.

"Well, happy birthday," I croaked out before forcing myself to remove my hands from his rock-hard waist and taking a sensible step back. "Your present is ready."

Grabbing an oven mitt, I opened the oven door and checked on our masterpiece. "Well, shit." Removing the tray from the oven, I dropped it down on the draining board and sighed in dismay.

Hunter, who was hovering behind me, added, "It looks kind of..."

"Floppy?" I offered dejectedly. "That's because it sunk." Ripping the oven glove from my hand, I tossed it on the counter and spun around to face him. "That's never happened to me before."

"Hope, come on, don't look so sad. It's just a cake," Hunter coaxed. "It doesn't even matter, sweetheart."

"But it was your present," I moaned. "And it *sunk*."

"Then dance with me instead," he suggested. "That can be my present."

"Dance with you?" I narrowed my eyes. "Are you serious?"

He smirked. "Why not?"

"Because there's no music," I shot back. "And it's *weird*." I stared around the room aimlessly before refocusing my gaze on him. "I'm not dancing."

Hunter's brows shot up in what looked like a silent challenge. "You're not dancing, or you're not dancing *with me*?"

"Both," I shot back. "I'm not dancing – alone or with you."

"Oh, I think you'll change your mind," he walked over to the iPod dock plugged into the wall and began to fiddle around with the shiny black iPod touch attached to it, "when you hear this!"

Seconds later, music blasted loudly through the otherwise silence.

I raised a brow in disbelief when I recognized the song playing.

"Hozier?"

"What?" He looked comically wounded. "Hozier is a fucking genius."

"I agree, but *Jackie and Wilson*?" I shook my head, at a loss. "I guess I was expecting something... else."

"Come on," he teased, prowling towards me. "Let's go."

"No," I giggled, backing away from him. "No freaking way, Hunter."

"Oh, come on," he laughed, reaching for me. "What have you got to lose?"

My heart, I thought to myself as I dodged his interception. "I'm not doing it."

Chapter 73 | 405

"It's just a dance," he added, wrecking me with that smile. "Just one dance." When he reached for me this time, I wasn't quick enough to dodge. "Just two people moving in the same direction to some fucking fantastic music." His hands snaked around my waist, pulling my body closer to his. "What do you say, HC?"

"A big fat no."

"Oh, come on," he said with exaggerated exasperation. "How often do you get all dolled up and wear a pretty dress?"

"Are you saying I don't dress up enough, Mr. Casarazzi?"

"You're asking a man who'd prefer you to never wear anything at all," he shot back, not missing a beat. "I would say too much, Miss Carter." He flicked at the strap of my dress and waggled his brows.

"You are so infuriating," I laughed despite trying my hardest not to.

"Maybe," he agreed. "But I also happen to know how to dance."

"Oh, you do?"

"In all forms," he replied, grinning. "Vertically. Horizontally..."

"Fine," I conceded, allowing him to pull my body flush against his. "Anything for a quiet life."

He spun me out before pulling me roughly back to him and I swear I could feel every nerve ending stand to life inside of me when he placed his hand on my lower back.

And when he tipped my chin upward, I forgot to breathe.

"See?" he mused, grinning down at me. "We're dancing, and no one died." He feigned a gasp before adding, "And look, the world's still turning."

"Funny," I rasped, struggling to maintain my composure, as his body moved directly against mine, and just like every time he had laid a finger on me, my traitorous heart skipped a beat.

He was bringing to life a side of me I never knew existed,

406 | INEVITABLE

and it was a side I wasn't sure I should like, but most definitely *did*.

Jackie and Wilson rolled into *Cherry Wine* and we continued to dance.

Closing my eyes, I rested my cheek against his chest and sighed in contentment as we swayed to the melancholy music.

"You're my best friend," I half whispered, half slurred as I swayed in his arms. "How pathetic is that?" I laughed humorlessly then buried my face in his chest. "Aside from Teagan, you're all I have."

"It's not pathetic, HC," he replied, tone soft. "It's fucking beautiful."

"You were never supposed to be part of my plan," I muttered, more to myself than him.

"Plan?"

"I vowed myself to another man nine years ago," I choked out. "Being around you only complicates things, and I don't need any more complications in my life."

"Well, tough fucking luck, sweetheart," he chuckled. "Because I am not walking away from you." His arms tightened around me. "And I won't let you walk away from me."

"I'm so lonely, Hunter," I blurted out, burying my face in the fabric of his shirt. My words were a drunken admission, but one hundred percent true. "All the time."

"I know." His voice was low and gruff, his hands gentle, as he cradled my body against his, still swaying to the music. "I know, baby."

"I ache," I admitted, eyes still clenched shut. I could feel his heart hammering against his chest, the rhythm matching mine. "There's a hole inside of me," I breathed. "A hollowness, and it hurts me."

Hunter tipped my chin upwards, forcing me to meet his gaze head on. "I can make it go away, Hope," he whispered, blue eyes searing me. "I can make it all better."

I didn't doubt him.

Chapter 73 | 407

I knew he could.

And that's what scared me the most.

I was losing myself in this man.

I was forgetting who I was.

And who I belonged to.

He cradled the back of my head almost lovingly, using his free hand to stroke my cheek, as his blue eyes burned a direct hole to my soul.

"I can take care of you, Hope," he whispered. "If you just let me."

"I just want someone to love me," I breathed, leaning into his touch.

Hunter's eyes burned with sincerity as he said, "Someone already does."

His touch was so intimate, his words were so sincere and loving, that when he leaned his face closer to mine, I didn't step back or turn away.

And when his lips touched mine, I didn't pull away like I knew I should.

Instead, I knotted my hands in his shirt, and clung to his huge frame.

And when his tongue probed my lips, seeking more, I opened my mouth and granted him entrance.

The moment his tongue swiped against mine, a hot blast of pleasure ripped through my body, causing me to moan into his mouth and Hunter to growl.

He was kissing me.

Hunter was kissing me.

And I was *enjoying* it.

Worse than enjoying it, I was kissing him *back*.

The smell of him, cologne and cigarettes and mouthwash.

I should have hated it.

I didn't.

With every stroke of his tongue, I moaned and writhed in

unimaginable pleasure as the taste of beer, mint, and nicotine filled my senses.

His calloused hands on my body were entirely welcome as he touched me in all the ways I desperately needed to be touched.

Heat pooled in my core as I lost myself in him.

He thrust his hips against me as we kissed. I could feel his erection straining, pressing hard against my throbbing clit. I was under no illusion as to how strong this man was, how sexual and primal, and the fact that he wanted me over any other woman?

Knowing that I was turning him on like this drove me wild...

This is bad, my brain screamed, but my body was screaming *don't you dare stop*, and my heart? My traitorous heart was telling me that *wrong had never felt so right*.

His kiss was drugging me. I was losing control as his hands roamed over my body, squeezing, pulling, wanting more from me.

I wanted more, too.

I wanted everything I had been denied for so long.

He burned me with his touch and marked me with his tongue.

It was as if he was laying claim to something that wasn't mine to give or his to take.

I felt his hands move to cup my ass and I shuddered in delight.

With our lips still punishing the others in what had to be a bruising kiss, he lifted me clean off my feet.

And then we were moving through the apartment.

My back hit his bedroom wall with a thud, followed quickly by his body as he slammed against me clumsily, the alcohol in our systems making this messy and raw and fucking perfect.

The feel of him, so big and hard and strong pressed against

Chapter 73 | 409

my softness, caused a shudder of pleasure to roll down my spine.

Balancing myself on one foot, I hitched my other leg around his waist, drawing him closer. My pussy clenched painfully, the need to be filled by this man causing my physical pain.

When I fisted my hand in the waistband of his jeans and tugged him harder to my body, Hunter groaned into my mouth, his lips becoming more frantic against mine.

I wasn't the person I envisioned myself to be.

I wanted the dangerous.

I wanted his darkness and all he exposed me to.

I wanted to feel like I was the only woman in the world. Hunter made me feel like that. He made me feel special and elusive and one in a million.

I was so broken from my past. I wasn't sure what to do. My heart and my conscience were at war. The selfish and selfless parts of my soul battling it out, both bringing their A game.

Loyalty was embedded inside of me. It was how I was raised. But it was switching. I could feel it. Mixing inside of me. Blurring the lines.

I was ruined.

Drowning in the man I couldn't give my heart to.

But I couldn't feel remorse or guilt right now. The only sensations flooding my body were the ones Hunter was giving me.

"You're so fucking beautiful," he rasped, breaking our kiss. "Christ..." His gaze raked over my body from head to toe before finally settling on the hem of my dress that had moved higher up my thigh. He made a noise, almost like a sigh, before dropping to his knees on the floor.

My heart hammered wildly as I watched him watch me, his blue eyes dark with desire. He pushed my dress up to bunch around my hips before yanking down my panties.

410 | INEVITABLE

And then his mouth was there, in my most private of areas, where only one man had been before him.

"Oh god!"

The stubble on his jaw scratched against the apex of my thighs as he licked and suckled at my clit.

Moaning loudly, I sagged against the wall. "Hunter...god...I can't."

My legs shook so violently,

I didn't think I had the strength to stay upright.

But he didn't let me fall.

His lips never left my pussy as he hitched one thigh over his shoulder and continued his delicious onslaught, holding me up with the sheer strength of his shoulders alone.

My body shook.

I trembled violently.

I couldn't seem to contain myself.

I'd lost all control of everything inside me.

I'd given in.

Wholly and entirely.

Everything inside of my brain screamed at me to stop, but no words of protest escaped my lips.

No words at all.

Just breathless, panting moans of encouragement as I grabbed at his silky blonde locks and screamed in pleasure.

His hands; those tattooed, dangerous hands as they held me open for his mouth to lap and suck, violating my innocence, taking with them any chance of turning back now.

His tongue speared me, his teeth nipped, everything about the man was driving me closer to the brink of orgasm.

I was so turned on and equally disgusted with myself.

And he seemed to know it.

Every sob that tore from my throat, Hunter replaced it with a moan of pleasure.

He quite literally fucked the guilt away until I was consumed wholly in him.

Chapter 73 | 411

All I could *feel* was him.

Lightning had struck.

The world had ended.

And he was still here.

Making me feel so good.

So fucking good...

He seemed to revel in my pleasure and the more I moaned, the harder he seemed to work to make it *more*.

"I can't..." I cried up, bucking my hips against his face. "Oh, fuck..."

"You can," he growled as he drove me to the brink of insanity with his mouth. "Let yourself feel this...feel me."

My head fell backwards, slapping hard against the plaster of the wall, as shockwaves of pleasure jolted through my core.

Holding onto his hair, I felt my pussy spasm violently as I came hard.

On his face.

Helpless, I could do nothing but shudder uncontrollably as my orgasm tore through me.

This felt so good.

So right.

So fucking right.

But it was wrong.

So fucking *wrong*!

I was in the arms of a man and he wasn't my husband.

Closing my eyes, I allowed myself to absorb the intensity of having him touch me, having him hold me.

Wanting me.

Loving me.

Oh god...

"You feel like mine," he whispered, brushing his lips to mine, as he carried me over to his bed. "Be mine."

I didn't answer him.

I *couldn't*.

Vulnerable and exposed, I dragged my dress over my head and tossed it on the floor, my bra quickly joining it.

My heart hammered in my chest, my blood bubbled in my veins, my air caught in my throat. He was seeing me. All of me.

"You're beautiful," he whispered, eyes trailing over my naked skin.

I watched as he pulled his shirt over his head, letting it fall to the floor, before dropping his hands to the waistband of his jeans, revealing his staggeringly beautiful body.

The intensity of his gaze had me paralyzed to the bed as he stared down at me through dark hooded lashes.

I couldn't have moved if I wanted to.

I was hypnotized by this man, locked inside an inner battle of doing what was right and doing what I wanted.

The right thing for me would be to put my clothes back on and leave, but what I wanted was to take him inside of my body.

I knew I would never forgive myself if I walked away now.

He just looked at me, and in his eyes, I received everything I never knew I wanted but suddenly and desperately craved so much.

My heart was racing so hard in my chest, I found myself breathing faster, exhaling in short, puffy breaths.

I wasn't a virgin, but Hunter made me feel like I'd never been touched before.

The way his eyes roamed over my skin made me feel like his were the first to see my bare flesh. I felt incredibly vulnerable in this moment.

When his clothes were on the floor, he returned to me, and I kissed him hungrily.

Pulling his body down to mine, I allowed myself to sink into the bottomless lagoon of pleasure that was Hunter Casarazzi.

"Hunter." His name tore from my lips like a reverberated prayer.

"I'm here," was his simple reply as he kissed my neck.

Two words that gave me more comfort than was rational.

One moment he was above me, and the next he was *inside* me, sliding into my warmth in one swift move.

Broken and torn, I clung to his broad shoulders, immersing myself in every vivid sensation and feeling that had no business in my heart.

A sharp, erotic hissing sound tore from his lips seconds before his hands clamped down hard on my waistline. He hitched my thigh around his waist as he rocked inside me.

The feel of his hips gyrating above me was too much, bringing with it friction to my throbbing clit that he miraculously seemed to know I needed.

It was too much.

He was too much.

My feelings.

Everything.

Crying out, I dug my fingernails into his hard, tattoo covered chest and stared into his icy blue eyes, reveling in the feel of his abdominal muscles contracting under my touch.

He felt so good under my touch.

He felt so good, *period.*

The heat of his skin, the hardness of his muscles, the knowledge that I was in the arms of a man who wouldn't think twice about taking a life for the woman he loved... It was oddly empowering.

He filled me to the brim and I gasped at the pressure before whispering, "Oh god."

"Take me inside you, Hope." He pressed harder, pushed deeper, demanded *more* from me with every thrust of his hips. "Feel what it's like to be *wanted.*"

I threw my head back and cried out loudly as the familiar swell of desire pooled inside of my body, causing my pussy to clench and my body to tremble.

"To be taken care of."

I did.

I could.

Oh god...

"I'm *right* for you, Hope," he growled as his movements turned urgent. "And I'm mother fucking willing."

He was.

He was.

Oh god, he was everything to me in this moment.

"The bad in me is exactly what that good girl inside of you needs," he added as he plunged himself inside me, each thrust as merciless as the rest. "Stop fucking denying me!"

"Oh god," I screamed, clutching for an anchor to hold me down as waves of ecstasy crashed through my body. "I'm coming," I cried out. "Oh god, I'm coming..."

He pressed a thumb to my clit and I went off like a firecracker, jerking and shuddering violently beneath him.

Hunter continued to pump into me until he too found his release and collapsed on top of me, a sweaty mass of primal man.

When the ripples of illicit pleasure eventually faded, reality crashed down on me, joined by the image of my husband's face, and I balked in shame.

Mortified and using every ounce of self-control left inside of my body, I shoved him away from me.

"Oh my god." Stumbling out of his bed, I held the covers tightly around my body as a sharp sob tore through my chest. "What have I done?"

"I'm sorry," Hunter panted, chest heaving and eyes dark as night. "I shouldn't have done that"

"No," I whispered, batting his hand away when he reached for me. "You shouldn't have."

"Actually, fuck that," he shot back. Jerking out of bed, he slipped on his boxers and hissed, "I should have done that a long time ago."

Tears pooled in my eyes when I noticed my dress and bra

Chapter 73 | 415

on his bedroom floor. "Oh, Jesus, no..." Shame and guilt crept into my body and I heaved loudly.

"It's okay, Hope." I felt Hunter's arms come around me, but I couldn't accept the comfort he was offering me.

I didn't deserve it.

"I need to go home," I gasped, shoving him roughly away from me. "Now!"

"Calm down," he choked out. "It's okay –"

"It's *not* okay," I sobbed brokenly as I quickly dressed. "I need to get away from you."

"Don't do this," he croaked out hoarsely, running a hand through his thoroughly mussed hair. "Don't treat me like I'm fucking expendable."

"I'm not!" I screamed, turning my face away as I clumsily toed on my heels. "I just need...space!"

I couldn't look at him right now.

I couldn't *see*.

"You're not? Then what the fuck do you call *space?*" He shook his head in disgust. "I'm not doing this with you again. I won't. I refuse to stand here and listen to you lie to yourself and make what happened out to be a mistake because it wasn't a fucking mistake. You wanted it, Hope. You wanted *me!*"

"No." I shook my head, fiercely denying it. "I lost my head for a minute. But I *don't* want you."

"You're lying," he shot back, tone heated and fierce. "You want me and it fucking terrifies you."

"Stop it." Turning on my heels, I hurried out of his bedroom. "Stop pushing me."

"I have to fucking push you," he shot back, following close behind me. "It's the only goddamn way I can get you to be honest!"

"I'm not lying to you," I hissed, stung by his words.

"Not to me, but you're most definitely lying to yourself," he countered angrily. "You've *been* lying to yourself. For months

416 | INEVITABLE

now!" He shook his head and exhaled a frustrated sigh. "And that's the worst fucking kind of lie."

"What do you want me to say?" I screamed, tears flowing freely now.

"Admit it," he demanded, closing the space between us. Cupping the back of my neck with his large hand, he drew me closer. "Admit you want me, Hope." His chest was heaving, his eyes wild, as he pressed his brow to mine. "Admit it!"

"I can't," I whispered, trembling violently.

Hunter growled in frustration. "Why *not*?"

A sob tore through me as I whispered, "He loves *me*."

"*I* love you!" he roared, backing away. "Me, Hope. Me. I fucking love you!"

This wasn't happening.

This couldn't be happening.

I was dreaming – I had to be.

"Jordan needs me," I strangled out. "He needs me, Hunter!"

"And I don't?"

I shook my head. "No, you don't!"

"So, what?" he demanded. "You don't want me because I can cope? Because I'm strong? You get off on the broken in him? On his weakness? Then fine." Ripping off his shirt, he stalked towards me. "I can be broken, too."

Taking my hand, he placed it against the skin covering his hammering heart. "This here?" He stared at me meaningfully, his blue eyes piercing and full of heated emotion. "This stopped beating when I was eighteen years old and watched the life seep out of the girl I loved." He was shaking, trembling all over. "It kick-started in my chest twelve years later. When it found *you*."

"Why are you doing this?" I screamed, snatching my hand away.

I couldn't handle this.

I couldn't cope with the tsunami of feelings I had for this

Chapter 73 | 417

man that were threatening to drown me. "Why are you ruining *everything?*"

"That's right, Hope. I'm the fuck up. I'm the one ruining everything," he snarled. "I got attached. I fell in love with a married woman. I'm the bastard. I'm the horrible prick. It's all on me."

"You need to shush!" I hissed as I pressed my fingers to my swollen lips.

"Shush?" Hunter cocked a brow. "I tell you I'm in love with you, and tell me to *shush*?"

"Yes, shush!" Stumbling backwards, I blindly gathered my purse – and to my deepest shame, my panties – off the kitchen floor before rushing towards the door. "You need to shush and I need to go."

I needed to get out of this apartment before I made an even bigger mistake I couldn't come back from.

Like what? my subconscious sneered. *Falling* back *into bed with him?*

"Us being friends was a stupid idea," I breathed, chest heaving. "It was never going to work."

It pained me to say it, but I *had* to.

I *had* to stay away from him.

My marriage was on the line.

I couldn't risk everything for him.

I *couldn't.*

Even thinking about it was insanity on another level.

No, I needed to get my drunk ass as far away from temptation as possible.

"Hope, stop. You can't just run out of here like this –" Hunter called out, but I didn't wait.

Instead, I hightailed it out of his apartment as fast as my legs could carry me.

What the hell had I done?

Why in god's name had I allowed that to happen?

418 | INEVITABLE

And why the fuck was my heart screaming at me to *stop running*?

I managed to make it to the elevator before I was lifted off my feet and thrown over a pair of huge shoulders.

The scream that tore from my throat was one of shock, partially because Hunter was carrying me back to his apartment, but mostly because he could.

"You're not running out in the dark," he said calmly, still carrying me. "And especially not in your condition, you little lightweight."

"I wanna go home," I mewled pitifully as I stared at his jean-clad ass. "And I'm hardly *little*. You know, you should really put me down before you hurt yourself."

"Hurt myself," Hunter chuckled as he stalked back into his apartment with me slung over his shoulder.

He walked over to the leather couch and gently sat me down.

"I know you don't want to be around me right now," he said then, taking a sensible step back. "But I'm over the limit and can't drive, and there's no way in hell I'm letting you walk around the streets at night on your own. So just sit tight until your ride gets here."

I frowned in confusion. "My ride?"

"Yeah," Hunter confirmed. "I called your brother."

"My brother?" I wailed. "Which one?"

"Cam."

"Oh god," I whimpered, flopping back on the couch. "Shoot me now."

74

Lucky

*W*hen I watched Hope run out of my apartment, I felt my mind go into overdrive as I thought through my options.

The selfish and most appealing of those options was to chase her down and beg her not to leave me. Declare to her that I was disgustingly in love with her, admit the fact that the thought of not seeing her face every day caused me physical pain, and beg her not to leave me. Tell her that I didn't give a fuck about her moral obligations because I knew I could make her happier than her husband ever could, then drag her back to bed.

But I didn't.

She couldn't hear me right now.

She was too consumed in her guilt.

The least selfish thing was to let her go. Stand back and give her the time and space she needed to work this through on her own.

420 | INEVITABLE

I didn't do that either.

Because I wasn't that masochistic.

I settled on option number three; the one in the middle.

It took every ounce of self-control I had to sit her on my couch and call her brother to come get her.

Every instinct inside of me roared at me to push – that I was *this* goddamn close to cracking the wall she'd thrown up around her heart.

Her mouth, her breasts, her clit, every fucking part of her was *perfect* for me.

And I was the one she turned to when shit hit the fan.

I was the one she took comfort from.

I knew I was the second man to ever be inside her, but I had treasured the moment like I was the first.

That had to mean something, right?

She didn't play around, this girl. Whether she wanted to admit it or not, she'd given me something tonight that only one man before me had the honor of having.

And she called me by my real name.

No one did that.

Absolutely fucking no one, and when she did it, she reached inside and pulled on some part of me I had thought was dead and buried.

I thought I had done all the time I ever would behind bars in the state pen, but from the moment I met this woman, it felt like I had walked out of one prison and straight into another.

"Cam's going to be so pissed that you called."

I cocked a brow. "Oh really?"

"Really," Hope nodded, wide-eyed.

"I think I can handle myself, HC," I replied, sitting on the coffee table opposite her.

I knew it could go one of two ways when Cam got to my apartment.

He was either going to lose his shit on me for getting his

Chapter 74 | 421

sister drunk, or he was going to lose his shit on his sister for being alone in my apartment with me.

Either way, I was fully prepared to shut that shit down.

I liked Cam.

We were friends, but he had a horrible habit of treating Hope like a porcelain doll.

Hell, it wasn't just him; his entire family was guilty of it.

They seemed to be under the illusion that she was on a pretty pedestal and had to behave a certain way.

I wanted to break that fucking pedestal the world seemed to hold her on. I wanted to rip those fucking chains that trailed around her ankles and show her what *real life* felt like.

I wanted her to know it was okay to screw up sometimes and *not* be perfect.

Like being with her tonight. She had been so fucking into it until that misguided conscience of hers reared its ugly head.

"Seriously." Hiccupping, she pulled herself into a sitting position on my couch and frowned. "He has a lot going on right now."

Oh? "Like what?"

"Like fatherhood," Hope drawled and then quickly slapped a hand across her mouth. "Omigod," she breathed, hand still covering her mouth, as she stared at me wide-eyed and innocent. "I wasn't supposed to say that."

My brows shot up in surprise. "Tillie's pregnant?"

Hope nodded eagerly. "None of the family knows except for me." She paused and frowned before adding, "And now you."

"Well, my lips are sealed," I assured her. She was too fucking adorable. *Goddamn.* "I promise, I won't say a word."

"Promises mean nothing to me," she surprised me by saying. "Not anymore."

Because of him, I wanted to ask, but held my tongue.

I didn't need to ask the question anyway.

Of course, it was because of *him*.

422 | INEVITABLE

"Can we pretend it didn't happen?" she whispered from her huddling position on my couch. She flashed me one of those terrified puppy-dog expressions that usually made me cave and whispered, "Please? Can't we just go back to before?"

"Not this time, HC," I replied with a shake of my head.

The pain that flashed in her eyes almost broke me then, but I couldn't keep lying to feed this fucked up denial she seemed to drowning in.

"Tonight was...different," I whispered. *More.* "I can't go back to before." *Not after being inside you...*

I wasn't going to make it easy for her to leave me this time.

"Everything's changed," she whispered, looking over at me. "Hasn't it?"

I nodded. "Yeah."

"I don't want to lose you," she sobbed.

"You're not going to."

"I already have," she urged. "Don't you get that?" Shaking her head, she exhaled a choked sob and said, "It's all gone now."

"No, Hope," I countered, forcing myself *not* to go to her. "It's not."

"We can't be friends anymore," she sobbed. "Not after what we just did."

"I'm not walking away from you," I shot back without hesitation.

"But I have to walk away from you," she whispered. "It's the only way."

If she didn't have feelings for me, she wouldn't be acting so irrationally.

If this was purely platonic for her, like she said it was, she would have been able to brush this under the table and move on.

Knowing that she felt the need to cut me out of her life only assured me that I was affecting her.

Chapter 74 | 423

One of these days she was going to wake up and have a *come to Jesus* moment.

She fucking had to.

Because the thought of her wasting her life on a man she *thought* she loved while I was forced to watch from the sidelines, made me want to claw my fucking heart out.

"You can try and erase me all you want," I told her. She could build all the walls she wanted. I wasn't her husband. I wasn't the one who ran away from what he wanted. And I wanted her. "But we both know I'm not going to let that happen."

"I need some time."

"Time."

"Yes, Hunter. Time."

"You can take all the time you want. Keep rebuilding those walls and I'll keep smashing them."

"Why are you doing this to me?"

"Because you want me to."

"No. I don't."

"Who's lying now?"

"You're crazy to get involved with me," she whispered. "It's going to end badly."

"I know."

She raised a brow. "But you're not running?"

"I don't run."

The sound of a knock on my apartment door filled my ears then, breaking the moment between us.

"Oh, god," Hope groaned. Grabbing a cushion, she covered her face and whispered, "Don't let him kill me, 'kay?"

"Okay," I chuckled as I got to my feet and walked over to open the door.

"Care to explain what *my* sister is doing in *your* apartment, drunk off her face, at one in the morning? Cam Carter hissed, glaring at me like I was the devil incarnate. "Well?"

Okay, so his anger was directed at me.

424 | INEVITABLE

"Come on in," I drawled.

Shoving past me, Cam stalked into my apartment like a man on a mission. "Oh, I fucking intend to."

When his gaze landed on Hope, he exhaled what sounded like a sigh of relief and shook his head.

"You think you can hide from me?" He marched over to where his sister was sitting on the couch. Crouching down in front of her, he took the cushion she was still holding against her face and said, "You were always terrible at hide and seek."

"I'm drunk," she admitted, staring at her brother in shame.

"So?" he countered softly in a tone that sounded entirely unlike him.

"And sad," she added, biting down on her bottom lip. "I'm really sad, Cam."

"Don't be sad," he whispered, patting her knee. "I'm here to take you home."

"That's what I'm sad about," she whispered before throwing her arms around her brother, and damn if my heart didn't crack clean open at her confession.

It almost killed me to call him tonight, but I knew it was the right thing to do by Hope.

If I had my way, I'd keep her right here in this apartment and never let her go back. I knew with a little persuasion it could happen. She was miserable and unsure and starved for attention.

But I cared about her wellbeing too damn much to be selfish with her like that.

Besides, I didn't want her to wake up in the morning and hate us both.

"Come on, Hopey-bear," Cam finally sighed, tone weary and laced with concern.

He stood up in one swift move and tucked her under his arm. "Staying here won't make you feel better."

"I know," she sighed. "You're right."

Chapter 74 | 425

"I'm always right," Cam agreed as he walked his sister to the door.

When he reached the door, he turned to look me dead in the eye. "I'll be back to talk about this."

I didn't doubt it.

"I'll be waiting," I replied evenly.

And then they were gone.

75

Hope

"I'm in trouble, Cam." The words, hard as they were to admit, spewed out of my mouth, the urge to be comforted by the only other outcast in my family strong. "So much trouble."

"It's going to be okay," Cam assured me as he buckled me into the passenger seat of his Range Rover.

Seconds later, he was sitting beside me in the driver's seat and cranking the engine. He put the truck into gear and pulled out of his parking space.

"He kissed me tonight," I sobbed. "And I kissed him back."

"Lucky?"

I nodded in shame.

You did worse than let him kiss you, you little tramp...

"Well, shit," Cam muttered.

Yeah, shit!

"What am I going to do?" I wailed. Jordan's face entered my mind and I cringed in disgust. "I'm a terrible person."

"You're not a terrible person," Cam shot back.

Chapter 75 | 427

"Omigod." I paled. "I'm Bryan Adams in *Run to You*." Turning to Cam, I gaped at him. "George in *Careless Whisper*." Whimpering in horror, I choked out, "Hunter is *Dirty Diana* and I'm Michael!"

"It was a *kiss,* Hope," Cam scoffed.

I squirmed in discomfort, my face flaming with heat.

"It was *just* a kiss," Cam added slowly. "Right?"

I stared at him, unable to get the words out of my mouth and tell him what a horrible human being I was.

"Jesus, Hope," Cam groaned, reading the expression on my face like a book.

"I didn't do any of this on purpose, Cam," I whispered, forcing myself not to cry. "I feel fucking horrible."

"I know." He sighed heavily before saying, "Christ, I saw this crazy-train coming a mile away."

"You did?"

"Come on, Hope," Cam growled. "Anyone within a thirty-mile radius of you two this past year could have seen this coming. The guy adores you," he added. "Fucking worships the ground you walk on."

"No, he doesn't," I protested. "We were only supposed to be friends."

"Friends," Cam scoffed. "Let me tell you something, Sis. Luck's my friend, too, but I'd be seriously fucking worried if he looked at me the way he looks at you."

"Oh, god," I wailed. "It's all so *fucked* up!"

"Yeah, it is," Cam agreed.

"What do I do?"

"What do you mean?"

"How am I supposed to tell *Jordan*?" I choked out his name like it was poison on my tongue. "He's going to hate me."

"You're going to tell him?"

"You think I shouldn't?"

Cam shrugged. "Hell if I know, Hope."

"God," I sobbed. "I fucked up so badly."

428 | INEVITABLE

"I know."

"Then help me!"

"What am I supposed to do, Hope?" Cam shot back. "We're not kids anymore. I can't barge into the playground and kick their asses for upsetting you."

"I know. But I just... I need someone to fix me."

"You're not broken."

"I *feel* broken."

"You're drunk," he countered. "You'll feel better in the morning."

"I'll never feel better again."

"Don't be so dramatic."

"Tell me what to do here, Cam?" I begged. "Please, just tell me!"

"Just... follow your heart," Cam tossed out, shifting uncomfortably in his seat. "And don't worry about what anyone else thinks," he added, tone soft and reassuring. "Mom will get over it. And as for Dad?" Cam shook his head and exhaled heavily. "He's got your back, Hopey-Bear. Always. Same as the rest of us."

"I'm *not* leaving Jordan," I blurted out, horrified at the thought. "How could you even suggest that?"

"Listen, Hope. You're not the first person in the world to fall in love with two people," he stated calmly. "And you won't be the last."

"What are you talking about?" I shook my head in horror and held a finger up in protest. "I'm not in love with Lucky!"

"Of course, you're not," he shot back sarcastically. "You were begging me to leave you back there because you're not in love with him. You kissed him back tonight because you're not in love with the guy." He muttered a string of incomprehensible curse words under his breath before saying, "And you stare at him like he hung the fucking moon because you really don't love him. I'm not blind, Hope Carter, and you're not stupid."

Chapter 75 | 429

"I *don't!*" I slurred, twisting in my seat to glare at him. "I only love Jordan."

I didn't love Hunter.

I couldn't love him.

I *wouldn't* love him.

I refused to allow this man to disrupt my carefully compiled future.

He was wrong for me. Wild, unattainable, dangerous.

I did not want that.

"Goddammit, Hope," Cam hissed, losing his patience. "Don't you realize how fucking pathetic you look? Traipsing around after a guy who jilted you?" He slammed his hand against the steering wheel. "Do you think we're all blind and can't see how fucking miserable you are with him? Well, we do. I see it. And so does Dad."

There he was!

The Cam I knew and loathed.

"Goddammit, you're so stupid, Hope!" he continued to say. "So fucking stupid."

"Excuse me?"

"You want to have what Mom and Dad have so badly that you're blinded to the fact that you're fucking it up for yourself."

"You don't know anything about my situation, Cam!"

"I know you're miserable."

"Shut up, Cam," I growled, folding my hands across my chest. "I'm not talking about this with you anymore."

"Because you don't want to hear the truth," Cam hissed as he ran a hand through his hair. "Well, news flash, sweetheart; the truth hurts!"

"He was raped!" I screamed. "I can't just walk away from him because things are hard right now." Tears were beginning to fill my eyes. "It's going to get better – he's going to get better." *He has to.* "And everything will be like it was before."

"Cut the shit, Hope!" Cam shot back. "It's not going to get better. This is who Jordan is now. This is what his life has molded him into, and god knows I don't blame the poor fucking man for being the way he is. If it had been me in his shoes back then, I'd have slit my goddamn wrists a long time ago. But I'd be a liar if I said I don't think it's a fucking crime that you're basing your future on the guilt you feel for what happened in his past."

"Please stop, Cam," I whispered, pressing my hand to my forehead. "I can't hear this."

"No!" my brother hissed. "I won't stop. Someone has to try and talk some goddamn sense into you!" Raising a hand, Cam roughly dragged his fingers through his hair, his expression one of sheer exasperation. "You don't *have* to do what you're doing, Hope. You don't need to be with him because that's what people expect from you. Goddamn! One of these days, you're going to have to stand on your own two feet. You're going to have to live your life for *you* and no one else. Sure, some people may not like it, but guess what? You don't have to care. What they think about you is none of your business. Stop trying to please every damn person on this fucking planet. Step out from that golden girl shrine you've been hiding under your whole damn life and make a decision because it makes *you* happy – not him or anyone else."

"I *love* him," I choked out.

"Do you?" he countered. "Do you *really* love him? Be honest with yourself and think about it before you answer that question."

"I don't have to think about it," I screamed defensively, losing my patience. "I know my own mind, Cameron!" The fear of being hated and judged kept me from acknowledging what I truly felt inside – even to myself. "So just drop it!"

"Then I don't know what to tell you, Hope," Cam replied wearily. "I really don't."

He was quiet then, and didn't speak for the rest of the ride.

I turned my face away and stared out the passenger window, but his words wouldn't leave my mind.

Chapter 75 | 431

They continued to haunt me the rest of the drive home, and long after when I was tucked up in bed.

I was *not* in love with Hunter Casarazzi.

He had no part in my future.

And I refused to entertain the notion.

Even if my heart demanded otherwise.

76

Jordan

"You're a shitty husband, Jordan Porter," Annabelle declared when I walked into the kitchen at a quarter after six on Friday morning. "An amazing friend," she amended. "But a fucking awful husband."

Ryder was already seated in his highchair, digging into his breakfast, so I presumed he was the reason his momma was up this early.

"Wow, thanks, Annie," I muttered, heading straight for the coffee pot. I knew I would never win husband of the year, but having Annabelle tell me that very thing first thing in the morning was depressing. "I'm fairly sure you covered the topic of just how shitty I am weeks ago."

More than covered it.

She'd given me a goddamn earful after the fight with Hope – and every day since.

She wasn't telling me anything I wasn't already very aware of though.

I was shitty.

Chapter 76 | 433

In every fucking way.

"I heard you in there," she clarified, dropping her hands to her hips. "Talking to O Malley on the phone in the living room? You took another double shift." Annie shook her head and glared at me with obvious disapproval. "I know you're new to the whole marriage deal, Jay, but it's kind of mandatory to discuss these things with your wife before making decisions."

I thought about defending myself, but decided I needed caffeine in my system before taking on the force of nature that was my best friend.

Besides, deep down I knew she was right. I should have talked to Hope before I took on another shift at the hospital, but I wasn't used to talking to anyone about anything to do with my life. I loved my job. I needed to work. It was my way of staying clean and focused.

Besides, we weren't talking much about anything anymore.

She was still mad as hell with me for fucking up the night she'd organized for us.

I wanted to fix things between us, but I didn't know how.

And I was still dealing with her telling her family about my past.

I *couldn't* get past it.

I felt so fucking tired from all of it.

Every day I woke up weary and went to sleep exhausted.

The medication I was on for my *issues* was strong enough to knock out a horse. Going about my day to day routine was all I felt able to do.

Pathetic an excuse as it sounded, I was too worn down to put up much of a battle.

"You've barely been home this week," Annie continued to quip, saying my thoughts aloud and making me cringe. "Actually, scratch that. You've barely been home since the girl got here!"

"It's not your business, Annie," I snapped, pouring myself a mug of coffee. "You don't know anything about it."

434 | INEVITABLE

"Do you know what day it was yesterday?" she demanded.

"Thursday."

"Funny," she deadpanned. "Really funny."

"Fine," I conceded wearily. "What day was it?"

"It was your wife's birthday," she exclaimed angrily. "And *you* didn't remember!"

My heart sank.

I snatched my phone out of my pocket and checked the screen.

Friday, May 13th.

"Shit," I whispered as guilt coursed through me. "Yesterday was the twelfth. I forgot."

"I know you forgot," Annabelle shot back angrily. "And it's not good enough."

"I'll make it up to her," I whispered, feeling sick to my stomach. "I'll... figure something out."

"Don't blow smoke up my ass, Jordan Porter," Annabelle shot back, not giving me an inch. "I know you better than you know yourself."

Yeah, she was probably right there.

Her no bullshit attitude around me was why we'd managed to remain friends for so long.

Annabelle had always given it to me straight, and I had always loved that about her.

Not so much this morning, though.

"You won't make it up to her because you're *avoiding* her," she stated. "You've been snatching up extra hours at work every chance you get and spending next to no time at home with your family."

"I need the money," I said, trying to argue my point, or at least give myself an out.

"Not that badly," she chimed in, blue eyes locked on mine. "Go ahead and lie to yourself if it eases your guilt, but we both know you're using work as an avoidance technique." Her voice softened slightly when she added, "You know what happens

Chapter 76 | 435

when you burn out – and you will crash and burn if you don't *slow* down."

Yeah, I knew what happened.

She did, too.

"That's not what's happening here."

"Are you sure?" Annie countered. "Because I've seen this behavior in you before. I've watched you use avoidance techniques to cope with stress, and I've also seen what happens when it blows up in your face." Sighing, she added, "It never works, Jay. You know that. Do you really want to end up back –"

"Don't," I interrupted, holding up a hand to warn her off.

I couldn't talk about *that*.

Not with Hope upstairs.

"Please. Just...*understand*..." Pausing, I inhaled a calming breath before squeezing out, "I need your support here, Annie."

"And you have it," she replied vehemently. "Always. But that doesn't mean I can sit back and say nothing when I see you falling into old patterns."

"I'm not going back there," I promised her, and it was a promise I wished I could keep.

Setting my mug down on the counter, I walked over to where she was hovering and pressed a kiss to her cheek.

"I've got this," I told her before pulling her into a hug. "I'm in control this time."

"I really hope so," she whispered, squeezing me back. "I really do."

77

Hope

I woke to the world's worst hangover and a conscience laden down with guilt.

I couldn't face Jordan.

Not after what I'd done.

I was disgusted with myself.

I didn't recognize myself anymore.

I wasn't the woman I used to be.

I didn't have the same morals or sense of right and wrong.

Everything was blurry now.

I was blurred.

My phone vibrated beneath my pillow. I didn't need to check it to know who was calling me.

Hunter.

He wasn't supposed to come into my world and turn everything on its ass.

There was no room, no extra space in my heart for a man like him.

But my heart, my traitorous heart, let him in all the same.

Chapter 77 | 437

I didn't put up a battle.

I didn't fight him off.

I let him in – wholly and completely.

His was a friendship that turned into something more, something much deeper than he or I had ever anticipated.

My face flamed as I thought back to last night.

The memory of being in Hunter's arms, having his lips on mine, his hands touching me, pulling me closer, pushing inside me, wanting more from me than I knew I could give...

It was *haunting* me.

Being in his arms.

Craving his touch.

Reveling in the intimate way he caressed me.

His lips on mine.

His tongue in my mouth.

His tongue *inside* me.

Having *him* inside me.

I could blame my behavior on the alcohol, but it would be a lie. Because the truth of the matter was I *wanted* him to kiss me. And I was *glad* when he did.

I couldn't erase him.

I couldn't escape him and, worse, I *didn't* want to.

My brother's voice filled my mind then...

"...You're not the first person in the world to fall in love with two people, and you won't be the last..."

Blanching at the thought, I threw my covers off, and forced Cam's words away.

Rolling out of bed, I bolted out of my room and straight into the shower.

I *had* to get a grip on this.

Wash it all away.

Force myself to forget about Hunter Casarazzi.

But how could I do that when he was so completely embedded in my world?

Even if I wanted to erase him, I *couldn't*.

My feelings for Hunter had hit me like an explosion.

It was like a light had been switched on inside of me, exposing me to sensations and feelings I had no idea what to do with.

And now? I couldn't switch it back off.

I hadn't been expecting him to walk into my world and turn everything on its axis, and now I was standing in the carnage, desperately trying to sort through my emotions and clear my mind.

Hunter saw something inside of me, the part I kept hidden from the rest of the world, and he brought it to life. He made me feel like it was okay to be who I was.

He made me feel like it didn't matter how badly I screwed up, or how many mistakes I made, because he would be there to love me through it all.

That was strange, terrifying, and addicting.

He was simply riveting to me.

And that *terrified* me.

Feeling numb, I remained in the shower until the water ran cold and my fingers turned blue.

Shivering violently, I continued to torment myself with my thoughts...

"...I just want someone to love me..."

"...I love you! Me, Hope. Me. I fucking love you..."

He brought me to life.

Things I never knew I could feel.

I felt them for him.

I felt them when I was *with* him.

This man set me on fire.

He made me feel wild and daring and free.

I'd never had that before.

He was bad and dangerous and worse than all my nightmares rolled into one because he had the potential to break me worse than Jordan ever had.

Jordan.

Oh god, my heart constricted so tightly I felt like I was dying.

When I couldn't stand the icy coldness a minute longer, I turned off the water and stepped out.

Wrapping a ratty old towel around my body, I trudged back to my room to get dressed.

My phone was vibrating on the bed when I returned, and I couldn't stop myself from sinking down on the mattress and reaching for it.

My fingers shook as I held it in my hand and watched Hunter's name flash across the screen.

I was going to have to face him sooner or later.

Might as well bite the bullet and do it now.

Desire couldn't be in the driving seat of my decision making.

It wasn't real.

It wouldn't last.

Lust and passion and craziness could only take a relationship so far.

Eventually, we would crash and burn.

That was the inevitability of Hunter and me.

It *couldn't* last.

Feelings like the ones I had for him shone bright and crashed hard.

It wasn't solid or stable.

It wasn't permanent.

It *would not last*.

He wasn't my future.

He was just a... complication that needed to be squashed.

I wanted Jordan to be my first, last, and only love. That was the plan and Hunter Casarazzi was screwing with it.

Lines were blurring and I needed to keep them firmly in place.

I lost my head when I was in his presence last night.

I would not make that mistake again.

Swiping my finger across the screen, I pressed accept and pressed the phone to my ear. "Hello."

"So, you are alive," his familiar voice came from the line.

"Yeah," I whispered, pressing a hand against my hammering heart. "I'm still alive."

"Good," he replied. "For a while there, I thought you must have dropped off the face of the earth."

I sighed wearily. "Hunter..."

"Don't ignore me, HC," he interrupted, tone serious now. "We need to talk about what happened last night."

"Yeah. We do." I sighed, my shoulders sagging from the weight of my conscience. "But I don't want to do it over the phone." Cringing, I added, "Are you at home? I can come over."

"I'll be here," was all he replied.

"Okay, I'll see you in a bit." Hanging up the call, I flopped back on my bed and released a pained groan.

This was going to hurt.

But I had to cut him out.

Make the jump and erase him from my daily routine.

Even if the thought made me feel like dying.

78

Hope

By the time I reached Hunter's apartment, the sick feeling of dread in the pit of my stomach had increased to the point I could hardly form a coherent thought.

The entire ride in the elevator was spent on trying not to hyperventilate.

I had to do this.

I had to face him like a grown up.

I had to make it clear that what happened last night was a mistake and would never happen again.

Problem was, the moment Hunter opened his apartment door, and I was impaled by those icy blue eyes, my mind went blank.

His dirty blonde hair wasn't tied back in his signatory man bun either. Instead, it hung loose around his face, skimming his broad shoulders.

He was also shirtless, his tattooed chest and stomach on full display, though I assumed he'd been in the process of getting

442 | INEVITABLE

dressed when I knocked on the door because he had a white shirt in his hand.

The gray sweatpants he had on hung low on his washboard stomach, revealing those sexy indents on either side of his hips. *The V*, I thought to myself. The fucking magic *V* I wrote about in my romance novels – the one all of my heroes possessed. Hunter's was the best damn *V* my eyes had ever seen.

Wordlessly, he stepped aside and held the door open for me.

My heart raced erratically as I forced myself to walk inside in a somewhat composed manner.

He closed the door behind me, and the sound of it clicking shut was like overload to my already frazzled senses.

"Coffee?" he asked, breaking the awkward silence, as he shrugged on his shirt before sauntering into the kitchen area.

"No." I shook my head. "I'm not staying." Clasping my hands in front of myself, I strived to find the words I needed to say. "I... uh..." I cleared my throat before trying again. "I shouldn't have done that last night."

"Done what exactly?" Hunter replied with his back to me as he poured two mugs of coffee. Turning, he walked over to where I was standing and handed me a mug. "Enjoyed yourself?"

"Allowed myself to get so drunk that I thought kissing you was a good idea," I muttered as I frowned at the mug in my hands. "I told you I didn't want any."

"But you do, right?" he shot back, raising a brow.

The steamy, delectable aroma of caffeine was filling my senses, making it impossible for me not to take a sip. The moment the familiar flavor hit my tongue, I moaned in appreciation.

Dammit, he was right.

I did want the coffee.

I wanted all the fucking coffee.

"See," Hunter mused, taking a sip from his own mug.

Chapter 78 | 443

"Sometimes you don't always know what you truly want until it's right there in front of you." He took a sip from his mug before adding, "And you didn't just let me kiss you, HC. You came on my face."

"Hunter, don't," I whispered, mortified. "Last night was a mistake."

"Not for me."

God, he was going to make this hard.

"Well, it was for me," I replied shakily. "I can't – I won't be that woman who cheats on her husband." I exhaled a ragged breath. "I'm not a bad person and I'm not *unfaithful*."

Yes, you are!

"A bad person," he repeated slowly, as if he was chewing the word around for flavor. "You think what we did last night makes you a *bad person*?" he asked, tone wry, eyes flashing with barely restrained frustration.

He placed his hand on my arm then. It was one simple, miniscule touch, but it evoked feelings deep within me that I'd been battling for months to keep hidden.

"Well, it doesn't make me a good one," I choked out before taking a step back from him. "God, I shouldn't even be here right now." I gestured around his apartment and whimpered in dismay. "Back at the scene of the crime." Tears filled my eyes as I looked up at his beautiful face, willing him to understand me.

"Hope, it's okay," Hunter finally sighed. Reaching down, he gently brushed my hair back from face.

"It's my fault," he whispered, tenderly stroking my cheek with his thumb. "I pushed you for this – for *more*..." He stared hard at me, eyes burning with emotion, as he spoke. "Jesus, please don't cry. I can't fucking bear it."

His words only made me feel worse.

His taking responsibility for something I knew I had wanted just as badly only made my guilt more suffocating.

"Christ," Hunter muttered when a huge racking sob tore through me. He took our mugs and placed them both on the

444 | INEVITABLE

counter before returning and enveloping me in his strong arms. "Shh, it's okay," he coaxed, trying to soothe me. "No one has to know."

"*We* know," I wept. "And I can't be friends with you anymore... not with our history and...last night."

"I'll back off," he whispered, holding me tighter. "I will. I'll stop flirting. Just...just don't cut me out."

A voice inside of me screamed *Stop it, Hope, don't you dare go through with this!*

But I knew it was what had to happen.

It was for the best.

It was the right thing to do.

"I'm sorry," I whispered, pulling away from him.

Why did this hurt so much?

And why was it so damn hard to make my feet move?

Walk away, Hope. It's the right thing to do.

"This...whatever it is..." I pointed a finger between us and shook my head. "Is over."

"You think it's as simple as that?" he called after me, making me halt mid-step. "You think if you freeze me out of your life, your feelings for me are going to disappear?"

"I don't have feelings for you," I spat, lying through my teeth. I spun around to face him and glared. "I had a momentary blip in judgment. That's all."

"Bullshit," Hunter shot back, tone heated now. "Bull-fucking-shit, Hope Carter. I challenge you and you *love it*. You're *alive* when you're with me. You're *happy* when you're with me. And sure, you might hate the fact that you fucking love how I make you feel, but it doesn't change anything."

"You're wrong."

"I'm right, and you know it."

"No." I shook my head. "You're not."

"Then why are you here right now, talking to me?" he asked. "Why aren't you with him?"

"Because!" I hissed, flustered.

Chapter 78 | 445

"Because?" He stood opposite me, with his hands folded across his chest, taunting me with his eyes. "Because you *want* to be *here*," he filled in. "Because you want *me*!"

I shook my head. "It's not that simple."

"It's as simple as you make it, HC," he shot back angrily. "And right now, you are making it really fucking hard!"

"What would you do? Huh?" I demanded then, losing my cool. "If Hayley was here?"

It was fine for him to talk; the girl he promised himself to was six feet under.

There was no comparison.

I was his second choice.

The latter option.

He flinched from my words like I had physically slapped him, but I was too angry to back off. "Don't go there, Hope."

"Come on, Hunter," I urged cruelly. "You're full of advice. Tell me what you'd do if your precious Hayley made a miraculous rise from the dead? For Christ's sake, you *killed* for her, Hunter. You took a man's life to *avenge* her honor." I threw my hands up in sheer exasperation. "She's the love of your life, and Jordan's the love of mine!"

"I love you more!" he roared into my face, stunning me.

"Is that what you wanted to hear?" he added, voice torn. "What you wanted me to admit? That I love you more than I *ever* loved her?" His face distorted in pain and he took a few steps backwards. "That I gave up eleven years of my life for a feeling I can't remember?" He ran a hand through his hair and exhaled a broken sigh. "For a *face* that I can't fucking remember?"

Shame crept through my body, the urge to comfort him overriding everything else. "Hunter," I whispered, taking a step towards him. "I didn't mean to hurt you –"

"Yeah, you did," he countered without a hint of hesitation in his voice. His blue eyes were locked on mine, searing me. "You're basically saying that because I was in love when I was

446 | INEVITABLE

eighteen, I don't deserve another shot at it." Hunter glared at me like he didn't know who I was anymore. "Is that it, Hope? I don't deserve another chance at love? I'm incapable of loving you because I loved her first? Is that it?"

"No. I'm not saying that!"

"You think any of this is easy for me?" he roared, losing all control of his temper. "I've been through this before, Hope, and I *lost*. Do you think it's easy for me? Putting myself out there again?" He took a step towards me and cupped the back of my neck, dragging my body roughly to his. "I'm here because you are worth it." He pressed his forehead to mine and stared right into the darkest parts of me. "I am fighting an unbeatable battle because I am so damn deeply in love with you that none of it matters. Nothing else matters to me. Just you."

"Hunter..." a sob tore from my chest, the sight of the pain in his eyes unbearable.

"You think I don't know how this ends?" he croaked out. His hand moved to cup my tear stained cheek. "You think I don't know what your hand of cards looks like? What the fucking endgame looks like?" He wiped a traitorous tear away and exhaled shakily, never taking his blue eyes off mine. "I know I lose, Hope. In the end. I fucking know that. But I'm still here. Do you know why? Because I *can't* walk away from you. And I *won't* walk away from you."

What could I say?

I wanted to heal him.

I wanted to take away his pain and stop him from hurting.

It was my fault.

Unable to stop myself, I stepped forward, placed my hands on his face and kissed him.

"You're going to be the death of me," he whispered, tone pained, eyes dark with barely restrained desire. "Fuck," he hissed harshly, breathing hard against my lips. "What am I talking about? You're already killing me."

He trailed his calloused fingertips across my cheek, settling

Chapter 78 | 447

on my neck. Pausing, he looked down at my face with the loneliest blue-eyed expression and whispered, "I should have known you'd be bad for me." He pressed his forehead to mine and exhaled heavily. "I should have run in the opposite direction." His tone was light and almost playful, but I could see the sadness in his eyes.

He was unhappy.

Because of me.

Because of my inability to let him go.

He was suffering.

I needed to stop it.

"I'm going to fix my marriage, Hunter," I whispered.

I pressed one final kiss to his lips before backing away from him.

"I need to do this," I added quietly, trying to make myself believe the words my mouth was saying and *not* the way my heart was feeling.

I was in pain. I was burning up.

The hurt and the anger, crushing my windpipes, making it hard for me to breathe.

Exhaling heavily, I whispered, "Please, let me do this."

"You want him?" Hunter croaked out, voice laced with anger. "You honest to god want him down to your bones? Then go for it." Shaking his head, he waved a hand in front of him and snarled, "Have at it. Don't let me stop you. Enjoy your picket fence and sweet tea sipping on your porch swing and playing second best to everything else he decides to put before you."

Blinking back my tears, I whispered, "Goodbye, Hunter," before rushing for the door.

"He won't make you happy, HC," he called out after me. "Not really. Not deep down inside where it counts.

79

Lucky

I watched her walk away from me.

I'd laid it all out there for her.

I'd poured my goddamn heart out.

And she still walked away.

Sinking down on the couch, I threw my head back and groaned.

What the fuck did I expect?

She was never going to leave him.

And I was always going to be the one that lost.

The sound of my phone ringing in my pocket drew me back to the present. I debated ignoring it, but then I thought twice about it. It could be her.

When I slid it out of my pocket and saw Kyle's name flash across the screen, I frowned.

"Kyle," I acknowledged, placing my phone to my ear. "What's up?"

"Is Hope with you?" he came straight out and asked.

Chapter 79 | 449

"No," I lied, for her sake more than mine. I had no fucking problem laying my cards out there for the world to see, but she wouldn't want that. "I haven't seen her."

A string of muttered curse words came down the line then.

"Why?" I asked, tone level. "What's going on?"

"He's out," Kyle choked out, voice torn.

My brows shot up. "Your father?"

"If that's what you want to call him," Kyle sneered. "Bastard was released first thing this morning."

Well, shit.

I'd been forewarned all about the piece of shit that was David Henderson back when I'd been asked to watch the boys last month.

"What do you need?" I asked without hesitation.

Kyle was a proud man. Making this call couldn't have been easy for him. He needed something from me, and I wasn't about to make him crawl for it. Regardless of the fact that I was in love with his daughter, I respected the hell out of him. He was Noah's brother. Noah was my family, and my loyalties extended to every member of his family.

"I have a cabin in Vale. I'm taking Lee away there until the dust settles and I can figure this shitbomb out," he announced. "Cash and Casey, too." He paused and then exhaled a heavy sigh. "Chances are I'm overreacting, and he won't bother with us. But I can't take the risk. Not with *her*."

I got it.

One hundred percent.

"What do you need from me?"

"My kids, Luck," he said gruffly. "I need to know they're safe." He paused again and exhaled another ragged breath. "It's not that I'm *not* worried about the triplets, but they've been around the block a time or two and I know they can handle themselves. But Hope? She's not like me or her brothers She's...vulnerable –"

I cut him off by saying, "I won't let anything happen to her."

"I know you won't," he replied after a long pause. "That's why I'm asking you."

80

Hope

I drove blindly for hours, trying to make sense of everything that had just happened, while trying *and failing* not to break down.

Tears flowed freely down my cheeks as I drove, and I gave in to the gut wrenching pain in my heart, allowing myself to cry hard and ugly.

I was sure anyone who pulled up alongside me when I was stopped at the red light would think I was a raving lunatic, but I didn't care anymore.

"I love you more..."

"You think any of this is easy for me? I've been through this before, Hope, and I lost. Do you think it's easy for me? Putting myself out there again..?"

"I'm here because you are worth it. I am fighting an unbeatable battle because I am so far deep in love with you that none of it matters. Nothing else matters to me. Just you..."

My phone continued to ring loudly, but I didn't dare answer it.

452 | INEVITABLE

Even when my father's name appeared on the screen, I sent him straight to voicemail.

I couldn't talk to anyone right now.

My heart felt like it had cracked clean open and was now oozing poison into my other organs.

I felt utterly ruined.

When I walked through the front door of Jordan's house later that night, I was still reeling. Dropping my purse on the bottom step of the staircase, I trudged into the living room to where Jordan and Annabelle were sitting around the coffee table eating pizza.

Numb, I stood in the doorway watching them.

"Hey, Hope," Annabelle greeted brightly when she noticed me. "Are you hungry?"

I shook my head, still numb.

Jordan frowned at me in concern. "Are you okay?"

Again, I shook my head.

I wasn't okay.

I didn't think I would ever be okay again.

He stood up and walked over to me. "What's wrong?" I could see the concern in his green eyes as he stared down at me. "Hope?"

I don't want to be here... The words were on the tip of my tongue, but I didn't have the courage to voice them. *I'm in love with another man.*

Because I was.

I thought he was a passing attraction. A kiss that I would remember in the middle of the night. A heartwarming notion I would cling to as I grew older as Jordan's wife.

Little did I know, he was going to pull the rug from beneath me and turn my world upside down.

I was in love with Hunter Casarazzi.

I was recklessly, senselessly, and completely in love with him.

Chapter 80 | 453

I thought back to that night on the phone when he told me not to fall in love with him, either.

I had been so naïve back then.

And even though it was only a few short months ago, it felt like a lifetime.

"I just realized I forgot my phone at Teagan's," I choked out, needing to be anywhere but in this house, looking at *him*. Forcing down the lump in my throat, I added, "I'm going to go get it."

I didn't wait for his response.

Instead, I turned on my heel and rushed back out the front door.

Emotionally drained, I collapsed in the driver's seat of my truck, covered my head in my hands, and desperately tried to force my mind to go blank. To think of anything but the two men who were pulling me in opposite directions.

I was in love with two entirely different men.

One was wild and unattainable and willing to attach his flag to my messed-up mountain.

The other was broken and I had already attached my flag to his.

Fuck...

I couldn't be here.

Not tonight.

I needed to get away.

I needed to leave.

Do a Teagan on it and haul ass out of the country.

Seemed like the perfect solution right now.

But then I thought of the seven miserable long years we had endured alone.

I couldn't do that.

I couldn't go through that pain again.

Not without Teagan at least.

But she was loved up and married now. I doubted she wanted to uproot her world and move back to Cork with me.

In fact, I knew the answer would be a hell no.

I debated driving straight to South Peak Road and curling up in a ball on her lap, but I couldn't do that.

I couldn't put them in this position.

Hiccupping loudly, I cranked the engine of my truck and drove off in the direction of the only place I wanted to be right now.

Thirteenth Street.

I was going home.

81

Hope

When my childhood home came into view, I mentally sagged in relief.

All I wanted to do was slip into my old bedroom and hide from the world – from my problems.

I needed the sanctuary while I tried to make sense of my life. Of my guilt. Of how I was going to move forwards now.

I wanted to make things work with Jordan, but the thought of losing Hunter caused me physical pain.

I wasn't pleased with this side of my personality.

I'd been raised to be better than this.

I had grown up expecting to have a love like my parents shared. A fierce, lifelong, unconditional connection. I had it now, but I had it with two men.

One, my husband.

The other, my lover.

I was going to crash and burn over this.

I could feel it.

For the rest of my life, there would be a hole in my heart.

456 | INEVITABLE

Either way, I lost.

It wasn't about who I loved more.

It was about who I *couldn't* hurt.

And I couldn't hurt Jordan.

I couldn't do it…

Pulling into my parents' empty driveway, I killed the engine and just stared up at the house.

The house was in complete darkness.

Nobody was home.

Relief seeped through me.

At least I could sneak straight up to my room without the third degree.

I let myself in using the house key and just stood in the hallway for a moment, revering in the silence. I needed this. Some time to gather my thoughts and compose myself.

My phone continued to vibrate in my sweatpants' pocket, and this time I slid it out and looked at the screen.

Four missed calls from Dad, two missed calls from Jordan, nine missed calls from Hunter, half a dozen voicemails, and a string of text messages.

Dad: I have something to tell you. Call me.

Hunter: Where are you?

Dad: Call me ASAP.

Hunter: I need to see you.

Hunter: Tell me where you goddamn are, HC!

Hunter: You need to come over here. I need to talk to you.

Hunter: Answer me, dammit!

CRINGING, I TAPPED OUT A TEXT MESSAGE, FIRST TO MY FATHER, then to Hunter.

> Hope: Dad, I'm home and nobody's here?
>
> Hope: I need some time, Hunter. I'm staying at my parents' place tonight. Please give me space.

AS SOON AS I PRESSED SEND, I SWITCHED MY PHONE OFF AND headed into the kitchen.

I just needed *space* from everyone.

I needed to figure out what the hell I was going to do now.

Flicking on the kitchen light, I made a beeline for the coffee pot.

I needed caffeine.

Badly.

Something to warm the coldness growing inside of my body.

Everything was *more* with Hunter.

He wanted me to be myself.

I felt oddly free around him, immersed in emotions I had only read about in storybooks.

Because Hunter Casarazzi didn't want the diluted, censored version of me.

He wanted the ugly, X-rated, uncut and unedited version of my heart.

The part he owned entirely.

Because somewhere along the way, I had lost a piece of myself in Hunter Casarazzi and I didn't think I would ever be able to replace that piece.

It was only when I heard this strange clicking sound come

458 | INEVITABLE

from behind me, followed by someone roughly clearing their throat, that I realized I wasn't alone.

I spun around and yelped in surprise when my eyes landed on the stranger sitting at the kitchen table. "Jesus Christ," I strangled out, clutching my chest with my hand as panic laced through me. "Who the hell are you?"

"Hello, sweetheart," the man said, cold blue eyes locked on mine. "Remember me?"

My heart hammered violently only to stop dead in my chest when I noticed the gun on the table. My gaze flicked from the gun to the man then back again.

Horrified awareness slapped me straight in the face as I put two and two together and came up with a big fat *four.*

"David?" I choked out, as I slowly began to piece together the resemblance between the man I'd seen when I was a child to the man sitting before me. He was older now, more weathered, but it was definitely him. "What the fuck are you doing here?"

"Now, now," he tutted as he slowly rose to his feet, gun held firmly in his right hand. "Is that anyway to greet your grandfather?"

"Probably not," I agreed, edging towards the door. "But I don't see any grandfather of mine in this room. And you don't look sick"

He smiled. "I'm not."

Shaking my head, I gaped at him. "Then how are you out?"

"It's good to have friends in high places," he mused. He cocked the gun at me then, aiming at my chest, before muttering a string of curse words. "The quality of this C9 is really beneath me," he explained. "I hate cheap products."

"Are you serious?" I strangled out. Was I hearing this right? Was he seriously debating the quality of the gun he had, no less than a minute ago, been aiming at my chest?

Oh, screw this...

Chapter 81 | 459

My survival instincts kicked into gear then and I dove for the kitchen door, my only thought being to get *away now...*

The words, "I wouldn't do that if I were you," caused me to freeze on the mortal spot. "I would hate to have to shoot you, Hope. But I will, if you leave me no choice."

Forcing back the sob that threatened to tear from my chest, I spun around and glared at him. "What do you want?"

"Don't act so obtuse, Hope," David scolded with a shake of his head. "You know what I want."

I did.

Revenge.

"I have nothing to do with any of this!" I hissed, desperately trying to keep a handle on my nerves. "Whatever happened between you and my father has nothing to do with me."

"True," David mused. "But *she's* protected."

My jaw fell open. "My *mother*?"

He nodded.

"You'll never get to her," I spat. "*Ever!* So, you might as well just give up now."

"That's true," he replied calmly. "He loves her most. Getting within breathing range of your father's precious little wife was never going to happen."

"Then why –"

"Why you?"

I nodded.

"Because you're next," he explained, tone emotionless. "The two great loves of Kyle Carter's life; his wife and his daughter." Shrugging, he added, "Can't get the wife, so..."

He said the words so calmly, so cool and unattached, that it terrified me. I was in the presence of a true sociopath.

"So, what?" I cried, unable to stop the violent tremors that were racking through my body. "You're going to kill *me*?"

"Of course not," David soothed. A second man appeared in the kitchen doorway, this one much more frightening than my grandfather. He was young, late thirties, and the biggest man

I'd ever laid eyes on. "This is Carl," David added, gesturing to the huge man. "He's going to kill you."

I tried to dart towards the back door, but the man caught me by my hair, dragging me roughly towards him.

"Please don't –" I began to say, but my words were lost when he knocked me to the ground with a savage blow to the face.

Crying out in pain, I cupped my jaw and scrambled away.

Fear like I'd never known flooded my body, adrenalin coursing through me.

I was going to die here.

He was going to kill me.

"Please," I croaked out, pleading for my life, even though I knew it was pointless. "Don't do this."

Please god, don't let this happen to me.

Please god...

"I wish I could tell you it will be quick and painless," David called out as he walked out of the kitchen. "But we both know that's a lie." He turned to the man and said, "Call me when it's done."

And then he was gone, leaving me alone with my potential assassin.

"You don't have to do this," I coaxed, scrambling away from the man. I dragged myself to safety, huddling in the corner. "Please – ooof..." The air was knocked clean out of my lungs when his boot caught me hard in the stomach.

"You're a pleasant surprise, bitch," the man snarled, towering over me. "Real fucking nice." His hands dropped to the buckle of his belt. "Bet that pussy of yours is nice and snug."

Winded, I used every ounce of strength I had to kick him away. "Don't you dare!" I gasped, desperately trying to drag air into my lungs, as I scrambled away.

Fisting my hair, he roughly dragged me back to him. "Don't bother trying to run, Cunt!" Forcing me to the ground, he straddled my body, kneeling down on my hands so hard, I was sure

Chapter 81 | 461

the pressure would shatter the bones in my wrists. "It only makes me hard."

"Fuck you," I hissed, spitting and kicking at him with everything I had inside of me. Bucking beneath his unbearable weight, I desperately tried to free myself from his hold.

"Fuck me?" he snarled. Rearing his arm back, he punched me full force in the face. "Fuck you, bitch!"

Everything went hazy then.

Pain scorched through my face as blood trickled from my nose.

Coughing and spluttering, I turned my face to the side and gasped for air, but he grabbed my chin in one beefy hand and roughly forced me to look at him. And then, he hit me again, this time with so much force, it felt like my eye socket had detached from the rest of my face.

A sob tore from my throat when I watched him pull a knife from his back pocket. "What do you want inside you first," he sneered, gesturing towards the sharp blade. "My cock or this knife?"

"No," I cried out, struggling relentlessly even though I knew it was pointless.

I don't want to die.

I don't want to die.

"Get off me," I screamed, trying to twist sideways.

It was no use.

He was too big.

Too powerful.

This man was going to do what he wanted with me, and I couldn't stop him.

I'd never felt more helpless in my life.

"This is for your daddy's benefit," he snarled, as he pressed the tip of the knife to my cheekbone. "David said your father would appreciate the irony; like mother, like daughter."

Then he cut me.

462 | INEVITABLE

I screamed out in pain as the knife sliced through my flesh, opening me from cheek to jawline.

I think I passed out then, the pain and the smell of blood was too much to comprehend.

When I came around several minutes later, my clothes were gone.

With the exception of my panties, I was naked as my torturer knelt over me with his pants down and his penis in his hands.

Cold to the bone, and feeling weaker than I ever had, I feebly tried to shove at his chest. My hands were free now, but too numb to do any damage.

Out of the corner of my eyes, I noticed the knife he'd use to torture me was laying on the floor beside us. I tried to reach for it, but it was too far away and I was too broken to get my body to move. "Please," I croaked out, begging for mercy. "Don't do this..."

"What did I tell you about begging, bitch?" the man sneered as he reached for the hem of my panties. "It turns me on."

Whimpering, I desperately tried to press my thighs together in a pathetic bid to protect myself.

It was no use though.

He was going to rape me.

And then he was going to kill me.

He dragged my panties down my legs and grinned darkly before saying, "This is going to hurt."

Tears streamed down my cheeks, mixing with the blood clotting on my face, as I thought about my father finding my body like this.

I clenched my eyes shut and braced myself for the pain I was sure would catapult through my body.

It never came.

I heard my tormenter roar out in pain.

Seconds later, the weight of his body was gone.

Light headed and petrified, I forced my eyes open and cried out in shock at the sight before me.

Hunter.

I had prayed for divine intervention and it had come in the form of my lover.

"You sick fuck," he snarled as he dragged my tormentor away from body and pounded his fists in his face. "You sick, mother fucking bastard!"

I watched in what felt like a dream-like state as Hunter pinned the man to the kitchen floor and beat his fists into his face over and over and over.

The sound of bones crunching filled my ears.

Blood sprayed from the man's face as he made a gurgled protest and tried to push him away

Hunter didn't stop.

He continued to hit him until the man's head smacked loudly off the kitchen tiles.

He looked over to where I was huddling in the corner and I swear I had never seen fury like I did in his blue eyes.

Without a word, Hunter stood up, walked over to where the knife was laying, and picked it up. He walked back to where my tormentor was writhing in agony.

And then *Hunter* began to cut.

And the man began to scream.

He started with his face, slitting him from his temple to his jawline.

He didn't stop there.

I watched in horror as Hunter roughly grabbed the man's exposed penis and lowered the knife.

Blood sprayed everywhere and I heaved, knowing full well that the screams that came from my tormentor's mouth would haunt me until my dying day.

I was screaming, too.

I couldn't stop.

Hunter silenced his screams with one final slash to the

464 | INEVITABLE

throat, and watched with dark eyes as the life slowly bled out of him.

Only when my tormentor stopped twitching and gurgling did Hunter finally stand up.

Gasping for air, I mirrored his actions and scrambled to my feet, while gaping in absolute horror as Hunter stood over the lifeless body.

There was blood everywhere.

On me.

On him.

Everywhere.

Hunter dropped the knife on the floor and slowly turned to face me. His chest was heaving, his face and body drenched in another man's blood

I watched him watch me as my body trembled violently.

Wordlessly, he stepped over the lifeless man on the floor and grabbed a hand towel from the draining board. He approached me almost cautiously, like he wasn't sure what I was going to do, and pressed the towel to my bleeding face.

None of the earlier violence was in his eyes now.

All I could see was love.

He never spoke a single word as he yanked his blood splattered hoodie off and gently slipped it over my head before feeding my hands through the too-long sleeves.

My body shook from head to toe as he dressed me; the tender show of affection too much for my heart to take.

"Oh god," I strangled out as a sob tore through me. "Oh god!"

My eyes flicked from his to the lifeless body on the ground.

"Oh god, Hunter," I choked out as fear threatened to overtake me. "What have we done?"

"Shh." His arms came around me, and it felt just like I remembered. I was cocooned in his embrace, cloaked in his love. "It's okay." He held me tight with one hand and stroked my hair with the other. "Everything is going to be okay."

Chapter 81 | 465

"You killed him," I sobbed, clutching my chest. "You killed him for me."

"I love you," he whispered brokenly. "There isn't anything I wouldn't do for you."

"Wait – don't leave me," I whispered in horror when he took a step back from me. He refused to meet my eyes as he ran a hand through his hair and choked out a pained sound. "Please." I was sobbing now. Crying real hard and ugly. "Please don't go."

"I'm not going anywhere," he replied, voice torn and weary. "I just need to make a call."

"Who are you calling?" I demanded, chest heaving, as I stumbled after him.

"The cops, Hope," he whispered. "And an ambulance."

"The cops?" I balked and shook my head. "They'll arrest you."

"I know," he whispered.

This man was vicious.

He'd committed crimes.

He had blood on his hands.

What I'd just witnessed him do should have been enough to send me running.

I should let him make the call.

But I *couldn't.*

"Hang it up," I strangled out. When he made no move to put his phone away, I staggered towards him and smacked his cell out of his hands. "Hang up the fucking phone, Hunter!"

"Hope," he whispered, voice pained. "I have to call them, sweetheart."

"No," I shot back fiercely. "No!"

"What do you want me to do here, Hope?" Raking a hand through his hair, he exhaled a heavy sigh. "There's a body in there, sweetheart, with my prints all over it." He shook his head again and said, "And you need to see a doctor. Your face..." His voice broke off and I watched him take several short breaths before adding, "Goddammit, Hope, that piece of shit raped–"

"He didn't!" I strangled out, head spinning. "*You* stopped him, Hunter. You *saved* me!" I hissed, clutching his shirt in my hands. "That man was sent here to kill me! If it weren't for you, he would have. And you are *not* going back to prison for saving my life."

"What are you saying?" Hunter shot back, eyes wary and locked on my face.

Inhaling a calming breath, I looked up at his face and said, "I'm saying we get rid of the body."

Crazy as it seemed, tonight's events had shed a direct light on my future.

I knew who I was now and I had finally come to the conclusion that I would much rather live a broken life with Hunter than one without him.

Was I ready to walk away from my marriage for him?

I didn't know the answer to that.

But I couldn't give Hunter up.

I needed to be with him, whatever the cost.

Regardless of what everyone thought, or what it cost my conscience and moral fiber.

I wasn't giving him up.

I was keeping this man.

That was all I knew for now.

THANK YOU SO MUCH FOR READING!

Hope's story continues in Altered, available now.

Please consider leaving a review on the platform you purchased this book.

<u>Carter Kids in order:</u>
Treacherous
Always
Thorn
Tame
Torment
Inevitable
Altered

OTHER BOOKS BY CHLOE WALSH

The Pocket Series:
Pocketful of Blame
Pocketful of Shame
Pocketful of You
Pocketful of Us

Ocean Bay:
Endgame
Waiting Game
Truth Game

The Faking it Series:
Off Limits – Faking it #1
Off the Cards – Faking it #2
Off the Hook – Faking it #3

The Broken Series:
Break my Fall – Broken #1
Fall to Pieces – Broken #2
Fall on Me – Broken #3
Forever we Fall – Broken #4

470 | *Other books by Chloe Walsh*

The Carter Kids Series:

Treacherous – Carter Kids #1
Always – Carter Kids #1.5
Thorn – Carter Kids #2
Tame – Carter Kids #3
Torment – Carter Kids #4
Inevitable – Carter Kids #5
Altered – Carter Kids #6

The DiMarco Dynasty:

DiMarco's Secret Love Child: Part One
DiMarco's Secret Love Child: Part Two

The Blurred Lines Duet:

Blurring Lines – Book #1
Never Let me Go – Book #2

Boys of Tommen:

Binding 13 – Book #1
Keeping 13 – Book #2
Saving 6 – Book #3
Redeeming 6 – Book #4

Crellids:

The Bastard Prince

Other titles:

Seven Sleepless Nights

PLAYLIST FOR INEVITABLE

Playlist for Hope:

Of Monsters and Men – I Of The Storm
James Vincent McMorrow – We Don't Eat
He is We – Skip To The Good Part
Noah Cyrus/Labrinth – Make Me (Cry)
Adele – Hiding my Heart Away
Fever Ray – Keep the Streets Empty for me
The Civil Wars – Poison & Wine
Switchfoot – On Fire
Miranda Lambert – Mama's Broken Heart
Ingrid Michaelson – Over You
Joan Armatrading – The Weakness in Me
Alex & Sierra – Little Do You Know
Swedish House Mafia – Don't you Worry Child
Jack Johnson – Sitting, Waiting, Wishing
The Chainsmokers – Don't Let Me Down
Cam – Burning House
Rachel Platten – Beating Me Up
Banks – Beggin for Thread

472 | *Playlist for Inevitable*

Lissie – Go Your Own Way
Little Mix – DNA
Kate Nash – Nicest Thing
Haley Reinhart – Can't Help Falling In Love
Counting Crows – Colorblind
Rachel Platten – Stand by You
Sia – Footprints
Taylor Swift – Haunted
Anne-Marie – Alarm
Nicki Minaj – Anaconda

Playlist for Hunter (Lucky)

Mourning Ritual – Bad Moon Rising
Hozier –Cherry Wine
Hurt – Somebody To Die For
Noah Gundersen – Day is Gone
Alexander Stewart – Make Me (Cry)
He is We – Kiss it Better
Hungry Eyes – Eric Carmen
Jaymes Young – I'll Be Good
Eric Arjes – Find my Way
Amy Winehouse – Will you Still Love Me Tomorrow
Sam Hunt – Make You Miss Me
Shawn Mendes – Treat You Better
The Script – Nothing
Semisonic – F.N.T
Maroon 5 – My Heart is Open
+44 – When Your Heart Stops Beating
Uncle Kracker – Smile
Hinder – Lips of An Angel
Switchfoot – Dare you to Move
Travis – Re-Offender
Aaron Krause – Only You

Playlist for Inevitable | 473

Bush – Glycerine
Every Avenue – Only Place I Call Home
Damien Rice – Accidental Babies
Hozier – Jackie and Wilson
The-Dream – Code Blue
Justin Timberlake – Mirrors
Blake Shelton – Sangria
Nine Inch Nails – Hurt

Playlist for Jordan

Kesha – Praying
Lady Gaga – Till it Happens to You
Sam Smith – Too Good at Goodbyes
Sheryl Crow – I Shall Believe
Nickelback – How you Remind me
Tom Odell – Heal
The Script – You Won't Feel A Thing
Bruno Mars – When I Was Your Man
Walking On Cars – Flying High, Falling Low
Hozier – Take me to Church
Otis Redding – Stand by Me
REM – Losing my Religion
Radiohead – Creep
Matchbox Twenty– Unwell
Sam Smith – Stay With Me
Ed Sheeran – Happier
Joel Adams – Please Don't Go
Within Reason – We'll Have It All
Michael Schulte – You Said You'd Grow Old With Me
Black Veil Brides – Lost it All
Tim McGraw – Don't Take the Girl
Jamie Lawson – I'm Gonna Love You
Staind – Outside

474 | *Playlist for Inevitable*

Paramore – The Only Exception
Gavin DeGraw – More Than Anyone
Boyce Avenue – Titanium
Imagine Dragons – Demons
REM – Everybody Hurts

ABOUT THE AUTHOR

Chloe Walsh is the bestselling author of The Boys of Tommen series, which exploded in popularity. She has been writing and publishing New Adult and Adult contemporary romance for a decade. Her books have been translated into multiple languages. Animal lover, music addict, TV junkie, Chloe loves spending time with her family and is a passionate advocate for mental health awareness. Chloe lives in Cork, Ireland with her family.

Join Chloe's mailing list for exclusive content and release updates.
http://eepurl.com/dPzXMi

Printed in Great Britain
by Amazon

34641755R00273